IN DEFIANCE OF HEAVEN

THE FORSAKEN COMEDY
BOOK THREE

KEVIN KAUFFMANN

IN DEFIANCE OF HEAVEN

Kevin Kauffmann

Front cover image by Andy Belanger.

Book design by Peter J. Wacks.

First printing edition 2014.

Second printing edition 2024.

www.kevinkauffmann.com

10 9 8 7 6 5 4 3 2

CONTENTS

PROLOGUE: STRANGERS IN A STRANGE LAND

William Combe scowled as he looked at his father's castle, a small, insignificant little speck in the King's marshland. The outer walls were covered with moss and ivy, ramparts had fallen into disrepair and the chains to the drawbridge had been rusted to the point of uselessness. If any marauder had wanted to invade Castle Combe, they would have found it an easy victory.

An easy victory over a strategically worthless swamp.

However, considering how William's father acted around his vassals, it would be hard to tell how insignificant it really was. Richard Combe had made a habit of throwing around his weight—which was considerable—and it more than just bothered William. In fact, almost everything about Richard Combe bothered his son, and it was becoming apparent that old Richard didn't deserve his position of strength. Unfortunately, since Richard was still the lord of the castle, his word was law, and William had to suffer his father as long as they lived under the same roof.

That was the reason William had not lived at Castle Combe for five years.

Still, Richard had summoned him and William had obeyed. Even if he preferred to avoid thinking of him as a father, Richard Combe was still his lord and could have him hunted down if he wished. Only two years ago he had done just that, and although he could probably avoid the dogs now, William looked down to the scars on his arm that they had left behind. As much as William hated the man, it was easier to give into his demands than hide out in the marsh for a week.

"The prodigal son returns, eh, William?"

William looked down from his arm to find a familiar face, a guardsman who had been in his family's service for the last thirty years, and he looked it. His eyes had retreated behind the folds of his skin and only black pupils could be seen, in contrast to the bushy white eyebrows that were arched in skepticism. His face was covered in a scraggly white beard and his mouth was open just enough for William to see the old man had lost even more teeth since he had last visited. With a smile, William set his hand on the guard's muddy shoulder plate and smiled.

"Only long enough to see what my lord father wants from a no-good mercenary. How have you been, Garret?" William slid off the saddle of his horse and joined him on the muddy path.

"Same as always. Nothing ever changes round here and you know it." Garret coughed as he extended his hand to gather the reins to William's horse. "It's been more than a year this time, you know that? Old Combe hates it when you don't come to visit."

With a disappointed grunt, William knocked away the guard's hand and nodded forward.

"I can lead my own horse to the stables. I'm not my father."

"That, you're certainly not," Garret said with a soft chuckle. "As you're so fond of pointing out. Eventually, though, you're going to have to admit that you're going to be the lord of this castle. Old Combe isn't going to live much longer."

"Look at you, talking about my father like he's going to keel over from old age," William said with a sly smile. "You have at least twenty years on Richard and you're not dying anytime soon. Hell, he still has you on guard duty."

"I might not last too much longer myself, but your father has gotten so fat that breathing has become a daily battle," Garret explained as they passed underneath the archway into Castle Combe, the portcullis falling apart above them. It would have been a death trap if the counterweight had not been chained to the ground. "Stressful thing, lordship. Eating is how your father gets through the day."

"It's too bad he doesn't let his subjects eat a whole sheep like he does every Sunday. I'm sure there would be less grumbling in the taverns if our lord was more generous with his storeroom."

"There would be less grumbling in the taverns if they didn't get tithed at church, but they get tithed all the same. One of these days, you're going to learn that life isn't fair and that you do the best you can. Nothing ever changes, Will, believe you, me. You were lucky enough to be born higher up in the chain." Garret sidled up to the entrance of the stables, watching as William gave his horse's reins over to a mud-covered teenager. With a nod, William tossed a copper to the lad and turned his attention back to the old guard.

"Maybe that means I can change it, Garret. They don't deserve the piss and shit we give them," William said before glowering at a man he had known for his entire life. Shaking his head, Garret looked over his young master with a sigh.

Although William was only twenty years of age, he had not had the life of a noble's son.

Over the years of his self-imposed exile, William Combe had become more of a man than his father had ever been. Sandy brown hair was cropped short to keep it from getting in the way, and the gaze from his dull green eyes made it seem like he had met Death many times but somehow managed to keep living. A dark green cloak clung to his back, but he was armored in a mix of hard leather and iron so he could fight bandits at any time. From his belt hung a loose assortment of daggers, tools and his long sword, and on his back was a worn longbow for hunting. If Garret hadn't spent more than a decade teaching William everything he knew, the young man would have been a stranger.

Instead, he was the next lord of this castle.

"Piss and shit, young William..." Garret grumbled as he stepped forward and met William's gaze, "What else do you expect to find in the marsh?"

They held their staring contest for a moment—Garret looking at him with grim determination—but then William finally broke and started laughing. The old guard joined him before clapping him on the shoulder and pushing William toward the Great Hall.

"Fair enough, old man. Fair enough. So," William said as he finished laughing, breathing in deep through his nostrils before turning to face his friend. "Do you know why I'm here?"

"I assume because of the visitors. They don't tell me much about the politics, but your father is quite impressed with these ones." Garret yawned and stretched his jaw. "Well, impressed by their money, in any case."

"Money... at a time like this," William growled as he looked at the entrance to the Castle. "His subjects are dying horribly, the Black Death is tearing us apart, and my precious father wants nothing more than the gold of strangers."

"Gold may help us yet, young sir, and if the fields aren't plowed by the sick, we need to buy our food from elsewhere." Garret let out a breath of desperation. "It's hard times, Will. Hard enough that you don't want to be sick *and* poor. On this, I don't blame your father. Heard all they want is a guide, anyway."

"A guide... the letter said as much. A guide to what?"

"That I don't know, young sir—"

"Stop that," William interrupted, but the old man continued undeterred.

"I will not, *young sir*. You're gonna have to get used to the titles again. I wasn't kidding about your father. May not last the winter. So," Garret said before nodding to the door, "you be nice this time.

4

Your father may not be the best lord, but he did one right thing with *you*. You gotta get used to this stuff so that you can rule the right way."

"Garret, I have no intention of—"

"Don't much care what you intend. Someday you're going to remember that you have a duty to these people and you're going to come back. Maybe before Old Combe eats his last meal, but I've seen too much to hope for that. All I'm trying to say is that—for the good of the people you like so much—it might be best to swallow your pride just for a few years."

"Where is this coming from?"

"Seen a lot in my time, Will, but... these last few years... Seems like it could be the end of the world. I just know, well, I know if anybody is going to stop it, it's going to be someone like you. Just don't want you hiding out in the woods when you can be a lot more useful here." Garrett avoided eye contact with his young master, and William's resolve melted.

"We'll see, Garret," he replied softly, not sure what he would do after all this. His father was insufferable, certainly, but Garret would not have asked him to stay if he didn't think it best. He was as much a part of this family as William; the uncle God had never seen fit to give him. "Are you coming with me, or am I to face my father alone?"

"No, young sir, you won't get me in that room, but you won't be alone, either." Garret huffed, looking back to William in trepidation. "He's entertaining the visitors right now."

"Anything I should know? You've never been the kind of man to back down from a stranger," William said, setting his forearm against the rotting planks of the door. Visibly shuddering, Garret walked to William's side and set a hand on his cloaked shoulder.

"These are... I don't know. Something about them gets under my skin. Friendly enough, but... you'll see," Garret said before moving past his master and walking to the gate. "I'll see you again before you set off, I'm sure."

"Yeah, sure," William said with some concern as he watched

Garret walk away. Grunting softly, he turned back to the entrance and pulled the door open—the edges of the wooden planks dragging through the mud and putting up some resistance—but soon he was through the doorway and had to let his eyes adjust to the light.

Once he did, he found his heavyset father in his lackluster throne as always, but there were four strangers standing in the hallway who made much more of an impression. They were all oddly dressed, but when the dark-haired man in the center turned back to look at him, William's breath caught in his throat.

A bright green eye was staring at him, *through* him, and he felt like his entire life was being judged. Although it made his stomach turn, William's judgment was interrupted by his father, who sat up and pointed to him with glee.

"Ah! There's my son. There is my William," Richard said, causing all the strangers to turn and join the green-eyed man in judgment. However, the other man closest to him—dressed in a grey cloak and black leather armor—gave him a thin smile.

"A pleasure, William. My name is Cadmus, and this is Niccolo." He waved at the dark-haired man before motioning toward the two women in their company. "And these young ladies are Paimon and Cimeries."

Before William could do much more than take in the sight, Niccolo sniffed with hostility.

"We need you to lead us to Stonehenge."

"Eat! Eat. You're all my guests here," Richard Combe said between mouthfuls of roast chicken, gobs of meat and fat slipping down the jowls of his face.

William had certainly seen worse from his father, but time had let him forget and now he was fighting the urge to be sick. Crossing his arms and doing his best to seem hostile, William looked at his father's guests with a skeptical eye.

They were all gathered around the high table of Castle Combe, only a few wooden planks lashed together surrounded by well-worn chairs. Refusing his place at his father's side, William was sitting at one end of the table, the traveler with the unkempt black hair directly across from him. On William's right, opposite his father, sat the other three visitors, each picking at the food on their plates in order to be polite. Even if the dark-haired stranger was acting hostile, William almost appreciated his rude behavior for being so direct.

"Thank you, Lord Combe," a surprisingly confident voice came from Cadmus, who was sitting across from William's father. After setting his knife down, the cloaked man spoke as he interlaced his fingers in front of him. "Your hospitality in such trying times is quite appreciated."

"Oh, no bother, no bother." Richard waved around a chicken leg, loose skin falling to the ground. "I love to help out fellows in need, especially when they are so willing to part with the contents of their purse."

"Well, we try to make sure we're wanted," the blonde woman said with a flirtatious smile. That earned a big grin from Richard Combe, whose second chin quivered in anticipation.

"That you certainly are, my dear Paimon," he said before gesturing toward William with the chicken leg. "And as the lord of this realm, I am pleased to offer the services of my son to help you find this Stonehenge."

"I haven't agreed to anything, Richard."

Cadmus looked at William with shock and his father's eye twitched in anger, but the brunette woman sitting closest to him offered a smile.

"That is fair. He did not say he would help us," she said before stabbing a chicken thigh with her knife and bringing it to her lips. "How would we convince you, William?"

"Cimeries, wasn't it?" he replied, looking straight at the woman.

From the armor hiding under her clothes, it was obvious that she was skilled in warfare. "It's a strange name."

"I find it difficult to believe you care about my name, ranger. Get to the questions you want answered."

Gaining a new respect for the woman, William turned to face the rest of his audience.

"I'm curious why you want to go to Stonehenge. It's a relic from another time in the middle of nowhere. There is no profit in this for you," he said, at which point Paimon set her chin on her hand and shrugged.

"There's profit for *you*. We're willing to pay you and your father handsomely for the service. It's important we get there." There was something off about her, but her golden eyes seemed to drink him in and it was hard to argue against her.

So, finding that a fool's prospect, William turned his attention to Niccolo, who was still scowling.

"Why is it so important to you? It's a pile of stones. Nobody knows how they got there."

Niccolo's hair was matted in front of the left side of his face, but William could see that something was wrong with his skin. William had traveled and seen what the swamp could do to a man after enough exposure, and he knew that blight did not make a man any less dangerous.

"What does it matter to you why we need to go? Why can't we just be tourists?" Niccolo replied, gaze unwavering. Mustering his courage, William leaned forward and set his elbows on the table.

"You're not tourists. You have blood all over you and you can only wash so much of it off. *All of you.* My father may not see it, but you spend enough time in blood and dirt and you can see one of your own. Forgive me if I don't believe you're just *taking in the sights.*"

"You *insult* our guests like this, son!" Richard exploded, almost falling out of his chair.

"They are not *my* guests, Combe, and you know that word

doesn't belong to you," William stated simply, but his father was already trying to climb to his feet and waving his knife.

"I will teach you manners, mongrel!"

"Enough."

The soft word was enough to stop father and son from going further, and they turned to see Cadmus sitting with his eyes closed and still resting his chin on interlaced fingers. After a sigh, the traveler opened his eyes and then beckoned Lord Combe to take his seat. Forgetting that he was the lord of the castle, Richard took his seat as he stared at the grey-eyed man.

"We did not come here to unearth old feuds. We simply need passage to Stonehenge. If you can provide that for us, William, we will pay you for the efforts. Can you help us?" Cadmus asked, turning to face the ranger without emotion.

William was still trying to work through this development. He had never expected any of the travelers to come to his aid.

"I'm not sure I should. I may not agree with my father, but these are my lands as well," William said, remembering his conversation with Garret and all the responsibility he was trying to avoid. "I need to make sure that our subjects will not suffer because of your actions."

"Hah, trust us, we want nothing to do with your subjects. Call it intellectual curiosity," Niccolo said, using the finger of his right hand to scratch the table. "We want a guide, that's all."

"Then why me? Why the son of a lord? Why can't you get some shepherd's boy to get you there? It's only a few days travel from the castle." William tried to ignore his father's silent fury. He wouldn't let it show, but he enjoyed the anguish he was causing.

"You were a correct judge of character, William," Cimeries said after swallowing down a mouthful of bread. "We have blood on our hands, and we will surely bathe in it again. Our guide needs to be someone who can handle himself on the field. A shepherd's boy would not last the journey."

"Then you've made it clear that I have no reason to help you. Not only guide, but to fight for you? Why did you think I would agree to this?"

"Because we know that you're just the same as us," Paimon interjected, shocking the young lord into silence. "You're no stranger to violence. We've heard all the tales from your father. He's proud of you, you know."

"Why should I care what he's proud of..." William trailed off as he looked at the great doors leading outside. "How much are you going to pay me?"

"More than enough, considering," Cadmus said, bringing out a small pouch that jingled as it swayed. After drawing out a golden coin from the bag and holding it up to the light, Cadmus threw the pouch at William, who caught it in his hand. "It's no guarantee we'll meet anybody on the way, but that should cover a week of normal mercenary work. After we meet our goal, we'll give you another pouch and provide your father enough gold to operate the castle for a month."

William eyed this Cadmus, who had withdrawn into himself over the course of the meal, and wondered why they were paying so much just for an escort. Cadmus was still leaning over the table—William could see that he had been trying to hide the fatigue in his voice—and it made it seem like they had been on this journey for decades.

Although extremely skeptical that this would be a standard escort, William's greed got the better of him and he looked at the money in his hand.

Opening up the pouch, William found that there were at least thirty golden coins just like the one Cadmus had set on the table. Lifting his gaze back up, he found five sets of eyes staring at him. He didn't trust any of them, but he could tell that they were no danger to the subjects of his father. These people had a clear goal that had nothing to do with Combe lands.

Staring hard at Niccolo, William made his decision and opened his mouth to speak.

"Give my father's reward to me and we'll make a deal," he offered, his father's arms falling to rotund sides. On the other hand, he could see from Niccolo's wicked grin that *someone* appreciated the comment.

"You scoundrel..." Richard said as he shakily climbed to his feet. "Where... why—what makes you think you can get away with this? What makes you think that I won't make the castle guards kill you for this insult?" He slammed his arm against the table, sending plates scattering and crashing to the floor.

"Please, Richard, they like me more than you. If you're curious, I was going to turn around and give it to your subjects. I want to make sure it gets to the right people." William added a dose of venom to that last statement before turning to face Niccolo, who was pleased by his antics.

"When will you be able to leave, William?" Cadmus asked, drawing away from the table and a still-spinning plate. Contrary to Richard's wishes, none of them seemed to pay him any mind, and so he slammed both of his hands against the high table once more.

"I will not suffer this in my own castle! You are not allowed to make this deal!" he shouted, grease and spit coming out of his mouth in equal measure. In response, Cimeries set down her knife on the plate and stood slowly, letting her cloak fall away from her armor as she did.

"Lord Combe, as much as you might prefer it otherwise, we will not allow you to stop us. That was the first and last time you command us to do anything," she stated before walking to the great door. His vision shaking in his fury as she left, Richard Combe roared and turned to his other disrespectful guests.

"I will hunt you down! I will hunt you all down! Even you, you ungrateful waste of seed," he threatened as he turned to his son. At the challenge, William jumped to his feet and his hand flew to his sword, but almost immediately a strong arm was pushing against his chest and keeping him back. Looking to his right, he saw that Cadmus had somehow come between them.

It was as if the man had appeared there instantaneously.

"If you hunt for us, you will only lose your hunters. We will leave your castle without violence, Lord Combe. That is our gift to you, along with some coin," Cadmus said as he grabbed another pouch and tossed it onto the table. "Thank you for your hospitality."

"You..." Richard started, but his confidence departed once Niccolo rose to his feet and stared through him.

Before long, William was being pushed along by Cadmus as Paimon and Niccolo walked with them. Once Cimeries pushed open the door, William realized how much had happened in the last few moments and started to resist Cadmus.

"Wait, I never agreed to anything," William said, but then a light chuckle came from Niccolo on the far side of their group.

"Yes, you did. Trust us, we know *just* what declaring war looks like." Before William could say anything, Paimon leaned forward and gave him a pleasant smile.

"Welcome to our merry band of adventurers, William Combe."

WILLIAM KNEW this was all kinds of stupid, but he continued to put one foot in front of the other. Stonehenge wasn't much further, and every step he took tightened the knot in his stomach. After climbing across the root of a great tree, William looked back at his fellow travelers and wondered what he had gotten himself into.

Cimeries was directly behind him and kept constant watch on the forest surrounding them. At first, the woman would go off on her own and come back—as if she knew exactly where she was going—and that only made William more nervous. It made him think that he was not here to guide them at all, but eventually Cimeries settled into walking by his side and waiting for his lead.

The others, however, lagged behind. Cadmus walked with difficulty, using a walking stick to help him get over the tangled roots of the forest and keep from slipping on loose moss and mud. Paimon, in contrast, was a spritely little thing and made her way through the path without the slightest amount of effort.

At the rear of their party was Niccolo, his left arm still held in the sling underneath his cloak, and this also made William nervous. He would have much preferred Cadmus or Cimeries as their rear guard —especially if they were expecting to be attacked—but Niccolo had insisted on keeping to the back. It only took a few moments of discussion before William knew it wasn't worth fighting the decision.

Even though Niccolo only had the use of one arm, the scowl on his face told William that it wasn't under debate.

"So's there any chance you'll tell me why you need to go to Stonehenge?" William asked as he turned back to face their destination. He could see the hill rising up before them and realized it wouldn't be much longer before he fell into whatever potential trap was lying in wait. They had been quiet so far, but William could not justify going further without an answer to his question.

"We're almost there, William. Do you really need to know when we're this close?" Cadmus asked, his breaths slightly labored, and William turned to him with a frown.

"How do you know we're almost there, Cadmus?" he growled, and that was enough for the stranger to stop in his tracks. Looking at him with tired eyes, Cadmus sighed and leaned on his walking stick.

"Well, *that* ruse is over. I'm sorry we lied to you."

That prompted William to turn back to his companions, his hand on the hilt of his sword.

"What's going on? Why am I here?" he asked, but Cimeries stepped to his side and caught his attention.

"You knew this was more than a mere escort mission. We hired your services because you are a mercenary, William. You are being paid handsomely, if you recall." She stepped back and set her spear into the moss at her feet.

Falling away from the woman, William tried to keep his eye on all four people at the same time.

"I was hired with the mindset that there was only *potential* violence," he said, trying to think his way through the situation. If he tried to run, he would have to cripple at least one or two of these strangers. Luckily, this was his homeland, so he could likely lose them within the woods.

"If it's more money you want," Niccolo said as he hopped over a log and continued toward his guide, "we can give you more. What's it matter what excuse we used for you to help us? We wanted your sword and you agreed to use it."

"You asked me to be a guide. *Apparently*, to a place you've been before. I don't have the patience for this. Stonehenge is up there," William said before pointing behind him with his free hand. "Pay me now and we'll be done with this."

"We can't do that," Cadmus said as he stepped forward, within striking distance of William's sword if he chose to draw it, and it was becoming difficult for him to keep it sheathed. "No more lies. We do need your help, and we don't need it at the base of this hill."

"Why do you need *my* help? Why are we here?" William demanded, but his anger emptied out of him once Paimon stepped out from behind Cadmus and made eye contact with him. Those golden eyes destroyed whatever willpower he had.

"We looked for you for a long time, Will. You weren't chosen at random. We need you to come with us... help us get past this obstacle. Then, if you want, you can go home. We won't keep you any longer than we need," she said, and it almost convinced him.

However, Niccolo sighed with disgust and brought William out of his daze.

"Forget it, let's just grab him by the scruff of the neck and we'll be done with this," he muttered, and William instantly knew he had to escape. Drawing his sword fast enough to make it scrape against the scabbard, William brought it across his body and intended to hack into Cadmus' midsection. However, Cadmus quickly brought up his walking stick and stopped William's sword mid-swing.

When William looked at Cadmus, instead of grey, he found

bright blue eyes looking back at him. William tried to turn his attention on the others, but his gaze stopped on the curved blade that had appeared at the end of Cadmus' walking stick. Panicked, William hopped back and finally realized that Cadmus now held an ornate scythe with a skull etched onto the head of the weapon.

"Who are you?" William asked, his voice shaking as he walked and tried to keep all four travelers in his vision. Cimeries had lowered her spear and adopted a balanced stance, but the other three weren't making any hostile motions.

"Come with us, Will. We'll explain everything soon," Paimon attempted, but William wasn't going to listen to the siren anymore.

Seeing that his options were limited—and that he certainly did not want to retreat up the hill—William tried to figure out some way he could escape. With a quick movement, William jumped to his left and sprinted away from the others, but before he made it a few yards, a wall of flames burst into existence and blocked his way. In shock, William looked back to his escorts and saw Niccolo leering at him with a twisted sense of satisfaction.

"What is this?" William demanded, retreating from the fire and wracking his brain for a solution. He was stalling—he had never encountered anything like this before—but that wouldn't stop William from doing everything he could to survive.

"Please, William, don't make this difficult," Cadmus insisted, holding his scythe to his side as he advanced. It was then that William realized he had no choice, that these killers and dark magicians would not let him go back the way they had come. Sheathing his sword, William turned around and sprinted up the hill, hoping that if he put enough distance between them that he might be able to escape.

However, every time he tried to break away from his path and run around the ruins, a new, blazing wall crackled into life and cut off his escape. Fear overtaking him, rational thought abandoned William and he tore his way up the hill. He stumbled and clambered along with his hands, grabbing tufts of dry grass and mud and flinging them into the air once the roots tore away from the soil.

When William could finally see the tops of the stone monoliths, he momentarily felt relief, but then a spear with a second, hooked blade underneath the head sank into the ground beside him. Unable to understand where it had come from, William picked himself up and worked his way up the hill, his thighs hurting as muscle fatigue threatened to make them useless. However, his life—the only thing he had left—was more important than the pain affecting his legs. It was only a few more frightening seconds before William had made his way to the top of the hill.

Unfortunately, a specter in a grey cloak was standing in the center of the stone circle, and in his hands was a brilliant, white scythe.

"No..." William muttered, the fight departing from him as he realized that this was all planned. This was where they had intended to kill him.

"Sadly, yes, William Combe. None of us wanted this to happen," the shrouded figure said before pulling back its hood. When he let his hand fall, William saw an old man with a marble-white beard and short hair. "I am sure they had hoped to bring you here without any unnecessary pain."

"Unnecessary... pain?" William asked, repeating words he did not understand and looking into the man's pale blue eyes. "Just... tell me. Who are you?"

"My name is Solomon. I hope you can learn to forgive us for this," he said with a tinge of regret, but William could only shake his head and look at the ground. When he looked back up, he saw something he couldn't have believed only five minutes ago.

Descending from the sky was a man bathed in fire, the heat coming from him intense enough to drive the air from William's lungs. When the figure's feet touched the ground, the flames abandoned him and a small, brown man with curly black hair was staring at him with pure-white eyes. Whatever he was, William could tell that this man regarded him with contempt.

"You should know by now that you cannot run, human," the newcomer spat, but he was interrupted by a voice from behind William.

"You're scaring him, Phenex. That doesn't do us any good," Cadmus said as he walked into William's field of vision, continuing forward until he could put his back to one of the stone monoliths to William's left.

"Why should I care if he's scared, Horseman? We don't need him for his bravery," the fiery demon said as he turned his attention to Cadmus. For a moment the words abandoned him, but William swallowed and tried to muster some courage.

"Horseman? Why..." he tried to say, but his throat was so dry from the heat that he couldn't continue. However, from his heavy sigh, it was obvious that Cadmus immediately understood what William was asking. With a wave of his hand, the reaper summoned a creature from the ether, a swirling mass of dust which solidified into a pure white horse.

"William, I'd like you to meet Mercy. And, well, I should introduce myself correctly," Cadmus said as he walked toward the creature. "My name is Cadmus. I'm the Horseman of Death."

"Horseman of... Death? The..." William muttered before apocalyptic visions tore through his mind and caused him to panic. It was obvious now. This was no mere stranger; this was the *Pale Rider*. This was the demon responsible for the end of the world.

Jumping to his feet and fully giving into fear, William tried to back away from the man who had tricked him into these very ruins.

"Please, William, we mean you no harm," Cadmus tried to argue, but William wasn't listening.

He turned away from the Horseman and found that Cimeries had blocked his exit. Turning away from her and trying to find an escape route away from the other demonic entities, he found Paimon standing between twin towers of stone. This time, however, her pupils and irises had abandoned her and golden knives had taken the place of her fingernails. Gulping down fear, William did the only thing he could and drew his sword, which shook in front of him.

"Why am I here?" he yelled, turning quickly to face each of the threats coming against him. None of them had moved an inch, but that did nothing to alleviate his fear. "Why the *fuck* did you bring me here?"

"We needed a defiant soul. A rebellious man whose entire being was devoted to justice. We found *you*," Cadmus explained, fatigue dragging down every syllable. "I'm sorry, William, but we needed you. We needed your soul."

"M—my soul?" William shouted, his fear giving way to anger. These demons had tricked him, lured him with the promise of gold and riches, and now he was going to pay.

However, this would not stand with William Combe. Almost snarling, he shook his head and gripped his sword tighter. "What makes you think I'll let you have it?"

"You don't have a choice," another voice broke into the conversation, and William turned to meet it. Just making his way past the crest of the hill was Niccolo, his every step a declaration of violence. As William watched him approach, the blighted man threw off his cloak with his right hand before undoing the knot of his sling. William stared as Niccolo lifted his bandaged arm and saw how massive it was. Then he grabbed the end of the bandage and let it fall away, revealing the grotesque monstrosity of his demonic arm.

"What the fuck are you?" William asked, ignoring the terror that had already worked its way through his muscles and bones. He kept his weapon at the ready as Niccolo advanced, stretching his arm and flexing wicked fingers.

"I *was* just a man. Now I am so much more." As Niccolo made eye contact, a gust of wind picked up and pulled matted hair away from the side of his face, revealing the blight along his left side.

Wondering if he even had the skill to back up his claim, William dug his heels into the dirt and breathed in deep.

"I'm not afraid of you, demon," he stated, his voice only wavering toward the end. With a malicious grin, Niccolo continued forward as if he was being threatened by a child.

"That makes me like you all the more, Combe. Unfortunately, it changes nothing."

By the end of the statement, Niccolo was within striking distance and William realized that it was his only chance. Swinging his blade at Niccolo's neck and hoping to end the demon quickly, William knew he was fighting for his eternal soul.

Niccolo merely swatted away his blade with his human hand before rushing forward and burying demonic claws into William's guts.

"Don't feel too bad about this," Niccolo said before lifting William into the air by the hole in his midsection. "You never had a chance."

"Wh—" William started, but blood drowned out his question. His consciousness already fading, William grasped Niccolo's twisted forearm with both hands and stared directly into his eye. "Why are you doing this?"

"You're no use to me alive. When you fall, tell Barbas that Niccolo sent you."

"Bar..." William murmured weakly, but he couldn't finish the name. When Niccolo lowered his arm, William slid off of his hand and fell to the ground, his eyes unfocused as blood drained out of him.

William screamed as he was bathed in hellfire, his afterlife only just beginning.

CHAPTER 1
HELL AND BACK AGAIN

Barbas felt the ground shake from the new soul's impact, but he was currently distracted by a dozen new recruits fighting among themselves. Seeing two leaders among them, the old Fallen walked forward until he was in the midst of the struggle and within striking distance of each aggressor. With an expert hand, Barbas brought the gnarled end of his staff across the face of the larger man before spinning around and shoving the other end into the gut of a fat recruit. Once he did, the other souls backed away in reverence.

"You make me come down here and break up another squabble, and I'll make sure someone harvests your soul. We don't need soldiers who can't respect orders," Barbas said as the larger man picked himself off the ground and spat into the dirt at his feet.

"I ain't no soldier, old man, and I don't take no orders."

The ancient Fallen lowered his staff to the ground and set weathered hands across the top, cocking his head to side.

"And I'm no babysitter. I'm here to get you ready for the Apocalypse, and I don't have the patience to deal with every stubborn bandit. You follow what I say—"

"Or what?" the brute interrupted, his fists clenching hard enough to make the veins on his arms pop out. His temper flaring, Barbas had to resist striking the man again.

"Or you see what happens when you cross a fallen angel," he threatened, but the giant man was a stranger to reason.

He rushed forward recklessly—determined to strike Barbas' head with a hammer blow—but the old demon merely stepped out of the way and grabbed the back of his neck with his right hand. Immediately, the flesh withered and as the man screamed, Barbas forced him to the ground before looking up at a balding, gangly soul nearby.

"Draw your sword," Barbas gave a gruff command, but the man stood there for a moment. With some annoyance, Barbas released his hold and squinted at his recruit. "You've been here long enough, Tommaso. Draw your sword and stab him through the heart."

"Wa—wait," the giant protested, but Barbas was deaf to his words. He only stared at Tommaso until the man drew his blade and approached the sacrifice kneeling on the ground. Although he hesitated, Tommaso eventually forced his blade into the recruit's chest and took the life from him.

With a grunt, Barbas turned away from the new corpse and looked at each of the new recruits for the Pestilence Quarter.

"This is what happens. I see you fighting again, I'm going to make sure someone doesn't walk away. Now practice your archery drills, I have somewhere I need to be," Barbas said before turning away from his audience and walking toward the impact crater. He was getting tired of this—half the recruits falling from the sky had little use in Niccolo's war—and he especially didn't like having to slaughter the inevitable rebellious souls. However, this was his duty; this was exactly why he hadn't given up and ended it all those centuries ago.

Barbas was still making his way toward the new soul when he saw a formidable man running to intercept him. This soldier was also scarred by Niccolo's plague—something which constantly made Barbas uneasy—but this was how it had to be. Since Niccolo had started this Black Death, millions upon millions of people had died horribly, but it had also flooded Hell with new soldiers who could be used in his Apocalypse.

It was the old Fallen's job to make sure that the weakest were harvested by the mighty, creating stronger warriors with the sacrifice. It would have been detestable if it didn't make so much sense. Barbas hated the means and he was not sure about the ends, but his hands were tied.

This was war, and blood had to flow.

"Sir! Barbas!" The man skidded to a stop in front of his master, hyperventilating once he had a chance to breathe. "You need to come quickly."

"It's just a new soul, Adam. We've got time—"

"It's not *just* anything, sir. Just—come on," he said before turning and running back to the crater in a hurry.

Seeing his subordinate's reaction, Barbas quickened his pace and made it to the new soul within a minute. There was already a substantial crowd gathered there, but it parted once Barbas made his presence known. When he came to the lip of the crater, Barbas looked at the new arrival in wonder.

Already standing, the short-haired man looked up in a rage at all the gathered souls. What was most alarming was that the man was still fully-clothed; most souls arrived in Hell completely naked. He stumbled in place, dropping to his knees and breathing out in pain, but soon he got back to his feet and his lip quivered in anger.

"Where the fuck is Barbas?" he asked, at which point the fallen angel had no choice but to step forward.

"That would be me, young man. Who are you?"

The stranger stepped forward and climbed out of the crater, coming to a stop in front of Barbas.

"My name is William Combe. I don't know who the fuck he is, but that demon said to tell you that *Niccolo* sent me," he snarled, shocking Barbas into dropping his staff to the ground.

Looking over this new arrival, Barbas realized they were finally at the end. There were no more preparations to be made.

"They finally did it..." he breathed out, at which point William grabbed Barbas by the robes around his neck.

"They finally did *what*? Who are they? Who are you? Where the fuck am I?"

Barbas stood there as the man let loose his barrage of questions. Once he recovered, he pried William's fingers off his robes before bending down to pick up his staff.

"I'm sorry, young man, truly, but your sacrifice was necessary." Then he turned and started toward the palace at the center of Dis.

"You're not going anywhere," William declared, grabbing at the demon's back, but the Fallen would not be taken by surprise again. He whipped around and battered William's hand with his staff, cracking his knuckles with the strike.

"You—you broke my hand!"

Sighing, Barbas turned around and continued on his path.

"You'll be fine in a minute, just follow me. We don't have time to sit around and explain everything."

William was about to fight him—condemn this old man for breaking his hand—but then he felt his bones rearrange themselves and heal within a few seconds. Unable to keep himself from following after the demon, William looked at his hand in amazement.

"What... what just happened?" he asked, and with that Barbas had to stop and address the poor soul. He turned and set a veined hand onto his shoulder, seeing that William's rage had departed.

"Perk of the afterlife. Unless someone kills you, you can pretty much come back from everything."

"After... life? What—what's going on? Am I... what happened?" William asked with tears in his eyes, which pained the Barbas' heart. He bit his lip in consideration, but then gave William the answer he deserved.

"You died, Will. And I hate to be the one to tell you, but you stopped being human the moment Niccolo killed you," he said before patting William's shoulder and waving his hand at the palace and all the lands surrounding it.

"We're in Hell, and you've just been recruited into a war against God."

"THIS IS INSANE," William said as he fought the stress headache throbbing in his forehead, looking at the stairs beneath him. This new destiny was too much to take in. As Barbas led him through the Pestilence Quarter and up the stairs to the palace, William still felt like this was all a dream. He was going to wake up in his hovel in the swamp and he would have to go out and hunt for his lunch as soon as he could wipe the sleep from his eyes.

It was only made more surreal when he walked into an aging centaur holding an armful of scrolls. The creature sighed in dismay as it pushed glasses up to the bridge of its nose.

"What have we here, Barbas? I was just about to bring these scrolls to you and instead I find you leading a stray human to the palace?" he asked, staring down at William with academic curiosity. White and grey streaked through his black hair, and suddenly William was reminded of Garret and his other teachers.

"You may as well drop the scrolls, Buer," Barbas replied. "Niccolo and the others finally established their end of the link. I need you to—"

"No need to go further," the centaur interrupted, cracking his neck and sniffing. "I'll run on ahead and tell Astaroth to light the beacon. I only wish I had enough time to put these away."

"I know they're precious to you, but do you *really* think they'll matter after we rise up against Adonai?" Barbas asked. With a sigh, Buer turned to face the palace before looking over his shoulder, sorrow wrinkling his wizened features.

"I have to hope, brother. I have to hope our history will matter when all is said and done, even if we don't make it back," he replied somberly, taking a moment before galloping up the stairs at blinding speed.

William stammered after the creature, but then Barbas wrapped an arm around his shoulders and led him forward.

"Brother... Just who—"

"Don't let his shape fool you. Buer is one of the Fallen, just like me. You're going to meet a lot of them today and I don't blame you for being confused. Just... keep an open mind," Barbas said, trying to coax William out of his shell. Remarkably, it worked.

"Where is he going? Why are we heading into this palace?"

Laughing softly, Barbas looked at the entrance to the courtyard fifty yards away and remembered why they had rebelled.

"Astaroth has made the palace his base of operations and is in charge of everything now that..." Barbas hesitated, remembering his lost brother, but he fought back the tears. "Buer went on ahead so Astaroth can light the beacon and we can get your group together."

"My *group*? I have a group? Why am I so important?" William asked, causing Barbas to breathe in deep.

"Well, you're the reason they're going back to Earth, Will. We've been waiting for you to arrive for... well, this might not be easy to hear." After a moment's hesitation, Barbas cleared his throat and continued.

"They killed you at those ruins in order to create a link between Earth and Hell. Now that the link's established, our friend Moloch can create a portal leading directly to Stonehenge and we can send Buer and the others to finish the job."

"Sorry, but Moloch... Stonehenge... what is all this—" William said as he slipped out of Barbas' embrace, but he was interrupted by a giant column of white light bursting from the center of the palace. It shocked William into silence, but Barbas had been expecting this for months.

"Well, there it is," Barbas mused as he watched the light flare and then dissipate. Looking back down at his charge, he offered William a warm smile. "Moloch is an ancient creature—something like Adonai—and he's going to help us get our troops on the ground. He's not much for the end of the world, either."

"As far as your Stonehenge..." Barbas groaned before continuing up the stairs, his knees creaking in protest. As he tapped his staff against the ground, he looked over his shoulder. "Well, that's a modern name. Us Fallen know it as the entrance to Purgatory."

"Purgatory..." William trailed off as he remembered the name, and then all of his church lessons came flooding back. "You mean *the* Purgatory? Where souls atone for their sins before entering Heaven?"

"A fairy tale," Barbas growled, gritting his teeth subconsciously. "It's a prison for things Adonai didn't like. No mistake, there's plenty human souls stuck there, but all kinds of terrors and horrors lurk in the shadows." He paused on the stairs and looked behind him, past the Pestilence Quarter and to the darkness beyond. "And there are plenty of shadows."

"Why go there? Why—"

"I have to explain everything?" Barbas asked flippantly before continuing up the stairs, William trailing behind. The Fallen remained silent as he climbed the rest of the stairway, but once he neared the palace courtyard, he sighed and turned back to his companion.

"Angels can get to Heaven however they want. It's harder if you don't have the key. Purgatory is a back way in," he explained, breathing out heavily as William joined him at the top step.

"So it really is a war against God," William muttered. As he mulled over his response, Barbas walked through the gate and into the courtyard, dragging his feet across the tiles.

"That it is, though you may want to stop calling him God. 'Round here, we know him as Adonai. Takes away some of the absurdity of fighting a god if you don't call him one," Barbas added, and William was nervous enough to bite his lip. They walked to the doors in silence, but once Barbas pulled open the door and stepped inside, William could hold his tongue no longer.

"Why should I help you, or *them*? They killed me. If this is a fight against a god, I have no part in it," William paraphrased, inside his own thoughts as Barbas led him into the hallways of the palace. "What's my stake in this fight? Why should I forgive them?"

"They're doing the best they can!" Barbas shouted abruptly, shocking William out of his indignation. The old Fallen's voice wavered as he continued.

"Niccolo—they... they're all doing the best they can with the shit they got. They have the fate of the world on their shoulders and they're doing... they're doing everything they can to save you animals," he said, a tear forcing its way out of Barbas' eye as emotion overtook him. He jabbed a gnarled finger into William's chest at the end, but there was no force behind it.

"If Adonai has his way—like he's *had* his way—" Barbas said as he broke eye contact, shaking as he continued, "then you humans are no better than slaves. Dolls he plans to destroy before making a new playground, just as soon as he decides he's done with this one. They —*we* are fighting for humanity. And I'm sorry, but one life, *your* life, means nothing in the grand scheme of that."

"Barbas..."

"*Adonai* never wanted you in the first place," Barbas said, resuming eye contact as his lip quivered. "Scratch... Lucifer gave you everything and... and it cost him everything. And so help me, Niccolo and Cadmus are doing just the same, those bastards. So you forgive them. If not for them, you—just... you forgive them, alright."

"I..." William started, thinking up a hundred arguments, but the pain on Barbas' face destroyed every single one. It had only been twenty minutes since he had met this fallen angel, but William knew he could trust him completely. And if that old man believed in the people who had murdered him, William realized he might have to believe in them, too.

"I'll try, Barbas."

At his promise Barbas nodded a few times, wiped the tear from his eye, and then continued through the hallways of the palace.

William still had a thousand questions swarming through his head, but he wouldn't drag Barbas through them.

Eventually, Barbas led him to a doorway and pushed through, exposing a dark staircase that led even deeper into the bowels of Hell. William held his tongue most of the way, but once he was able to see the full expanse of his surroundings, his jaw dropped and he couldn't believe his eyes.

"This is... this is insane," he muttered, losing control over his mouth. He could only look at the giant archways above him, the columns of lava springing from beyond the cliff, and he was amazed that all of this was underneath an already-impressive palace. However, when he turned his eyes to the bottom of the staircase and saw the figures waiting for him, William stopped caring about his surroundings.

Buer was standing there talking to a giant creature with four arms, but the white mask on its face drew William's eyes. There were seven interlocking triangles displayed on the alabaster mask, and William could tell that they faintly glowed with golden light. The creature noticed William's arrival, but almost immediately turned back to Buer and murmured in a low voice. From his vantage point, William could not hear, but he wasn't sure he would want to.

Then, once Barbas and William had reached the ground floor, he noticed the bald figure standing at the edge of the cliff, light shining from his very skin. Lustrous wings stretched out from his back, but otherwise the man was completely nude. Coiled around his arm was a green serpent, its black tongue flicking in and out. William was still staring as the creature noticed him, which caused the demon to turn around and look at him with golden eyes.

"Lucifer..." William said without thinking, causing a twitch of annoyance in the Fallen's lip. Once the fallen angel turned around completely and walked forward, William realized he had made a mistake. Gold and white armor manifested around the man's skin and his wings disintegrated, making him look even more hostile.

"Not quite," the Fallen said as he moved to the center of the clearing, Barbas leading William to meet him. "I'm guessing this is the one, Barbas?"

"Yes, it is. You'll be able to leave soon," he replied as he set his hand on William's shoulder, trying to reassure the young man.

It didn't help.

"Astaroth, this is William Combe. William, this is Astaroth, the Duke of Hell," Barbas said, only making William feel worse for his mistake.

"I'm—I'm sorry. I just assumed that I would be meeting Lucifer."

Barbas gripped his shoulder tighter and Astaroth's face immediately filled with anger, but William felt grateful when the Fallen turned his gaze on Barbas.

"You didn't tell him," Astaroth growled, certain of his statement, and then he turned back to William. "Lucifer's dead. Killed by one of our brothers. For now, I'm in charge of Hell."

"I—I'm sorry," William started, but Astaroth sighed in disgust and turned his gaze to Moloch and Buer on the other side of the platform.

"Save it. Moloch, how soon can we get started?"

"Now, angel, but Moloch assumes the angel wishes to wait for others. Purgatory is danger and fragile creatures need to band together," Moloch stated, crawling forward with its massive knuckles. Astaroth crossed his arms before replying.

"Call me fragile again, Moloch, and I'll tear off one of your arms." Every word was tinged with violence, but the giant creature laughed in a low murmur.

"The angel is funny. Moloch will start once they are ready," it said before retreating to the edge of the cliff overlooking the lake of lava. With a sneer, Astaroth faced the others in the center of the clearing.

"I hate that he's always right... Anyway, Buer, you know what you need to do, right?"

That prompted a scoff from the centaur, who had come closer over the course of the conversation.

"Of course, I do. I've been studying Moloch's designs ever since we came up with this plan. When we leave Purgatory, I'll draw the sigils and we'll create the portal. There will be no issues on my end," he summarized, waving around his hands in absent gestures, and Astaroth looked at him with mild approval.

"Good. Now we just need to wait for—" he said as he looked past William and Barbas and toward the stairway, "...nevermind. Guess we're done waiting."

With a deep breath, William turned to find that the rest of their party had finally arrived. While two of them seemed to be normal humans, there was one creature who stole the breath from his lungs.

The two who looked most human were the first to reach the bottom of the stairs; one a woman in an almost-transparent dress, the other a lightly armored brute holding a giant hammer on his back. They each had black hair—the woman's reaching to the small of her back and the man's coming down to his shoulders—and they seemed to be in their late twenties. At first, William couldn't look away from the woman, who had gold and silver spun through her hair, but something was off about her and he couldn't quite place it. Soon, however, William's gaze fell on the man, who looked like he might be Egyptian, and it became apparent that he was someone important.

His chest was covered in a leather cuirass, a harness was lashed around his midsection and belts held his shoulder guards in place. All along his left arm were overlapping pieces of armor which kept it safe from harm, and he had a spiked bracer on his right arm. He wore a leather skirt with knives scattered along his belt, and great iron grieves covered his lower legs. Upon second look, William noticed that the great hammer on his back was blunt on one side and an axe blade on the other, which was something he had never seen before. After looking it over for a moment, William glanced back down to see the giant man leering at him.

"Like what you see, little man? Maybe I'll let you hold it if we have the time."

"Seere, that's enough, you can flirt with the new animal after you get to Purgatory," Astaroth said before turning his attention on the woman, who had wrapped her arm around Seere's tree trunk of a right arm. "And Sitri, why are you even here?"

"Moral support, cutie. I'll let you all go without a fight."

William would have been confused at her statement, but then he finally noticed the giant mass of cloaks that was still descending the staircase. Its sheer size was enough to make William breathe faster, but what drew his eye was the golden, three-foot long mask with a blue cross on it, blue orbs of fire burning low in the dark recesses where its eyes should be. If not for a low growl coming from behind him, William would have kept staring at the giant creature indefinitely, and he unintentionally jumped a few inches into the air once Moloch slammed a hand into the ground.

"The angel did not tell me *the Leviathan* would be going through the portal," Moloch snapped, its head jerking toward the radiant demon beside him. Astaroth merely shrugged.

"What does it matter? You should be able to send him through. You told me this portal could create a passage for hundreds of souls, if you wanted. The completed portal to Heaven is supposed to let the *entire army* through." Astaroth stepped forward, his upturned face only inches away from Moloch's mask. "Are you telling me you lied?"

"No, angel. Moloch does not lie." A deep snarl filled the air. "The portals will be stable. The angel's plan, however, is in danger. The creatures should not trust one such as the Leviathan."

"Why should they doubt, cousin?" twin voices soaked the air above William, one a whisper and the other a deep rumble, and with some anxiety William turned to see that the shrouded creature had somehow snuck up on him. The giant mask hung ten feet in the air above him, and by the end of its question, it had noticed the human standing beneath it. Tilting its mask, the creature looked at him with eyes of fire. "Hello, young one."

"Uh... hi," William muttered, and a quick flare of blue flames lit up the darkness behind the mask. He didn't know why, but William had a feeling the creature was pleased.

"Moloch knows this hunger, monster. The Leviathan has no need to help the angels or humans," Moloch replied, causing everyone to look back at it. These creatures were beyond all of them, and William stepped to the side in case they decided to come to blows.

Instead, warped laughter shook the air.

"No. No, I do not," a rasp tore through the air as the whisper became dominant, but the deep rumble took its place as it continued. "But their goal coincides with mine. Adonai must be reminded his place."

"And it hopes to educate the cousin? Is that the Leviathan's plan? It will consume everything, will it not?" Moloch asked, the golden light from its mask waning as anger filtered through its words.

The Leviathan shuffled forward, revealing twisted, six-fingered twin hands as its cloaks shifted and causing William to stare at it in horrified curiosity. Soon, it was just a few yards away from the other creature, Astaroth and Buer standing off to the side.

"I will consume what I want," it declared in twin voices, filling the giant chamber with echoes, "and I want a taste of angels and gods."

"Which is all we need, Moloch," Astaroth interrupted their conversation, pointing at a dark line trailing away from him. William looked at it and realized for the first time that the entire floor was covered in a spider web of markings; a giant circle forty yards in diameter.

A pit grew in his stomach once William realized he was standing in the exact middle.

"His goals are currently aligned with ours, and so it doesn't matter who he is or who you are, Moloch," Astaroth stated. "I don't care if he wants to dismember an entire legion of angels and lick the meat off their bones. If it gives us a tactical edge, I'll give him the salt to make them taste better."

"Angel, Moloch gives this warning for their benefit. The angel will come to regret this decision by the end."

"I'd rather regret my decision *then*. Thank you for your words, Moloch. Now please, get this started," Astaroth said as he stared at the alabaster mask above him. It was a tense moment, but then Moloch lifted his head and backed away from the defiant Fallen. Looking beyond him, directly at William, Moloch grunted in dissatisfaction.

"The human will stay in the center, the others will take their place along the edge of the sigil in each of the cardinal directions," it said before crawling toward the cliff.

Shaking, William worked through all of the options in his head and whether or not he was about to be sacrificed in some dark magic.

"You heard him. All of you take your place," Astaroth commanded, but William wasn't listening. Lifting his head back up, William panicked and looked all around him, watching as the Leviathan, Seere, Astaroth and Buer took their places along the edge of the circle. When he turned—desperate to find some escape route —he found Barbas staring at him from beyond the circle.

"You'll be fine, kid. Don't panic. You're the focal point, but you're going through *with* them. This is safe." Barbas' reassurance almost worked, but then a low murmur filled the air and William recognized it had come from Moloch.

"Nothing about this plan is safe, angel."

William finally decided it was time to run as fast as he could from the symbol, but he was too late to react. The creature slammed his hands down on the outer edge of the circle and white fire spread from where his hands struck, filling out the design. As soon as the first flare rose out of the sigil, William realized his feet were moored to the ground.

"I bet you wish they told you that before, right?"

When William turned to look at the source, he found Seere laughing at the ceiling. After a few seconds, the warrior looked back at William and winked. "They just keep fucking you over, don't they? How's it feel to be a sacrifice?"

"Don't listen to Seere!" Barbas yelled over the crackling of fire at their feet. At this point, the entire sigil was burning low with white flames and it had become difficult for William to see the old Fallen. "He's screwing with your head!"

"Hopefully not just your head by the end of this," Seere added with a smirk, and William realized what kind of man he really was.

Gulping down air along with his anxiety, William looked to his right to see Astaroth with his arms crossed, the snake on his arm coiled around brilliant armor. The angel was looking at the ceiling, light reflecting off his eyes, and in curiosity William joined him. Above them—spreading from a single point—was a swirling mass of purple and black energy. Crackles of violet lightning tore across the surface as the cloud grew in size, and William's fear was replaced by wonder.

"Wait!" a shout tore through the air, the voice a stranger to William. He lowered his gaze and looked to the entrance of the room to find something flying down from the doorway, its skin so dark that he could only see the bright blue electricity snaking through its torso and arms.

"Crocell, what are you doing here? Go back!" Astaroth shouted, and suddenly William realized something had gone wrong. He watched as the stranger dove through the air, and a bright flash of lightning from the maelstrom above them illuminated the new arrival. He had blue skin and wore black trousers, and the magnificent black wings stretching from his back let William know this was another fallen angel.

"I will not let you leave without me!" he shouted, the lightning along his skin flaring brighter with the statement.

William could tell Astaroth had meant to stop this Crocell, but they were interrupted by a loud crack above them. Without another thought, William looked above them and saw the giant mass of energy had imploded, creating a swirling tunnel of bright energy of all colors. Then he felt the wind whipping around him and his feet leaving the ground.

With no way to fight the pull, William was lifted into the air and unable to breathe as he saw impossible creatures and sights just beyond the walls of the vortex. If he could have thought with clarity, he would have seen his companions joining him as they entered the tunnel, but rational thought was beyond him. As he entered the portal, William realized that he could die satisfied, that he had seen the other side, even if he could not comprehend it.

And just as they were about to leave Hell, Crocell flew into the chaos and looped his arms around William, forcing his last coherent thought to be one of fear.

WILLIAM'S EYES OPENED, pain enveloped his senses, and he gasped in air that burned his lungs. He tried to sit up, but his strength abandoned him and the only thing he could do was roll over and support himself on his knees and elbows. Immediately, nausea overtook him and he retched into the grass beneath, his stomach cramping violently and forcing him to regret he had ever existed. His muscles continued to seize for a crippling moment—even if there was nothing in his stomach—and it took a few shaky breaths before William realized he was no longer in Hell.

When he looked up, he saw Paimon crouched on the ground and offering him a knowing smile.

"Glad to see you're back with us," she said before rubbing his back with her hand. Even though she had terrified him at the end of his short life, William felt comforted by her touch and closed his eyes as the cramps in his torso subsided. Once he reclaimed his senses, William leaned back and sat on his knees before spitting out the bile still clinging to the back of his mouth.

When he was able to see his surroundings, he found the familiar stone obelisks of Stonehenge encircling him. It was a beautiful day, barely any clouds in the sky, and it only served as a contrast to the creatures nursing their injuries as they recovered from their brutal landing. William was able to see Astaroth grimace in pain before shoving his arm back into place—it had apparently been dislocated after they had gone through the portal—and it only reinforced the idea that he wasn't someone William wanted to cross.

Looking to his left, he saw the Leviathan heaped over itself—the flames of its eyes burning low—and it seemed to be ignoring everyone around him, including Cimeries, who was glaring at the creature with concern. Turning around, William noticed Seere stagger into one of the giant stones surrounding them.

"What the hell just happened? Did Moloch do the spell wrong?" Seere asked as he buried his head in his palm. Before William could do much more than breathe, he heard someone stir behind him. Once he turned, he found Buer steadying himself on a nearby monolith with one hand, using the other to massage his right temple.

"No. No, I saw what he was doing and it was perfect. I helped him create the seals myself. No, this was—"

"Crocell," Astaroth growled as he rose to his feet and looked past William. "This was all because the slayer interrupted the spell."

"Why did he do that?" William finally entered the conversation, his mind swarming with questions as he looked to Paimon, who was frowning just in front of him. "Who is Crocell?"

"A coward."

Niccolo's voice had come from a few yards away, instantly throwing William's mind into chaos. He looked over at the man who murdered him and gritted his teeth, fists clenching so hard that his bones ached. As he knelt on the ground—Niccolo watching him the whole time—William was almost unable to restrain himself.

"He's not so cowardly anymore, it seems," Seere said from his vantage point, standing up to his full height and stretching his arms above his head. "The slayer was willing to risk everything by going through the portal. Must have been trying to make up for not helping out with Azazel."

"That sounds like him," Cadmus said as he walked into the circle of stones, earning their attention. "Did he not make it through?"

"I don't see him." Seere dropped his arms and set his hands on his hips. "Hell, I couldn't see much of anything once the portal opened."

"He..." William started, swallowing his anger and trying to concentrate on the matter at hand. Almost immediately he regretted it, since he gained the attention of every one of the hellish creatures. "He was holding onto me when I entered the portal, but I—I blacked out."

"Not surprising," Astaroth said, sighing as he looked to the centaur on the other side of the circle. "For now, we'll just have to forget about him. Buer, get to work on creating the portal. We'll get out of your way."

"Are you kidding? You're just going to give up on him?" Paimon asked in indignation. Astaroth merely looked down at her and scoffed.

"He was never part of the plan. Hell, he almost ruined it. I don't have the time or patience to deal with a penitent slayer. If he's alive —if he even *made it* through the portal— he'll be lucky. Now, let's get out of Buer's way so we can start this suicide mission of ours," Astaroth explained before turning away from his sister and walking out of the circle of stones.

Paimon was about to argue with him, her fingers growing in fury, but then she doubled over in pain and collapsed to her knees, coughing up blood.

"Paimon, what is..." Buer muttered as he walked toward her, concern evident on his face, but she threw out her hand and shook her head.

"It's nothing. Just... get on with your preparations. I'll," she said, wiping the blood from her mouth and picking herself up. "I'll be fine."

"Once we're in Purgatory, we're going to talk about this."

"Yeah, sure. We'll gossip once we have the time," Paimon replied with a weak laugh as the centaur walked over to one of the obelisks and drew a piece of chalk from the pouch held on his belt.

As Buer started his work scrawling designs onto the ancient relics, everyone vacated the circle except for William, who was still kneeling in the dirt in the center of Stonehenge. There was so much to take in, and these former humans and demons were talking as if this was normal behavior. Only a day ago, William would never have thought any of this possible.

"Get up."

William looked up to see Phenex staring down at him. Taking a deep breath, William ignored his command and watched Paimon depart from the circle.

"What's wrong with her?"

"She was poisoned, human. Yet *she* still got out of the way," Phenex said before picking William up by the armpit and glaring at him with disdain. "Now what is *your* excuse?"

If he had still been sane, William would have been frightened by the heat coming from Phenex's eyes—by any of the individuals who were just speaking—but his anger came back to him and he slapped the hand from his shoulder.

"My excuse? How about the fact that you bastards just killed me?" William said, standing up straight and acting indignant. In response, tendrils of flames wrapped around Phenex as he seemed to grow taller. It didn't much matter to William—he was too angry to care—but Phenex was hovering so he could look down on him.

"It was necessary, human. Did they not explain that to you? Your life means nothing compared to what we're trying to do." Phenex's tone was patronizing as flames licked at his cheeks, but William would not be intimidated. He only squinted before responding.

"My name is William. Remember that," he said, and a bitter laugh broke through the air. Both of them turned to see Seere leaning against one of the slabs, a smile on his face.

"I like that spirit of yours. You rebellious ones are just too much fun. And Yeshua," he added while looking at Phenex in disappointment, "don't pretend you're not human, too. What kind of precedent does that set?"

"*That's not my name anymore,*" Phenex said as he rose further into the air and wrapped his limbs in an inferno. "*Why are you even here? Aren't you supposed to be defiling Sitri?*"

"Touchy..." Seere pushed himself off the stone and crossed his arms, still smiling at the airborne man. "Why *wouldn't* I be here? I'm the new Horseman of War! This is *literally* my fight. Oh," he added before grinning wider, "and Sitri defiles *me*, if we're going to bring all that up."

"You're... the Horseman of War?" William asked, and Seere looked back at him in surprise.

"What, you didn't know? They really were just fucking you over..." he mused as he lazily set a hand on his hip. "Yeah, for about the last year. Once Niccolo declared himself the new Devil and came up with this plan, they kinda forced me into the role. I mean, I should have been the Horseman from the beginning, but I don't much like responsibility."

"The *Devil?* Niccolo is the *Devil?*" William asked, his eyes widening as he contemplated everything that had happened in the last day. He had been gutted by that man only a few feet away from where they were standing.

However, Seere's grimace told him Niccolo didn't deserve the distinction.

"Well, kinda. He *was* the Horseman of Pestilence, but then his horse died and he somehow got Lucifer's powers so... well," he said before hesitating and then twirling his finger in the air by his temple. "He's gone a little..."

"*You have no right to talk about him like that!*" Phenex shouted as he slammed into the ground and stalked toward the Horseman, scorching all the nearby grass once he was within a few feet. He was about to strike at Seere, who was getting into a ready stance and smiling, when a declarative voice rang out.

"That is *enough!*" Buer shouted from the other side of the ruins, drawing the gaze of all three humans. The centaur had somehow transformed over the course of the conversation and seemed much more imposing. New muscle stretched under his skin and he appeared twenty years younger, but what was most disconcerting was the armor that had formed over his loose clothing.

"All of this posturing has gone too far," Buer said as he walked over and pointed at each man in turn. "This is childish behavior and I will not have humans fighting and possibly destroying our one chance to enter Purgatory."

"Buer," Phenex started, but the centaur stamped one of his hooves and formed a great lance out of nothing so he could sweep it across the air in front of him.

"Stay here and I will be forced to remove you. *Have I made myself clear?*"

Completely intimidated, William nodded before backing out of the circle of stones. Seere joined him, unwilling to fight a fallen angel, but Phenex lingered for a moment and scowled.

"Fine," he muttered, and he flew into the air above them before departing in the other direction. Seeing that he was alone, Buer let his armor and weapon fade to the ether before taking his chalk back up and continuing his work.

William watched him draw for a moment, but eventually he turned to face Seere. The new Horseman was looking down the hill at Niccolo and Cadmus, who were sitting by themselves and seemingly refusing to look at each other.

"I thought there was a lot of drama in Hell, but that's nothing compared to this little group. I mean, I stirred it up a *little*," Seere said offhandedly to William, looking at him out of his periphery with a smirk, "but everyone here is on edge."

"Just who *is* Phenex?"

"Well, this is a bit of a secret but..." Seere said before turning to William, glancing around to see if anyone was nearby before leaning in to whisper in his ear. "You'd know him as Jesus."

"He's *who*?" William whispered back, almost unable to stop himself from shouting, but he was fortunately able to contain his reaction. Even then, Seere shushed him and raised a finger, but then he nodded behind them at the fiery demon flying around in the air hundreds of yards away.

Once they were looking in that direction, William noticed that Paimon, Astaroth and Solomon were having a very heated discussion on the ground. It even seemed like Paimon was stopping Astaroth from attacking the old reaper, but William couldn't focus on them once Seere continued.

"Phenex is exactly who I said he was. Used to be an alright guy, but when he lost Judas back during the fight with Azazel and Beleth, Yeshua went batshit and now he thinks he's one of the Fallen. I tell ya, between Phenex and Niccolo, our leadership is questionable." Seere only turned back to William by the end of the explanation and noticed that he was understandably confused. "Oh, Judas was a demon, too. One of the few guys I could fight without holding back. I'm gonna miss that guy..."

"Judas... Jesus... I don't..." Too many thoughts raced in William's head, but then Seere set his great hands on his shoulders and forced him to look up at him.

"Shh, you'll be fine. They're just people. Well, except for Astaroth, Paimon, Buer, the Leviathan and Crocell if we ever see him again. Even then, they mostly act by the same rules." Seere wrapped his armored arm around William's shoulders and pointed at the Leviathan with his thumb, who was still withdrawn and resting fifty yards away. "Though you should be careful with that one."

"I will. He... I don't like him. Or it. Whatever the Leviathan is," William mumbled before looking back at Niccolo and Cadmus, who had been joined by Astaroth, Solomon and Paimon. "So Niccolo and Cadmus were human once?"

"Yep, squealing babies and all. Cadmus is one of the brooding types, but he's a decent guy once you get him to talk, and Nico used to be hilarious. Real standup guys, those two..." Seere trailed off as he remembered the better days. As William watched, he wondered just what had happened to Niccolo to make him do such evil things. Barbas told him that Niccolo had caused the Black Death, that he had killed millions of people so he could raise a hellish army.

It wasn't exactly something William would have considered from a standup guy.

"He killed me. Smiled as he did it. I'm not seeing the joke," William said as he looked up at Seere, who avoided eye contact as he withdrew his arm from William's shoulders. Scratching the back of his neck, Seere bit his lip and turned to face him.

"Niccolo... Phenex wasn't out of line. I didn't have any right to talk about him like that. I'm sure that wasn't pleasant for you, but he is a good guy, deep down. Life fucked him over more than you can believe. Exiled from his home, ostracized for years, lost a devil who was like a father to him." Seere paused as he looked back at Niccolo, who seemed to be yelling at Astaroth as he swept his arm across his body. "Then he lost Plague."

"Plague?"

"His horse. They're tied to us, our horses," Seere said before a bundle of blood and tissue bubbled into the air beside him. Before William's eyes, bone formed into a massive frame and muscle lashed around it, tendons forming just before skin wrapped around the new tissue.

After a moment, a giant, red horse with black hair was standing next to Seere.

"If they die, part of us dies with them, Will." Seere was sympathetic as he lifted his hand and set it against the neck of his horse. "Since he bonded with me, I haven't been able to imagine how it would feel if I lost Fury, here."

"You won't have to know. I'm sure you'll die first," a throaty scream ripped through the air, shocking William momentarily, but then he saw Seere roll his eyes.

"He's been bitchy ever since his last Horseman died. Fury, this is William. William, this is Fury, my *war* horse," Seere said with a smile, a disgusted sigh filling the air.

"You know that was old even before you said it the *first* time. I'll be glad to have a new master once your corpse is in the ground," Fury responded, whipping his head hard enough to cause his mane to fall to the other side of his neck. Seere made a puckering sound with his lips before grinning.

"Love you, too. Now," Seere started, but before he could say whatever he intended, something struck the ground behind them with enough force to stagger William. Turning around quickly, he found a blue creature had fallen hard into the earth, creating an impact crater that spread out for a yard in all directions. Looking up at them with dark eyes, Crocell huffed before standing to his full height and gripping his trident tighter.

"Crocell? Glad to see you made it," Seere offered, but one look from the slayer was enough to stop him from continuing. Pointing behind him at a black cloud on the horizon, Crocell seemed to stare through the Horseman of War.

"Where is Astaroth? Michael is here and he has a dozen angels from the vanguard behind him."

"*MICHAEL IS HERE?*" Astaroth shouted in fury as wings burst out of his back and his armor formed in a flash of golden light. Within a moment, he had Crocell by the throat and lifted him in the air. "And you led him to *us?*"

"I did what I had to do," Crocell responded before letting lightning crackle through his skin, which literally shocked Astaroth into dropping him. Water flowed out of his back before solidifying into wings, but Crocell's black eyes were somehow more intimidating. "I was not going to let you leave me behind."

"Why would I want a coward like you in my strike force?" Astaroth asked, but Crocell scoffed before picking up his trident and pointing at the black specks that were growing by the second.

"I am about to show you why. Do you want to intercept them, or wait until they are closer?"

Astaroth merely fumed as light seemed to solidify around his hands. Instead, Cadmus was the one to speak up.

"We need to wait. Only half of our forces can go airborne, and we need to stop them from reaching Buer at all costs. If we draw the vanguard in where all of us can fight, we'll have a much better chance at defeating them," he suggested, causing the slayer of Dis to look at him with skepticism. Then Crocell nodded and let his weapon fall toward the ground.

"Fair enough." He looked at his colleagues and his eyes finally wandered over to William, who was standing between Seere and Paimon. Pointing his trident at the new soul, Crocell stared with black eyes lacking emotion.

"And this one? What do we do with him?"

After a moment, Astaroth sighed and shook his head.

"Who cares? His part is over."

"I'll take care of him," Niccolo offered to everyone's surprise. When he noticed their reaction, he merely looked back at the approaching angels, who were just starting to become distinct from one another. "What? I feel bad for killing him."

"You're going to be in the air, Nico. Did you forget that you fly now?" Astaroth had been patronizing and drew a snarl from the former Horseman as brilliant wings materialized from his back, but their conflict was interrupted before it began. Solomon stepped forward and waved at William from his place across the circle.

"I will keep guard with him as Buer completes the portal. I'll be no good in this fight as it stands, and each of you will be much more useful without having to worry about William," he explained in his calm manner, but Astaroth seemed like he was about to tear off the man's head just for speaking.

"Damn straight you'll be no good. You're lucky I haven't already killed you," he started, but a whistle pierced through their bickering and caused all of them to look a little further down the hill. Standing off on her own, Cimeries looked over her shoulder at them.

"There is no time for this. Solomon will take him to the circle and we will fight. It is that simple," she declared before turning back around and waiting for the angels to sweep down from above.

Without another word, the warriors from Hell prepared for the coming battle. Those who could fly jumped high into the air, and Cadmus and Seere summoned their horses and got into better positions where they could stop the advance of the angels. Their purpose was to create a wall between them and Stonehenge, and they would kill as many angels as they needed to do it.

Soon enough, William was standing at the base of the hill with only Solomon and Paimon, who beckoned for him to come with them to the safety of the stone circle.

"Wait," William said, following and making eye contact with Paimon once she looked over her shoulder expectantly. "Why aren't you..."

"Going with them?" she offered, causing William to nod. She shrugged before turning back around and starting up the hill. "You saw what happened up there. I'm... not well."

"I—I'm sorry," William said, not knowing what else to say, but he wished he had stayed silent.

"Not your fault, sweetie," she muttered, and they were quiet as they continued their way up the hill. They did not speak until they reached the edge of the stone circle, seeing that Buer had been busy with his chalk. Eldritch designs covered almost every slab, including the ones propped up by other monoliths, and it seemed like Buer only had a few left to cover on the opposite side of the circle.

"Is it alright if we take shelter here?" Solomon asked, his voice tinged with mild tension, and it caused Buer to look back at him in annoyance.

"As long as you stay over there, reaper. We cannot afford your *interference*." Buer emphasized the last word, but the meaning was lost on William.

"That is not my intention, Buer. I hope you realize that," he said softly, but Buer had already turned back to his work.

"We'll soon see if my hope is misplaced, *Solomon*. For now, I do not have the time to second-guess your intentions," he said before resuming his drawing. This led to an awkward silence, but then William turned back to watch the battle now underway.

On the ground, he saw Seere swat an angel out of the air with his hammer, his horse carrying him further before turning around. When he rode back past the recovering angel, Seere sank his axe head into the angel's body and split the poor soul in half. William was amazed at the brutality, but then a wave of fire crashed into the ground behind Seere and forced William to look skyward.

There, holding a burning sword almost as big as his own body, was an angel diving toward the fleeing Horseman.

"Michael," Paimon muttered beside him, and William turned to her before realizing that they were watching *the* archangel.

William looked back in time to see Astaroth intercept his brother and slam his fist into the archangel's face, sending him crashing through the dirt and creating a deep trench in the ground. Astaroth followed up that strike by sending a beam of energy after Michael, but something streaked into the air just before the impact. Although a large explosion occurred where the energy hit the ground, it was obvious that Michael had escaped.

"That's who we're up against?" William asked in desperation.

"Just one of them, honey," Paimon said, causing William to realize just how outclassed he was in this war. If any of these angels came after him, the only possibility was William's second death. It was enough for him to back away from the spectacle—every instinct telling him to run away—but he was stopped by Solomon's stern voice.

"Running will not help you, William Combe," he said, turning slightly so he could look at William out of the corner of his eye. "Fear will not help you survive."

"How—I can't be part of this. If any one of these angels..."

"Are you sure about that?" Solomon said, turning around

completely and propping his scythe against the ground to his left. "If they came against you, would you lay down your life for them, or would you fight? Would you try to survive by any means necessary?"

"I—I'm no coward, but—" William started, but his argument abandoned him once he made eye contact with the reaper.

"That is correct. In this very circle, when you first encountered demons beyond your imagination, you held your ground. You swung your sword against a Horseman of the Apocalypse, purely because you were too defiant to turn craven when it mattered most."

"So what? I still died." William looked at the ground with tears in his eyes, but then he felt a gentle hand on his shoulder.

"And you were reborn stronger for it. Make no mistake. You have something to contribute to this war, William," Solomon said, waiting for the young man to respond.

Standing up straighter, William nodded in return before they both resumed watching the battle at hand. He still thought it was hopeless, but William's resolve had been strengthened by the old reaper's words, and as they watched their friends fighting against Heaven's vanguard, William thought they may have a chance in this war after all.

That was until five angels, including Michael with his burning sword, broke away from the action and headed straight for them.

"Shit," Paimon muttered before turning back to yell at her brother. "Buer, please tell me you're almost done."

"A few more signs and then the only thing left is the incantation, but I need to wait until everyone is ready. Why do you sound so panicked?" Buer asked as he turned away from the last monolith. "Oh, that's why."

"Don't worry, we'll take care of it. You just finish what you're doing." Paimon extended her fingers into claws and let pointed teeth descend from her jaws.

"Because that is working out *so well*," the centaur replied sarcastically, but one look from Paimon's transformed face was enough for him to turn back around.

As she backed into the center of the circle, Solomon joining her, Paimon remembered that William was standing there and swept her arm across her body. "Hide! Step behind one of the columns!"

"But…" he started, unsheathing his sword as he spoke, but then William realized he would only get in the way. Before the angels had a chance to spot him, William ran between two of the pillars and then put his back to the ancient slab. It was just in time, as five angels arrived shortly after that, a torrent of wind sending waves among the grass and causing Paimon and Solomon to guard their faces.

"Sister, I had no idea you were part of this," a tenor called out to Paimon from the air, but William was unable to see him because of the stone blocking his view. "And you—Why on earth are *you* here?"

"I go where I please," Solomon said, holding his scythe with both hands. Paimon looked equally defiant; crouched and ready to slash at whatever angel came too close.

"Same goes for me," Paimon added, her words slightly warped by the excess of teeth in her mouth. A soft sigh came from the air, and William had to resist the urge to peek out from behind his hiding place.

"I would have preferred not to face either of you. Why must you continue to rise against him?" he asked, and William had to assume it was Michael talking. He couldn't see any of the archangel's subordinates being so familiar with Paimon.

"Why do you continue to act like his lapdog?" she asked, pointing a clawed finger into the air. "I know you, Michael. I've known you for millions of years. You're a *good person*. How do you not see Adonai's evil?"

"It's not up to me to judge whether or not our father is evil. I must carry on his will. Our brothers and sisters die as they distract your companions, but my priority is to destroy this portal. Our lives mean nothing, if not to serve him."

At that point William could no longer resist.

Peeking past the corner of his hiding place, he was able to see

Michael hovering there along with his fellow angels in the vanguard, each of them lazily flapping their wings in order to maintain their altitude. Michael was looking down at his sister with golden eyes, his short brown hair hanging loosely about his face. From his expression, William could see the archangel truly did regret this confrontation.

"You can choose to ignore him, Michael. You know right from wrong," Paimon tried once more, but the archangel slowly shook his head.

"Right and wrong have never mattered, and you know that. If they had, Lucifer, Tamiel and I would have ended up on the same side. I'm sorry, sister, but we must end this before it begins."

Michael held his burning sword above him and seemed ready to swing it down, but then a loud roar shook them all and a huge grey shape seemed to float through the air before spindly limbs grabbed two of Michael's fellow angels. When it landed in the center of the clearing, William realized what had come to save them.

"*The Leviathan?*" Michael asked in horror, lowering his sword as he realized what had come from the depths of Hell. With another roar—its mask splitting vertically to reveal long teeth and three tongues—the creature stood up on six of its hands, the faces of its victims screaming in silent torture and stretching against the skin of its distended belly.

After the horrific display, Michael tried to recover and brought up his sword, but the Leviathan merely swatted at him with one of the angels in its hands and sent Michael flying through the air. The attack broke the neck of the angel he used to strike Michael, but the other one was still alive when the Leviathan shoved the warrior's upper half into its mouth and slammed the mask shut, dismembering him before throwing the rest of his corpse into its throat.

The other, the Leviathan merely swallowed whole.

Before anyone was able to react, the giant creature used its eight powerful limbs to clamber over the stone monoliths of Stonehenge and pursue Michael, leaving only two angels for Paimon and Solomon.

Although the odds had shifted in their favor, the Leviathan's antics were enough to shake even them, so when the angels rushed forward, Paimon and Solomon were ill-prepared to deal with their attack. While Solomon was able to parry the numerous sword strikes of one of the angels—eventually countering with a horizontal sweep of his scythe and relieving the angel of her head—Paimon had less luck.

She tumbled away from the angel's initial spear thrust and slashed at her opponent's armor, but the angel parried it with his gauntlet. He pursued her with another series of thrusts, which Paimon deftly avoided, and eventually she contorted her body to use her foot to strike at the man's head.

Instead of taking it off, it was merely a glancing blow that knocked off the angel's helmet, revealing his dark skin. They backed away from each other after the exchange—neither side drawing blood—but eventually the angel was proven more fortunate. Paimon collapsed to her knees and into a coughing fit, blood coming out with each painful breath, and the angel used this as an opportunity to advance.

"No!' Solomon yelled as soon as he noticed, hoping to close the distance between them, but it had only alerted the angel to his presence. Instead of killing Paimon like he had intended, the angel hit her with the butt of his weapon, knocking her out, and then threw her like a ragdoll into Solomon, who was slammed into the monolith across the circle. Seeing that his two opponents had been taken out of the fight, the angel turned his attention on Buer, who was still furiously trying to finish the sigils on the last slab.

William watched as the angel drew back his arm holding the spear and prepared to throw it directly into Buer's heart. In fact, William was only a few feet behind the warrior and was holding his breath—trying to escape unnoticed—but then he realized just what he was doing. If he did not act, Buer would die. If he stayed with his back against the stone like a coward, their only chance to enter Purgatory would perish and William would die soon after that.

In that instant, William realized that he would not accept another death so soon.

As the angel brought his arm behind him, William jumped out from his safe haven—his sword now held in both hands—and he closed the distance with a few powerful strides. The noise was enough for the angel to turn, spotting William out of the corner of his eye, but he didn't have time enough to do anything else. William threw his blade across his body, attempting to sever the angel's neck. Only at the last second did he remember that when he had tried the same thing with Niccolo, he had died for it.

However, this time, William's blade cut into the angel's flesh, through the muscle and spinal column, and divine blood spurted out of the angel's arteries as his head fell to the ground.

His momentum carried William forward and he crashed into the angel's headless body shortly thereafter, rolling over the corpse and coming to a stop in the center of the clearing. It took a moment before William realized he was still alive and that he had accomplished his goal. Still surprised by what he was able to accomplish, William picked himself up just in time to see Buer staring at him in complete shock, the chalk previously held between his fingers falling through the air.

"I really hope you're ready for this," he murmured, looking past the human soul, who had been relieved only seconds before. With halted breaths, William turned around to see golden energy leaking into the air from the angel's corpse. It gathered in a small cloud for a moment—the spirit floating without a destination—but then it seemed to realize where it needed to go.

Before William knew what was happening, the power of the angelic warrior surged forward and tore him away from reality.

"Do you think he's dead?"

"He should be."

"He's the only reason we're all still alive, so you can all just stop it. Buer would have died if he hadn't stepped in," Paimon's voice echoed at the edge of his perception.

"Our sister is correct. William saved my life and I didn't know until it was too late. I... was fixated. Damn it all, if I had noticed, he wouldn't have had to take our brother's soul. It was too much for him," Buer added, and that allowed William to focus.

He had forgotten who he was, but they had given him a name.

"That's not your fault. If these two had been more capable, the human wouldn't have had to do anything."

"Oh, would you just quit it with that *human* crap? His name's Will and he just saved all our asses. Give him enough respect to call him by his name," Seere's voice joined in, bringing William back from the brink of oblivion.

Sucking in air, eyes rolling back even as his eyelids opened, William's back arched and his fingers curled as he rejoined the land of the living. Once his muscles stopped clenching, William was finally able to see his surroundings and found that almost a dozen souls were watching him with trepidation.

"Holy shit, he's alive," Seere said as he jumped back, and William tried to stand up, no matter how awkward he felt. He faltered— almost stumbling back to the ground as his legs gave out—but Crocell had leaned down and caught his arms, pulling William to his feet without a word. After a moment, he was strong enough to stand on his own, and he shakily pulled away from the Fallen's embrace.

"Um," William mumbled before breathing in and trying to collect himself. He felt tingly all over—and something certainly had changed—but he didn't quite understand what happened. "Are they gone?"

"Yes, William, after the Leviathan entered the fray, the vanguard was dispatched quickly," Solomon said. "Michael escaped, but that is no great surprise. That he had to retreat without stopping us is due entirely to your selfless act."

"Oh, that's... good to know," William replied, pursing his lips as he tried to understand that outcome. "So why did I pass out? What happened to me?"

"You," Cadmus started, pausing to consider his words. "You inherited the soul of an angel. Not just a former human, but an angel of Michael's vanguard. Whatever power he held in life is... well, now it's yours."

"It's mine? What the hell does that mean?"

"It means you're as strong as that angel," Niccolo said, making eye contact and letting his approval obvious. "It means you're one of us, now."

"I'm one of... you?"

"If you want to be," Solomon added, drawing William's gaze. "We always intended to give you the choice to return to your home once we established this portal. That choice is still yours."

"Choose quickly," Astaroth said in a clipped manner, looking over this newly powerful human. "We don't have time to waste and Michael can return here with a hundred angels within minutes," he added before turning to Buer. "Open the portal now."

"Astaroth, we should give him some—" Paimon started, but her brother shook his head dismissively.

"We've already spent too long waiting for him to recover. This is how it has to be."

Buer muttered a few curses at his brother, but then he turned toward the center of the ruins. As they watched, the centaur raised his hands to the heavens and hummed in a low voice. Then he started to speak words in a language William couldn't understand at first, though a nagging sensation tugged at the back of his mind. Soon, he understood a word here and there, and he had absolutely no idea why he could translate any part of it.

However, before William could truly consider that absurd notion, the chalk lines along the monoliths brimmed with dark power. After a moment of this, the lines warped and shifted around before floating off the walls and streaking toward a single point in the air. Once they joined together, a dark sphere appeared five feet in the air, only a few inches across. Then the pitch-black mass grew in size until only its top half was above the ground, the apex of the sphere fifteen feet in the air. At that point, Buer turned to face his companions and let out the breath he had been holding.

"The portal to Purgatory is open."

"So who's first?" Seere turned to face Astaroth, but the fallen angel was staring straight into the abyss. As stubborn and as strong as he was, it seemed like Astaroth had run out of confidence. He merely stood there, dark lightning reflecting off golden eyes, before a weary sigh filled the air.

"You were the one speaking of wasting time, Astaroth," Cimeries said as she stepped forward, pausing as she stood at the edge of the sphere. "It is ridiculous that you would stop now."

Then, without another word, Cimeries passed through the portal and disappeared into another dimension.

"Oh, man, that's gotta sting," Seere added with a laugh before walking up to the surface and breathing in deep. "Let's just hope *this* doesn't." The Horseman was a little more cautious than his predecessor—extending an arm first—but once Seere realized that it wasn't painful, he shrugged and then passed through the barrier.

Sighing, Cadmus followed after, Astaroth right behind him, and then each of their companions passed through the barrier. The Leviathan was so large it almost couldn't fit, but the creature ducked down so that its large body could pass through the surface of the sphere.

Within just a few moments, William was staring at the portal and still trying to make his decision, Buer watching him the whole time.

"It is not a coward's act if you decide to stay behind, William, but we don't have time to spare. The portal will stay open for one minute after I step through, so you must make your decision by then. I know that is not enough. I've had millions of years of life and I still fear the realm lying beyond this portal, but this is the reality of the situation."

"I... do you think I'll make a difference if I go?" William asked, giving the centaur an anxious look. However, that anxiety was unwarranted, as the centaur had a warm smile on his face.

"You already *have*, and history has a habit of repeating itself," Buer said before nodding and turning to face the portal. Within a few seconds, the centaur walked through the black surface and into Purgatory, leaving William Combe alone with a portal and an extremely difficult choice.

He only had a minute and it was obviously not enough time. Thoughts that were not his invaded his mind, battled against him, and William still didn't know what he should do. A day ago, he had been hunting in a marshland. In those twenty-four hours, William had met the Horsemen of the Apocalypse, died, escaped Hell, and stopped an angel from killing a demonic centaur intent on establishing a portal to Purgatory.

Now, if he was truly insane, he might follow all of these creatures into a war against Heaven. If he did not, William would be the petty lord of a kingdom devoid of worth, but he would be safe. For the first fifty seconds, William didn't know he would do. Then, just as the portal was about to disappear, he knew he could not forgive himself if he did anything else.

"Fuck it," William Combe muttered, and then he ran headlong into the unknown.

CHAPTER 2
MORE THAN A FEELING

"Michael. Michael, Michael, Michael..."

The archangel clenched his fists tighter as he looked down in a show of humility. Ahead of him was his father, long, black hair obscuring his face as he leaned forward, his legs covered by a loose white skirt hanging from his hips. After the deity leaned back in his golden throne, he crossed his legs and propped up an elbow on the arm of his chair. Now that Adonai was finished brooding, Michael made eye contact with his creator.

"I did what I could, Father. Once the Leviathan entered the fray, it became obvious that we were woefully unprepared. Within a few moments, he took out four of my vanguard. That I escaped with Muriel was a miracle." Michael motioned at the angel to his left, who was shaking despite her millennia of training.

They both knew the consequences of failing their god.

"A miracle? My baby boy, miracles only happen through my interference. You merely failed," Adonai said before looking to the shorter angel at Michael's side. "*And* you ran away with your tail between your legs. What kind of message does that send?"

"Father—"

"It sends a *bad* message, Mikey. It shows us as weak, it gives those traitors and murderers confidence. It gives them *hope*," Adonai said dismissively, uncrossing his legs just so he could lean forward and place his fingertips together. Behind him lay the expanse of his throne room, golden clouds and light radiating from a hundred sources in the pocket dimension, but Adonai dominated Michael's vision. "*Why* would we give them hope?"

"My lord," Muriel spoke up, her voice trembling before she stood up straighter and puffed out her chest. "It is not Michael's fault. At every turn he faced our enemies with bravery and strength. The vanguard was not prepared to find humans as strong as this group."

"You're saying it's the vanguard's fault? Is that it, Muriel?" Adonai scoffed. "You're taking the blame for my son's mistakes?"

"I..." she started, her breath halting in her throat before she peered at Michael out of the corner of her eye. With that one look, Michael knew exactly what she was about to do and he wanted to stop her. However, she jerked her head and stopped him before he could speak, looking back to their father with a determined gaze. "I am."

"That's cute. How long have you been rutting around with your sister, Mikey?" Adonai asked with a smile, shocking both angels, but he merely sat back in his throne and sighed. "You're supposed to keep your sword sheathed until I need it."

"It's not like that!" Michael protested, taking a panicked step forward. "She's just taking the blame so you don't punish me!"

"Then you should be grateful I'm going to let her do it," Adonai said with a cruel smile, and Michael heard a wet sound followed by a pained cough.

Turning, he found that Muriel had been stabbed through the midsection with a golden spear, its owner standing behind her with malice stretching the features of his long face. After a moment of dwelling in his satisfaction, Muriel's killer looked at Michael and swept long, brown hair behind his ear.

"Do you see now, Michael? This is what happens when you use

inferior angels and humans in your vanguard," the other archangel said before using his leg to push Muriel's body off of his spear. Disgusted, he took the time to crouch down and use the ancient warrior's tunic to wipe her blood off his weapon. "I would not have been found in this position."

"Uriel," Michael growled as he turned to face his sadistic brother, his right hand going to the hilt on his belt. "What have you done?"

"Only what our father wished," Uriel quipped, a light smile on his face as he rose to his feet. Behind Uriel, Adonai's throne room extended for a hundred yards; marble flooring beneath them, dozens of golden pillars stretching up to infinity and set against a backdrop of miniature suns floating through the air, and a giant white set of double doors at the end.

In that hall of radiance, this smiling angel was a source of darkness.

"Really, Michael, you should count yourself lucky that he did not order *you* to cut off her head."

"That's correct," Adonai added, causing Michael to whip around in fury, but his god was still sitting on his throne and watching the drama unfold. "I spared you that, since I know you cared for her."

"You didn't have to do that! Muriel was just being loyal to me! She was just being loyal to *you*!"

"What use is loyalty if it comes from a weakling?" another voice joined the conversation, and Michael turned to see his brother Sabrael walking from behind a purposeless pillar. He was shorter than Michael, stout, and wore purple robes, which contrasted everything else in the room. Still, he appeared as apathetic as always, ignoring Muriel's corpse and instead running fat fingers along the length of the column.

Once he was finished admiring the architecture, Sabrael turned to his brother with a shrug. "As far as we are concerned, Muriel's loss only means another vacancy in your vanguard."

"As far as *we* are concerned?" Michael lifted the sword from his belt and brought it to his right side, flames pouring away from the hilt. "Since when does *my* vanguard concern you?"

"Since the Apocalypse is now so very close, my brother, and since you failed in your mission." Sabrael didn't bother to care about Michael's hostility or the blade forming from his hand. He merely looked it over once before turning back to their father. "If it pleases you, I might be able to replace his ranks."

"It would please me if we replaced him entirely," Uriel added, walking past his brother and coming to a stop near Adonai's throne. "It's clear that he is incompetent. He could not subdue a handful of humans."

"That is true," Sabrael mused before joining his brother and father, taking his place on the other side of the throne. "Uriel and I were able to handle Niccolo and Cadmus easily some time last year."

"You faced them when they were weak." Michael drew his sword across his body and let flames condense until they became a single blade as long as his body. "And you didn't have to contend with Astaroth or the Leviathan."

"Really, brother? You use Lucifer's lesser twin and a monster as your excuse?" Uriel asked, using his spear to hold up his weight. "You brought twelve angels with you, and you brought *one* back. If I had been in charge of this operation, we would no longer be facing their threat and we would not be mourning twelve of your' inferior officers."

"You arrogant son of a—"

"Remember who your father is," Adonai interrupted, making Michael balk. Seeing his frustration, Uriel gave another smile and narrowed his eyelids.

"Yes. Remember, Michael. *Remember your place.* You are the flaming sword—God's weapon—and if a weapon cannot be used to kill his enemies..."

"...then what use is that weapon?" Sabrael added, a thin smile on his face. "I will choose the members of your vanguard and your next mission will not end in failure."

"You are not allowed to choose my soldiers! I was the General of the First Rebellion and I can destroy you in seconds!" Michael shouted as flames spiraled around his blade and he brought it to bear, his temper getting the better of him. Before he could jump forward, a low chuckle filled the air.

"He is allowed if *I* allow it," Adonai said, forcing Michael to falter in his step. With a smirk, Adonai leaned forward and tilted his head. "And I see no reason to stop him."

"Our father knows reason, Michael." Sabrael clasped his hands together, where they disappeared into the folds of his purple sleeves. "And we have no patience for your antics."

"Indeed. How about this," Uriel said before facing their creator. "We allow him to choose his own second-in-command? For a fellow archangel, it might be too much for his pride if he has no choice."

"I see the reason in that," Sabrael added, turning to face Michael with a nod. "He has provided for you in the past. It might be too much to ask to deprive him all agency."

"Too much to ask, my son?" Adonai said as he looked at Sabrael, who merely shrugged before responding.

"My apologies. A poor choice of words. Of course, you need not ask anything of your servants. However, he may fight with more determination if he is given... the illusion of choice," Sabrael said, staring straight into Michael's golden eyes.

Michael gritted his teeth, but he knew that the fate of his vanguard was in this archangel's small hands.

"The illusion of choice," Michael muttered, swallowing his pride and stepping back to his place beside Muriel's corpse. After letting his sword dissipate into the air, Michael placed the hilt back on his belt and let out a resigned sigh. "I *have* no choice, Father. Do what you will."

"Oh, Michael," Adonai said, leaning back in his throne. "That's *all* I wanted to hear. Sabrael will give you your vanguard."

"And his second?" Uriel asked, confident that a compromise would be reached.

"Will also be assigned by Sabrael," Adonai stated, surprising all three of them. "Michael, you've proven that you have poor judgment when it comes to your vanguard. I have no desire to let you do it again."

"My lord." Uriel turned to face Adonai, but one sidelong glance from their creator was enough to make him reconsider his words. "You are wise, of course. I am certain Sabrael will provide the best soldiers to use against these ruffians."

"I will, Michael," Sabrael said as he nodded toward their brother. "You have my word that your new vanguard will not disappoint."

It was all Michael could do to hold his tongue, but he knew that Adonai was merely looking for an excuse to punish him further. Clenching his fists at his sides, Michael bowed low before standing back up. Then, with one last nod at his brothers, Michael departed without another word. Anger built inside him with every step, but Michael tried to focus on what he could change.

And Adonai's will was definitely not something he could change.

MICHAEL WAS through the white double doors and in the entrance hall to Adonai's palace before he let himself feel grief for his fallen brothers and sisters. None of his vanguard were supposed to die in this mission; none of their enemies were supposed to be this strong. When Heaven's scouts had seen Crocell break through the Veil, Michael had not realized what would be waiting for him. Astaroth had been one of the strongest angels before the war, but these Horsemen were much more formidable than he had thought possible.

Setting his back to a nearby pillar, Michael let the emotions overtake him. He had known five of his vanguard since their birth, since the First Rebellion. The others Michael had picked by hand, Muriel being the youngest angel of them all. Michael had counted it a blessing when he had been able to retreat with her after the Leviathan had started his feast. At least *she* had made it.

And their father let Uriel kill her like a dog.

"I'm sorry, brother," Sabrael said from Michael's periphery, and he looked up to see his fellow archangels approaching. Pushing his back off the pillar, Michael crossed his arms and glared at them.

"You're sorry? You're *sorry*? Why should I believe that?"

"Because it is true," Sabrael offered, his face betraying the slightest amount of compassion. "I only wanted to help and I was... somewhat certain that you would not take my assistance."

"That is true, Michael." Uriel inspected his fingernails as he spoke. "That is why we suggested that you choose your second. We didn't expect Father to go against it."

"Oh, I can understand, Uriel. I do get that," Michael growled as he walked within just a foot of his brother and towered over him. "Except that you killed my second *right in front of me*."

"And you owe me a favor for that." Uriel's lip curled in disgust even as he stood in Michael's shadow. "Our sister should have already died on her sword in shame. I could almost say the same for you."

At this insult, Michael could take no more and swung his fist at Uriel's head. He would have succeeded if not for Sabrael, who knocked away his arm with a well-timed swipe of his staff. Snarling, Michael turned his attention to the squat angel and shook his head, pointing back at the doors leading to the throne room.

"Father would not approve. We already have enemies, Michael, and Uriel is not one of yours. I'm sure our brother will forgive you for this little outburst."

"Oh, he doesn't need to worry about that," Uriel added. Gritting his teeth, Michael turned to look at him and saw a smug smile on his face. "I understand why he might be a little sore. That temper of his... the frequency of his mistakes. I mean, he could have killed Lucifer and Astaroth two million years ago and he just *let them go*. He needs our guidance, brother. That is all."

"You..." Michael muttered, thinking up a hundred insults for Adonai's lapdog, but he swallowed them all down and stepped away from Uriel.

The First Rebellion had cost Michael more brothers and sisters than he could count, but it was only more painful that his favorites —the angels he *trusted*—were the very people who had risen up against Adonai. What siblings remained were not worth a fraction of the blood he had been forced to spill.

"...will be leaving," Sabrael finished Michael's sentence for him, motioning to Uriel with a nod. "We can see that our presence brings you anger and that is not our wish. I will contact you soon about your new vanguard, and again, our apologies."

"*His* apologies," Uriel said as he stepped to Michael's side and glared at him out of the corner of his eye. "You and I are merely even."

"We will never be even." Michael hoped to cause a fight, but Uriel smiled and patted his shoulder before continuing past him. Michael stood there as his brothers walked slowly to the end of the hall, the entrance doors opening before them. When they closed behind them, Michael thought he was alone.

Once he was by himself, Michael let the fury flow out of him and screamed, flames gathering around him. After his roar of indignation and frustration, Michael dropped to his knees and started to sob, grieving for all of the brothers and sisters he had killed or led to death over his millions of years of existence.

Flashes of memories came back to him; Lucifer laughing in the sun, Tamiel flying with him over the ocean, Muriel sparring with him in the light of Heaven. Those moments were all lost to time, but they would forever be burned into his mind.

"I'm sorry, Michael," another voice came to interrupt him, but he was glad to hear this one. Lifting his face and wiping tears from his eyes, Michael tried to recover himself as he saw another archangel walking toward him. Holding a golden staff decorated with twin serpents wrapped around it, his little brother had golden curls for hair and a tiny frame, and in contrast to their fellow archangels, his face was full of compassion.

"You have nothing to be sorry for, Gabe, and you know it. Our brothers' depravity knows no bounds." Michael sniffed back the snot from his sobbing and pushed himself to his feet, letting out a deep breath as he looked at Gabriel's chubby face. "It's not your fault that you're the only other archangel with a conscience."

"But that's exactly why I need to apologize *for them*," Gabriel responded with a warm smile, walking up to Michael with the aid of his staff. Michael frowned as he saw the angel limping toward him.

"After what you've done—after what Adonai did to you—you never need to apologize. *Especially* for the angel who caused that," he said as he pointed at Gabriel's leg. "How did you ever forgive Uriel?"

"I *didn't*," Gabriel responded with a short laugh. "I don't have to forgive either of them for anything they've ever done. We're just forced to live with their continued existence. Our father never had much in the way of taste."

"It's not up to us to forgive, Michael," Gabriel continued as he set a small hand on Michael's shoulder. "Our job is to balance them out. *We* are here to make sure that not all of the angels are terrible creatures. We serve as an *example*."

"An example people choose to ignore," Michael muttered as he looked away, but Gabriel lightly slapped his cheek.

"They were given free will for a reason," he said with a smirk, walking away a few steps before beckoning Michael to follow.

"What planet do you live on, Gabe?" Michael asked in dismay, crossing his arms as he kept pace with his brother. "Free will's a myth. We're all his slaves."

"*Are we?* I know a few thousand angels who refused to be just that," Gabriel said, his staff clinking against the stone underneath them. "It may not align with Adonai's wishes, but it still exists."

"And it causes a war every time." Michael said it under his breath, but Gabriel heard every word.

"Some wars are worth fighting. Anyway, that wasn't the example

I was trying to make," he said, causing Michael to look at him with skepticism. "I'm talking about humanity. Most are kept under control through the church's influence and the feudal system, but every once in a while, you find some worthwhile people. *Individuals.* There are those who stand up for what they believe in, no matter the cost."

"I'll believe that when I see it."

"Then you should open your eyes, Michael. They're out there. Trust me."

Shaking his head, Michael placed his hand on the door and pushed, the golden suns burning in the sky drowning both of them in light. For a moment, Michael closed his eyes and enjoyed the warmth on his skin, but it was spoiled by memories of his lost brothers and sisters. So many of them would never feel that warmth again; so many had been forced to live in Hell just to escape Adonai's cruel domain. Gabriel was right, there *were* people who stood up for something.

Unfortunately, they were all on the other side of this war.

NICCOLO OPENED his eye and saw grey clouds blanketing the sky. He sat up with a groan before propping himself up on his elbows and grinding the heel of his palm into his right eye. When he brought it down, he tried to look at his surroundings.

Instead, a three-foot long mask dominated his vision.

"Ah, the new god awakens," twin voices said as the Leviathan drew back, the fire of its eyes reduced to slits. Niccolo knew from experience that it was pleased, so he instead focused on what the creature was saying.

"New god? I wasn't aware I had reached godhood," Niccolo replied as he set his feet on the ground. A deep rumble filled the air as he did—the Leviathan was obviously laughing—but Niccolo was more concerned with their empty surroundings.

66

Dense fog obscured everything around them and, besides his monstrous companion, Niccolo could only see lifeless, cracked ground and withered saplings in all directions. He turned his attention back to the monster just in time for it to stare down at him with interest.

"You should hope you have become a god, if you plan to attack my cousin. Besides," the Leviathan whispered as it looked off to the right and sniffed the air. "You have changed. You are no longer human."

"I'm no longer human?' Niccolo asked, but the Leviathan shuffled off in the direction it was sniffing.

Unwilling to be left alone in this new realm, Niccolo jumped to his feet and followed after the otherworldly creature. Without looking at Niccolo, the Leviathan dismissively waved with a twin set of hands.

"You did not need me to say this. You have not been human since Lucifer's death," it explained, pausing as it considered its own statement. "Not entirely, at least."

"How do you know that?" Niccolo asked, causing the Leviathan to look over its shoulder and give a bemused laugh.

"You have been special since the first time we met. Inheriting Lucifer's powers only makes it obvious. To call you human would be an insult," the Leviathan responded before resuming its crawl, the mass of cloaks and robes covering it even as its entire body undulated with each step. Niccolo ran forward so he was at the creature's side before continuing the conversation.

"What does that mean? Does that mean I have the power to stop Adonai?" That drew a quizzical look from the monster, who stopped in its tracks.

"Possibly, though I do not understand why you want to stop him."

"W—why?" Niccolo asked, thankful that the Leviathan had stopped while he spoke. He was having trouble keeping up. In anger, Niccolo lifted his demonic arm and almost growled out his response.

"Because he manipulated me my entire life! He gave me this arm, took me from my family, and then he was responsible for Lucifer's death. He wants to destroy the world!"

"There are other worlds," the monster said—the deep rumble now dominant—and continued on its path. "Why do you care about this one?"

"Why do I care? Because this is *my* world! Because humanity deserves to exist, to be free!" Niccolo had forgotten that the Leviathan had a talent for upsetting him.

Chuckling softly, the monster continued on its path.

"Is that why you caused a pandemic and killed so many of those humans?" The Leviathan picked up speed, almost fast enough to lose Niccolo in the fog.

Cursing, he let out Lucifer's wings and flew forward, catching up to the Leviathan but shocked to see it crawling forward at top speed, its mask opening slightly and letting out trails of drool.

"Where are you going?" Niccolo asked, trying to shout over the impacts of the Leviathan's hands against the ground, but the words disappeared in the wind. He pumped his wings harder, trying to get in front of the creature, but he was surprised once the Leviathan again stopped in his tracks, and he was forced to bank hard and turn around.

After a few mighty flaps of his wings, Niccolo reversed his momentum and flew back to see the Leviathan standing over someone. Its mouth was open, exposing long teeth as the mask opened up wider.

Then Niccolo realized that the Leviathan was drooling over a defenseless and unconscious Crocell.

"What are you doing?" Niccolo asked once he landed a few feet away from the monster. When the Leviathan looked up at him with curiosity, Niccolo realized he had gotten there just in time.

"I am hungry. This one looks like he would taste interesting," it said, both voices wrapping around each other, but otherwise sounding like an innocent child.

Stomping forward, Niccolo tried to figure out some way to convince the simplistic monster why he shouldn't eat Crocell, but he was having difficulty forming an argument.

After all, Niccolo realized that if he had not woken when he did, he could have shared the same fate.

"He's one of our friends! We need him in the coming fight," Niccolo argued, causing the Leviathan to back away and close its mouth, tilting its head in confusion.

"You claimed he was a coward. He almost ruined the portal to Earth. He is not awake," the Leviathan responded, drawing in on itself as it looked at its potential meal. "If he does not wake, he will have to be carried. I am *hungry*, Niccolo."

"Then find something else to eat," Astaroth's voice came from the distance, and Niccolo realized he had never been so relieved to hear the arrogant Fallen. Breaking through the fog, Astaroth made his shining appearance before landing hard—cracking the lifeless ground beneath them—and then walked with purpose toward the Leviathan.

"I thought I smelled you," the monster commented, its eyes showing twisted satisfaction, but Astaroth was unbothered. He stepped between the Leviathan and Crocell and shook his head.

"Any of us who made it through the portal are not to be eaten. I need all of them, even the idiot who stowed away. Have I made myself clear?" Astaroth asked, and it shocked Niccolo to see the Leviathan shrink into itself and seem afraid.

"I am so hungry, angel. I was promised food, and it has been *hours* since my last meal," it argued, but Astaroth stamped his foot and nodded behind it.

"I will *not* have this argument again. When we *find* food, you will be fed. We're not exactly alone down here, so I don't want to hear it. Hands off anybody from Hell."

He jabbed his finger into the Leviathan's mask before turning around and crouching next to his brother. As Astaroth examined Crocell, Niccolo was filled with awe for the fallen angel. So many were afraid of the Leviathan, but Lucifer's twin just didn't seem to care.

"You want something, Nico?" Astaroth asked, not bothering to look away from Crocell. Now that he had been noticed, Niccolo approached them and crouched on Crocell's other side.

"What do you think is wrong with him?"

Astaroth only sighed and swept his hand over his face.

"I have no fucking clue. There are a thousand possible reasons. Too much travel over dimensions. Maybe he got attacked before we got here. There's a fair amount of blood here that already seeped into the ground, if you didn't notice." Astaroth motioned at dark stains around the body. "Though I'm not sure that's it."

"Why do you say that?" Niccolo replied, at which point Astaroth finally made eye contact with him.

"There would be evidence of a battle, especially since it's Crocell. I give him a lot of shit, but my brother is tough. Even if he got surprised, he would still get a few hits in on an attacker." Astaroth inspected Crocell's ribs, where small lacerations were slowly healing. "And it looks like the wounds are staying open much longer than they should be."

"Wasn't..." Crocell's voice interrupted them, which caused Astaroth to reach over and flip his body. Then he held his brother's head up so they could speak easily. "...wasn't anybody."

"What are you talking about?" Niccolo asked, but one stern look from Astaroth made him stop talking. Crocell's eyelids fluttered open, but then he grimaced in pain.

"I will be fine," he said while sitting up. Once he was able, Crocell climbed to his knees and cradled the wounds on his right side. "It was only a poor landing."

"Don't you lie to me." Astaroth rose to his feet, but Crocell laughed softly and set one foot against the ground.

"Then stop asking questions," he muttered before standing up with Astaroth, who was not entertained. There was a moment of silence as they stared at each other, but Crocell eventually relented.

"I lost the ability to heal properly after I fell out of the transportation spell's influence."

"You idiot..." Astaroth muttered, but soon he turned back to face the Leviathan, who had regained his confidence and was standing at its full height. "You're still not allowed to eat him."

"How did you lose—" Niccolo started, but Crocell looked back at him and sighed.

"I do not know how, Niccolo. I just know that it is gone. I was torn away from the human and had to force my way through the Veil, and something happened while I was there. I got these wounds," he said as he pointed at his ribs, "during the fight against Michael and his vanguard, and the fall after arriving in Purgatory forced me unconscious. I am not proud."

"You shouldn't be," Astaroth quipped. "What am I going to do with a Fallen who can't heal?"

"The same thing you were going to do beforehand." Crocell leaned down to pick up his spear before speaking again. "*Absolutely nothing.* I am my own master and you do not command me."

"Oh, I don't? How about I let the Leviathan eat you, then?"

"You don't let *it* do anything, either. I will be *fine*. Thank you for your concern."

"What are we going to do now?" Niccolo asked, gaining the attention of three intimidating celestial beings. However, this time Niccolo was not going to be silenced; he merely crossed his arms and waited for an answer.

Breaking first, Astaroth looked at the ground and rubbed his face before replying.

"We should find the others. They're probably all scattered like we were, but there is strength in numbers. Something we desperately need," he explained before resigning himself to a troublesome option. Turning around, Astaroth looked up at the Leviathan and sighed. "Can you sniff them out like you did Crocell?"

"Possibly. The blood made his scent much stronger."

"Desperately? Why do we desperately need strength I numbers?" Niccolo asked, drawing a scoff from Astaroth.

"Because, Nico, Purgatory is where nightmares make their home."

"WE DON'T NEED to do this now," Paimon claimed, but then another spasm ripped through her and instantly destroyed her case. Although she had already been kneeling when the fit took her, the pain was enough to cause her to fall to her side in agony.

"Stow it, Paimon. I won't let you stop me," Buer stated, kneeling over his sister and preparing a number of items. With only a nod, he threw a pack of materials at Seere and motioned to a series of runes ten feet away. "Place a crystal at each of the five circles at the edge of the design I drew. Then I'll need you to stand above the sapphire in the other sigil."

"Buer..." Paimon protested, but one stern look from above the frame of his spectacles was enough to finish the argument before it had started.

"This infection has to be taken care of, and that's all there is to it. I did not realize it had gotten this far or I would have told you to come to Hell so I could have fixed it sooner," Buer explained, drawing a blue vial out of a satchel on his belt and inspecting it. After a moment of watching the bubbles dissipate, he took out the cork and offered it to Paimon. "Drink this."

"I'm not going to," Paimon started, but then another stomach cramp hit her. With a sigh, Buer grabbed her chin and forced her to look at him.

"It's an anesthetic. This is going to hurt, sister, and I would rather you don't feel the brunt of this pain. We're literally cutting off parts of your soul." His tone was grave, and he poured the contents of the vial into her mouth, which she accepted without fighting. "Beleth was cruel. He found some way to rot you from the inside. I'm afraid the only method to cure you is a sort of... amputation."

"We're wasting time. We're in danger."

"We were in danger before. Only William's interference saved my life once this infection crippled you. It's better we do it now, before we encounter anything down here." Buer looked up at Seere and found that the Horseman had placed the crystals in the designated areas. "Excellent, Seere. Now go stand above that sapphire and we can get this underway."

"Buer, please, the Nephilim are down here," Paimon said in a panic, but Buer only groaned as he picked her up and walked to the chalk outlines he had drawn moments before.

"Which is exactly why I need you to have your strength before we encounter them. I'm through arguing." He lowered his sister to the ground and then pushed her back down when she tried to sit back up. "We're doing this now."

"Who the fuck are the Nephilim?" Seere asked, causing Buer to look at him in confusion. Soon, however, the centaur shook his head and waved off the question.

"After, Seere, please. Just be prepared for Paimon's transfer." Buer walked over to the third circle, where he would have to manipulate the spell and, hopefully, be safe from harm.

"Why is he... why is he part of the spell? What is this transfer?" Paimon asked from the ground—her hands cradling her abdomen—and Buer looked back at her with sympathy. Sighing, he took his place in his circle and then raised his hands, pointing at the others as he collected himself.

"Simply put, Paimon, I need somewhere for the corrupted energy to go. It seems humans are not affected by Beleth's poison." Buer could tell that Paimon was about to fight again, but he couldn't afford to waste more time. She *was* right about the Nephilim.

Speaking words he had been forced to relearn in the depths of the Infernal Library, Buer manipulated reality and felt the power of the ancients.

Before he could perceive the change, Buer saw thin wisps of energy that were already flowing from Paimon and into the crystals set into a pentagon around her body. It took him a moment, but he eventually found the dark energy coiled around his sister's soul and cursed Beleth once more. Pulling at the corrupted energy with his mind, Buer watched as the darkness poured into the five crystals, the light of her energy blinking out as Paimon screamed.

With all the mental energy he could summon, Buer pulled at the energy and then tried to shove it into the sapphire, but then he saw some of the corrupted soul flow toward him. Gasping, Buer pushed out and did everything he could to halt the progress of the black energy, and it was almost not enough. However, the energy soon stopped in the air and hung there for a moment, the screams of corrupted humans and angels echoing across the Void.

Ignoring his empathy, Buer focused and then pushed the energy toward the sapphire underneath Seere, who was obviously amused by the entire display. Buer would have laughed if he had not just avoided poisoning himself—he assumed he looked like an idiot while this was happening—but this was not a time for laughter. Instead, he gathered the energy residing in the sapphire and prayed that he was correct.

Then he shoved the corrupted energy into Seere's eternal soul.

With that last act, Buer was thrown out of the ether and back to reality, watching as Seere looked at his hands and trembled. After a moment, the Horseman anxiously looked up at him.

"So what the fuck just happened?" he asked, and Buer had difficulty finding the right way to say it. He approached the human and looked him over, hoping to avoid seeing any indication that Beleth's poison had affected him.

"Well," Buer said as he pushed his spectacles onto the bridge of his nose, looking over every inch of the Horseman's frame. "I removed a portion of Paimon's soul—what had been affected by the corrupted souls of the chimera, and I, well..."

"He just used you as a trash can," Paimon snarled from the

ground, and they turned to see her pick herself up and crack her neck before glaring at Buer. "He put you in danger just to save me."

"*Really*, Buer?" Seere asked, crossing his arms and frowning at the centaur. "I thought we had a mutual respect thing going on."

"We do, Horseman, we do," Buer said as he busied himself with gathering materials and throwing them back in his satchel. Avoiding eye contact, the centaur tried to offer an explanation that would stop them from being so hostile. "Every piece of evidence showed that humans were not affected by Beleth's poisons. Something about the human soul's makeup meant there was some natural mechanism—"

"What he is neglecting to tell you," Paimon interrupted him, making the centaur's lip tremble, "is that he had no idea what would happen if you absorbed the corrupted soul of a *fallen angel.*" She crossed her arms and shook her head in dismay. "If you had just waited until Nico or Cadmus was around, I would have let you do it without an argument."

"Well," Buer stalled, backing away from these clearly upset people, but then he relented and dropped his gaze to the ground. When he looked back up, his face was morose, which threw Paimon for a loop. "I... I didn't want you to die before we reached them."

"Buer..." Paimon muttered, her resolve breaking as she considered his feelings. "I wasn't going to *die*. We would have found them first."

"*Would* we have found them, Paimon?" Buer asked, fidgeting and running his fingers along the surface of the sapphire in his hands. "Would we have found them before we ran into one of our enemies? Before we found a settlement of Nephilim? Before this infection went too far?"

"We—"

"You didn't see it," Buer interrupted, looking her in the eye before pursing his lips. "It had already infected you more than I had thought. It could only have been hours before it had progressed too far. I made the right decision, Paimon." He looked back at the gem in his hands and worried his thumbs over its hard ridges. "I made the right decision."

"You big softie," Paimon said, surprising Buer by throwing her arms around his midsection. After throwing the sapphire back in his satchel, Buer brought his arms around his sister and enjoyed her warmth. When Paimon looked up at him, she gave him a bitter smile. "You always take care of me."

"I will never stop," Buer said before Seere cleared his throat. They looked over to find that he had summoned Fury and was leaning against the massive stallion. With a marked note of disappointment, Seere looked to his horse and waved at his fallen friends.

"These guys risked my life and haven't even thanked me yet. Can you believe that?"

"I wouldn't either," Fury somehow screamed in a whisper, causing Seere to grunt before turning back to the Fallen, who looked sheepish after his comments.

"I mean, *I* didn't want to risk your life. That was all this guy." Paimon nodded at her brother, but she gave Seere a warm smile after that. "Thank you. Seriously."

"Yes, thank you, Horseman. I honestly did believe you would be safe," Buer claimed, but Seere looked at him skeptically. Hoping he would not be caught in the lie, Buer was prepared to go further into his reserves of false evidence, but Seere shrugged and then climbed onto his horse.

"Good enough for me, and it looks like I'm stronger for it. I'll give you a pass," Seere said before grabbing Fury's reins and then patting the saddle behind him. "Get on, girlie, and we'll go about finding the others."

"Sounds like a plan," Paimon replied, but before she could take another step, Seere slapped his forehead and then motioned for her to stop.

"Wait, wait, you have to tell me about these Nephilim first. You're not keeping me out of the loop on this one."

Paimon grimaced when he said the name. Biting her lip, she held her elbow with her other hand and looked more awkward than Seere had ever seen her.

"I'll tell you on the way."

"You'll start now," he said, but he also reissued his invitation to Fury's saddle by extending his huge arm. Seeing the motion, Paimon nodded and approached the red horse.

"That's fair." Paimon grabbed Seere's outstretched arm and climbed onto the black saddle, which was a little too wide for her comfort. After wrapping her arms around his midsection, Paimon launched into her confession.

"The Nephilim were... well, they were the humans before there were humans," she said, Buer nodding along as he kept pace with them. "They were a giant warrior race and they held Adonai's favor for a long time, but then they decided they didn't need to worship him anymore."

"That's... close enough," Buer muttered, gaining Seere's attention before waving it away with his hand. "They started to worship themselves and their achievements, and since they were immortal, they thought they were gods."

"They weren't," Paimon interrupted, reclaiming her story. "You'll find that a lot of gods have forgotten that they're just more powerful than the other creatures around them."

"Anyway," she said, resting her chin against Seere's shoulder. "Once Adonai heard the Nephilim weren't paying him tribute anymore, he decided to throw them into Purgatory and teach them a lesson."

"And he's still teaching them their lesson?" Seere asked, drawing a scoff out of the centaur walking beside them.

"Adonai's only lessons are pain, cruelty and reminding people how powerful he is. The lesson has already been taught." Buer made eye contact with Seere after that. "He just forgot his students."

"Wait, so Adonai doesn't even know the Nephilim are still in Purgatory?"

"Probably not. He gets distracted easily, and there has been a lot going on since we rebelled and humanity started to evolve. I don't think he ever thinks about the Nephilim, even if the rest of us remember." Paimon leaned back, sinking into her own memories and regretting it. "Not sure we can ever forget. There were thousands of casualties on both sides and it was such a needless war. The Nephilim were just trying to live in peace, and we ruined that..."

"So you were there, huh?" Seere looked over his shoulder and watched her lost and looking into the distance, even if the fog was impenetrable. A tear formed and rolled down her cheek, and he realized he never should have asked.

"I was in charge of their genocide."

CADMUS LOOKED DOWN at William and wondered if they would be responsible for this boy's second death. It seemed like Cadmus couldn't get away from this blight on his soul; he could not escape from this destiny. When they had first risen to Earth, Cadmus and Niccolo had done everything they could to avoid spreading their plague and hurting innocent people. Now, millions of people had died for Niccolo's vengeance and it didn't seem to bother him at all.

The boy unconscious beneath him was hopefully the last one to die, but Cadmus had learned that hope was a fool's prospect, especially where Niccolo was concerned.

"William," Cadmus said as he crouched down and placed his hand underneath his head. This young man did not deserve what they had done to him, but Cadmus tried to justify it. They had needed their link from Stonehenge to Hell, and killing a defiant son was the best way to do it. It had never sat well with Cadmus, but now that they were in Purgatory, he could at least justify the end, if not the means.

"You realize that it does not matter if he dies." Mercy's rasp had come from the ether, and Cadmus looked up to see the white horse standing at his side. With a shrug, Cadmus looked down and rubbed his fingers through the boy's hair.

"One soul among many," Cadmus said before reaching up to Mercy's saddle and grabbing a skin of water from the pack. "I know the statistics, Mercy, and you don't need to convince me that I shouldn't feel guilty."

"That is good."

"Because it doesn't *matter* that I *shouldn't*. I'm going to feel guilty and you know it. Allow me my selfish compassion."

"I do not allow you anything, Master." Mercy peered into the distance. "That is not my place."

"Good," Cadmus said as he took the skin of water and placed it to William's lips. "It's one of the few things left to me. It's... one of the few things that let me know I'm still human."

"You have no need to explain that to me. I... sympathize, if nothing else," Mercy rasped before nuzzling against Cadmus' shoulder. "I just wish to relieve you of some of that burden."

"It's a burden I wish to keep. That's all it is," Cadmus replied before lifting the container and letting liquid bubble out, splashing against William's lips. Almost immediately, the water was spat back out and William thrashed in the reaper's arms, but eventually he sat up and frantically looked around.

"And this is your reward." Mercy let out a weak laugh, causing William to back away from them and hyperventilate.

"Clearly." Cadmus used his cloak to wipe away water and saliva from his cheek, and then he pushed himself to his feet with his sigh. Once he was standing, he offered William a hand. "Come on."

"Uh... thanks," William said, hesitating on the word before grabbing the arm and getting yanked to his feet. Soon, he was standing on his own and looking around their surroundings. "So this is Purgatory, huh?"

"Unless Buer made a catastrophic mistake," Cadmus said before looking over Mercy's saddle and noticing that the ground just *ended*. He turned—about to tell William he was going to inspect it—but then he saw a tall shape coming out of the mist. Once he saw the white blade, however, he knew who had joined them.

"He did not. This is Purgatory. This is exactly where we need to be," Solomon declared as he approached, coming to a stop when he was just five feet away. "It's good to see that you made it through unharmed, William."

"Was that in doubt?"

"Dimensional travel is always tricky. I barely made it through the last time I tried," Solomon said, earning skepticism from Cadmus, but he returned a look that meant any questions would go unanswered. Unfortunately, Cadmus had become used to that look, so he decided to ignore the reaper's mysterious past and focused on his surroundings.

Walking around his horse, Cadmus inspected the drop-off he had found earlier and realized he could not see past twenty feet in this fog. Summoning a fair bit of power, Cadmus swept his scythe across his body and let out a blue wave of energy that took the fog with it. What he saw was enough for him to gape in wonder.

The ground literally fell away to reveal a deep abyss with no end in sight. If they fell off, Cadmus had no way of knowing if they would ever hit the ground. Looking into the distance, he saw that small islands hung in the air—with pathways miles long—but the fog consumed them again after just a moment. Stepping back from the edge, Cadmus looked at Solomon and nodded behind him.

"If we fall?"

"*We do not fall,*" Solomon said, firm, the gravity of the statement enough to make Cadmus feel even worse about their situation.

Stepping back around Plague, Cadmus looked at the older man and then to William, wondering what their next step should be. They were here to find the entrance to Heaven, but Cadmus hadn't expected to be separated from the rest of the group. He wondered if the others still existed or if they had fallen into the abyss, their quest already a failure.

"Do we have any way of finding the others?" William asked,

surprising both reapers. When they turned to look at him, William realized what they were thinking and crossed his arms, looking offended. "Oh, because I'm the new guy I'm not supposed to think ahead?"

"Sorry, we're used to Niccolo," Cadmus provided, smiling slightly. "Explaining things comes naturally to us."

"Well, I'm not him." William turned around and shifted his weight to one leg. "So do we? Have any way of finding them? Can you do that scythe trick again?"

"I probably shouldn't." Cadmus laughed wearily as he considered the consequences. "I could cut our friends in half."

"That would only be a little productive," William said with a smile, which in turn made another appear on Cadmus' face.

Something about this boy was bringing out the lighter side in Cadmus, but he had no time to dwell on levity. He turned to Solomon and waited for him to contribute, but found the man looking skyward. Joining him, Cadmus saw what had grabbed his attention.

"It could be something dangerous, but it could be exactly who we need," Solomon mused, and Cadmus immediately knew they did not have a choice. Breathing in deep and gripping his scythe tighter, he didn't wait for Solomon to agree and instead turned his attention to the orange light beyond the grey clouds.

"*Phenex!*" Cadmus shouted at the top of his lungs before throwing the scythe across his body and aiming a projection of energy to the side of where they saw the dim, orange light. The clouds parted as the distortion continued, but it wasn't enough to expose the source of the light. However, whatever it was noticed *them*, and the light grew brighter and brighter with each second. Holding their weapons ready, the reapers prepared for whatever horror came out of the clouds, William joining them once he stopped gaping up at the sky.

Their fears were proven groundless, as the fog burned away to show Phenex descending from the sky, coming to a stop just a few feet above the ground.

"You almost cut me in half, Cadmus," he said, but a knowing smile betrayed the false annoyance. Seeing that Phenex was in a lighter mood, Cadmus placed the handle of his scythe on the ground and supported himself on his weapon as usual.

"If I had tried to cut you in half, you probably would have been completely destroyed," he teased. "I'm glad that you were flying around, though. We were just wondering how we were going to find the others."

"What does that have to do with me?" Phenex adopted a somewhat hostile stance, but Cadmus was unintimidated.

"You can burn away the fog, which means we won't have to worry about falling off into the abyss," he explained, interesting Phenex enough that he abandoned his flames and touched down on the ground.

"The abyss?"

"We're surrounded by it," Solomon stated, waving behind them to the cliff Cadmus had found earlier. "One misstep and you could be lost forever. Well, unless you fly, of course."

"Of course," Phenex added with a satisfied nod. "So I'll lead the way?"

"Yes, that will be best, but I must warn all of you about what we may face now that we are in Purgatory," Solomon said, all of them turning to face him. "The abyss is not our only danger. Purgatory is full of monsters and nightmares."

"We've heard this before, Solomon." Phenex sighed, but the old reaper shook his head and halted him with a free hand.

"No, we did not brief you as well as we should have, and William has had no warning," he said before continuing and gripping his scythe tight. "Purgatory itself is a living creature. It will see inside you—see what you *fear*—and it will bring that out. It will manipulate you and force you to see the worst aspects of yourself, and there are entities who will amplify this effect. Purgatory wants you to lose your humanity."

"Humanity is not exactly something we need anymore," Phenex

muttered, but Cadmus took the warning to heart. He had seen what it was like to lose too much humanity; Niccolo was a constant reminder of that.

"Your humanity gives you strength, Phenex, even if you refuse to see it," Solomon argued before looking at each member of his audience, including Mercy, where he stalled. "Well, for most of us."

"So what do we need to do?" William asked, earning the old reaper's gaze. Solomon seemed to appreciate the thought and approached, placing a weathered hand on William's shoulder.

"Stay true to your self. You will each have to confront the worst in yourself, the worst in others, but if you stay strong—if you maintain your sense of self—we will all make it to the other side."

"This is stupid," Phenex jabbed, but one glare from Solomon was enough to make him stop talking.

"You will see. You will understand, eventually. However, I cannot hope to convince you now. Experience will be a better teacher. Lead on, and we will follow."

"Hmph, fine." Phenex huffed before letting flames wrap around him and then floated into the air. Setting off at a walking pace, Phenex sent tendrils of fire into the mist, evaporating the dense cloud and giving them much greater visibility. After a moment of this, Cadmus jumped onto Mercy and then motioned to the spot behind him in the saddle.

"Solomon?"

"No. No, thank you, Cadmus. These old bones want to enjoy some walking while they still have the time," he replied, so Cadmus turned to William.

"I've never been one to sit behind anyone on the saddle..."

"I'm just trying to be nice, Will," Cadmus said, and William realized he might have offended him.

Hesitating for a moment, William walked forward and then jumped into the saddle, awkwardly wrapping his arm around the reaper's midsection.

"Thank you," he muttered, at which point Cadmus laughed and then urged Mercy forward.

Since Solomon was walking, they kept a slower pace than Cadmus or Phenex would have preferred, but—seeing as they did not know where they were going—it didn't matter how fast they traveled. Noticing that Solomon had wandered off a bit, inspecting bits and pieces of the world around them, Cadmus turned to look over his shoulder and start a conversation with their new companion.

"I'm sorry about all of this, William, but I'm glad you decided to come with us," he said, but his passenger refused to make eye contact with him.

"It's... I didn't really have a choice."

"I..." Cadmus hesitated, looking down at Mercy's neck. "I know. I know we said that you did, that you could have gone home, but your hands were tied. If you decided to stay and we were successful, people would have noticed how you never seemed to age. If we weren't successful, there... there wouldn't be a kingdom for you to rule anyway."

"I'm glad you understand."

Cadmus wished he could convince William that it was all worth it, but he was not so sure, himself. After breathing in deep and letting the air back out, Cadmus lifted his head and looked at Phenex, who was issuing bursts of flames in all directions.

"I do understand. As many choices as I've made with Niccolo, I've always been reluctant. I've always felt like my hands were tied, that I didn't have a choice, even though I did. That's... I think that's the essence of this struggle," Cadmus said before looking back over his shoulder. "It's that—because of how we see things—it doesn't even seem like a choice. To someone like Adonai, to the Leviathan, to someone without a conscience, they could see both sides.

"But I don't see the other way, Will," Cadmus said as he turned back around and closed his eyes. "Adonai needs to be stopped. We need to stop the end of the world. I can't just sit back and watch it happen, especially since I *know* that I can help."

"That's well and truly noble, Cadmus," William replied, but Cadmus could hear from his voice that he hadn't convinced him of anything. "Did you use that same reasoning when you tricked me into becoming your sacrifice?"

"Yes," Cadmus said quickly, even though he felt awful for doing so. "This struggle isn't just about life and death. It's about freedom, and it's about making sure humanity has a future. Even if it means losing *our* humanity... even if it means causing the Black Death..." he hesitated again, breathing out shakily as he recalled the malice in Niccolo's eyes.

"That's... I think I understand," William admitted, but Cadmus didn't feel like he had won any argument. "Do you think you've lost your humanity?"

"No, not completely. Not yet..." Cadmus trailed off. "At least, I hope so."

"And what about Niccolo?" William asked, which shocked Cadmus back into the moment. Over the last year, he had seen Niccolo commit atrocity after atrocity, enough cold-blooded murder to remind Cadmus of some of the worse souls he had reaped.

"I..." he mumbled, remembering Niccolo's promise after Tamiel's death. He had claimed to be the new Devil, and in this last year he had lived up to that claim. Unable to look back at William, at anyone, Cadmus stared at the cracked ground before him. "I don't know."

"I was afraid of him," William said softly, causing Cadmus to turn back in his saddle. "When he came to kill me, I thought I was seeing pure evil. He didn't hesitate at all."

"No. No, he didn't," Cadmus admitted, dropping his gaze. "He wouldn't have."

"And why is that?" William asked, and Cadmus didn't have the strength to lie.

"You were the third man we tried to sacrifice at Stonehenge... and the only one to make it back."

CHAPTER 3
GHOSTS OF LIVES PAST

Blood ran down the other side of Gabriel's arm, and his breath caught in his throat as he tried to turn his arm over and stop wasting his sacrifice. The rebellious trail of blood collected at his elbow before a glob of blood became too heavy and fell. Gabriel watched as it splashed against the floor, splattering and marring the partially completed sigil at his feet, but he should not have wasted time on saving errant drops.

Falling to his knees, Gabriel flexed his wrist—bringing new blood to gush out of his slit veins—and went to work finishing the sigil. It was a large pattern, but Gabriel had no need for the blood in his body and rushed through the rest of his preparations before using the sleeve of his robe to wipe away the scarlet that clung to his elbow. Sitting back on his knees, Gabriel looked over the design and nodded before wrapping a bandage around his wrist. Once he stemmed the flow of blood, Gabriel stood up and looked over his shoulder, paranoia destroying his nerves.

He hated doing this—especially now that Adonai had started the war machine of the Heavenly Host—but delivering information was Gabriel's purpose. Walking over to the doorway of his modest apartment, Gabriel watched as patrols of angels flew through the sky, as former humans marched their way through the streets. Anyone with sense knew these drills were useless, but it kept most souls busy and unconcerned with Adonai's plans and the antics of his archangels.

Unfortunately, it meant creating a communication portal between Heaven and Hell was a risky endeavor.

Letting out a deep breath, Gabriel turned away from the door and walked back to the blood sigil on the floor. Satisfied that the angelic runes were all in the right place, Gabriel lifted his staff and slammed it into the middle of the design before backing away. Speaking just above a whisper, Gabriel uttered the words that would allow him to transcend the barriers between dimensions, watching as the snakes coiled around his staff unwrapped themselves and then stretched out in opposite directions. Turning back in on themselves, the golden serpents arched back together to form a circular window flickering with energy.

"Buné," he commanded, and all at once the blood on the floor bubbled as if a fire had been lit beneath the ground, some of the new bubbles popping before the blood took on life and rushed toward the staff standing upright on its own. Gabriel's sacrifice ran up the grooves of the golden staff before covering the serpents, continuing on until it came to the joining of their mouths.

Once his blood ran along the edge of the staff, the empty circle flickered and showed an image of the Void—twisted energies threatening to break through—before it shifted and Gabriel saw an armored man reading a scroll. Upon seeing his fallen brother, Gabriel cleared his throat and waited for Buné to take notice, and he was disappointed to see him raise a finger.

"Just reading the end of a sentence, brother." Buné's grey eyes were focused on the ink in front of him, but Gabriel had no time to waste.

"I doubt it's as important as what I have to say to you," he said, but Buné held up his finger until he was ready. After setting down the scroll, Buné sighed and made eye contact with his heavenly brother.

"You would be surprised what happens down here, Gabe. Thousands of humans die every day and it's my job to keep up with the casualties of our new recruits, delegate to the reapers, et cetera." He lifted his hand and wiped fatigue out of his eyes. "Not to mention playing babysitter to the demons Astaroth left behind. Asmodeus is furious that they snuck out without him. Looks more like a lizard every day."

"I don't have much time here, Buné. I'm risking a lot bantering with you," Gabriel replied, and Buné dropped his hand and looked at him expectantly.

"Well, you should have interrupted, then. What's going on?"

"If only it was that simple, reaper. Anyway, the team made it through."

"How would *you* know that?"

"Because they didn't go through without incident." Gabriel nodded in the direction of Adonai's palace. "Michael saw Crocell break out of the Veil and followed him to Stonehenge, where he encountered the strike force."

"Damn it all," Buné replied under his breath, leaning forward so he could prop himself up on his desk. "How many died?"

"Twelve," Gabriel said, watching as Buné's eyes wandered away from the portal in mourning. "All of Michael's vanguard."

"*What? How?*"

"Our friends were able to drive all of them back. It helped that the Leviathan was there to terrorize them." Gabriel saw the confusion on Buné's face mixing with relief. "It seems like the plan is still on track, so you can tell everyone to continue preparations."

"And what's the bad news?" Buné asked, cutting right to the heart of it. Shocked for an instant, Gabriel recovered and shook his head. After so many years, Gabriel had forgotten his brother's talent for reading subtext.

"Because of his apparent failure, Michael has fallen from favor.

He's not going to be the leader of the Host this time around, I'm sure of it." Gabriel looked at the floor as he considered their options. "Adonai is depending more and more on Uriel and Sabrael. He even let Sabrael select Michael's new vanguard."

"That's... not good." Buné leaned back in his chair and crossed his arms. "It would be much better if we only had to contend with Michael's leadership. He always did favor a direct assault."

"Yeah, that's what we had hoped for, but obviously we need to rework our plans. Uriel would act the same way, of course, but—"

"Sabrael is a bit more cunning than that," Buné finished the statement, pursing his lips. "Thank you, Gabriel. I'll have Eligos revise the battle plans and see what we can do to anticipate the change in leadership. Is there anything else?"

"That's not enough?" Gabriel asked, raising an eyebrow, but Buné did not seem amused.

"Like you said, you're the one at risk for this conversation. I would assume you wouldn't open the portal unless you had something more substantial to say," he explained in a dry tone, and he was right. Gabriel shouldn't have opened the portal without something more to say.

"It's a—a feeling I have," he said, looking away from the portal. "About Michael."

"What about him? Does he have a weakness we can exploit?"

"It's nothing like that," Gabriel said before looking back at his brother. "The conversation I just had with him made it seem... it made it seem like he regretted his actions during the Rebellion."

"We always knew he had a conscience." Buné clasped his hands and supported his chin once he leaned forward. "Michael only fought for Adonai because he didn't know what else to do."

"I know that. I know." Gabriel replied, pausing as he considered how to say it. "But it really seems like he's had a change of heart, especially after Adonai ordered Uriel to kill the last angel of his vanguard in front of him. I think... well, I think we might be able to get him on our side."

"Interesting, I hadn't considered that." Buné looked down, his brow furrowing as he contemplated having another archangel allied with them. After a moment, he looked back up, but then his grey eyes opened in alarm.

"Close the portal now!"

Gabriel turned around to see what had spooked his demonic brother, but then he joined Buné in his panic. Standing at the doorway was an imposing brute, piecemeal silver armor set about massive shoulders and along his torso, but the look on his face was more frightening than his physical threat.

He had seen Gabriel communicating with the forces of Hell.

"Sir Gabriel," the soldier muttered, looking from the portal to Gabriel, his lip quivering as he tried to understand. Gabriel took that moment to pick up his staff—the image of Buné flickering out of existence as the weapon reverted back to its normal shape—but it was already too late.

"Kushiel, it's not what you think," Gabriel started, walking within a few feet of the giant angel. "I'm a messenger for Adonai! I was speaking to one of the Fallen and trying to establish codes of conduct during the final battle."

"Sir..." He paused, looking down on the archangel in disappointment, "I'm sorry, but I don't believe you."

"What are you—"

"I heard a great deal of that conversation before I walked in the door," he said, glaring down at his superior officer. "You are a traitor, Sir Gabriel. You use blood magic to make plans with the enemy. You are on *their side*," he emphasized, which made Gabriel realize that there was no talking his way out.

He had literally been caught red-handed.

"Kushiel," he muttered, but the large angel brought out a mace as tall as Gabriel's entire body.

"There is no convincing me, sir. I hope that you will come quietly for his judgment." Seeming the coward, Gabriel backed away and pointed out the window.

"He—Adonai would never have let you exist. If they hadn't fought against him, you would never have been born a human, died or become an angel. Why would you help him in this war? Why would you not rise up with me?"

Kushiel stepped forward and towered over him.

"He is *God*, Sir Gabriel. I have no choice," he said, raising his mace in violence, but Gabriel was prepared for that. Abandoning his fear, the archangel looked up in sorrow.

"Neither do I."

Gabriel quickly rolled underneath his legs before turning around and slamming his staff against Kushiel's neck. The giant man was unable to react before the twin snakes on Gabriel's staff slithered around his neck and then rejoined their mouths just above his Adam's apple. Once they made him a gilded collar, the bodies of the snakes flattened and became a sharp blade pressing against his neck, and—with a silent prayer—Gabriel pulled on his weapon and cut through Kushiel's throat and spine, relieving the giant angel of his head. As he turned to see the giant fall, Gabriel's staff reverted back to its normal shape, but it was covered in innocent blood.

"I'm sorry, Kushiel," Gabriel said, closing his eyes and crossing his chest as he prayed for the human's soul. After a silent moment, Gabriel made a simple rune in the air, which burned gold as his finger left the pattern. Muttering out another spell, Gabriel set his palm against the sigil before pushing it against Kushiel's body, where it seemed to disappear into the ground.

"I'm sorry for that, too, but I can't do you the honor of a proper burial. I... you deserved better, noble one," Gabriel said before scrawling another rune into the dirt now covering Kushiel's body. It flickered out of existence quickly, and soon Gabriel was left alone in his apartment. With that many wards in place, no one would find him; Kushiel would be just another unaccounted-for angel in the Host's records.

It was unfortunate, but Gabriel knew he had done the right thing.

Trying to assuage his guilt, Gabriel prepared himself for another meeting with Adonai as he took care of the remaining evidence. Once he took the bandage off his wrist—the wound already healed— Gabriel looked around for any other clues to his misdeeds before nodding and tossing the bandage into the air. With a snap of his fingers, the fabric burst into flames, not even leaving ashes to scatter on the floor. After that, Gabriel's apartment looked exactly like it had before.

Although he felt guilty, Gabriel knew what was at stake and why he couldn't have let Kushiel escape with his knowledge. Focusing instead on what he *could* accomplish, Gabriel stepped through the doorway of his apartment and walked along the shining path leading to Adonai's temple, his thoughts on how he might be able to recruit Michael to their side.

But as he walked away, Gabriel did not see the blue wisps of energy rising from Kushiel's makeshift grave.

***

"It's been hours since we've started," Niccolo said, looking at Astaroth out of the corner of his eye. Although his eyes narrowed, Astaroth looked ahead as they marched through the fog, their visibility down to just ten yards.

"And what do you suggest? We can't exactly just sit around and twiddle our thumbs." Astaroth gritted his teeth while the serpent on his arm flicked out its tongue.

It regarded Niccolo with interest, but he knew it was just a fragment of Astaroth's soul, mere decoration. Instead, Niccolo pointed to the sky with Lucifer's sword and let out his wings.

"Why don't we fly? All three of us can search in different directions," he said before pointing back at Crocell, whose ribcage had healed on the exterior, but the slayer was acting as if his bones were still mending. The snake on his arm hissing, Astaroth turned to face Niccolo with fury etched into the lines of his face.

"What, and lose *each other*? I don't think so." He closed the distance and whispered so only Niccolo could hear. "And we don't want to leave the Leviathan behind."

"Why not?"

"Because if we don't keep him in check, we're gonna have a lot more problems. Between you and me, we might be able to handle him, but if it gets hungry and we can't talk it down, we'll have another monster on our hands," he explained before drawing away. Doing his best to avoid looking at their monstrous companion, who was shuffling forward on eight hands, Niccolo caught up with Astaroth.

"What do you mean, *between you and me*? You always talk like you can handle him yourself."

"That's what it is, Nico. *Talk.* I can't hope to match the Leviathan alone. He'll eat me alive. Even though I don't like it—and even though you're a piss-poor substitute—you do have Lucy's powers, which is what I would need to subdue it. Basically," he said before making eye contact, "if I want to take him down, I need your help."

"You'd need *my* help?"

"Trust me, I'd have it any other way. An animal dressed up to look like my brother isn't my idea of an ally, but we do what we have to do." Astaroth kept walking, the mist sweeping around his legs as if it wanted to devour him.

"Then why do you talk to the Leviathan like you do?" Niccolo asked as his wings shattered into light and disappeared.

"What do you mean?"

"You talk like you can take him down at any moment. Just a show of dominance?" he asked before looking back at the Leviathan. The blue fire of its eyes gave an ethereal light to the mist surrounding them, making the monster seem even more eerie. Niccolo may have come from the depths of Hell, but this creature was more fearsome than anything else he had encountered.

"You can't dominate the Leviathan, you just have to appeal to its baser instincts," Astaroth explained in a low voice. "It wants to eat, so I promise it food. That's the best I can do. The rest... the rest of it is just me."

"Just—"

"I would rather die than back down, Nico," Astaroth stated, not bothering to conceal his words. When Niccolo looked back, he found a Fallen who had never lost his defiance. "That the Leviathan could eat me whole means nothing."

"So you're just stubborn?"

"You're one to talk," Astaroth growled, lowering his gaze so he could stare at the mist pooling about his feet. There was silence for a moment and Niccolo thought the conversation was over, but once he moved past the fallen angel, Astaroth lifted his head. "We'll both need that, Niccolo. That stubbornness."

"Yeah?" Niccolo asked over his shoulder, pausing to look back at Lucifer's brother. With the mist surrounding them, the golden eyes shined through the atmosphere and it was easy to see the resemblance.

Only when he spoke did Astaroth betray the similarities.

"It's the only way either of us will make it through to the other side. You can't stop in Purgatory. You can't think. You just have to push forward, *keep* pushing until we're at Adonai's door. Anything less, any doubts, and you'll be stuck down here." As punctuation, Astaroth let his wings appear and stretched them out to their full span.

"Now you're just being dramatic. Why bring out the wings if we're not flying?" Niccolo asked, but Astaroth had no patience for him.

"Clearing the way, you idiot," he said before bringing forth his wings and creating a gale wind that almost knocked Niccolo off his feet. Only by materializing his own wings and flapping against the current did Niccolo stay standing, and when he looked back up at Astaroth in rage, he was just about to summon Lux from the ether.

However, he stopped once he saw that the mist had been banished from the ground between them. Turning around, Niccolo saw that Astaroth had carved a path for them; a great divide had appeared between the clouds that had covered Purgatory for miles. Seeing a number of shadowy figures standing in the mist, Niccolo assumed that they had found the others and ran forward.

"Nico, you idiot!" Astaroth shouted after him, but Niccolo wasn't listening. He just continued, hoping their forces would soon be bolstered, and for the first few seconds wondered what he would say. The mist fell around him as he ran, and soon Niccolo was alone if not for the shadowy figure that was now standing just a few yards away.

"Who is that?" he asked, skidding to a stop so he would not barrel into his friend. However, once he spoke, he saw the figure's head jerk, as if it had been surprised to hear anything at all. It stumbled forward on two legs that barely seemed to support it, and Niccolo realized why Astaroth had warned him. Letting out his wings and forming his weapons, Niccolo prepared himself for whatever he was about to see.

"Who is that?" he repeated in a low voice, but the figure only jerked its head to the side again. Realizing his own mistake, Niccolo took a cue from Astaroth and stretched out his wings before giving a great flap, pushing away the mist obscuring the mystery figure. When he was able to see who had come to greet him, Niccolo found it difficult to prepare himself for battle.

Emaciated arms lying limp from weary shoulders and rot and decay evident from the spider web of veins on his face and exposed skin, the man looked like a shambling corpse. Niccolo had seen so many awful things since he had started his plague—untold amounts of dying men and infected creatures rotting from the inside—but this was worse than any of his crimes against nature. That was because this was a different crime; a man whose death had been long before Niccolo's turn to darkness.

Shuffling toward him, mouth held open unintentionally as his jaw muscles were too weak to keep it close, was Giovanni Simonetti.

"My God," Niccolo mumbled, reverting to old habits as he watched the man stumble.

"Your... fault," Giovanni choked out, green liquid trailing from the corner of his mouth and dribbling down his chin and neck, and it had stained the faded yellow collar of his ruined clothes. "You did this... to me."

"I..." Niccolo stammered, his sword falling to his side as his arms became heavy. It all came back to him, memories of that last duel flashing before his eyes. He watched from his own perspective as he disarmed Giovanni's guards, defeated the bloated noble and cut him with a poisonous blade. Niccolo could see it all now; how the venom had coursed its way through Giovanni's veins, destroying his body over his last painful days.

"You filthy—" Giovanni choked and doubled over, letting out a stream of brown muck before looking back up at his killer. "You filthy peasant. You killed me like a coward."

"I needed—I needed to do it," Niccolo replied as Giovanni closed the distance, but he was still seeing Camilla from that memory. He remembered her pleading, the ring she tried to give back to him. That was when he remembered how Giovanni had stabbed him through the back; that was when he regained his confidence and anger. "I did exactly what I wanted to do, Simonetti."

"Just like you did... to them," the living corpse said before jerking around, letting his emaciated arm fling around in a reckless gesture. Looking beyond his killer, Niccolo saw the group of souls who had gathered at the edge of the mist.

Most of these he did not recognize, but he saw that they all held something in common. Swollen buboes were scattered along their skin, black from the plague Niccolo carried with him. They were covered in rags, peasants all, but then more filled their ranks. Niccolo could see men and women from all walks of life, all of them staring at him in condemnation.

"You killed all of these people, Niccolo Vespucci da Firenze," Giovanni said, his words still coming out of his throat even though his jaw had gone slack. "Because you are selfish. Because you wanted revenge. They were victims who did not deserve their fate, because you wanted an army that has little hope to succeed."

"I don't care—"

"You killed *me*." Foul saliva splattered out of Giovanni's mouth and sprayed Niccolo in the face. "You killed me because you wanted revenge, but did you stop to consider who else would be hurt? Did you not consider what would happen to Camilla?"

"I..." Niccolo muttered, unable to stop that guilt from washing over him.

"Because of you, she was forced to fend for herself. With me, she would have at least had a life, *Vespucci*," Giovanni said, jerking his arm around again. "Without you, all of these people would still be alive."

"I don't..."

"You killed them, Vespucci! You killed me! And we want *our* revenge!"

Giovanni lunged forward with his mouth, his teeth latching onto the skin of Niccolo's neck. Flinching in that moment, Niccolo fell away as he tried to push off his attacker, and his skin tore as Giovanni chomped down and fell back. Covering his wound with his hand, Niccolo looked at Giovanni as he spat out a chunk of skin and smiled.

"Are you so much a coward that you will not face our wrath?" he said, enmity in his eyes, but Niccolo recovered once he heard another voice coming from the sky.

"Nico, goddamnit, where the fuck did you go?" Astaroth yelled, and Niccolo remembered just who he was.

Giovanni was no man to condemn him; none of these souls were of any consequence. In Niccolo's mind, he was a new devil; he was a scourge who would be responsible for killing God.

And if he could kill a god, he could kill these people again.

Bringing up his weapons, Niccolo stretched out his wings and threw them forward in a mighty flap, screaming with three voices in harmony with each other. Light burst out in all directions and solidified rays of light lashed out and drove away the mist, some of them even impaling the living corpses that had gathered around him. Niccolo let the light burn away from him for a few moments longer—reveling in Lucifer's inherited power—but he soon collected himself and turned his attention back to his victims.

When he looked back down, Giovanni was staring at him in terror, and eight of the plague victims were already writhing on the ground. Malevolence twisting his heart, Niccolo stalked forward, the buckler on his left arm pulsing with bright light that burned away the mist. Once he was within a foot of his killer, Niccolo towered over him and breathed deep.

"You'll die, Vespucci. I will die again with confidence, as long as I know that," Giovanni said, already shrinking away in fear and betraying his promise.

"And I will count myself lucky that I get to kill you again," Niccolo replied before planting Lux deep into the noble's heart, twisting the blade and letting Lucifer's light burn through the disgusting man who had stolen the love of his life. As Giovanni turned to ash, Niccolo turned his attention to the other souls who had gathered to condemn him. They all stood there, pained expressions on their faces, and Niccolo almost allowed himself to feel guilt.

Then he remembered why he had sacrificed them in the first place; that these souls were so worthless that they had not even made it to Hell.

Letting Lux brim with divine energy, Niccolo swept the blade across his body and sent out a radiant arc that cut through dozens of the miserable creatures, as if he was merely a farmer in a field of grain. As soon as they fell to the ground, his victims turned to shadows that leaked into the cracks of purgatory, and Niccolo realized that it was all an illusion. Not noticing the smile on his face, Niccolo continued his slaughter, detached from any compassion he might normally have. For the moment, he was truly enjoying this, no matter who might be watching.

And as it watched from a nearby hilltop, the Leviathan found a kindred spirit.

———————

PAIMON SLID off the saddle before Seere could do much more than gape in wonder, but as he saw her stumbling toward the huge skull —its jaw open to the sky—he realized that she needed the moment to herself. Stopping her would be an intrusion, so he looked over the giant skeleton, seeing the bones of its arm rising ten feet in the air.

Five thousand years in Hell and the Horseman had never seen anything like it.

"We are cursed, Horseman," Buer said, and Seere broke his gaze away from the giant corpse and saw the despair on Buer's face. "We have already stumbled into their territory."

"*Whose* territory? How is there any territory at all down here?"

"The Nephilim," Paimon muttered in a daze, drawing closer to the gaping jaws of a former enemy. When she raised her fingers to touch a tooth as big as her hand, Paimon hesitated—feeling like she could be crossing a line—but she needed to know if it was real. Pressing her skin to the rough surface of the yellowed teeth, Paimon knew for certain and wept.

"That's a Nephilim?" Seere asked in alarm, standing up in his stirrups so he could look at it better. "It's massive! That mouth could swallow Fury and I together!"

"Only if you allow us to be eaten, weakling," his horse replied, but Seere disregarded the insult and turned to Buer.

"But it's dead, right? They're not walking skeletons, are they?"

"Don't be absurd," Buer said as he walked over to Paimon, who had pulled away from the ancient skull and was holding her elbow to her side. "This one has been dead for years, at the very least. He—"

"She," Paimon interrupted, turning to him as a tear rolled down her cheek. "This one was a woman named Gerhun. She killed more than a few angels in her time."

"How do you know it's her? She doesn't even have skin," Seere asked, prompting Paimon to point up to the empty eye socket of the giant skull.

"See those three lines at the brow? I gave her that during the Fall of Jotunheim. Would have taken her eye, but their leader called for a retreat before I could tear it out," she explained, turning to face her old enemy once more. "From the defeat in her eyes, I could tell she wanted me to kill her. I thought I was giving her mercy by letting her go."

"But then Adonai banished them all down here," Seere murmured.

"We thought he would be more lenient on our cousins," Buer said, placing his hand on Paimon's shoulder. "We could not have known he would be this cruel."

"And this was our first lesson," Paimon said before a roar filled their ears. She whipped around to find the incoming threat, but the mists prevented her from being able to see beyond a few yards.

"Who disturbs the grave of my sister?"

An almost unintelligible voice shook the air around them, and Paimon finally was able to see where it was coming from. The force from his voice was enough to make the mists depart, and standing thirty yards from them was a great silhouette forty feet tall. Letting her fingers turn to knives and allowing golden armor to cover her skin, Paimon hoped Buer's surgery had not weakened her too much.

"Travelers!" she shouted back. "We did not mean to stumble upon this grave!"

"I know that voice," the giant man said as he stepped forward, each great stride bringing him a few yards closer. Once he was beyond the haze of mist, Paimon could see exactly who it was. Missing an eye and an ear on his left side, greying patches of hair scattered around his face, and loose, dark scraps hanging from his shoulders and his hips, another old enemy stood before her. As he leaned down and stared at her with a pale eye, Paimon realized she could not hide her identity.

"Jormun." She transformed her knives back to fingers and held her palms out in a display of peace. "Forgive me for not recognizing you sooner."

"The Butcher?" he shouted, the power of his breath enough to cause a stiff breeze. "How is it that an enemy has invaded our home? Has she come to gloat?"

"No, Jormun!" Paimon swept her arms in front of her. "I have no use for gloating and you know this!"

"Then why does the Butcher dance on my sister's grave?" he roared, slamming a giant fist into the ground and shaking them all where they stood. "This one has no decency!"

"I did not intend to come here, Jormun!" she shouted, her voice wavering as sorrow took her. "I never thought I would ever see you or Gerhun or any of the Nephilim ever again! I am just as upset to see what has happened to your sister!"

"I doubt that, Butcher! You took from me an ear. You took from Gerhun her honor!" He lifted himself to his full height, dwarfing the fallen angel beneath him. "And now I will crush you and reclaim it."

"I don't want to fight, Jormun! This is not why we came to Purgatory!"

"Then you should not have come at all."

He raised his foot and brought it over Paimon's head, determined to crush her body. For a moment she stood there, staring at the giant's tortured eyes, but then she felt a strong arm pull her off the ground and through the air just before the Nephilim's foot crashed down where she had been standing.

"It would be a waste to die here, sister," Buer said as he turned to place her on his back, which was already covered in demonic armor. Although she instinctively wrapped her arm around his midsection, Paimon was still lost in her past.

"We just need to get through to him," she muttered, but Buer laughed at her as he banked to the left and materialized a lance in his right arm, another sword in his left. As he maneuvered around the

Nephilim, Paimon could see Jormun frantically looking through the cloud of dust he had created with his last strike.

"As much as I would like a peaceful option, I fear it is much too late for that," Buer stated, resigned to their fate. "You led the charge that destroyed his people, Paimon, and he has just found you desecrating the monument to his fallen sister. We also have no idea to what extent his mind has deteriorated in this mad place.

"He will not stop until you are dead," Buer concluded as he turned back to run at the giant warrior, who yelped when Seere rode past him with his axe and sliced through his calf. "There is no getting through to him."

"I don't want to kill him, Buer. Not after what I did." Paimon tried to fight, but she had subconsciously surrendered, her fingers turning to knives and her teeth becoming dagger sharp. Already, she had brought her feet up to Buer's back and was crouched and ready to strike.

"After what you did, my sister, you have to."

Buer leapt into the air and threw his lance into Jormun's gut before taking his sword in both hands and slicing through the Nephilim's hamstring, just as he rode through his legs. Before he had even thrown the lance, Paimon had sprung from his back and flipped through the air, catching the talons of her foot on Jormun's lowest rib.

"The insects think they can defeat Jormun?" the Nephilim asked even as dark blood flowed out from his wounds, but Paimon knew it was not just boasting. As she clambered up his torso—using Buer's exposed lance as a springboard once she realized that the giant was sweeping his arm along his body—Paimon tried to remember forgotten tactics. Landing gracefully on Jormun's still-moving arm, Paimon used her claws and talons to dig through his flesh and climb up to his shoulders.

"Jormun! Stop fighting us! We are *not* your enemies anymore!" She shouted at the top of her lungs as she made her way to the giant's remaining ear, but when he turned to face her, she finally realized that Buer spoke the truth. At this point, Jormun was little more than a beast that vaguely looked human.

This was proven immediately when he headbutted her off his shoulder and then followed it up with a fist slamming her out of the air and into the ground, where her body made a trench fifteen feet long.

"I don't care what you are." Jormun snarled, looking for his other enemies. When he turned to his left, Buer was bearing down on him with lances in both hands. Chuckling at the direct tactic, the Nephilim turned to face the centaur, but then he felt a blade tear through his Achilles' tendon, forcing him to his knee in time for Buer to send both of his lances into his upper torso.

"Paimon," Buer muttered as he turned away from the kneeling giant and galloped toward the trench made by his sister's body, but then a massive hand barred his way. Before Buer could materialize another sword, the hand closed around his torso and picked him off the ground, forcing the air from his lungs. Grimacing in pain, Buer turned to see Jormun looking at him with hate in his eyes.

"You will not save this day, angel," he growled, his voice resonating through Buer's body.

Frustrated and unable to move, Buer could only watch as Jormun brought him closer to his face and opened his mouth to reveal rotten teeth dripping with saliva.

"Yeah, but I might!"

The Nephilim turned as Seere leapt off Fury's saddle, hammer held above him, and then slammed the blunt end of his weapon into Jormun's face. The force of the impact was enough to issue a small shockwave and Jormun's nose immediately shattered, sending him to the ground and onto his belly, where he released his hold on the centaur.

However, Buer was likewise unprepared and spent the next few seconds rolling to a stop.

"Who are you? You are no angel!" Jormun tried to roll over but couldn't, and his words were muddled from the blood flowing out of his nostrils.

Seere chuckled before breaking into a sprint, turning his weapon so he could strike with the blade of his axe. Then, leaping high into the air, Seere rotated his body and sent himself into a spin as he fell back to the ground. He plunged the blade of his weapon deep into the Nephilim's ribcage, just above the heart.

"I'm new," Seere teased before he lifted his weapon perpendicular to Jormun's chest and then used both hands to force it deeper into the Nephilim. Jormun seized at that, but Seere clung to his weapon as the giant thrashed. After a panicked moment, the Nephilim stopped trying to throw him off and just focused on staying conscious, wheezing as he lay on his back.

"Still alive? Do these guys not have hearts?" Seere turned to face Buer, who was still getting to his feet.

"You've only punctured it." Buer materialized a lance so he could assist the Horseman, but Seere quickly turned back to his own weapon before standing up and stomping the exposed handle, burying it completely.

This time—because he had nothing to hold onto—Seere was thrown from the thrashing Nephilim and sailed through the air, making Buer panic. However, his fear was proved groundless as the warrior curled in on himself and flipped through the air, bundles of muscles and flesh wrapping around each other and turning into a giant horse beneath him. Creating an impact crater once they landed, Fury screamed in bloodlust and Seere issued a war cry to the heavens.

In that moment, Buer realized Seere had always been the true Horseman of War.

"Is he..." a weak voice came from his side, and Buer turned to see that Paimon had survived her ordeal, even if she looked worse for it. Her golden hair was sullied with clumps of dirt and her arms were covered in bruises and scratches, but Buer could see the pain behind her vacant eyes.

However much Jormun had hurt her in that strike, her soul had taken much more damage.

"Yeah, he's dead." Seere slid off Fury's saddle and walked up to Jormun's body. "At least, I hope so. This will go very poorly, otherwise."

"He didn't have to die," Paimon said, her voice shaking. "He was just guarding his sister's memorial. I drove him to this."

"Well, sometimes we don't do things we're proud of," Seere said dismissively as he climbed up the Nephilim's corpse and then walked up to the entry wound. "I can't count how many people I killed that had no business being dead. Though that might be because I'm terrible at math."

"Seere, you shouldn't joke about this," Paimon said as she walked forward. Once Seere crouched down next to gaping hole in Jormun's chest, he turned to her with skepticism.

"It's how I cope." Then Seere turned back to the giant's body and threw his arm into the darkness. He was up to his shoulder in gore before his fingers wrapped around the handle of his weapon, and he pulled it out of Jormun's chest with a hearty amount of blood. "How about you take the next one if you take issue with how I do things?"

"Seere," Paimon growled, but the Horseman leapt into the air and landed in front of her, swinging his axe to the side and flicking away a trail of Nephilim blood.

"Darling." He closed the distance and offered her a sad smile. "My dear, sweet Paimon. It had to be done."

"You didn't have to kill him."

"*Someone* had to. Because you didn't cut off his head when you had the chance, he almost ate Buer whole. Between you and me, I prefer Buer over a lunatic pre-human," Seere joked, but Paimon still glared up at him.

"That's—that's not," she tried to argue, but Buer's hand fell on her shoulder and she looked back at him.

"You know what is at stake, Paimon. Some people cannot be saved."

Paimon shrugged off his hand before turning to face him.

"You want me to kill them all over again? I've killed thousands of the Nephilim, Buer. Their blood will never be washed from my hands, and I've only *just barely* handled that over the years. It's my *constant* regret." Tears formed despite her defiance, but her companions looked at her in sympathy.

"I know that need for redemption," Seere said softly, drawing her gaze. "I will never be able to atone for the death I've caused, or the death I will cause. That is what comes with being a warrior."

"Seere—"

"But you *know* that. You've been fighting a thousand times longer than I have. And there is one constant rule that I know you can't forget." Seere abandoned his sympathy and looked at her with determination. "You can't fight a war if you're not willing to kill."

"So you think we need to fight a war against the Nephilim, too?" she asked, but Seere burst out laughing and had to back away, recovering only after a few moments.

"God, no! That was good, though," he said as he resumed his full height. "Just don't get lost in your guilt. We see other Nephilim, we'll deal with them however we have to. That *includes* killing them. This Jormun wanted to kill you. That means we had to kill him first. It's that simple."

"Is it really?" Paimon asked, crossing her arms, but then Buer cleared his throat.

"He's a simple man, this Horseman, but I have to agree with him." Instead of backing down from her scorn, Buer maintained eye contact with his sister. "You agree, as well, even if you are choosing to draw this out longer than necessary."

"I..." she started, determined to make her point, to try to find some way to deal with her guilt and grief, but then she realized the cruel truth. It had taken the words of an insolent human for her to see it, but Paimon finally saw that she had been acting the hypocrite. They were in the middle of a war, she had been a warrior for millions of years, and it would be absurd for her to stop now.

"Damn it all. Just... damn it all," she muttered, at which point Seere offered her a warm smile. "What? You're going to rub it in?"

"Nah, not at all. We just haven't fought side by side for a long time, and I was getting worried that you had lost your touch," he teased, at which point Paimon extended her nails and narrowed her gaze.

"Keep talking, and you'll be wishing I *never* touched you."

"Oh, my dear, sweet Paimon, it's good to finally see you again. Now we just need to find Cim and the team's back together."

BLOOD WAS warm on the Amazon's fingers, flowing into the creases and gaps of her gloves and spreading along her hands while she readjusted her grip. Glowering at the woman laying beneath her for a split second, Cimeries backed away from the other three warriors advancing on her and wished she hadn't allowed her corrupted sister to get so close. The blood that had poured out of the specter's gut could potentially cause Cimeries to lose her grip.

Even in her second death, Cimeries' sister might have her vengeance.

"It is your fault we died, Hippolyta," the tallest of the Amazons said as she held her spear in front of her. In the mist it was difficult for Cimeries to see her face, but she recognized the voice immediately.

"My fault, Ophelia? It was my fault that you gave our kingdom to a foreign king?" she replied, holding her pike out in front of her. "You made your bed, my sisters, and you gave me up to do it."

"If you had surrendered when you had the chance..." Ophelia motioned at her fellow Amazons to flank Cimeries, but the former queen did not let her continue.

"You surrendered *for* me, my sister, and see where that got you. My way, we would have died in battle and given ourselves to glory. Instead, you turned our women into subjects, slaves or worse. I have no patience for your pathetic words," Cimeries declared before lunging forward with her pike.

Her sister tried to parry the lunge with the shaft of her spear, but she had never experienced combat against anyone wielding such a weapon. Bringing the curved edge of her pike to Ophelia's neck, Cimeries drew back and cut through the woman's arteries, letting out a spray of blood, but she knew her sister would not die so easily. Thrusting up again and through Ophelia's chin, Cimeries destroyed her brain before retrieving her weapon and whipping around to face her other sisters.

She was soon confronted with a spear thrusting toward her midsection and another coming around from the side, determined to slash through her neck. Using her pike to knock away the strike aimed at her abdomen, Cimeries then ducked underneath the other spear before grabbing the shaft. Immediately her sister started wrestling with her while the other woman tried to thrust again, but Cimeries pushed forward and launched her foot into her sister, knocking her off balance before using her bracer to deflect the other strike.

She then brought the curved edge of her weapon down onto the back of the standing warrior's neck, severing her spine, and turned around to see that her other sister had regained her balance. Pulling hard on her weapon and then pivoting to face the warrior, Cimeries brought her arm back and thrust her pike forward. Before the Amazon was able to do much more than gasp, the pike tore into her chest and into her heart, forcing the life from her.

Once the woman crumpled to the ground, Cimeries walked calmly over to her and retrieved her weapon from the body, scowling at the corpse when it dissolved into shadows and fell between the cracks of Purgatory.

"That was a nice show, Hippolyta," a male voice came from the mist, and Cimeries immediately jerked around and readied her pike again. Snarling—spit gathering at the corners of her lips—Cimeries knew exactly who stood just beyond the edge of her vision. The silhouette stood there for a moment, most of his weight on his right leg, but soon the figure shook its head and approached, light falling on his face once the mist departed.

A rather unintimidating man with curly, light brown hair was standing there with hands in his pockets, a smug smile on his face.

"You dare to face me like this, cretin?" Cimeries asked, squeezing tighter on the shaft of her pike and feeling her sister's blood flowing through the empty space of her gloves. "You dare to show your face when I am not in a cage?

"I always did like you, Hippolyta. Fiery. So very strong, so very proud." He stepped closer, but still well outside of striking range. Looking down at the pools of blood surrounding Cimeries, he chuckled in appreciation. "Your sisters didn't fare too well, I see."

"Of course, they didn't. They were mere shades of the real thing, imitations and mimicry," Cimeries said, violence in every word. "I did not need to see them turn to shadows to know the truth of them.

"Bright as always," he replied in a wistful tone. "Gods, if only you had surrendered and become my queen, we would have ruled all of Greece. No one could have stopped us."

"I would have rather died, Theseus." Cimeries spat out the name in anger. "Greece was not yours to rule, and I would not have allowed you to sully the honor of my sisters."

"No... No, they did that themselves," Theseus said, sorrow on his face before he looked back up at her. "I was a bit out of line. I will admit that, Hippolyta. You nor your sisters deserved what I did to you."

"We did not deserve it, coward? They did not deserve to be sold off and turned into slaves? I did not deserve to be crippled, hobbled and turned into a piece of meat for your enjoyment?" she asked, emotion filtering through and making her voice shake. "You are so *benevolent*, Theseus. My, what a king you would have made if only you had chosen to think before acting."

"It was a different time," Theseus said, waving off Cimeries' sarcasm. "You were an enemy; a spoil of war. My actions—though regrettable—well, they were from another era."

"Because that should be enough of an excuse?" she shouted, advancing on the man until her pike was at his throat. The ancient king had the decency to face her, but he still looked down his nose at her.

"These are no excuses, woman!" he shouted, grabbing the pike just behind the spearhead and pressing it against his neck. "I did what I did for a reason. I would have done it the same way every time. Was I cruel? Yes. Did it intimidate my other enemies? *Yes*."

"My nightly abuse? That was just to show your power to the other kings?" she asked in disbelief, but she could tell from his stare that he was not lying.

"You know the game as well as I do, Amazon. We were all barbarians back then. We were all monsters."

"*Some things do not change,*" she said before inching forward, the point of her weapon pushing further into his flesh. "What was this for, coward? Do you expect me to give you mercy now that you have justified your actions?"

"Absolutely not, Hippolyta," he said in a soft voice, surprising Cimeries. "I expect you to kill me."

"Then why do you not fight against it?"

"Because I have wandered around Purgatory for millennia, denied even the option of suicide." He pulled Cimeries forward and pricked through his own skin with her weapon. "This place is for those who would atone for their mistakes."

"And you think you have?"

"Not in the slightest," he admitted, looking hard into her face. "My list of crimes is long—never-ending—and my sentence is eternal. For the rest of my days, I will wander the mists, knowing the pain and misery I caused just to provide for my people."

"For your people?" Cimeries scoffed, but Theseus bristled with anger.

"Of course, for my people!" he shouted, pushing her away and shaking in place. "That is the purpose of a ruler! We take on countless sins so that our subjects don't have to!"

"You expect me to believe that?" she asked, skepticism in every word, but her tormentor merely rolled his eyes.

"You *should*. You were a ruler as well, Hippolyta. You were the Queen of the Amazons, as much a part of legend as myself. You *know* the responsibilities that come with the crown."

"I understand, Theseus," Cimeries said, squeezing tighter on the shaft of her weapon. "I have committed my own crimes. However, I *never* enslaved another; I never took their freedom. I never cut their tendons and used their body as a toy."

"That is because you were a woman, and softer for it," Theseus said, prompting a low growl from Cimeries. "You had mercy, respect for others, and it cost you a kingdom and your freedom.

"Although, after our brief time on Earth ended, you were given a much greater reward. You are now a warrior of Hell come to Purgatory, my eternal prison. You have been given a gift," he said, looking up at her with long overdue respect. "You have been given the chance to take your revenge. To kill me."

"To kill you?" Cimeries advanced on him. "You offer your life to me?"

"It is the only way I can truly atone. You were by far the most tragic of my victims. It is poetic justice that you come here now; a fitting end to a cruel life. Whenever you are ready, Amazon," he said before closing his eyes and setting his arms to his sides in supplication. Seeing the extent of his surrender, Cimeries brought down her weapon and stood in front of him.

"I will not allow you your poetic justice," she said, causing Theseus to open his eyes in confusion.

"What? What are you talking about?"

"I will not allow you to atone, coward. I will not allow you to end your wandering, to end your pain. As much as I would like to kill you, it pleases me *so* much more to know that I leave you here to suffer for eternity," Cimeries explained, watching as Theseus seemed to shrink in fear.

"Wh—why would you..."

"Is it so hard to understand? You left me in a cage, crippled, where I was not given the option to end my own life. I am merely returning the gift you gave me so many years ago," Cimeries said before walking past him and leaving him to the mists.

"Hippolyta! Come back here!" Theseus shouted after her, but she wasn't listening. Cimeries continued forward, ignoring his pleas until his voice was swallowed by the mists of Purgatory. This was the way it had to be; this was the revenge she truly needed.

After all, she had never surrendered to his demands in life. She would never surrender to his wishes in death.

"GABRIEL!" Michael shouted as he fell from the sky, his wings arresting his momentum until he landed gracefully on the street outside his brother's apartment. A dust cloud spread from his landing and scattered against the rough outer wall of Gabriel's home, and Michael wondered again why the archangel chose to live out here in what could be considered the slums of the Capitol. Gabriel was one of the original seven archangels—Adonai's messenger—and deserved a position of status among all his children.

His thoughts falling on dark times, Michael realized just why Gabriel might shun life in the palace grounds. His brother had never been one for grandeur while others suffered.

"Gabriel!" Michael shouted again as he walked to the small doorway to Gabriel's apartment, the white paint on the dark wood already chipping away before he started knocking. Slivers of paint fell through the air once he rapped his knuckles against the cheap wood. "Gabriel? Are you there?"

"Are you sleeping?" he asked. Michael realized that Gabriel could be out playing the messenger, but he also knew that Adonai was resting and did not want to be disturbed. Since Gabriel had a nonexistent social life, that meant he was probably on the other side.

"One last chance, Gabe," Michael said—waiting for a few seconds for his brother's reply—but no answer came from beyond the fragile door. Apologizing silently, Michael pushed and threw the door off its hinges, causing it to fall back and slam against the dirt floor of his brother's apartment.

Sighing in disgust once he saw Gabriel's squalor, Michael shook his head and then stepped over the broken door. It was darker on the inside—Gabriel had drawn shut the curtain for his sole window—so Michael brought out his weapon and let a dagger of flame burst into existence.

Using the dagger as a torch, Michael made his way through the apartment. Although he noticed the lack of furniture, he put it down as one of his brother's eccentricities. Once he turned the corner, he found Gabriel's bedroom and saw the modest, somewhat small bed his brother used for sleep. It was the only piece of furniture in the entire apartment.

Sighing, Michael crossed his arms and hoped this was not some symptom of a deeper problem. Ever since the rebellion, his brother had become withdrawn and refused to spend time with any of his other siblings for lengthy periods of time. In fact, Michael was one of the only people who could make him smile, and Michael knew it. He wanted so much better for his brother; he wanted to be able to help Gabriel if he was hurting.

Then he realized that Gabriel wasn't just absent from his home. Adonai was not sending him on an errand, either. Gabriel must be doing something he *wanted* to do, and that revelation made the archangel smile. After all of these millennia, he must have found some purpose or something he enjoyed, even if he did not tell his dear brother.

Smiling, Michael turned around and headed back to the entrance of the apartment, snuffing out the dagger from his hilt and stowing it back on his belt. He still had his doubts, but he would ask Gabriel what he was up to the next time he saw him. With most of the war effort taken from him, Michael had little else to do.

Just before leaving, Michael saw Gabriel's door and felt a wave of regret. His brother didn't deserve to have his privacy invaded, and Michael panicked. He did not have the skills to fix this and—when he picked up the door and looked at the broken hinges—he grimaced at the sight. At the very least, Gabriel would know someone had intruded.

"*Michael.*"

Turning around and retrieving the hilt from his belt, Michael let it burst into flame as he faced the apparent threat. As he watched blue energy rising from the dirt, Michael wondered who would appear to him like this, but then he saw broad shoulders and that stoic face. Dropping his weapon to his side, Michael stepped forward and gazed at the apparition.

"*Kushiel?* Kushiel, what are you doing here? What happened to you? Why are you in Gabriel's apartment?" His thoughts were chaotic, but the worst of it was because Michael had been training with Kushiel only hours ago, trading blows and evading the giant angel's strikes. Michael had been looking forward to seeing the former human improve the next time they fought.

"*Gabriel is the answer to all those questions,*" the ghost said, his mouth unmoving as he looked down at Michael with blue eyes. "*Your brother killed me right where you are standing.*"

"That's absurd!" Michael's wings spread out from his back in his fury, the crests scraping against the ceiling of Gabriel's apartment. "Gabriel wouldn't kill a fly!"

"*Then he must consider me less than one. He took my head with that staff of his... buried me... the dirt swallowed me whole.*"

"I don't believe you..." Michael trailed off, anger coursing through him, but Kushiel laughed, the blue wisps of his soul fading in and out.

"*See for yourself. I am not buried deep,*" he said, drifting back as an invitation.

Narrowing his eyes and fear replacing his anger, Michael turned his gaze to the floor. He swept his burning blade across his body and sent a cloud of dust and dirt through the shade of his fellow angel. Once it all settled on the far side of the apartment, Michael was horrified to see a decapitated body lying just a few feet below the surface. Unable to comprehend it all, Michael fell to his knees and stared into Kushiel's lifeless eyes.

"Why... Just—why..."

"*He conspires against your father. Gabriel is allied with the Devil. He is an agent of Hell,*" Kushiel explained, but Michael refused to look at the ghost once the truth came out. "*I stumbled upon him leaking information to the enemy, a blond angel in grey armor.*"

"Buné..."

"*Is that his name? No matter. The traitor must be killed for his crimes. We will go to God together,*" Kushiel declared, at which point Michael looked up at him.

"I—I need to think," Michael said, climbing to his feet and almost losing his balance, but then he heard Kushiel scoff.

"*What is there to think about? Gabriel must die.*"

"He's my brother, Kushiel," Michael argued, looking back up at the ghost and breathing in deep. "*They* are my brothers. Maybe... maybe Buné is their traitor. I need to talk to Gabriel."

"*There is nothing to talk about! If you do not go to Adonai with this, I will find a way!*" the ghost shouted, his ephemeral lips unmoving.

"You can't! One word of this and Adonai won't hesitate to kill Gabe! He let Uriel kill my subordinate right in front of me just to teach me a lesson!" he argued frantically, but he could already tell that Kushiel had no intention of stopping.

"*Then perhaps it is time for another lesson. I will do what you cannot, archangel, even if I am just a ghost.*" With that, Kushiel turned from Michael and drifted toward the outer wall of Gabriel's apartment.

Panicking, Michael tried to think of another argument, another way, but then he remembered Gabriel's smile and his pain.

Michael did not think as he jumped forward and sliced through Kushiel's ghost with a blade made of fire, the angel's soul burning away with an unearthly howl. Immediately, Michael felt pain tearing through his head and he placed his free hand up to his temple. Although Azrael, the Angelic Reaper, had always been able to take souls without difficulty, any other angels would suffer from the ordeal.

However, it was a necessary suffering. Michael would not allow Kushiel to threaten Gabriel's life like this. His brother deserved better than Adonai's supposed mercy; deserved better than getting skewered by their sadistic brother in a show of power. When the headache of absorbing Kushiel's soul subsided, Michael was able to breathe again and straightened up. Stepping to the other side of the angel's makeshift grave, Michael flapped his wings and let the dust cover Gabriel's transgression once more. There would be no saving Gabriel if someone stopped by, investigated the broken door and then found a corpse.

And as he stood by himself in Gabriel's apartment, covering up his brother's crime, Michael realized that he may be trying to save a traitor.

CHAPTER 4
A PIECE OF STRAW

"I knew you were interesting, Horseman," twin voices said from above, and Niccolo had to force himself to stay his hand.

"I am *not* a Horseman, anymore. I am *the Devil*. I am Lucifer's heir." He gritted his teeth as the pain of Plague's death bubbled to the surface. Nothing had been the same since Azazel tore out the animal's heart.

"You are nowhere close to the end of that journey, Niccolo. I can help, if you wish," the monster replied in a whisper. After looking skeptically at the Leviathan, Niccolo turned away from the bundle of rags and waved off the statement.

"I don't need your help," he replied, causing the Leviathan to let out a low chuckle.

"It is not about needs. It is about what you want," the creature teased. "You wish to become a devil? A rival to a god? Do you not want the power to defeat one such as Adonai?"

"And you think I don't have that power?" Niccolo said as he turned to face the Leviathan, not noticing the fallen angels flying in from above. Instead, the Leviathan lowered its mask and dominated his vision.

"Not yet. You hold yourself back. You still hold onto humanity. Adonai has no such issues."

"I am *not* holding myself back," Niccolo replied, but the Leviathan's eyes burned brighter and made him doubt.

"You are starting, Niccolo, this is true. I watched, I saw, I *see* it burning itself out of you. The more you give up your old life, your old ways, your human... *morality*, the better you can stand up to my cousin. Adonai would not stoop so low to show mercy."

"I—"

"Just as you showed those illusions no mercy. You cut them down as if they were nothing. Less than ants."

"I knew they weren't real—"

"Not at first!" the Leviathan's whisper dominating its voice, and its mouth opened in excitement. "You burned that real soul to ashes! You destroyed men and women you had infected in their first lives! No compassion! No mercy!"

"What are you telling him, monster?" Astaroth demanded as he landed a few feet away, marching between them and pushing Niccolo back to make room. "He doesn't need your foul words in his ears."

"He *needs* nothing," the Leviathan replied as it towered over its audience, the deep voice trading places with the whisper. It looked past Astaroth and made eye contact with Niccolo. "It is merely what he *wants*."

"Don't listen to him," Astaroth said as he faced Niccolo. "He'll twist anything to his own goals."

"That is the opposite of true, angel," the Leviathan commented, not noticing Crocell landing silently at his side. The slayer's wounds had eventually healed, but Niccolo saw him wince as his feet touched the ground. "My goal is obvious. I wish to eat. You continue to deny me."

"That will be resolved soon, monster," Crocell spoke up, drawing the attention of the shrouded beast. "There are more than enough enemies ahead for you to consume."

120

"I get nothing from eating illusions, slayer," it replied with annoyance, drawing its mask closer and opening its mouth, a tongue venturing forward and almost touching Crocell's face. Niccolo was surprised to see the undisturbed Fallen look up at the Leviathan with black eyes.

"No shades; no tricks. You know well that real souls find their way to Purgatory. One of the creatures I found will keep you fed for days," Crocell claimed, his arms still crossed as the Leviathan's tongue extended one of its fingers and traced the line of Crocell's jaw. At the touch, a blue hand shot up and grabbed it, clenching further. "I am *not* an appetizer."

"What do you mean *fed for days*?" Astaroth asked, prompting Crocell to release his hold on the creature's tongue and turn so he could point in the direction he had come.

"There are two Nephilim three miles that way, near the cliff-side entrance to a large valley. I am not sure *why*, but they are fighting each other. With the other groups nearby, we should be able to easily take them down and feed the monster."

"The other groups nearby?" Niccolo asked.

"Paimon, Buer and Seere are between us and the Nephilim; the reapers are with Phenex a short distance from them. With all the energy that man is using to burn away the mists, I am sure they will find each other soon," Crocell explained before flexing his wings and yawning.

"You left out the part where you flew down and told them where we are," Astaroth said in a low tone, already knowing what the slayer would say.

"You know I did not forget. We will meet them soon enough."

"And you didn't think to warn them about these Nephilim? From what Paimon told me, they're not something they want to stumble on," Niccolo said, but Crocell only looked skeptically at him.

"If she told you about the Nephilim, then you should know that Paimon was responsible for their wholesale slaughter. *She* should carry the title of slayer instead of me. I tire of this." He looked at

Astaroth expectantly. "Would you like to warn them, or do you wish to follow me?"

"One of these days, Crocell, that attitude of yours is going to get you killed," Astaroth said as he let his radiant wings burst out of his back. "And I'm not exactly sure it's going to be one of Adonai's angels who kills you."

"Perhaps it won't," the Leviathan said, causing Niccolo to look back at it. Even though it didn't have the right kind of mouth to show it, Niccolo felt like the creature was smiling at him.

Pushing the thought out of his mind, Niccolo materialized his wings and jumped into the air, the fallen angels rising with him, and with a flapping of angelic wings and a shuffling of twisted limbs, they left to rescue their friends.

However, the Leviathan's words echoed through Niccolo's mind. That monster seemed to think that he was capable of terrible things, that he *needed* to be capable of terrible things in order to accomplish his goal. For a split second, Niccolo wondered how much stronger he would become if he harvested Crocell's soul, but he immediately pushed the thought out of his head. He was not like the Leviathan; he was human.

And as he flew to join his friends, Niccolo realized that might be his biggest obstacle.

"Dead end," Phenex said, airborne and looking back at Cadmus expectantly. "There's an island within a stone's throw of here, but it might be better to turn around."

"Another one," Cadmus mused as he looked around. William and Solomon were on the ground, the curious human looking over the edge, and Cadmus wondered if they would ever find their companions. Turning to face Phenex, Cadmus shrugged and nodded to his left. "Let's keep following the cliff's edge. At least then we'll be able to keep track of where we've been."

122

"We have already had to turn around once because of that thinking," Phenex argued, but he could tell from Cadmus' defeated expression that there was no argument. With a heavy sigh, Phenex floated back from the edge and continued along the cliff to his right, burning the mist in front of them.

"I'm with you on this one," William spoke up from behind Phenex, shocking him into focusing on their new companion. As he walked up to Phenex's side, William nodded back to Cadmus and shook his head. "With your powers, we can cover a lot more ground and see much more if we headed inland."

"And why do you think you know better than a Horseman of the Apocalypse?" Phenex asked, his eyes smoldering in a show of intimidation. Instead of backing away, William shrugged and looked ahead.

"He's *still* just a man, and I have a lot of experience with swamplands covered in fog. We can keep going like this, but I doubt we're going to be making much progress if we keep to the outer edges of an island," William explained, but then he looked at Phenex and gestured forward. "You gonna light up our path?"

"I could use *you* as the torch, human. Would you prefer that?" Phenex asked, but William only smiled. Grunting, Phenex let out a cone of fire that burned away the mist in front of them before sputtering out.

"I understand, by the way," William said, causing Phenex to look at him out of the corner of his eye. "I understand why you might want to cut all ties to your past."

"What do you know of my past, human?" Flames surged around Phenex, but William continued without the slightest hint of fear.

"The highlights—Cadmus and Seere filled me in—but you can tell me more if you want. I know that the Bible did a piss poor job at telling your story; I know what they did to Judas. Basically," he said before making eye contact. "I know why you want to run away."

"*Be very careful, human,*" Phenex threatened, flames covering him completely and hiding him in an inferno. *"This is your only warning. You will not call me a coward again."*

"Who's calling you a coward?" William asked in return, the flames of Phenex's armor reflecting off his eyes. "If you're a coward, then I am, too. And between you and me, cowards don't try to piss off demons wrapped in fire."

"Why do this? Why are you not afraid?" Phenex asked, the blaze around him weakening as he looked at this child.

"Because I've been there, and it took a good man to get me back out. Wow," he said with a laugh, looking forward and breathing in deep. "I just realized that Garret outlived me."

"You have *not* been where I have been." Phenex floated closer and pointed at William with a burning finger. "I lost my people, I lost my faith, and I killed my best friend."

"So have I," William replied, shocking Phenex into abandoning his flames entirely. "Did you forget that I just *died*? Did you forget that you and your friends forced me into an apocalypse? You didn't know about my best friend—it was my brother, in my case—but we can add it to the list."

"Human..."

"And seriously, stop with the human thing," William said, gesturing forward again. Without thinking, Phenex let out another fountain of flames before floating alongside the boy. "You can separate yourself from your past as much as you want, but everyone sees how painfully obvious *why* you refuse to acknowledge your humanity."

"Why do you think you can talk to me this way? Why do you think I won't burn you where you stand? I ask again, why are you not *afraid*?" Phenex was so distracted from his anger that his pupils returned for the first time in a year.

William did not know the significance of this, so he gave the demon his answers.

"You're a good man, Yeshua. You aren't going to kill any of us." At the old name, Phenex's anger resurfaced, his pupils disappearing as the fire returned. "And like I said, I understand. I ran away from my life and tried to forget my past."

"You ran away from your father and lived in the swamp," Phenex commented with a dismissive wave of his hand.

"It's still *running away*," William replied, unbothered by Phenex's flippant disregard. "I refused to be a lord, became a mercenary, because I was ashamed of who I was... who I had been. When my father sent my brother after me and he drowned in the swamp, it only got worse. Only after my teacher knocked the ale out of my hand and talked me out of it did I even understand."

"Oh, and what does the child have to teach me?" Phenex asked, hovering in place and looking down at his companion. Without an ounce of fear, William met his gaze and continued.

"We can't run from our pasts. It's part of us. Whatever mistakes we've made are there even if we change our names, even if we abandon our morality, even if we run as far as we can and kill as many people as we can because the *anger never goes away*," he said, inching closer with every word. "And as long as we hold onto it, Yeshua, it *never* goes away."

"*That is not my name.*" Flames leaked out of Phenex's skin as he closed the distance between them. He had expected William to back away in shock or even in pain, but the young soul just stared at him, the reflection of Phenex's flames dominating even his eye color, almost as if the fire had been there all along.

"Just because *you* deny it doesn't mean I'm using the wrong name," William said before continuing on their path. Phenex's flames threatened to burst out of him—he even gathered an inferno in his hand to send at the insolent creature—but then a wail of pain echoed through Purgatory.

Deciding he could destroy William at any time, Phenex instead hurled the flames forward, waiting until it was hundreds of yards away before letting it explode. When the energy erupted and created an inferno in the sky, Phenex was able to see two giant creatures finish grappling with each other and look up at the explosion.

With a smile, Phenex realized he had found an outlet for his misplaced anger.

THEY HAD all been silent since the fight with Jormun, but when an explosion rocked through Purgatory, Paimon looked up and saw a sphere of fire burning in the sky. As the flare illuminated the Nephilim gaping up at it from below, the heat evaporated the mist around them. Then, when she saw a blazing figure streaking toward the giant creatures, Paimon realized they had found their missing companions.

Or, at the very least, Phenex.

"Oh, goddamnit, we need to help him!" Paimon shouted. Buer was already galloping faster—he knew exactly why Paimon was worried—but Seere scoffed once Fury caught up with them.

"Who, Phenex? He can go toe to toe with Astaroth and I heard he became another sun when Marchosias was killed. I'm pretty sure he can handle himself," he argued, but Buer looked over at him just as a war helmet formed around his face.

"Against most creatures, yes, but the Nephilim have an affinity for fire. They were born in it, living during a time when the Earth was still covered in active volcanoes and clouds of ash. Phenex..." he said before turning his attention back to the giants, who had stopped fighting. "He may as well be an insect."

"Who is about to get squashed," Paimon added, readjusting her hold on her brother's torso as demonic armor covered every inch of his skin. "How fast do you think we can join him?"

"Not soon enough, I fear," Buer muttered as Phenex hovered in the air above the Nephilim, a burning speck dwarfed by his opponents. A blazing typhoon formed around him before he let loose a torrent of flames on the closest giant, who raised an arm to his face to ward off the attack. As Buer and Fury galloped even faster, they watched as the Nephilim brought down its arm in confusion, unaffected by Phenex's unleashed fury. He even smiled at the man's antics.

Then, before Phenex really understood what was happening, the giant swatted him out of the air and sent him crashing to the ground.

"Alright, I see what you mean," Seere muttered as he grabbed the hammer from his back. It would still take them a minute to reach where Phenex had landed, but the Nephilim were already pursuing their prey, still smoldering in his crater. With their great strides, the giants would be upon Phenex before they could even hope to intercept.

"We're not going to make it," Paimon said under her breath, but then she heard a rumbling come from behind them. Looking back, Paimon saw a monstrosity shambling forward on eight limbs— bringing with it no small amount of terror—but then she recognized the men flying above the creature.

"We *will*, sister," Astaroth declared as he flew past them, his hands wreathed in light. Niccolo and Crocell followed after him, but they broke off to each side once they were within a hundred yards of the Nephilim closest to Phenex, just as they had planned. The giant was already leaning forward to inspect their companion, but Astaroth dived in from the side and landed between Phenex and the curious Nephilim.

"I will not lose another!" Astaroth shouted as he pushed off the ground with all his strength, raising into the air and slamming his fist into the Nephilim's jaw with a powerful uppercut that forced its body off the ground. Before the creature could land, Astaroth flew underneath its body and raised both of his hands up and then let out a massive column of energy.

His unleashed power was enough to force the mists of Purgatory back for miles.

"Seems like *he's* not holding back," Seere muttered, dropping the arm holding his axe. The power of the blast was enough to force the Nephilim further into the air, but its body fell back to the ground once the energy dispersed. A cloud of dust enveloped Astaroth as he stood there panting, but Seere was no longer watching Astaroth or his target. Another radiant display was already taking place.

As the first giant fell, Niccolo and Crocell flanked the other Nephilim, who was roaring at the sudden appearance of these pesky creatures. Pausing in the air on either side, Niccolo let out a blinding flare of energy from his buckler as Crocell lifted his trident to the sky and gathered surges of lightning in the weapon, and it seemed like they would make short work of the Nephilim. However, as Niccolo brought back his sword, the Nephilim lashed out and grabbed him, pinning Niccolo's arms to his sides.

"No!" Crocell shouted as he pointed his trident at the creature, a bolt of lightning crackling forth and burning its way through the Nephilim's entire frame. Although Niccolo was shocked in the process, it seemed like a necessary sacrifice to Crocell; he only let up his assault once he ran out of electricity. Realizing the Nephilim was not finished, Crocell started the process again by lifting his trident to the storm clouds above him, but then a radiant mass slammed into him and sent him rocketing through the air.

"What was that?" Paimon asked, squinting and trying to see further, but her answer came from an unlikely source. As it crawled further and faster than Buer and Fury, the Leviathan peered at her, three tongues already trailing behind its face.

"It was Astaroth, angel. Is your vision so bad?" it asked, but it was already running past them, saliva spraying from its open maw. Shaking her head, Paimon hoped the monster was incorrect, but she could already see Astaroth's giant opponent rising above the dust cloud. In a few moments, she would be able to pay the creature back for what it did to Astaroth, but then she heard the cry of pain coming from Niccolo.

Anger falling away, Paimon could only watch as the Nephilim clenched his fist and broke too many of Niccolo's bones. The human let out an anguished cry—though Paimon could tell at least half of it was from frustration—but then she saw the panic filling his face. The Nephilim was drooling and bringing his broken body closer to its mouth, and Paimon knew then that she would not be able to help.

It seemed like Niccolo's reign as the Devil was almost finished, but then a blue streak of energy carved through the Nephilim's forearm, cutting through the bone and most of its flesh. As Paimon watched, the creature howled and fell to his knees as the hand holding Niccolo fell to the ground and uncurled its fingers, allowing Niccolo's broken body to roll from the Nephilim's phantom grip.

A hopeful smile on her face, Paimon looked to her right and saw Cadmus with his arm outstretched and his fingers grasping for something outside his reach. Turning back to the screaming giant on his knees, Paimon watched Cadmus' scythe get pulled back in time and fly back toward its owner, slicing through the Nephilim's head and relieving it of its jaw.

"Since when could Cadmus do that? That's totally unfair!" Seere shouted, bringing up his weapon in indignation. Turning to look at him, Paimon gaped at him even as she sharpened her fingers and readied for battle.

"It's... *unfair?*"

"What? I'm *supposed* to be the strongest, Paimon." Seere's gaze narrowed as he looked over the Nephilim cradling the ribs on his right side. "What use am I if the Pale Rider can destroy a giant that easily?"

"It takes a lot out of him, Seere," Paimon replied as she looked back at the reaper, who was now huddled over Mercy's neck and struggling to stay in the saddle. A year ago, it would not have affected him that much, but Paimon knew why the reaper never slept, never recovered.

Nothing had been the same once the Black Death had started in earnest.

Realizing she could not change anything now, Paimon set her feet on Buer's back, launching herself into the air just as Buer slammed a conjured lance into the Nephilim's calf. Due to the centaur's velocity, Paimon was only in the air half a second before she had to hook her fingers and toes into the Nephilim's back. The creature screamed, but Paimon ignored the sounds as she crawled further, trying to make her way to the creature's ear. This time, hopefully, she might be able to talk the creature out of carrying on this fight.

Her hopes were dashed once something big hit the Nephilim from the other side and forced her to dig her claws in deep, struggling just to hang on. Looking up, Paimon saw three grey hands wrapping around the Nephilim's left side before she saw the Leviathan's mask peek out from over its shoulder. Its blue eyes burning bright, the monster slammed its vertical mouth into the meat of the Nephilim's shoulder, letting out streams of dark blood.

Panicking as the Leviathan started to eat it alive, the Nephilim whipped around and slammed its fists into the monster, his erratic movements enough to force the Leviathan off his chest—letting out gouts of blood in the process—but it also loosened Paimon's grip on the creature.

Once her claws came loose from the Nephilim's back, Paimon was suddenly forced airborne, which was not unexpected. Turning and trying to find some way to land gracefully, Paimon realized that there was no ground for her to land on. Instead, the ground fell away, leaving Paimon to stare at the abyss below. At that moment, Paimon realized she was about to fall into oblivion.

And for the first time in a few million years, Paimon was absolutely terrified.

However, that fear abandoned her once she felt strong arms wrap around her and redirect her momentum. Looking up, Paimon saw the angry face of Astaroth looking past her, his golden eyes focused on the battlefield.

"Thanks, Roth," she said, the pet name making him flinch.

"Don't call me that," he growled as they circled around the battlefield, allowing Paimon to see the state of their companions. Phenex had picked himself up from his impact crater, but she could see Solomon and William keeping guard over him. Cadmus was still hunched over his saddle, but the way he was holding his scythe made it seem like he would soon rejoin the battle.

His last opponent was not so fortunate; the wounded Nephilim was still kneeling down and holding his severed forearm, trying to reconnect the tissue and failing.

As Astaroth banked to the right and back toward the battlefield, Paimon watched as Buer rushed headlong toward the other Nephilim, who had a dozen wounds but was still moving around. Before Buer could throw his lance at the creature, the Nephilim leaned down and slammed his palm into the centaur, sending him tumbling to the side.

"I guess it's up to us once again," Astaroth grumbled as he dived toward the Nephilim, who had turned his attention to the eight-legged monstrosity circling around him. "You remember the execution maneuver?"

"I haven't forgotten everything, *Roth*," Paimon replied in a snide tone, but he disregarded her attempt to get on his nerves.

"Good, then do it," he said before unceremoniously dumping his sister midair. However, Paimon was prepared for it and tumbled into a controlled descent, her trajectory lining up perfectly. After a few seconds of freefall, Paimon slammed into the back of the creature's neck, digging her talons deep into its flesh just below the point where its shoulders began.

It screamed in pain and forgot the Leviathan in front of it, but there was nothing it could do. As Paimon held on with her feet and braced herself, she saw her radiant brother circling around again and starting a flight path leading directly toward their position. Letting her fingers grow into longer, riskier knives, Paimon prepared herself even as the Nephilim reached behind and tried to swat her from his back.

The Nephilim stopped screaming as it saw Astaroth descending from the sky, the Fallen's right arm held behind him and brimming with light. It only gaped up at him as Astaroth slammed his fist into its nose, Paimon shredding through the back of its neck at the exact same time. Between the two of their strikes, the Nephilim's neck separated from its body, the force of Astaroth's strike sending its head flying through the air and out of sight where the mists of Purgatory would claim it.

The giant's body stood there unassisted for a moment, but then Paimon felt gravity claim it, and she held on as it toppled forward, the impact almost enough to shake her loose. Only by biting into the creature's flesh did she not lose her grip, and once the dust settled, Paimon pushed herself off the Nephilim and spat out foul blood.

Looking around, Paimon found that all of her companions were still alive, even if their pride had been damaged. Crocell had finally made his way back to the battlefield, but he was bleeding from where bone had torn through the skin, possibly from Astaroth slamming into him. However, he had already reset it and had used the sash of his trousers to form a makeshift bandage.

Everyone else seemed to have superficial wounds at worst, even Niccolo. The former Horseman was shakily getting his feet—his bones already healed—but Paimon could tell that he didn't feel satisfied with his part in the battle. He would not make eye contact with anyone and stared into the middle distance, lost in anger and frustration.

"Is everyone finally together?" Cadmus asked as he slid off of Mercy's saddle and looked at their companions. It didn't seem to matter to him that the Nephilim he had wounded was still alive and whimpering at his lost arm.

Perhaps that was because Cadmus knew he could easily destroy it with just another strike of his weapon.

Paimon had been walking toward the creature, determined to find some way to reason with it, but she paused once Cadmus asked the question. Looking at her brothers and companions, Paimon tried to figure out who may be missing. Already feeling like something had gone wrong, Paimon bit her lip and turned to Cadmus.

"I don't see Cim," Seere suggested as he walked around the group, hoping to find the warrior crouching behind someone.

"She's not here," Cadmus said before burying his face in his empty hand. Once he drew in a deep breath, Cadmus turned to Astaroth for guidance. "What do you think we should do? Just keep going?"

"Of course. You didn't need to ask me that," Astaroth said as he crossed his arms. "One spearwoman lost in Purgatory isn't exactly a priority."

"How can you say that?" William shouted as he made his way into the circle. His sword was still drawn—even if he had no intention of using it—but he swept it across his body in anger. "She's one of us! If any one of us fall, are you just going to leave us there? Do we matter *that* little?"

"Yes," Astaroth stated, meeting William's anger with indifference. "Literally every one of us except Buer, Niccolo and Cadmus is expendable. We're not going to jeopardize the mission for a single warrior."

"Nice to see you care, Roth." Paimon turned back to face the Nephilim, who was now trying to reattach its jaw. It was enough to pull on her heartstrings, so she approached the creature with palms out in a show of peace.

"We don't want to hurt you," she started, but then a diagonal arc of divine energy tore through the Nephilim and caused it to scream from a jawless mouth.

Before Paimon could do much more than stare at it, the top half of the creature slid away and fell to the ground as dark blood gushed out of its torso, some of it reaching Paimon's feet before it trickled into the cracks of Purgatory. In disbelief, Paimon turned to face Niccolo and found him panting, shaking and gritting his teeth.

"Why—why did you do that?" Paimon asked, weak at first, but then fury broke through her composure and she glared at Niccolo. "It was crippled!"

"It crushed my arm, Paimon," he replied, looking to her with scorn. "I will not suffer a mindless creature like that to live."

"They are *not* mindless, Nico." She stomped over to him,

subconsciously letting her nails grow sharp. "They can think and they can reason!"

"They just tried to kill every one of us!" Niccolo's weapons shattered to light as he pointed a diseased index finger at the newly-made corpse. "You expect me to give mercy to our enemies?"

"I expect you to think before you fucking act, you child!" she screamed back, her teeth growing to points even if Niccolo did not notice. The leper closed the distance until he was only a foot away, looking down at her with eyes burning green.

"Don't you *dare* call me a child! *Especially* when you don't have the nerve to kill a Nephilim," he said, his voice tinged with violence. "You told me once that you killed hundreds of these things. Where is *that* Paimon?"

"Keep going, Nico, and you'll see *that* Paimon in all her glory. There's a reason they called me the *Butcher*," she threatened with a mouth full of dagger-sharp teeth, but then they were pushed away from each other and lifted into the air by their collars.

"Enough!" Astaroth shouted as he held both of them aloft, turning to face each of them with a glare. "You're *both* acting like children, and I will *not* entertain this."

"You can't stop me, Astaroth. I did what was necessary," Niccolo growled, his weapons starting to materialize, but the fallen angel jerked him around and shocked him into silence.

"Killing a crippled giant who could give us information, Nico? Not *exactly* necessary. Lucifer would not have done *that*."

"I am *not* Lucifer," Niccolo said, considering breaking Astaroth's hold and beating him to a pulp, but the fallen angel released both of them and looked at him with disappointment.

"That's pretty fucking obvious," he said before turning to Paimon. "Now can we stop this? We have the fate of the world on our shoulders, and I'd prefer not to break up squabbling couples every five minutes."

"Fine by me," Paimon said as she shoved Astaroth's arm away. "Nico and I were *never* a couple."

"Could have fooled me," Seere muttered from the outside of the circle—Buer slapping him on the shoulder for the comment—but the fight seemed to be over.

Clearing his throat, Cadmus broke the silence and looked at Astaroth.

"So what do we do now? Do we have any sort of clue as to where we should go?" he asked, at which point Solomon turned to him and folded his hands over his scythe.

"Well, there is a valley leading away from us, that seems—"

"Why don't we ask this guy?" Seere interrupted, pointing at the entrance of the valley. Turning to face whatever new threat was coming out of the mists, Niccolo saw a dark shape stumbling toward them, the sound of his heavy breathing already reaching them. Letting out his inherited wings and materializing Lux in his hand, Niccolo was ready for another fight.

"Who are you? What do you want?" He let loose an arc of radiant energy, sending it above the silhouette's head and dispersing the mist surrounding it.

What he saw was enough to make Niccolo's jaw drop, his sword falling from his grip and shattering into light.

"That voice... that—is that... is that you, Nico?" the overweight man asked as he stumbled forward. Dirt was caked on his face, but not enough to obscure who it was. His clothing was in shambles, a relic of what he may have worn in life; tattered and covered in soot, dirt and blood. However, none of that mattered to Niccolo. He just saw the relief of the man's face; the joy in his gleaming eyes.

"No, it can't..." Niccolo started, but the words abandoned him. Within just a few moments, the man was able to come within a few feet of him without any resistance, and his companions were so confused that they did nothing to stop him. With tears in his eyes, the man set his hands on Niccolo's shoulders and almost collapsed into him.

"Is that you, my son?"

"GABE," Michael said, watching as his brother turned to face him. The smaller archangel had been standing at a precipice looking over the expanse of Heaven, oblivious to his brother's arrival. When Gabriel first saw him, he offered a thin smile, but then he realized Michael was not happy to see him. Within seconds, Gabriel's face went dark, and he cradled his staff in both arms.

"I—what's the matter, Michael?"

His voice was already shaking, and Michael knew that Kushiel had been telling the truth. Shame was evident, and now it fell to Michael to find out why Gabriel had murdered a fellow angel. Pursing his lips, Michael approached his brother.

"Gabe," he repeated, crossing his arms and looking at the marble floor beneath them. He didn't want to have this conversation, but it was his duty as an archangel. Looking back up and making eye contact with Gabriel, Michael breathed out his despair. "Why?"

"Why what, Michael?" Gabriel replied, trembling so much that his golden curls swayed in front of his face.

"Kushiel, Gabe. His ghost came out of your floor," Michael hesitated, his own voice trembling with this confrontation. "Why did that happen?"

"He was... he," Gabriel stalled for a moment, thinking up a thousand lies, but once he stared into Michael's eyes, he knew they would all be useless. "He found me out, Michael. You already know, so there's no point in hiding it. Kushiel stumbled onto something he was not meant to see."

"Something you were not meant to *do*, Gabe!" Michael shouted before realizing that others may be listening. Closing the distance, Michael continued in a whisper. "Why the *hell* were you talking to Buné?"

"He—he saw that, huh," Gabriel said before looking at his feet and dragging his toes along the floor. Frustrated, Michael uncrossed his arms and grabbed Gabriel by the chin, forcing the archangel to look up at him.

"It doesn't matter *what* he saw. You betrayed us. *Why?*"

"Why? *Why?*" Gabriel asked as he knocked away his brother's hand and swept his arm behind him. "Did you not see what happened during the Rebellion? Did you not see what Adonai did to the Nephilim? Are you not watching what he does to the humans? Adonai is a *monster.*"

"He is our *father,*" Michael replied, but Gabriel rolled his eyes at that.

"And that *absolves* him? You haven't seen everything, Michael. Not like I have. You get to fight people honorably on the battlefield; he makes me do all the dirty work. He makes me relay messages— threats mostly—and he brags and goes on and on about all the atrocities he's committing."

"It is not our place to judge," Michael muttered, but his brother surprised him by grabbing him by the shoulder.

"If not us, then *who?* Who stops the monsters if the angels just stand and watch? That I didn't stand up with our brothers and sisters during the Rebellion has been a *constant* source of guilt, and I *know* you understand."

"Gabe—"

"No, Michael! You're one of the last few angels up here who *has* a moral compass! *You* are most of the reason I didn't switch sides!" he shouted, so intimidating that Michael forgot he was larger and more powerful than his brother. "You're the only reason I have any hope left for this forsaken place."

"Gabriel, this is wrong. You betrayed all of us," Michael said, tears in his eyes, but Gabriel couldn't accept his words. Releasing his grip on his brother, Gabriel turned away and stood at the precipice.

"Think about what I *betrayed.* Our father let our sadistic monster of a brother kill Muriel right in front of you. He banished the Nephilim to Purgatory just because they wanted to think for themselves. He's subjugated the humans—turned them into playthings—just because he can."

"Gabe—"

"*Listen* for once, Michael," he interrupted, whipping around and closing the distance. "He's been holding them back for millennia. And now—now that they're *just* showing signs of progress—he's going to wipe them clean and start another universe. One where *we* don't exist, either, no matter what nonsense he's throwing around about taking people with him."

"He's *God*, Gabriel," Michael stated, regaining confidence and standing tall. "It doesn't *matter* what we think or what we want. It doesn't matter if he kills everyone or keeps them under his control. He is *beyond* our comprehension."

"His cruelty is beyond comprehension, at least," Gabriel said as he backed away, shaking his head in disbelief. "I know exactly what kind of person he is, because I have known him for *millions of years* and *You. Have. Too.* Just because he had the power to create us doesn't mean that we can't understand him."

"We... we can't fight against him, Gabe. He'll destroy us without even trying." Michael buried his face in his palm, but Gabriel yanked his hand away and forced eye contact.

"*Us*? Definitely. But *them*? I honestly think they have a chance! The Horsemen... their power is growing day by day; they're fighting and destroying fallen angels and monsters that *should* have destroyed them easily. They have the potential—"

"That's nonsense, Gabriel!" Michael replied, but his brother dismissed the claim and a hopeful smile stretched his face.

"It's *not*! You've seen them yourself! The reaper, Cadmus, he has control over *time*! The other one has Lucifer's powers! Buné, he told me all about it, the plans, everything! He and Lucifer set this all up *centuries* ago!"

"That's enough!" Michael backhanded his brother and regretted it instantly, but he did his best to maintain his anger. Whimpering slightly, Gabriel backed away in confusion and fear. "I didn't want to think it was true, but Kushiel wasn't lying. I need to bring you to Father."

"You hit me..." Gabriel squeaked out, and Michael felt an instant pang of conscience.

"I—you weren't listening to reason." Breathing in deep and mustering his resolve, Michael turned his attention back to his brother. "Will you come with me peacefully?"

"Michael..." Gabriel muttered, turning to face the precipice and leaning heavily on his staff. "He'll kill me."

"He—I'll make sure that won't happen. You know the last thing I'd ever want is your death. You're my *brother*," Michael emphasized, stepping forward to set a hand on Gabriel's shoulder, but the archangel flinched at the touch. "You betrayed us, but I'm sure we can work something out."

"If... do you promise?" Gabriel replied, looking up at him like a hurt puppy. Seeing that display, Michael had absolutely no choice.

"Of course, Gabe. You were tricked; it was all just a moment of weakness. I'll make sure Father knows this." He almost fooled himself in the process. Seeing the hope on Gabriel's face, Michael had to smile.

"Thanks, Mike. I really do appreciate it," he said before turning back to the precipice and looking at the golden expanse of the Capitol. "Can I stay here for a moment longer? Just... just in case? I've always liked this view."

"I—" Michael started, hesitating as he considered what Adonai would say, but he could not force his brother to judgment in this state. He had to offer him at least this small consolation. "Of course. Just—promise that you'll stay here?"

"Yeah, yeah I will," Gabriel said, sniffing back tears. His heart straining against him, Michael considered lying to Adonai, but he knew he wouldn't be able to live with that guilt.

"Alright, Gabe. I'll come back with them and we'll get you through this in one piece," he joked, trying to keep his tone light, but his thoughts were dark as he turned toward Adonai's palace. As he let out his wings, he could hear Gabriel trying to hold back a whine.

When he jumped into the air, Michael swore to himself that he would not let any harm come to his brother.

"Niccolo, who is—"

"It *is* you, it is!" the lost soul interrupted Cadmus, shaking Niccolo by the shoulders and letting tears flow freely down his face. "I thought I would never see you again, Nico."

"This is your father?" Astaroth said, walking forward so he could see the man from the side. At the question, the man released his son and turned to face Astaroth with a smile.

"Yes! Yes, my name is Carlo Vespucci da Firenze! I'm Niccolo's father." He walked forward and grabbed Astaroth's hand with both of his, shaking it profusely. "And you are?"

"Above this," Astaroth said dismissively as he reclaimed his hand and inspected the grime that covered his marble-white skin. The serpent on his arm approached it before flicking out its tongue and hissing in response. Seeing the effect he had on Astaroth, Carlo tried to avoid conflict and turned his attention back to Niccolo.

"Oh, it is so good to see you, my son! I have been wandering here for years, maybe decades. I've been running away from monsters ever since I've been here and it's been such an ordeal. I just—"

"You can't call me that," Niccolo muttered, looking at the ground, trembling as emotion overtook him. At his reaction, Carlo stopped speaking and then tried to maneuver himself so Niccolo was forced to look at him.

"Whatever do you mean, my boy? I—"

"*You can't call me that!*" Niccolo roared, clenching both of his fists and hyperventilating in rage. After a moment—everyone watching him in anticipation—Niccolo gathered his thoughts and shook his head. "Not after what you did. You can't claim me as your son."

"After what I..." Carlo muttered, but then he remembered his crime and his hands dropped to his sides. "Oh, Niccolo... I forgot. I was so glad to see you, to see something that wasn't a monster... I almost thought that had all been a dream. Niccolo, I am *so* sorry."

"Sorry for what?" Seere asked, completely oblivious, and he was rewarded with Niccolo turning to face him, wings bursting into existence and his sword and shield materializing on his arms. With his fury barely contained, Niccolo pointed at Carlo with his demonic arm and shouted in three harmonious voices.

"This man was my father, my teacher, and he abandoned me when I needed him most!" he declared before turning back to face the small man. "The last time I spoke to him, he threatened to cut me down with a sword. Sabrael might be responsible for my leprosy, but this is the man who ruined my life."

"Nico..." Carlo mumbled, backing away from his son and shaking his head. "What happened to you? You have... wings. Are... are you an angel?"

"No, I am very, *very* far from being an angel." Niccolo advanced on the small man, stretching out his wings to their full span. "When I died, I was damned to Hell. I became a Horseman of the Apocalypse."

"A Horseman—"

"And when my horse was *killed in front of me*," he continued, ignoring his father's words and grabbing him by the throat with his rotten arm. "When Plague was *murdered*, I found out that I was merely a pawn in some game. *Your* God gave me this arm that is squeezing the life from you; Lucifer, who was a better father than you *ever were*, gave me his wings and his weapons. All so I could kill Adonai for him."

"*That,*" he said before releasing his father and pushing him to the ground, "Carlo Vespucci, is what happened to your son. And *so much of it* is because of *you*."

"Nico," Cadmus said softly, appearing by his side and walking in front of him. "I know this is difficult..."

"It's *not*," Niccolo replied, the trembling of his voice betraying his words. "This man might as well be a stranger. I just wanted to correct him. Tell him his place before I left him to *rot*. Just like he did to me."

"Niccolo, no," Carlo begged, climbing to his knees and offering his hands forward in prayer. "You can't leave me here! There are monsters in that valley and ghosts everywhere else! There are hundreds of those giants and I've seen them eat men whole!"

"*Good*," Niccolo replied, looking down at his father in disgust. "You're big enough that you'll provide a decent meal for them."

"He could provide a decent meal for *me*," the Leviathan said, shuffling forward and into Carlo's vision. Falling away from the bundle of robes and cloaks, Carlo stammered as he pointed at the creature.

"My God, what is that?"

"That is a real life monster," Niccolo said as he pointed at the Leviathan, "and I *still* think he's better than you. I have half a mind to let him have you."

"Nico, no," Cadmus argued, earning Niccolo's fury in an instant. "This man says he has been in that valley; he's seen the Nephilim up close."

"So?" Niccolo asked, but Cadmus sighed and annoyed him further.

"We might be able to use him as a guide. If he tells us what he knows, we might be able to avoid the rest of these Nephilim completely. From what we just experienced, it would be wise to at least try."

"You're kidding, right?" Niccolo shouted, pointing at his cowardly father with the shining blade in his hand. "This man is beneath our notice. He can't help us!"

"Yes, I can!" Carlo interrupted, crawling forward so he could plead his case to Cadmus. Already, he knew that his son would not listen to another word. "I've seen their camp! If you can call it that, anyway..." he muttered before turning back to his potential savior. "If you help me out of here, help me get to Heaven—"

"Help you get out of here?" Niccolo yelled, turning to face his father with light burning from both healthy and ruined eyes. "Help you get to *Heaven*? We're here to *destroy* Heaven, you fucking piece of shit! We're not helping you do anything!"

"It's a good deal, yes?" Carlo asked Cadmus, ignoring his son's display entirely. "You will be my escorts and I will tell you the way. You won't have to deal with those monsters."

"You have no idea who you're talking to, old man," Niccolo said as he bent down and picked up his father by the throat, his entire body surrounded by light. "I'm more monster than any of those creatures. In fact, I think I'll just kill you right now."

"Nico, no!" Cadmus protested, walking forward and getting rewarded with Niccolo slamming Carlo into him. After being forced back a few yards, Cadmus shook off the strike and dug his scythe against the ground. "We need him to guide us!"

"No, we don't!" Niccolo pressed Lux to his father's throat as the man shook in fear. "I can harvest his soul and I can take the knowledge from him. I'd rather take that chance than consider a future where *he* goes free."

"That's really unlikely, Nico, and you know it! Stop this now." Cadmus approached his friend and tried to convince him to come back from this anger. "I know he hurt you, but you don't have to kill him. Let him rot; let him suffer. Just because you *can* kill him doesn't mean you should."

"Yeah, but I *really* want to."

"Nico, he's your *father*," Paimon stated softly, whatever anger she held toward him melting away. "Don't do something you're going to regret."

"I will not regret destroying the man who let me *suffer*! I will not mourn the man who turned me into a beggar! I will *enjoy* seeing the life depart from his eyes." Niccolo smiled toward the end, but he was distracted by words he thought he would never hear.

"Niccolo!" Cadmus readied his scythe, earning Niccolo's attention with his serious tone. "Stop *now* or *I* will stop you. I'm not going to let you kill someone who can help us."

"You—you're going to *fight* me?" Niccolo asked, dropping the arm holding Carlo but still holding his fat neck firm. "You're going to raise your weapon against *me?*"

"You've gone too far, Nico. I know you're hurting, I know that Plague's loss meant everything. I know that Adonai and Lucifer used you and I know that's too much to bear, but this is *too far.* You've killed millions of people to create troops that might not even make a difference." Cadmus was saying words he had been holding back for an entire year. "I'm your best friend, Niccolo, and I've been watching you sink further and further into darkness."

"And that's *my* fault." Cadmus stressed his share of the blame as tears built in his eyes. "I thought that maybe it was a phase; that maybe you were right and I just couldn't see it. I've been so tired, I haven't slept, so I put it down to just paranoia, but I can't see you do *this,* Nico! I can't see you kill your father, a man who could help guide us to the end of our journey! That's what *all* of this has been for! The Black Death, the revenge, *everything*, and if you kill him just to satisfy some petty revenge..."

"Then..." Cadmus hesitated, unable to believe this had actually come to pass. "Then I have to fulfill a promise I made to Lucifer a long time ago. If you do this, you're the monster he warned me you might become. And I'd rather stop you now than see that happen. Please, Nico. Come back to us."

"Petty... revenge," Niccolo repeated, looking away and smiling in frustration. Looking back up at Cadmus, knowing everyone was staring at him, Niccolo wondered what he should do. It had never come to this point—they had never come to blows—but his friend was serious.

When he turned to look at the overweight man still straining in his grip, Niccolo felt an odd mixture of righteous anger, pity and disgust, and he suddenly didn't know what he wanted. Turning back to face his friends, Niccolo tried to read their minds. Almost universally, they were all looking at him in anticipation, pleading with him to stop.

Except one. When Niccolo made eye contact with the Leviathan, he saw blue orbs reduced to slits. It was offering its own twisted version of a smile, and Niccolo immediately realized what it wanted, what it did not need to say. Looking back at Cadmus and reliving the reaper's speech in his head, Niccolo realized that whatever he felt for his father was a relic from his past, a connection to his fading humanity.

Deciding he had no use for that humanity, Niccolo shoved Lux through Carlo's skull and burned his father's soul to ashes.

CHAPTER 5
BOYS WILL BE BOYS

"Niccolo!" Cadmus shouted, so stunned by his friend's brutal display that he couldn't think up anything better to say. As the last of Carlo's soul burned away, Niccolo faced Cadmus as if there was no other option.

"What, Cadmus? Did you really think I would stop now? Did you expect me to stop myself from killing a man who betrayed me and threw me into the garbage?" he said, gripping his sword tighter. "And you *sympathized* with him."

"I didn't..." Cadmus hesitated, dropping his weapon lower in a show of defeat. "I didn't sympathize with him, Nico. I just didn't want you to kill him; I didn't want you to take that next step. I wanted to stop you—"

"From becoming a *monster*?" Niccolo interrupted, clenching his demonic fist so hard that his ruined skin creaked. "That's what you said, Cadmus. That's what you *promised* Lucifer. Tell me, since when were you his *lackey*? Just when did you decide to follow his orders, even if they were to kill me?" Niccolo bombarded Cadmus with questions as he approached with slow strides. "When did you even *have* that conversation?"

"Nico..."

"You're keeping secrets!" Niccolo roared, flapping his wings forward and creating a gust of wind that slammed into Cadmus and sent his cloak out behind him. "What was the *one* thing I asked of you? I told you to never lie to me, and here you are holding back *again*."

"I... I don't have an excuse for that," Cadmus said, regaining his confidence and standing up straighter. "But I don't need one. I keep my secrets because I need to. I hold back because if I *didn't*, you wouldn't be able to handle it."

"I wouldn't be able to *handle it?*" Niccolo yelled, so angry that energy surged from his eye. "Just who the fuck do you think you're talking to?"

"You're Niccolo da Firenze, *right?*" Cadmus gripped his scythe tight and stared at him with cold, grey eyes. "I've known you for two hundred years, Nico, and I've seen every side of you."

"Oh, fuck you—"

"You don't get to interrupt!" Cadmus shouted as he slammed the blunt end of his scythe into the ground and let loose a cloud of energy. "I've been your best friend—spent almost every day with you for the last *two hundred years*—and I'm telling you that I don't recognize the man in front of me! In this last year, you've crossed so many lines that I'm fairly certain you don't even *see* them anymore."

"*I've* crossed lines?" Niccolo asked, scoffing at the statement. "What about *you*? Every time you see the future, do you warn us? Do you tell us what was coming? When Marchosias died, can you honestly tell me that you didn't see it coming?"

"I..." Cadmus hesitated, recalling his vision of Phenex covering the sky with fire. "I don't see anything with certainty—"

"I wasn't asking for *certainty*, you pompous ass!" Niccolo yelled as he hunched over, gripping empty air as if it was Cadmus' throat. "I'm asking you—*yes* or *no*—did you see any clue, any goddamn hunch that Marchosias was about to die? Just answer me!"

"No!" Cadmus declared, his eyes flickering with blue light.

"What I saw had nothing to do with Marchosias! The only vision I had before that battle was about Phenex!"

"About me?" Phenex interrupted, confused upon hearing his name. "Just what about me?"

"Phenex..." Cadmus started as he turned to face his companion—trying to figure some way to evade this conversation—but then he realized he had no choice. "I saw what happened after his death. I saw you turn into that inferno."

"And you didn't think to tell me?" Phenex's voice wavered as he considered an alternate future where Marchosias could still be alive.

"It was obvious that I couldn't change a thing," Cadmus admitted before turning back to Niccolo. "That's the cruel part. No matter what I see, no matter whose death I want to avert, it never matters. Lucifer was our first failure; we *helped* cause his death."

"Don't give me that bullshit," Niccolo replied, throwing out his demonic arm and cutting through the air. "Just because you're scared to act upon your visions doesn't mean you can ignore them! You saw what happened to Phenex, there were so many things you saw and didn't tell us one goddamn word."

"Nico—"

"No! What about Tamiel? Did you see him, too?" Niccolo stood up straighter and looked like he was prepared for war. "You did, I know it. There was no way you couldn't see something that monumental."

"I don't have to answer that—"

"Yes, you *do*! I'm sick of this shit! For once, tell me the goddamn—"

"Fine!" Cadmus interrupted his friend and joined him in anger. "I did see it! I saw Tamiel rushing at Sabrael, I saw what happened just before you *gutted* him! Is that what you wanted to hear? Is that the truth you so desperately wanted me to tell you? Do you feel *better* knowing that he was destined to die the moment he met you?"

"At least I know you're telling the truth now." Niccolo drew his blade and settled into a loose stance. "At least I know that I can't trust you."

"You can't trust *me?*" Cadmus said as he raised his scythe and dug his heel into the dirt. "I've been your best friend—sometimes your *only* friend—and *everything* I do is to help you!"

"Which is why you promised Scratch that you would put me down like a rabid dog the moment I stopped playing along?" Niccolo slowly circled to his right, which Cadmus mirrored.

"It wasn't like that, but it has become apparent that I may need to. I've watched you change into this... *thing,* and I can't justify *any* end by these means. You're not the same man I followed to Earth."

"You're damn right I'm not," Niccolo growled before slashing across his body, letting loose a powerful arc of white energy aimed directly at his friend. Their audience stood breathless as the energy roared toward Cadmus, but the reaper wasn't frightened in the least. Once it was within range, Cadmus swept his weapon up against the wave of light and sent it into the clouds.

"And that means I don't have a choice," Cadmus said as he rushed forward, closing the distance and then digging in his foot a few feet away from Niccolo, who had raised his shield in order to fend off his attack. Pivoting with his foot, Cadmus threw his scythe into a horizontal spin that Niccolo parried easily.

"Did you really think—" Niccolo started, but Cadmus continued the spinning motion and lowered his scythe before bringing it up into a rising slash. It swept under Niccolo's guard and was about to impale Niccolo through the scale armor covering his midsection, and only by flapping his wings and forcing himself backward did Niccolo avoid having Cadmus' scythe buried in his gut. From a few feet in the air, Niccolo watched as Cadmus slowly returned to a ready position.

"No, Niccolo. I didn't think that would work." Cadmus dropped his guard entirely so his scythe was planted against the ground. "But I know how you think. I know just what to do; just how to manipulate you. The only reason you're not dead right now is because of those wings."

"Good thing I have them, then!"

"Yes, it's good. They're a great strength, but you're entirely outclassed. Give this up now, admit you were wrong, and we'll go on like we did before. I'm trying to bring you back," Cadmus said, and Niccolo became so angry that he spat out his next words.

"*Outclassed?* I'm the fucking *Devil*, Cadmus! I have Lucifer's powers, his weapons, his *wings*. Why do you think you can beat me?" he asked, rising higher into the air as Morningstar flared with light.

"You can't just claim you're the *Devil*, Niccolo. You may have thrown away your bow, but that doesn't change who you are. Just because you borrow his wings and his weapons does *not* make you Lucifer. Since you inherited his powers, have you even thought about how much it limits you?" Cadmus asked, motioning up at Niccolo with his left hand. "It's not *your* strength; it's *his*."

"What *difference* does it make?" Niccolo asked, disappointment on Cadmus' face.

"Because Lucifer couldn't beat *Adonai*, Nico. He fought a war and lost with those powers. I know he meant a great deal to you, but he wanted you to depend on your own strength, your own power, your own *character*. Stop pretending to be someone else; stop pretending to be a scourge of humanity," Cadmus said, sincerity in every word. "Become Niccolo again. Be our friend."

"I never stopped being *me*. This is who I *am* now. I *am* this scourge you talk about," Niccolo said just as Morningstar shattered into light and was absorbed back into his body. Raising his demonic arm, a green handle manifested in his grip before he swung it through the air, a sickly bastard sword bubbling forth. "But if you want me to use my own powers, I'll entertain you."

"This isn't entertaining," Cadmus said, tired. "This is just *sad*. I'm *going* to defeat you, Niccolo."

"We'll see about that." Niccolo swooped down, Lux in his right hand and a bastard sword in his left. Gritting his teeth, Niccolo was about to slash through Cadmus with both blades, but then a blue distortion enveloped the reaper. Then Niccolo felt a sudden impact from his back and was slammed into the ground.

After sliding for a few yards and spitting out a mouthful of dirt, Niccolo picked himself up from his elbows and then turned to look behind him. From where Niccolo had first met the ground, Cadmus calmly approached and used his scythe as a walking stick like always.

He almost looked bored.

"I told you, Nico. I'm going to win this battle. I can stop time itself. No matter how powerful you are, you're not going to be able to fight that."

Throwing his arms forward, Niccolo rose into the air and pivoted before settling on his feet, bringing both blades to bear once he faced Cadmus.

"You're not more powerful than me. We were *both* made into weapons for this battle. I'm supposed to defeat Adonai!" Niccolo screamed, but Cadmus shook his head and looked at him with sympathy.

"No, Nico. *I* am supposed to defeat Adonai. You were merely Lucifer's back-up plan," he stated, but that calm response caused Niccolo's body to erupt in white light, the sight almost enough to burn Cadmus' eyes.

"*I am no one's plan!*" he shouted in three voices before rushing at his friend, flapping his wings to run even faster. Cadmus was almost unable to react before Niccolo was upon him, attempting to crush the reaper with both blades.

Raising his weapon, Cadmus blocked both blows with the handle of his scythe, but he had not anticipated Niccolo using his redirected momentum to flip over him and land on the other side. Cursing, the reaper focused on slowing time and turned to see Lux just an inch away from cutting through his neck.

Letting out a breath heavy with anxiety, Cadmus slammed the head of his weapon into Niccolo's midsection before releasing his hold on time, knocking the wind out of Niccolo's lungs and propelling him through the air.

When he crashed against the ground, Niccolo fell to his knees and tried to regain his breath.

"Give up!" Cadmus commanded, but he was winded by the exertion and paused before continuing. "You're not going to be able to trick me! You're not going to be able to fight someone who can stop you midair!"

"I..." Niccolo faltered and cradled his torso, but then he looked up at Cadmus with a malicious grin. "I just need to outlast you."

"What?"

"You think I didn't notice? You think I don't know the extent of your power? You've been watching me and you think I don't watch you, *too*?" Niccolo asked, chuckling softly as he released his side and stood up, pointing both of his weapons down and away from him. "As useful as your time manipulation is, it's only useful as long as it doesn't make you pass out."

"Niccolo..."

"I'm not *stupid*, Cadmus. You're smarter than me, but that doesn't make me stupid." Niccolo pointed his bastard sword directly at Cadmus. "When you first started being able to stop time, you could handle it, but staying awake all night, getting haunted by all those souls burning their way through you..."

"Face it," Niccolo said, abandoning his smile and gripping his swords tighter. "If you don't kill me with the next attack, you're not going to be able to stop time again."

"Niccolo, don't," Cadmus protested, but Niccolo was already running toward him.

"This is your one chance to kill me, reaper," he declared, planting his foot just a couple yards away from Cadmus and then sweeping Lux up and across his body, which let out a radiant crescent of energy. Cadmus countered the strike by slamming his scythe into it and sweeping the attack to the side, but then he saw Niccolo descending from the air in a controlled spin. His body was horizontal in the air and, if he had his way, Niccolo was about to tear through Cadmus in a whirlwind of blades.

When Cadmus focused on the moment and stopped Niccolo midair, he could see the anger in his healthy eye; he could see the violence Niccolo intended. It radiated off him, tainting the air, and Cadmus knew there was no saving Niccolo from his fate. No matter what he might say, he would not be able to stop Niccolo from turning into the monster Lucifer had foreseen. Raising his scythe, he prepared to reap his best friend, the one person who understood him. The soul that Cadmus had somehow lost along the way.

However, as his breath ran out, Cadmus could not bring his weapon down.

And just like that, the moment was over, they were both jerked back into the normal flow of time, and Niccolo slammed his bastard sword into Cadmus' torso, a splash of blood escaping as the edge cut through his leather cuirass and an inch into his skin. Drawing back and feeling dizzy from both the time manipulation and the blood loss, Cadmus was only able to breathe and stay standing as Niccolo picked himself up from the ground, dark hair shrouding his face.

"You lost your chance. From here, we're on even footing. You versus me," Niccolo muttered, his hair falling away from his eye and letting him glare at his friend. "The worst of it is that you were *right*. You would have beaten me."

"Nico..." Cadmus groaned, but there was nothing he could say. He watched as Niccolo threw away his bastard sword and let Morningstar take its place.

"What stopped you?" Niccolo asked before launching into a line of cruel questions. "Was it the hundreds of years of memories we shared? Was it that empathy that Beleth manipulated so well? Did you see some vision where I needed to be alive? What was it that stopped you from reaping me when you had the chance, you *traitor*?"

"I didn't..." Cadmus started, but he looked back at his friend and realized just how far they were from home. "I couldn't do it. Even with the world at stake, I couldn't..."

"You're weak, Cadmus," Niccolo interrupted, every confident step forward displaying his arrogance. "This is why you can't beat Adonai. When you fight a monster, you can't offer mercy. To fight a monster, you must become a monster."

"Nico, there is another way," Cadmus argued, but Niccolo scoffed at the suggestion.

"No. There isn't. Thank you, Cadmus, because without you, I would never have fully appreciated how much our humanity makes us weak. You are so much stronger than me, so much smarter, so much *better* in so many ways, but because you hesitate, because you don't want to sacrifice your morality—because you stubbornly hold onto your humanity and our friendship—you *lost*." Then Niccolo slashed vertically and let out a wave of energy that tore through the air and let loose a wake of dirt and stones as it cut through Purgatory.

"Our humanity is all that keeps us from becoming just like Adonai!" Cadmus said as he diverted the attack with his scythe, but he could feel himself falter under the blow. Without rest for so long, without the time to recover, Cadmus could only defend against Niccolo's aggression.

Once Niccolo came within a few feet of Cadmus, he seemed to tower over his friend.

"And that's a *bad* thing? If I'm to rival a god, I can't bother to keep my weakness. You're not going to hold me back," Niccolo said before swinging at his neck, which the reaper parried even if it staggered him. However, Niccolo was merely toying with him, because he quickly followed it up with a haymaker from his demonic arm that Cadmus could not avoid.

"I'm not trying to hold you back! I just... I just want—" he replied after the blow, recovering only enough to look as this new Devil grabbed him by the bundles of his cloak.

"I don't care what you want..." he said, at which point Cadmus panicked. Throwing a forearm against Niccolo's hand, he broke out of Niccolo's hold and then slammed the handle of his scythe into his friend's torso, causing him to double over. Flipping the blade for a better hold, Cadmus threw the blunt side of the weapon into Niccolo's face, breaking his nose. Then, once he was stunned, Cadmus kicked out with his leg and sent Niccolo backward.

"Enough of this," Cadmus growled, fully realizing how far Niccolo had fallen, and he summoned enough power to cut Niccolo in half. Even though his consciousness was already fading from the effort, Cadmus brought his scythe above him and prepared to destroy his friend. However, he saw Niccolo pick himself up and glare at him once more, reminding him of those final moments in the Overlook when he was about to kill Mammon, and he realized that he had run out of time.

Before Cadmus could swing down his weapon, Niccolo raised Morningstar and let out a flare of light which drowned out every detail, blinding the reaper. Cursing, Cadmus swung his weapon anyway—letting out a distortion that would have destroyed everything in its path—but he already knew he had failed. Although he tried to blink away his blindness, Cadmus could only recover enough to know that something was diving at him from his right before he felt Niccolo's buckler slam into his face, sending him tumbling end over end.

Frantically, Cadmus tried to stop his momentum and grabbed at anything within reach—his fingers scrabbling against loose dirt and momentarily digging into the cracks in the ground—but he continued to flounder until he remembered the scythe he was still holding. Slamming the weapon down, Cadmus was able to bury the blade of his scythe into the ground and arrest his momentum. Still, before he stopped completely, Cadmus felt the ground fall away underneath his legs and panicked, holding onto the handle of his weapon as if it was the only thing keeping him alive.

Once he was finally able to see, Cadmus saw that it *was* the only thing keeping him alive. The head of his scythe was still buried into the ground, but his body was dangling halfway over the abyss.

Keeping hold of the handle with one hand, Cadmus tried to find purchase with his other hand, but loose dirt tore away from the ground every time. His entire body trembling, Cadmus just held on as Niccolo descended from the sky, landing gracefully a few feet away.

"Pull me back up, Nico." In his distress, Cadmus had almost forgotten that Niccolo was trying to kill him. Niccolo crouched down and made eye contact with Cadmus, smirking at the ailing reaper.

"I wonder what would happen to you. Would you just fall endlessly? Would you see Cimeries there? Will you relive all of your mistakes? I think that would be the most appropriate," Niccolo said, chuckling softly. "You stood by and witnessed all those horrible things, even though you saw them coming. It would be so fitting for you to relive all those moments for eternity."

"Nico, no more!" Paimon shouted, but he wasn't listening. He just laid his hand on the crest of Cadmus' scythe, running his finger along the back.

"Niccolo, this has gone far enough," Solomon's voice came from directly behind him, and this time Niccolo looked over his shoulder. The old reaper was standing there, looking down and judging him just like he had every day for the last year. "You two have had your little battle. You've proven yourself superior. Don't forget that we still have a god to destroy."

"I haven't forgotten, Solomon," Niccolo said, standing up and facing the old reaper. "I will *never* forget that. I do this *because* I have to kill a god. I have to remove this weakness—*his* weakness—from my soul."

"Who told you that you need to kill your friends?" Solomon asked, pain in his voice, but Niccolo did not answer him directly. The former Horseman had turned back to his oldest friend.

"I don't *need* to do anything, but I'm done. I just wanted Cadmus to know his *place*," he said, smiling in his misplaced confidence, but the smile fell away once Cadmus' scythe dragged back to the cliff edge.

Although it seemed like Cadmus had manipulated time, it was

only in everyone's perception that everything slowed down. As Cadmus' scythe slipped back along the ground, most of the group started forward before realizing there was nothing they could do. In that terrible moment as Cadmus slipped away from them, they watched as his scythe caught on the edge for just half a moment. Only Solomon was able to move, diving forward and grabbing the handle of the scythe, but he wasn't prepared for how heavy Cadmus was.

When Cadmus' scythe fell from the edge, Solomon was dragged down along with him into the abyss.

Niccolo was unable to believe it at first, but he had watched both reapers disappear into the mists, their bodies devoured by the yawning nothing beneath them all. In those last furious seconds, Niccolo had lost his best friend, his fellow Horseman, his one true rival, and he had been directly responsible for it all.

When he turned to face his companions, he saw all the emotion threatening to break through. He saw their anger, their frustration, their sorrow, their confusion, but he saw something more fascinating than all of it.

Fear.

After all this time, Niccolo was no longer the little human with a grudge match; he was no longer Lucifer's favorite. With one act of brutality, with one betrayal, all of these people finally saw him as the Devil Niccolo had promised them.

Seeing the Leviathan's pleasure at what had just occurred, Niccolo realized that he was one step closer to being the monster Lucifer had foreseen, that the Leviathan wanted, that Adonai did not know he should fear.

"Nico... what have you done?" Paimon asked as she ventured forward, the bravest of his audience.

"I didn't—" he hesitated, but then he realized he must play the part. Turning to face them, his wings spread out magnificently behind him, Niccolo claimed it all.

"I removed a thorn from my side," he said, but Astaroth shook his head and clenched his fists.

"You're going to regret that, leper. I promise you that. You're going to regret what you've done here today."

"I doubt it," Niccolo replied, looking to the Leviathan for approval. From the satisfaction glowing from the monster's eyes, he was well on his way to godhood, even if it meant traveling a forsaken path. Turning back to Astaroth, Niccolo did his best to continue without emotion. "My only regret is that I didn't harvest their souls."

"You're not human, you bastard..." William muttered, but the insults no longer bothered Niccolo. He simply walked toward the valley of the Nephilim without a response.

After killing his father and his best friend, Niccolo accepted both statements as truth.

"Adonai, I need to speak with you." Michael pushed through the double doors, marching toward his father's throne with a dash of irreverence, but then he saw Sabrael and Uriel flanking their father. "Oh, don't you two have *anything* better to do?"

"No, actually," Sabrael replied. "Which reminds me, your vanguard is almost prepared and I would like to show you my results."

"Prepared? What do you have to *prepare?*" Michael asked, but then he remembered he had more pressing concerns. Shaking his head and ridding himself of dark theories, Michael stomped across the room. "I'll deal with that later."

"Why don't you deal with it now?" Adonai asked, leaning forward and setting his elbows on his knees. "You were so animated last time we talked about the vanguard. Don't you care anymore?"

"Of course, I care," Michael replied once he was within a comfortable speaking distance, stopping and crossing his arms. "We have a problem."

"Well, speak." Uriel commanded his brother to continue with a flippant gesture and Michael's rage was almost enough to make his weapon ignite while it was still on his belt, but he restrained himself. Instead, he looked directly at Adonai, hoping he could find a way to persuade a god from his nature.

"Gabriel. He's been speaking to Buné."

"What do you mean he's been speaking to *Buné?*" Uriel asked, anger already flooding through his tone.

"He discovered some way to speak to our siblings in Hell, and..."

"He can only use the portal. That's what I told him he could do," Adonai interrupted, but then he beckoned his son to continue.

"He found another way, Father. And he's been using it to... he killed Kushiel once he found out." Michael tried to gloss over the worst of his brother's betrayal, but he was unsuccessful.

"He killed one of the Host?" Sabrael asked, shocked for the first time in Michael's memory. "Why would he do such a thing?"

"Because he got found out," Uriel growled, the rings at the end of his spear clinking as he set the blunt end against the ground. "That's what it was, right, Michael? He's betrayed us."

"That... seems to be the case, but he was misguided! I doubt he gave them anything of merit!"

"The Horsemen and your siblings, the ones who rose *against* me, have found their way to Purgatory. Instead of being good, little humans," Adonai said as he picked himself up and dwarfed his creations, "they have continually rebelled against me. They have continually *defied* me."

"That's what you wanted, if I recall correctly," Michael growled.

"I wanted it *my way!*" Adonai shouted, a shockwave spreading out from him once he stomped his foot like a toddler. "They keep screwing up the game, and now I know why! It's because your weakling of a brother has been giving them secrets! Telling them our weaknesses!"

"What *weaknesses?*" Michael asked, adopting a pleading stance.

"You are all-powerful, Father. What does it matter what Gabriel told them?"

"It doesn't matter *what* he told them!" Adonai roared back, the force of his breath enough to ruffle Michael's hair. "I will not have an archangel defying my will! Bring me that damned traitor and *I'll* deal with him!"

"I promised him mercy!" Michael claimed, but he was met with a scoff.

"You promised him something you could not give," Sabrael said, intending to speak further, but Uriel stepped forward and interrupted him.

"Why do you not already have him in chains, brother? What possible reason do you have for leaving him alone?" he shouted, but Michael would not back down again.

"He promised me he would stay. I trust him; he knows his fate. I didn't want to deprive him of one last moment to look out on Heaven," Michael explained, after which Uriel shook his head in disgust and walked forward.

"You are *soft*, Michael. I can't believe we ever stood together on the battlefield." He knocked his shoulder into Michael as he passed, and it was almost enough for him to grab Uriel's weapon and cut him in half with his own spear.

"Where did you leave him?" Adonai stepped down from his throne and stood over his son. Although he was a general of the Heavenly Host, Michael was intimidated by this god who stood at double his size.

"At his precipice," he replied, at which point Adonai stepped past him and followed Uriel. Michael turned just in time for Sabrael to join them, and it took him a moment to realize what was happening.

"Come, Michael," Sabrael said over his shoulder. "This is your duty as an archangel. We must all be there to witness the end of our brother."

"You can't kill him," Michael urged, his wings coming out of his back in an instant as he pushed off the ground, flying up and over the others marching to the doorway. Adonai looked at him in indignation for a moment before narrowing his gaze.

"*I* do what I *want*, Michael. Now lead us to this traitor and I *might* consider being lenient on *you*," he said, and that was when Michael knew he had lost. Gabriel was going to die, and he might have to be his executioner.

Surrendering, Michael turned around and flew through the doors that had opened on their own; Adonai had pushed them open with his will. Michael didn't even have the strength to look behind him as he made his way back to Gabriel's precipice, knowing full well that Adonai and his brothers were following him. It would only be a few more moments before they confronted Gabriel, before Michael had to betray his promise to his favorite brother.

However, when he was finally able to see the precipice, Michael realized there was no one waiting. There were only golden words burnt into the marble floor, angelic scrawls that were too hard to make out from the air. Landing and withdrawing his wings, Michael leaned down to read the message Gabriel had left for him.

"Thanks for trying, Michael, but neither of us could keep our promise," Michael read aloud, and he realized Gabriel never had any intention of waiting for him. It had only been one last desperate attempt; one last gamble before the end. Standing back up, Michael felt Adonai's anger leaking into the air around them.

"He escaped," Adonai said, and when Michael turned to face him, he realized this could be his last moment.

"I'll find him," Michael claimed, but Uriel slammed the blunt end of his spear against his temple and sent him tumbling to the side. When Michael recovered himself enough to look back, Uriel was fuming.

"You have failed our father too many times. Wait here; wait for your glorious *battle*," Uriel said, spitting at the end of the statement before setting his spear against the floor. "I will go deal with our treasonous brother and give him the fate he deserves."

"You will go get him, Uriel," Adonai stated, hatred flowing

through every word even as he stared directly into Michael's eyes. "But you will bring him back."

"Father—"

"You will bring him back," Adonai declared, crossing his arms and looking at Michael like he had been the one to betray them. "I have a great deal of pain in store for him."

"Father," Michael started, but their god sneered at the word and stopped him instantly.

"I am *God*, Michael. You forget that sometimes. You don't have free will; you exist solely to fulfill *mine*. You are *nothing* to me. If you ever—*ever*—fail me again, I will wipe you from existence. Do *not* test me!" Adonai's voice was loud enough to resonate through the entirety of Heaven. "I am your creator and the only reason you live. I am God!"

"Adonai—"

"*Repeat what I said*," he commanded, a thousand threats buried in the syllables. With that, Michael realized submission was the only option. It was the only option he *ever* had.

"You are God." That prompted Adonai to step closer and lean down, his face dominating Michael's vision.

"And *what are you*?" he asked, and at first Michael did not realize what he wanted to hear. However, after a moment of Adonai standing over him, it became clear what this supreme being needed from him. Looking down at his feet and resigning himself to his fate, Michael spoke just above a whisper.

"I am nothing," he admitted, and he was rewarded by Adonai's hand grabbing his head and slamming him down to the ground, forcing him to black out. However, with one snap of his fingers, Adonai brought him back to consciousness and pulled him back up by his hair, holding him high enough so they would make eye contact.

"Don't forget that, Michael. Don't you *ever* forget that," he commanded, but Michael's thoughts were not on how little he mattered. He did not vow to remember his place.

Instead, deep inside his mind where Adonai couldn't find it, Michael vowed to never forget this cruelty.

———

"Did you even get any information from that man's soul?" Astaroth asked abruptly, not even bothering to look at Niccolo as they continued through the valley. Cliffs rose on either side, and only after an hour of walking had the path opened up enough for even four of them to walk side by side. From his position at the front of the group, Niccolo looked over his shoulder to respond.

"From my father?" Taking Astaroth's silence as his answer, Niccolo turned back to the mist in front of them. "No, I didn't get anything. I'm starting to think he was just an illusion."

"He was not," Buer commented, the clacking of his hooves echoing off the cliffs flanking them. "Your father was a real person; a soul lost in Purgatory. You killed him with your own hand and ruined our chances of avoiding the Nephilim."

"If you say so," Niccolo replied. "It's not like it makes much of a difference."

"Makes much of a *difference*?" Paimon asked incredulously, waiting for Niccolo to turn back to her before continuing. "Just two of the Nephilim were powerful enough to give us problems. They almost *killed you* and that was back before you betrayed your best friend."

"Mind your tongue, Paimon. He betrayed us first."

"He did no such thing," Astaroth added with venom. "If he kept you in the dark, it was to stop—oh, *I don't know*—something *exactly like this.*"

"You have no idea what you're talking about," Niccolo said, walking up to Astaroth and pointing back the way they had come. "We lost so many people because he didn't tell us what he saw! Cim almost died because he played right into Beleth's hands! Marchosias would still be here if he had just opened his damned mouth! Tamiel—"

"What, you really think any of that would have changed if Cadmus had told you about some ambiguous visions without context that *could* have happened?" Astaroth interrupted, the viper along his arm coiling around tighter and hissing along with its master. "You're fucking absurd."

"He saw—"

"Nothing useful!" Astaroth interrupted him again, this time shocking Niccolo enough to back away. "You're putting *way* too much importance on what Räum and Amon gave him! You know what they gave us with those revelations of theirs? Fucking nonsense! And that was *after* millions of years of practice and exposure to their, *literally*, god-given gifts."

"Cadmus inherited all of that mess," Astaroth continued his tirade, "and he *somehow* didn't go nuts. That, *by itself*, is impressive by any standard, and that he was able to see anything at all and even make a guess is just *ridiculous*. That man you condemned to the abyss along with our solitary *guide* is worth far more of my respect than either of my prophetic brothers, and he was *certainly* better than you, no matter how powerful you get."

"Is that all?" Niccolo asked, trying to seem confident, but Astaroth's golden eyes saw right through him. He inched forward and dominated his view, reminding Niccolo entirely too much of his second father.

"Hopefully *not*. *Hopefully* that bastard pulls a miracle out of his ass and comes back to save us all, because if you're our best hope of killing Adonai, we're fucking screwed. But just in case," he said before drawing back, the viper loosening its hold and showing that Astaroth had calmed down. "Make sure you're ready when the time comes."

"That's all I'm trying to do," Niccolo replied, but Astaroth rolled his eyes as he walked past.

"And here I thought you were sabotaging us when we needed all the help we could get," he muttered, almost causing Niccolo to fly into a rage. He stopped, however, once he saw the looks of disapproval from everyone in their group. The only two who didn't seem to care were the Leviathan and Crocell, but it was clear the others had lost their faith in him. Even Seere shook his head at him as he rode past.

"What, you're going to get on my case, too?" Niccolo asked, at which point Seere pulled back on Fury's reins and looked down at him.

"Niccolo, you might have just killed two of us and one of them was a Horseman. He was your brother in arms and, really, the closest thing to a brother you've ever had. Hell, for a long time I thought you two were more than that, but I guess I'm just kinky." As he paused, Seere dragged fingers through the coarse black hair of Fury's mane. "We might be able to get over your mistake, but we're not going to forgive it."

"I don't want your forgiveness."

"Yeah, you do, even if you don't want to admit it. That was all passion, Nico, which I totally understand, but... that's going to cool off. You're going to realize what you did and you're not going to like what you see. I've killed a friend before." The ghosts of Seere's past haunted him as they made eye contact. "It never stops hurting."

"Enough of that," Crocell commented as he walked past them. "Cadmus and Solomon are gone. There is no point in standing around and drowning in guilt."

"You're one to talk," Niccolo commented, remembering how the slayer had knelt in the palace courtyard with hands covered in blood. He only vaguely recalled that it was one of Lucifer's memories.

"I am, Niccolo," Crocell said, his black eyes like mirrors. "I am *exactly* the one to talk."

"I... yeah," Niccolo said before breaking his gaze, which Crocell used as an excuse to continue on his path. After a second of feeling guilty, Niccolo looked back up to find that Paimon was just a few feet away, filling the position of rear-guard. Seeing the determination on her face made him remember just what he had done and what he had said to her. Instantly, Niccolo felt a whole new wave of guilt.

"Don't even. I don't want to talk to you right now," she preemptively tried to stop their conversation. Once she walked past, however, Niccolo regained his confidence and caught up to her side.

"Look, I know I said some things—"

"You think I give a shit about the things you said?" she asked, whipping her head around and growing out teeth in a subconscious show of anger. "This is not about you and me, Nico. Whatever happened between us has been over for a while. *That's* not why I'm upset."

"I know," Niccolo admitted, but that wasn't enough for the demon king. Though Paimon slapped him hard enough to make his jaw pop, it was her nails that did the most damage. His cheek was already healing by the time he finished staggering, but Niccolo still felt the four gashes she had left for him.

"Then why are we even talking, Nico? You disgust me right now."

Then Niccolo said the only thing that could make her still feel for him.

"I'm sorry, Paimon. For all of it. I didn't really mean to..." he said in a soft voice. Refusing to admit to any sort of sympathy, she clenched her fists.

"I know you didn't mean it, but *sorry* doesn't bring Cadmus back," she said before leaving Niccolo to his thoughts.

It was for the best, because Paimon's thoughts were currently chaotic. Shaking her head and determined to keep tears from coming to her eyes, Paimon tried to focus, tried to avoid any lingering emotions for the former Horseman. She had been too easily manipulated—too willing to see Lucifer in that blighted soul—and she had been hurt for it. By the time she caught up with the rest of the group, Paimon had fallen into painful memories of sharing both their beds.

"C'mon." Paimon looked up to see Seere offering his left hand. Although she shook her head at first, Seere pouted and she had to relent, grabbing his forearm and getting pulled into Fury's saddle as if she was nothing.

"I can walk on my own," she protested, but she leaned into Seere's back anyway. Chuckling, he looked at her with a mischievous smile.

"What, this can't be just because I want your arms wrapped around me?" he asked, drawing a resigned laugh from Paimon as she laid her cheek on his back.

"That was all a long time ago, Seere. I don't think you can handle me anymore," she teased, but the smile on her face fell away when he set his hand on hers.

"I don't know. Sitri and I have gotten pretty adventurous over the last thousand years. Though," he said as he ran a fingertip along her much smaller finger, "it's clear you don't have eyes for *me* anymore."

"Niccolo and I are over," she replied too quickly, too obviously.

"No, you're not. You have a type and *it's pretty specific*. Besides, you forget," he said as he closed his hand around hers and looked back with a slight smile, "I have part of your soul now. I actually kinda *know* what you're feeling."

"Shit, I forgot about that," she muttered, but he patted her hand and grabbed Fury's reins once more.

"Don't you worry, I can keep my secrets. And God knows I've had my fair share of contentious relationships."

"It never got to that point," Paimon said as she hugged the Horseman tighter. "Almost did, but... he lost too much, changed too much. He's fallen harder than any of us."

"Kinda makes him ideal to kill Adonai, doesn't it? He'll come back around, I think."

"For a second there, he fully intended to kill Cadmus. That's a line I didn't think it was even *possible* for him to cross. Those two... it would have been like..."

"Like Lucifer and Michael? Like Judas and Yeshua?" Seere asked, his voice dropping lower as he nodded at the biblical figure walking ahead of them. "There are cracks in even the strongest friendships."

"It wasn't like that..."

"That phrase gets said a lot around here," Seere said, turning back to raise an eyebrow. "I'm starting to think you guys have a communication problem."

"Oh, you think *that's* the problem?" Paimon asked, resigning herself to laugh at the absurdity. Seeing that he had accomplished his goal in making her smile, Seere winked at her and turned around.

"Couldn't hurt to try and fix it. I'm not sure we can afford to lose any others in this group. William can only kill so many angels," he joked, prompting Paimon to lean against his back again.

"You *like* him, don't you? Didn't peg you for robbing the cradle."

"He's cute, don't get me wrong, but oddly enough I'm not really in the mood," he said with a weary sigh. "He's just the only one who hasn't screwed up yet."

"Oh, and how have you screwed up?" Paimon asked. With a smile and a shrug, Seere let out a deep breath.

"Can't tell you. It's a *secret*."

CHAPTER 6
THE REASONS FOR FALLING

"Cadmus!"

The word was familiar, but the voice was almost a stranger. It was enough incentive for Cadmus to stir, roll over in the dirt and try to gather his chaotic thoughts into some form of consciousness. Even when he felt a sharp pain in his ribs, the man was still lost in the darkness of his own mind.

"Cadmus, you have to get up!"

The words were a little more jarring—he recognized the voice this time around—but it still wasn't enough to let him know what was going on. When he opened bleary eyes, the only light came from a source a few feet away. Raising his hand to his face, he tried to wipe the sleep away, but then he felt another impact in his stomach that forced the air from his lungs.

Cadmus, Mercy's voice rattled inside his brain, pulling him back to consciousness and causing him to sit straight up on the hard floor.

Once he gasped awake, his pupils focused and he was able to see his surroundings, his jaw dropping at the sight. Every part of his body ached, his brain felt like it was going to explode, but Cadmus saw three very familiar figures standing above him. One was

Solomon, Mercy another, but the last person was someone he had not seen in over a thousand years.

"Get up, you lazy bastard!" the living ghost said before kicking Cadmus in the arm and making the reaper withdraw, placing his back against the rough wall.

He was just as Cadmus remembered; a dirty brown tunic covering him from his shoulders to his knees—the material rough as burlap—his skin covered in long-healed scars and fresh scratches and bruises. Completely bald, the man was missing half of his teeth and the bottom of his right ear along with a few of the fingers from his left hand, but Cadmus knew the man had no need for any of them. Once Cadmus' eyes fell to the black whip in the man's right hand, he instantly transformed into the coward he used to be.

"Decimus... how?" He was rewarded with the man's maimed hand slamming into his ear, making the headache even worse.

"Don't you *how* me, slave! You is about to fight and you get up 'fore I use this to lick your back!" He brandished his whip before hitting Cadmus again with his fist.

Warding off Decimus' continued attacks with his arm, Cadmus saw that his scythe lay next to him in the dirt. Once he realized he was still dressed as a Horseman of the Apocalypse, Cadmus gathered his weapon and marveled at his situation.

"What is going on here?" He turned to face Solomon, who looked around Cadmus' cell and shrugged.

"I am not exactly sure. Once we fell past the mists, I lost consciousness," he said as Decimus leaned down and grabbed Cadmus by the shoulder, who replied to a statement not meant for him.

"What's going on? You kidding! You is about to die because you stupid enough to believe in wrong gods," he shouted before throwing Cadmus at the wooden frame of his cage. After recovering from the attack, Cadmus looked back at Solomon and Mercy, again ignoring the slave master still yelling at him.

"And after that?" he asked Solomon, not even looking at Decimus as the enforcer dropped the length of his whip.

"We found ourselves here," Mercy responded in a skeptical rasp. "I appeared as soon as I was able and saw that Solomon was already present."

"What's after *that?*" Decimus asked as he threw the whip forward, striking Cadmus with the end of the whip and cutting into his cheek. "What after that is you burn in Hades, you Christian shit!"

"And he can't see either of you?" Cadmus asked rhetorically, grimacing in pain for a moment before his cheek started healing. "Are we in my memories? Have we traveled to the past?"

"My guess is as good as yours," Solomon said before nodding at Decimus, who was almost snarling at the reaper's indifference. "You *could* ask him."

"What you *talking* about?" Decimus asked, and Cadmus was through with it. As the slave master drew back his arm to attack once more, Cadmus plunged his scythe into the man's gut and pushed him into the wall. Gasping in air, the man's stomach muscles clenched and he coughed up blood, which then dribbled out of his mouth.

"You have no idea how much I wanted to do that when I was kept here," Cadmus said to his companions, but then he turned his attention to the slave master. "You. What are you?"

"What—how...what you..."

"*What are you?*" Cadmus asked again, his eyes shining with blue light. At that, the façade of the slave master fell away, his irises and pupils vanished, and the man stopped shaking.

"A test." Decimus slowly raised his head to make eye contact with Cadmus. "This is all for you."

"*What* is all for me?" Cadmus asked, but Decimus just laughed before replying.

"Knowing that is *also* a test," he said, smiling weakly.

Cadmus was tempted to bury the scythe deeper and cut to the side, but he didn't have the opportunity. Just as he finished the statement, Decimus faded from existence and they were left alone in the cell. After seeing that it was just an illusion, Cadmus retrieved his scythe, which was buried partially in the wall, and then turned to his companions.

"At least we're not dead."

"That is not certain," Mercy said, drawing a nod from Solomon.

"Indeed, nothing is certain here, but I have the feeling this is just another part of Purgatory. I have never encountered anything like this, but I have also never fallen into the abyss." Solomon lifted his head and looked back at Cadmus. "This will be a new experience for all three of us."

"It's good to know we can still count on your expertise," Cadmus muttered before walking up to the door of the cage and pursing his lips. "So what kind of test do you think this is?"

"Well, Purgatory—in the stories—is supposedly a place where souls can atone for the mistakes of their lives. Now, we know that Adonai does not actually *allow* this, but we can count on some small portion of truth," Solomon explained, setting a wrinkled hand on a part of the latticework. "The trees and forests of legends all come from seeds of truth."

"I am curious as to how you know so much about all this," Mercy commented, walking up to the wooden frame and setting his nose against it. "I cannot imagine many souls move through Purgatory and have the capability to tell you these stories."

"I wouldn't imagine so, either, Mercy," Solomon said as he turned with a smile. From his connection to the horse, Cadmus could tell that it was not received well. "But there are always exceptions. I myself have been through that wasteland, even if it was only to make it to the Gates of Heaven."

"Tell me, reaper, why is it that you did not stay there?" Mercy asked, prompting Solomon to frown.

"Some find Heaven somewhat insufferable and I happen to be one of them. I'm curious. You and your friends have asked all of these questions before. Why is it that you ask again?" He looked directly into Mercy's blank eyes and they held their staring contest for a moment, but eventually the pale horse turned back to the cage and passed through it, dissolving and reassembling himself from the dust as he walked through.

"I am curious as to whether or not your answers will change, great Solomon, now that you are alone with Cadmus and his horse. In this place of illusions, I do not wish to be deceived by my companions, as well," he rattled, not bothering to wait for an answer. Solomon recognized this and instead turned to the horse's master, smiling at Cadmus as he pulled open the door to the cage.

"I have no intention of doing so. Come, let us find the truth of this place and be on our way." Realizing there was little choice in the matter, Cadmus walked through the threshold and then paused at the entrance of the barracks.

We cannot trust him, Master. He may be part of the illusion. Mercy's voice bounced around in his head, but Cadmus kept up an outward appearance of trust as Solomon walked up beside them.

So could you. We can't know what tricks Purgatory has in store for us, he thought back, already feeling the horse's revulsion at the comment. As they walked into the light, Cadmus tried to justify himself. *If he is real, we still have very few options. He's led us this far into Purgatory. Abandoning him now would be ridiculous.*

I would not trust him completely. Especially if he is the real Solomon. As they continued the conversation, Cadmus realized they were standing in the middle of an empty fighting pit.

I never have, but Tamiel did. That's enough for now.

Cadmus turned back to Solomon, who was looking at them with no small amount of skepticism. However, before he could comment, dozens of voices burst into existence all around them. Readying their weapons, the reapers looked at the empty stands and the elevated platform for the nobles before realizing the sound was coming from nowhere.

Although confused at first, the reapers watched as the sounds were given owners. Dirty peasants and Roman citizens appeared from the ether until the stands were full of crying spectators. Seeing the magic at work, Cadmus turned his attention to the platform across from the entrance and narrowed his gaze once he saw a familiar form take shape.

"Thank you, one and all, for attending our special event!" a declarative voice came from the platform before a wide silhouette appeared from nothing, stepping into the light once it solidified into a fat, short man with greying hair wearing a clean tunic. "This is a very special day, one where we commemorate the glory of our fighting rings!"

"Lucius..." Cadmus growled, hunching over and gripping his scythe tighter. Upon seeing the noble, hundreds of memories came flooding back, none of them good. When he saw the man's thin lips stretched into a smile—both of Lucius' chins wobbling as he spoke—Cadmus clenched his jaw so hard he almost shattered his teeth.

"You know this man?" Solomon asked, cautiously holding his scythe in front of him. Without bothering to look at the old reaper, Cadmus recalled far too many atrocities for him to explain.

"He owned me."

At that point, Lucius looked down from the stage and swept his arms out in front of him.

"As I owned your mother, your sister, and your young nephew." His black eyes were shining with malice. "Tell me, young Cadmus, did you imagine killing me when I fed that poor babe to my dogs?"

"I imagined more than killing you."

That earned a guffaw from the fat noble, who looked to the crowds gathered in the stands.

"Hah, this one was always so impertinent! So *defiant*," he said before making eye contact with Cadmus. "His sister was quite pretty for a Christian. They're mostly dogs—they are—but this one, she had a nice face. Why, when I took her to bed, I almost considered letting her keep the whelp I gave her! A pity a man such as myself cannot suffer an illegitimate child like that."

"A pity? A *pity?*" Cadmus roared, his grey eyes turning blue in anger. "You crucified her!"

"Which was good enough for your messiah, Cadmus. You should feel lucky! I set up her post in view of your window so you could see your sister's *piety*. That *was* for you."

"I'm going to kill you, Lucius," Cadmus promised, but the noble just sneered at him.

"My poor boy, you're much too late for that. I'm already dead! I merely arrived in this delusion for the memories." He lifted his hand and materialized a cup from the ether before taking a sip. "Well, that, and to administer this test."

"What kind of test is this?" Solomon asked, but Lucius kept his focus on his slave. Suddenly, Cadmus realized why his former owner was ignoring Solomon and almost slapped himself for not realizing it sooner.

"What kind of test is this?" he repeated, earning confusion from Solomon, but Lucius smiled even wider at the question.

"A confrontation with your past, to see what kind of man you have become in your afterlife. Purgatory has its own set of rules, its own goals, and I am here to administer its judgment." Lucius snapped his fingers and a chair formed behind him. "If you are found wanting, you will be lost forever."

"And what are these rules?" Cadmus asked, and the specter laughed at his audacity, taking another draught from his cup before replying.

"Come now, Cadmus, you must know by now that *figuring out* the test is *part* of the test. Poor Decimus told you as much. Whenever you're ready, we can begin." He yawned and looked behind him, beckoning to someone with an offhand gesture. As Cadmus turned to face his companions, a servant appeared from the shadows of the platform and refilled Lucius' cup.

"He can't see me, can he?" Solomon asked, Cadmus nodding along.

"It's my test. You're not supposed to be here at all." Before he even finished the statement, he felt Mercy's thoughts nagging at him.

*Which begs the question as to **how** he is here.*

Not now. We'll figure that out later, Cadmus thought back, but he did his best to avoid letting Solomon know they were communicating.

"What do you think the rules are?" he asked Solomon, the other reaper dropping his weapon and leaning on it just like Cadmus normally would. After a moment of thought, massaging his beard with his free hand, Solomon breathed out heavily and shook his head.

"I am not sure. It is obvious that this Lucius is a servant of Purgatory, that this is all some sort of deception. We must try to figure out what *Purgatory* might want in this whole ordeal."

"What do you mean? Wouldn't it want me to be trapped forever?" Cadmus asked, and Solomon perked up and shook his head.

"Not at all! For normal souls, yes, but you are not a normal soul, Cadmus. You are a Horseman of the Apocalypse and almost definitely the best option for defeating Adonai. You have a *unique* set of circumstances," he stated, breathing in deep before his conclusion. "This might actually *be* a test."

"Are you saying..." Cadmus hesitated, furrowing his brow in thought. "Are you saying that Purgatory itself wants me to... succeed?"

"I don't believe it's outside the realm of possibilities," Solomon said, waving around them with his free hand. "Purgatory has a mind of its own and, well, its own survival instincts. When Adonai decides to end the world, Earth is not going to be the only casualty. Heaven, Hell and Purgatory are now directly connected to the planet and, once it's destroyed, they will be thrown into the Void as well."

"So, for it to survive, Purgatory wants something to stop Adonai."

"I don't see any other reason why it might offer you a test. The problem now is figuring out what it wants," Solomon ventured, and Mercy took that as incentive to enter the conversation.

"I find myself asking the same question as before, great Solomon. How would someone like you know all of this?" he asked, drawing a frustrated sigh from the reaper as he massaged his forehead.

"Because, Mercy, I have been around for a few thousand years and have communicated with all numbers of spirits. Demons and angels are not the only sources of information."

"Stop it, Mercy. It's not doing us any good to treat him like that," Cadmus added, the betrayal already affecting his horse. Anticipating this, he whispered in his mind in order to avoid further negative emotions. *You're being obvious and we have more urgent concerns.*

"Thank you, Cadmus." Solomon offered his fellow reaper a warm smile. "Like I said, we must figure out the rules of this game."

"I am getting bored with this endless prattling. Are you ready or not?" Lucius asked, drawing out each word painfully, but Cadmus put up his hand without looking at the man.

"I will tell you when I am ready, Lucius," he said before dropping his hand and continuing the real conversation. "Do you have any theories as to what it's testing for, or are you expecting me to figure that one out?"

"It would be a nice change, Cadmus, but no. However, I have an idea. I believe," Solomon said as he looked at all the spectators to his companion's test. "I believe it is looking for something... more than human."

"What is that supposed to mean?"

"You might have to show Purgatory that you are no longer a man. That you could be a rival to Adonai," Solomon guessed before making eye contact. Cadmus pondered the idea for a moment—remembering his duel with Niccolo and how he had been given that same advice from the Leviathan—but Cadmus didn't have the time to truly consider it.

"Enough, gladiator! I was not given back life to watch you talking to yourself in the dirt!" Lucius shouted, waving his hand and spilling the contents of his cup in the process. "Prepare yourself!"

Before Cadmus could raise his scythe, something burst out of the ground in front of him, sending out a colossal wake of sand that filled the air. Once his ears registered the sound it made, the breath left Cadmus' lungs and he was left helpless as the creature blocked out the sunlight above him. The only thing that saved him from being crushed and torn to pieces was Mercy's hooves slamming into his side, sending him tumbling off to the far end of the arena.

Panicking, Cadmus watched as the creature fell onto Mercy and worried that he had lost him just as Niccolo had lost Plague. However, his panic turned to relief when Mercy turned to dust and collapsed into the sand, completely evading the death meant for his owner. Although Cadmus felt relieved that Mercy had somehow maintained his composure, dread filled his whole body once he saw the creature in full light.

Standing up on powerful legs and twice as big as he remembered was an African lion, which shook his mane and sent particles of sand in every direction. Gulping down fear, Cadmus watched the giant cat turn toward him, its lips pulled back to show fangs that had torn him apart in his first life. Once it noticed his presence, the lion turned to face Cadmus and its gaze burned right through him. Then, as it stood there in the center of the arena, the creature let out a roar that echoed across Purgatory and assaulted Cadmus from all sides.

Shrinking back against the wall, Cadmus remembered just what it felt like to be torn apart, to look desperately for someone to save him even as the cat ate its fill of his belly. He remembered every aching moment, every panicked thought as the lion made its way through his fellow gladiators and then finally settled its gaze on him. Each one of those memories caused Cadmus to withdraw further and further, desperately trying to become part of the wall behind him. At first, it was too much, and as the lion stalked after him once again, Cadmus closed his eyes.

*It is just a **cat**! Remember who you are!*

Upon hearing Mercy's voice, Cadmus finally realized that he was not the same person. He was no longer a slave, no longer a helpless Christian thrown to the sands; he was Death incarnate. His earthbound terror now falling away, Cadmus straightened up and faced the giant cat, which was only a yard away from him. Looking at the creature that called back to all the fears of his first life, Cadmus realized how absurd it was that he had cowered from a simple animal. He even laughed at the situation before picking up his scythe in both hands.

If this was Purgatory's test, he seriously doubted its merit as a teacher.

As the lion lunged forward to bite off his upper half, Cadmus stopped time and shook his head in dismay, wondering how he had ever let himself be affected. With a lazy swipe of his weapon, Cadmus cut through the flesh of the lion's neck and then hit the decapitated body with the blunt side of his scythe, sending the carcass across the arena in a tumbling mass of flesh. When time jerked back into its normal flow, the lion's head flew off to the side before exploding into a spray of blood, flesh and bone, and the main body closely resembled jelly by the time it came to a stop.

"That... that was certainly something, Cadmus," Lucius commented in wonder, sitting forward once he let the cup fall from his fingers. When Cadmus turned to look at him, the noble snapped his fingers and the attendant brought him another cup.

"I'm not the slave you used to know."

"You never were the type to lie, but that was only the first part of your test! Fear... it's unnecessary for gods. In fact, it gets in the way more often than not," Lucius said while sitting back in his chair and looking smug. "This next part will be much more difficult."

"Thank you, Lucius," Cadmus said, the noble giving him a confused look. "For confirming that Purgatory is trying to see if I can be a god. That settles some things."

"*Too clever*, Cadmus. Too clever," Lucius muttered, but then he waved his hand again and Cadmus saw three silhouettes form in the air surrounding him. At once he brought up his scythe, but then he saw the first shadow turn to flesh. Upon sight of her, Cadmus dropped his weapon completely.

"No..."

"What, you thought this was going to be easy?" Lucius shouted, standing up and approaching the edge of the platform. "Purgatory wants nothing of mercy, nothing of humanity! It wants a god to defeat a god!"

"I can't do it..." Cadmus said, looking into her grey eyes and seeing all the pain, all the sorrow and, most importantly, the love she held for him.

"You must!" Lucius declared, spit and wine coming out of his mouth in equal measure.

"It's alright, Cadmus," the woman said, knowing exactly what was required of him. "There are things we must do."

"I *cannot* kill my *sister*." Cadmus looked away from the pretty girl from his past and then saw something even worse. The resemblance was obvious even to Solomon and Mercy, this other woman looked so similar.

"Your sister and your mother, my son. The world does not need your compassion," his mother said, approaching Cadmus and placing a warm hand on his shoulder. At her touch—at the proximity to a woman he had not seen in thirteen hundred years—Cadmus started to cry. "It needs a firm hand, Cadmus. A strong hand. One that will show no mercy—that will not weigh one life over countless others."

"I can't kill my family," he muttered, and this time he felt a tug at his cloak. Looking down, Cadmus' heart broke all over again when he saw a healthy, smiling toddler at his feet.

"Pi' me uh, Unca!" he shouted in glee, his words half-formed since he had died too young to learn to speak properly. From the way he bounced and tugged at his cloak, however, Cadmus knew exactly what he wanted. Crouching down, Cadmus wrapped his arms around his nephew and wept, unable to restrain his emotions any longer.

"This is your test, Cadmus," Solomon's voice interrupted, causing Cadmus to open his eyes and look at the approaching reaper. He could tell that Solomon didn't want to do this—he didn't want to be the one to explain it—but it was the role left to him. "This is the path you must travel."

"Why?" Cadmus cried out, tears still streaming down his cheeks. "Why does it have to be this way?"

"Because, Cadmus, there is an essential truth to this universe, however cruel it may be." Solomon crouched down and joined Cadmus in his misery. "And Niccolo realized it in his own way."

"What, that I have to kill my friends and family? That I have to become a monster to kill a monster?" Cadmus picked up his nephew before standing with the rest of his family. Solomon followed him up, but he did not look at Cadmus like he was a student or someone to be scolded for his insolence. His face was full of compassion when he set a hand on Cadmus' shoulder.

"No, not that." His ancient eyes brimmed with tears. "The truth is thus. Sometimes, in order to best serve humanity, you must abandon your own. I truly am sorry, Cadmus."

"I..." Cadmus started, pain and misery contorting his face—his very soul crying out in pain—but then a calm came over him. He was too numb to hurt, to feel the heartbreak threatening to destroy him. "I believe you."

"Good, then you know what must be done." Solomon withdrew, holding his scythe at his side and bowing his head in reverence.

"It's fine, Cadmus. We know you cannot save us," his sister said, scratching the back of his neck just like she had when they were children. Looking into her eyes, Cadmus raised his hand to her face and tried to remember all the sunny days, all the afternoons spent fishing and heading to the market. He tried to remember how happy she looked on her wedding day.

"I'm sorry," Cadmus said as he turned to face his mother and set down his nephew, looking back to Solomon for just half a moment. With those words, Solomon lifted his head and made eye contact, realizing too late that the apology hadn't been meant for the reaper's family.

"I'm sorry," Cadmus repeated, reinforced with resolve, "because I'm going to try anyway."

Before anyone could react, Cadmus ran toward the platform and readied his scythe, looking more determined than Solomon had ever seen. Lucius backed away from the edge of the platform, but he couldn't anticipate Cadmus summoning Mercy from the sand, his body rising to meet the reaper's foot as he planted it down and pushed, propelling himself up with enough force to easily clear the wall.

"I *promised* you this, Lucius."

Cadmus slammed his scythe through the noble's left shoulder and carved through to his right hip, cutting his former owner in half in a spray of blood and gore. Although momentarily satisfied, Cadmus realized that he had thrown it all away in this act of vengeance and defiance, that any moment now he, Mercy and Solomon might be lost in the wasteland of Purgatory forever.

In *that* moment, Cadmus realized he didn't mind; he would have saved his family every time.

Then—when his feet were about to touch the floor of the platform—the entire arena disappeared, time and space warping around him. For an instant, Cadmus thought he might fall through the abyss for an eternity, but then his feet hit something solid.

As soon as he was able, Cadmus looked around and found that the mists of Purgatory surrounded him again. He was at the end of an abyssal peninsula, and when he turned to his right, he saw Solomon standing there with him.

"What happened? I... I failed, didn't I?" Cadmus whipped around to look at his surroundings and thought it must be another illusion, but then Solomon's hand landed on his shoulder and he turned to face the old reaper. In direct contrast to what he expected, Solomon was smiling at him.

"Cadmus, I said *sometimes*. You were human when it mattered most."

"But—Purgatory, it... it wanted a god! It wanted me to kill my family," Cadmus argued, but then another soul joined them. He looked past Solomon's shoulder to find his sister standing there with a serene smile on her face and wearing pristine, white robes.

"It wanted you to make up your own mind," Solomon stated. "It wanted to make sure you wouldn't lose yourself along the way."

"And..." Cadmus said before turning to face Solomon with anger. "*Did you know?*"

"Yes," Solomon admitted, wincing at the revealed truth.

"And you didn't tell me?"

"It was *your* test," he added, turning to face the ghost standing just a few feet away. "I couldn't help you. Just as you said to Niccolo, you must depend on your own strength, not mine."

"You..." Cadmus started, but then he realized the weight of Purgatory's lesson. It was something that could not be taught; it needed to be experienced. Instead of fighting Solomon further and wasting time, Cadmus turned to his waiting sister and stepped forward. "Claudia..."

"I am so proud of you," she said, at which point Cadmus could not stop himself. He closed the distance and wrapped his arms around her, burying his head in her neck as he squeezed tighter.

"I didn't want to fight. I couldn't stop them back then," he muttered, his words almost unintelligible, but she understood him perfectly.

"Shh... don't you dare. You didn't kill Titus on purpose, and you hold no blame for me, either," she said, pushing him back so she could look into Cadmus' eyes. "You did your best."

"It wasn't good enough," he argued, but Claudia shook her head and placed her finger against his lips.

"It was all I needed. You owe me nothing," she said, looking at him with love and affection. "You owe the *world* nothing. We can only ask."

"I will... try," he said, but his breath caught in his throat upon seeing her smile.

"I am sure that will be enough. Forge your own path, Cadmus," she said before escaping from his embrace. "I cannot follow, but you have our love, our respect and our hope."

"Claudia..."

"Goodbye, brother. If there is yet another life, perhaps we will see each other then," she said, and Cadmus realized their time was over.

Before he could take a step in her direction, her essence faded from Purgatory as if she had never been there at all. On that peninsula hanging in empty space, it was just Cadmus, Solomon and the white horse forming from the dust beside them.

"I am sorry, Master," Mercy rattled, but his voice came as a comfort. "I would take this pain if I could."

"I—I know." Cadmus lifted his hand and set it against Mercy's shoulder once the horse nuzzled against his neck. "But it's mine, and out of respect for them, I will bear it for the rest of my life."

"Noble, Cadmus, and neither of us could ever judge you for it," Solomon added, and when Cadmus turned to face the reaper, he saw the truth of those words. In that moment, Cadmus trusted Solomon —trusted that he would never betray them—and Mercy joined him in that feeling.

With a nod, Cadmus lifted himself onto Mercy's saddle and then breathed deep for a few moments, letting his grief subside until he could handle his emotions. Once he could breathe without shaking, Cadmus turned to Solomon and nodded again.

"No more wasting time. We can't save the world from here."

"Don't think about Gabriel and Uriel, brother," Sabrael said, turning slightly so he could speak to Michael over his shoulder. Although he walked much slower than Michael preferred, this was Sabrael's domain, and so he was left to follow. "It will only serve to make your thoughts darker. You have no need of more tragedy in such trying times."

"You speak as if you have no part in that," Michael muttered, but loud enough so Sabrael would hear. With a light scoff, the archangel in the purple robes turned forward and shuffled along, tapping his staff lightly on the bricks underfoot.

"I have done nothing to you, brother, except provide suitable replacements for your vanguard," he replied, but Michael turned his head so he could avoid looking at the door at the end of the hallway.

"We'll see about that. You were never one for martial prowess, Sabrael. Forgive me for thinking you will have *provided* anything of worth for the coming battle."

"A battle is not won merely by the number of troops, nor the skill of each individual," Sabrael said, causing Michael to look back at him and break his staring contest with the wall. "I merely wish to provide you with a strategic advantage."

"What kind of strategic advantage could *you* give me, Sabrael? The vanguard is just supposed to be a handful of angels that will be a spearhead for the Host," he commented, but then Sabrael looked at him with a malevolent glint in his eye.

"You have little in the way of imagination, brother, that much is sure. I find it amusing that you cannot conceive of any way for your personal vanguard to strike *fear* into the hearts of your enemies."

Michael stopped in his tracks, but Sabrael's comments were not entirely responsible for the feeling of his heart jumping into his throat. As he stared at the door, Michael could finally hear the anguished cries, the whimpers of the creatures being held in Sabrael's laboratory. This far underneath Adonai's palace, Sabrael's crimes had gone unnoticed, but Michael finally realized his brother was up to something more sinister than choosing his vanguard.

"What have you been doing down here?" Michael asked, and Sabrael turned to face him. Reading his brother's expression, Sabrael gathered his staff in both hands and looked at Michael with a note of dismay.

"Only what our God allows. I would not do something outside his wishes."

"You and I both know that he would allow a great number of terrible things on a whim," Michael said, walking forward to stand over his robed brother. "I'll ask again: what have you been doing?"

"And I will repeat myself: only what our God allows. I don't have the patience for this, Michael," Sabrael said dismissively, turning and closing the distance to the end of the hallway. "It is much easier if I just show you the results of my work."

"Fine," Michael replied as he stomped after his brother. "But don't be surprised if I see what you've done and you find yourself at the end of my sword."

"Then you must promise not to be surprised when I laugh at your childish antics," Sabrael said, sighing as he waved his hand over the handle—disengaging magical seals that locked it in place—and then opened the door. With a sly smile, Sabrael motioned for Michael to step through the doorway, and it was almost too much for him to stomach. However, Michael swallowed his pride and walked through, his jaw dropping once he saw the results of Sabrael's efforts.

"What is this?" Michael growled, anger already rising up his throat.

With a light chuckle, Sabrael walked past his brother and up to the glass tube holding an unfortunate soul in place. From what Michael could see, a man with four arms was suspended in a glass column filled with green liquid, a mask over his mouth. The only mercy Michael could see was that the man was asleep in his cage.

That changed once the man's eyes slammed open and he frantically started pawing at the glass.

"He's a recent addition. I'm not exactly sure he will be ready by the time Niccolo and his friends find their way out of Purgatory," Sabrael replied as he walked up to the glass and set his palm against the surface. Once he was close enough, the man in the tube stopped pawing at the glass and retreated as far as he could, which made Sabrael smile. "If he is, however, I'll make sure to add him to your team. His strength will be nothing to scoff at, at the very least."

"Why is he so afraid of you? Why is he held in that *glass*, Sabrael?"

Michael's brother didn't even bother to turn as he swept his finger across the glass, tracing a sigil that burst into activity after a moment, and electrified the column and its occupant.

"He is afraid because I have taught him fear. He is held in that glass because I am not finished with him," Sabrael said before turning to his right and heading to another part of the room. "In any case, that boy is not your concern right now. You have others to meet."

"Others? You've done this to *others*?" Michael asked, so shocked that he moved away from Sabrael's victim and followed after his brother, looking from side to side to see all kinds of blades and saws, medical tables and tethers whose purpose he could only guess at.

"Of course! Ten, so far. Depending on when this war starts, I could have as many as fourteen individuals for you to direct in combat," Sabrael commented, fiddling with the odd vial and scribbling in nearby notepads as he shuffled through the laboratory. In contrast to his pace in the hallway, Michael could barely keep up as Sabrael swam about in his element. "You're here to see my completed projects, after all. Your vanguard."

"Are they all like that poor boy in the glass? Just who were these people, Sabrael?" Michael was about to smack a nearby pot to the ground for effect, but his brother looked at him with condescension and shocked him into staying his hand.

"No one of importance until I got to them. You are about to fight a war that will determine whether or not *any* of us get to go with Adonai into his new universe. We want you to win, but more importantly, *I* do not want to be left behind. I am here to give you the weapons and tools you will need to defeat the upstart Horsemen and all of our deluded siblings." He drew closer until he was only a foot away from Michael, intimidating even though he was a foot shorter. "These souls are nothing but clay for me to use."

"So they're human," Michael surmised, Sabrael smiling slightly with his eyes before responding.

"They *were*. Now they are so much more." They headed to the far side of the laboratory, which led into a small hallway lined with iron bars on either side. "Gregorious was nothing before I got to him, and now he will kill a number of demons without much effort. His mass alone will be enough to crush them. You'll meet him very soon, but I wish to show you my prize before the others."

"Your prize?"

"I will introduce all of them, of course, but I am quite excited about her," Sabrael said as he walked up to the farthest cell on the left and swept his arm along the thick bars, a seal shimmering along the surface before it shattered. Michael watched something black slam against the cage and a dark mass reach out for Sabrael, but the archangel tapped his staff against the floor and electricity raced along the mass as it retreated back into the cage.

"*Her*? What have you done to her?" Michael asked, drawing closer, but Sabrael motioned for him to stay before backing away from the cell and beckoning its occupant to come closer.

"Nothing too cruel, I assure you, she is just not so pleasant upon waking. Come now," he said as he waved his hand, "the days of your punishment are long over, my dear. I am merely introducing you to your superior officer."

"Superior... officer?" a woman's voice came from beyond the bars, and Michael was too stupefied to do anything but watch as a slim woman with dark hair and olive skin stepped into the hallway, her lithe frame covered with a light set of shirt and trousers. "I'm sorry, Master Sabrael, I forgot my place."

"It's quite alright, my dear. Regression is expected from time to time," Sabrael said as the woman drew closer, stepping behind her so he could place his hand on her far shoulder. "Michael, I would like you to meet Camilla, your lieutenant."

"Who was she, Sabrael?" he asked, but the woman responded for the archangel.

"A mere servant of the lord, great Michael. I hope I may please you in the coming war." Camilla avoided eye contact for the entire statement, and when Sabrael noticed her humility, he tapped his staff against the ground, sending volts of electricity through her small body.

"Sabrael!" Michael shouted, but Camilla shook her head and put out her hand in protest.

"It is alright, archangel," she protested, lifting her head so she could make eye contact with him. Michael was shocked to see those eyes were completely black. "My master is just teaching me to look at you with confidence, to meet your gaze and manage my fear."

"He's teaching you the *wrong way*," Michael said, narrowing his gaze at his brother, but Sabrael was unaffected.

"I have my methods, Michael, and I do not need to explain them."

"Who was she really, Sabrael? *Why* is she my lieutenant? You have some scheme."

His brother did not respond directly, instead turning to his pet project.

"Who were you, Camilla? Answer your superior officer," he commanded, and the woman obliged.

"I was Camilla Simonetti da Firenze, formerly Camilla Gherardini. In my life, before... he came down with his affliction, I was betrothed to Niccolo Vespucci da Firenze," she said, and Michael watched her anger play out when she said his name. Each syllable was poisoned with venom, and it was obvious she could barely stomach the fact that they had intended to marry.

"You—you're using the woman he loved? *That's* your game?" Michael asked as he approached Sabrael, but Camilla threw out her arm and a dark mass grew out of her skin and slammed into the wall beside her.

"*It is not a game!*" she screamed, the darkness of her eyes leaking out into the lines of her face, her mouth stretching further than it should. "*That man is an enemy of God, a blight upon the Earth and I will rip him limb from limb!*"

"So you brainwashed her, too?" Michael asked, immediately regretting it. Within seconds, Michael was forced to retrieve his hilt and set it aflame as Camilla directed a torrent of black sludge in his direction. Even as an archangel of Heaven, Michael was pushed back a foot before Camilla retrieved the dark mass and wrapped it around her arm.

"My master has done nothing to my mind, archangel. Niccolo *ruined* my life, he killed my husband and the convent was the only option I had left," she stated, dark tendrils wrapping around her other arm and her legs, other tentacles pouring out of her back and fanning out around her. "I will gladly kill him with my own two hands."

"This is my lieutenant, Sabrael?" Michael asked, still holding onto his sword in case the woman tried to attack again. "This is the creature you want me to use against the Horsemen?"

"No, my brother. *This* is the creature I want you to use," Sabrael said before drawing a sigil in the air and tapping it with the end of his staff, which immediately forced Camilla to scream and hunch over, holding her hands to the sides of her head.

And as Michael watched, the true horror of Sabrael's experiments revealed itself; twisted limbs and bones stretched through skin, the dark extensions of her normal form became more terrible than Michael had thought possible. Even though he was in clear danger, the archangel could not help but drop his weapon to the floor and gape in horrific wonder at the creature Camilla had become. He wondered how much of it was even human.

"My God, Sabrael. Why would you ever do this?" Michael asked, but his brother replied with soft laughter before looking up at his creation.

"I only needed permission, and Adonai was kind enough to grant it to me."

"It's very quiet," Buer said, his words echoing off the high walls all around them. In just a few yards, the canyon walls fell away, the claustrophobic path ending abruptly and opening up into an empty plain covered in mist. A few withered trees were scattered along the road, but they gave no sense of life to Purgatory.

"What, did you expect it to be a bustling center of activity?" Seere asked, and he was almost immediately rewarded with a pinch from Paimon, who was still sharing his saddle.

"I expected a trap," Astaroth said as peered through the mists.

"You may still get one," Crocell replied as he ventured into the empty ground in front of them. "The only way to find out is to spring it."

"You would go forward without caution?" Buer asked.

"I would go *forward*."

Crocell's brief reply shamed his companions into following. Soon they were surrounded by the mists of Purgatory, their visibility reduced to ten yards. It was enough to make William nervous as he sat on Buer's back, but the centaur did not scold him.

"It is alright, my young friend. We sneak around in the land of giants, and there is no shame in fearing their presence." Although done out of kindness, William did not take kindly to Buer's patronizing words.

"That's enough." He slid off the centaur's back and hit the ground hard, but he quickly retrieved his bow and kept his finger on the string. "I'm not letting you coddle me."

"That was not what I intended, William," Buer replied, but the young man shrugged it off and continued forward.

"Shouldn't we have seen this city by now? These Nephilim are huge."

A deep laugh boomed through the air as an answer, and at first William thought it was the Leviathan finding another way to unnerve him. However, when he looked back at the creature, it was shuffling along and looking at the floor. Then William looked at his companions and saw how they were not amused, how none of them were laughing.

"Size is relative, little one. You're tiny to all of us." Once the deep voice resonated through the air, William and his companions drew their weapons and fell into a circle. They could not see beyond the mists so—resorting to his usual behavior—Niccolo let out his wings and yelled as loud as he could.

"*Show yourself, coward!*" he shouted in three voices, almost deciding to flap his wings and scatter the mists then and there, but that deep laugh broke through again.

"You angels are so rude. You sneak into the middle of New Jotunheim and you have the gall to accuse *us* of cowardice? If nothing else, you've lost little of your humor, Lucifer."

Then a thunderclap filled the air and the group was struck by gale force winds. Niccolo was forced to retract his wings in order to stay standing and held his hand in front of his face, but when he felt the wind subside, he lowered it and saw the mists had disappeared. However, what he saw gave him no relief.

As far as Niccolo could see, Nephilim had gathered around them —at least sixty—and they were completely surrounded.

"Wait. You are not Lucifer," the closest Nephilim said before crouching down to inspect him. He was older than the giants they had already encountered; long white hair fell down to the middle of his torso and a great beard covered his face. His right eye was covered in a huge patch held in place with what seemed like metal rivets, but his left eye looked over Niccolo's every detail.

"You're right," Niccolo replied, turning to face the giant with sword and shield ready. "My name is Niccolo, and I am the new Devil."

"What's a devil?" the Nephilim asked, shocking Niccolo into stammering.

"I—Lucifer was the first. I am the leader and most powerful creature from Hell," Niccolo explained, drawing a snort of laughter from Seere. Although he turned back to glare at the Horseman, the damage was already done. When he turned back to the Nephilim, Niccolo tried to recover his appearance by puffing out his chest. "That's what being the Devil means. That's who I am."

"You expect me to believe that you're a leader, insect? Are you—are you even an angel?" the Nephilim asked, crouching forward and turning his head so he could inspect Niccolo from all sides.

"No, you idiot, we're all from Hell." Niccolo was getting frustrated, but the Nephilim drew back on his knees and shook his head.

"You keep saying these words like I know what they mean. What is Hell?"

Niccolo was interrupted before he could respond with something equally foolish once Paimon jumped off Fury's saddle and stepped forward, earning the Nephilim's attention once she had walked past Niccolo.

"It's where we were banished, Ymir. It took some time for us to realize it, but many of the angels who were responsible for forcing you to Purgatory eventually saw the truth of Adonai's evil." She looked directly into the giant's silver eye, which had narrowed at her arrival. "Eventually, we rebelled against Adonai and soon found ourselves the victims of his wrath."

"Serves you right, harpy," Ymir said before sniffing and then turning to the side, spitting a huge gob of mucus which landed twenty feet away. "You know how hard it is to care about what happens to you, Butcher?"

"I know you don't care about me, Ymir, or any of the others

responsible for your exile," Paimon replied, dropping her hands to her side. "We're not here for your sympathy."

"Good, because you're not getting it." Ymir's voice turned to gravel as he readjusted his legs so he could sit on the ground. "You're lucky I haven't killed you yet."

"We're just trying to make it to the other side of Purgatory." Paimon set her hands on her hips and breathed deep. "As long as you don't get in our way, there won't be problems."

"See, I'm not exactly sure about that," Ymir grumbled as he waved at his fellow giants. "Because it looks like we're directly in your way and I'm not too keen on getting out of it. What do you say to that?"

"We'll fight you if we need to."

Ymir let out a deep bellow of laughter and shook his head, holding his face in his palm as he shuddered. After a moment, he withdrew his hand and leaned down so his face was just a few feet from Paimon.

"Forgive me for not taking the threat seriously. When you banished us last time, you had an army behind you, Butcher. You have—what?" He drew back and examined her companions. "Six angels, a creature with eight legs and a devil, whatever that is. I'm not sure I can care."

"Technically, she only has three angels," Seere added from horseback, leaning against his pommel with mild apathy. "The rest of us are lowly humans, along with that crusty man who's *calling* himself the Devil."

"Wait, the *monkeys*?" Ymir replied, turning back to raise an eyebrow at Paimon. "You're using animals to try and scare me? What's wrong with you, Butcher? You go insane after all this time?"

"Watch what you say, *Ymir*," Niccolo growled, his wings slowly stretching out from his back. "Or you'll see why you should fear us."

"You gonna poke me with a stick, monkey?" Ymir showed a slight smile with only a handful of teeth, and it was too much for Niccolo to take. After letting out a bright flash of light that made Ymir flinch,

Niccolo jumped forward and slammed his demonic fist into the giant's nose and sent him sprawling. Bellows of rage from their Nephilim audience filled the air, but none of them compared to the deep roar from Ymir as he pushed himself to his feet and then stared down at Niccolo.

"*I could eat you whole! I could grind you to dust beneath my feet!*" Ymir's voice shook the very atmosphere, but Niccolo held his ground.

"And I could cut you down before you get anywhere near me. You remember Lucifer, right? You remember the firstborn?" Niccolo brandished Lux and swept it above him, letting an arc of explosive energy soar into the air. "I have his powers added to mine."

"I was never scared of *him*, either," Ymir replied, standing up straight and bristling with anger. "You picked the wrong day to come to New Jotunheim, *Devil*."

After he spat out the last word, Ymir started toward Niccolo, pebbles clattering against the ground as he came closer. Niccolo was about to jump up to meet his new enemy, but he was unable to clear the ground before something hit him in the center of the chest and knocked him over. Springing to his feet, Niccolo looked up just in time to see Paimon running to intercept Ymir.

She must have been the one to knock him down.

Ymir saw that Paimon had decided to take Niccolo's place and brought his right arm forward, but Paimon was prepared. Hopping up quickly, Paimon landed on Ymir's arm and sprinted forward, using her talons to create footholds in his flesh. Already yelling in frustration, the Nephilim brought up his arm and tried to swat at her with his other hand, but she only used that as an opportunity to switch to his left arm, using that momentum to launch toward Ymir's face. After scrabbling up the remaining few feet of his cheek, Paimon settled her talons around the skin of his bottom eyelid and then held her extended fingers inches away from Ymir's pupil.

"That's *enough*, Ymir! We stop this now or I take your other eye!" she claimed, forcing the Nephilim to stop in his tracks. From the trembling of his eye, Paimon could tell the giant was afraid, but he recovered a false bravado.

"Wouldn't mind losing it if I could finally take you down, Butcher," he claimed, but he made no movement. Paimon let her claws grow just a little sharper, just a little closer to his uncovered eye.

"Forgive *me* for not taking the threat seriously," she said. "I'm not your enemy anymore, Ymir. None of us are. We're here to invade Heaven, to fight a war against Adonai."

"Bull fucking shit, Paimon," Ymir protested, but Paimon withdrew her nails and jumped off the Nephilim's face, flipping in the air before landing gracefully on the ground forty feet below.

"*No* fucking shit, Ymir. Even if our best chance is the kind of devil who might kill his best friend, it's better than the alternative. Adonai wants to destroy everything, start over from scratch. I've heard he makes promises of taking people with him, but I don't exactly trust him," Paimon explained, crossing her arms, and the Nephilim sneered at the thought.

"First reasonable thing you've ever said," Ymir said, easing off as the cuts around his face bled. "Is that all you want? Just to head through Purgatory and get to the other side?"

"That's it." Paimon waved at the giants still watching from afar. "We have no intention of killing any Nephilim. We'd just as soon leave them alive."

"I still say that we could take down your little ragtag group of angels and humans..." Ymir looked to the side as he muttered, but Paimon shocked him with her next words.

"I'm not sure you're wrong," she said as an idea formed in her head. When the giant turned to express his skepticism, Paimon decided it was worth pursuing. "It's an interesting point, though."

"Spit it out, Butcher."

"Come with us."

"I'm sorry, *what*?" Niccolo shouted, and that was enough for Ymir to laugh and point at Niccolo with his thumb.

"Answer your devil, Paimon."

"He's not *mine*." Paimon walked over to Niccolo and set her hand on his shoulder. "He could be ours, though. Niccolo here has the potential to kill Adonai."

"And who's been telling you that?" Ymir replied with a scoff, but this time Buer stepped forward.

"Humans have a potential we do not, Ymir. Their souls are not limited by a framework of Adonai's design. Their souls spring from living creatures," he started to explain, but Ymir crouched forward and squinted at the centaur before his eyes opened wide.

"Buer, is that you? Gods, last time I saw you, you didn't have legs at all!"

"That's... somewhat beside the point, Ymir," Buer said, but the Nephilim only drew back and shrugged. Seeing that momentary surrender, Buer cleared his throat and continued. "What I was saying was that the human souls have no real rules when it comes to their existence. What we've seen with Niccolo here and his frie— another Horseman, is that once they absorb the power of demonic and angelic souls, it becomes their own. For all his arrogance, Niccolo here is a great deal more powerful than any of us."

"You're saying he's stronger than all of you?" Pointing around the fields full of Nephilim, Ymir continued his questioning. "He could kill all of my supporters here?"

"Possibly. I wouldn't be surprised if Niccolo could take on two or three of your Nephilim at once," Buer mused as he ran his thumb and forefinger through his beard in thought. Although the others stared at him, Buer had not realized what Ymir had inferred.

"Then let's see it," Ymir said, nodding at three of his companions to come closer.

"What? *No*," Paimon said, but Ymir yawned through her protest.

"Not my fault you all make such crazy statements. That's the wager. If this devil of yours can kill three of my men, alone, then he can be our devil, too."

"Wait, are you serious?" Niccolo asked, earning the giant's scorn.

"I joke around sometimes, but this isn't one of those times. You kill three of us by yourself, then we can talk about joining your army. Think that stick of yours will be enough?"

Snarling, Niccolo stretched out his wings and faced the approaching giants.

"I'll be just fine."

WHEN THE FIRST giant slammed his forearm down on him, Niccolo quickly found out that he would *not* be just fine. Although Niccolo raised his shield above him to deflect the blow, the Nephilim was strong enough to force him to his knees, sinking further into the dirt as the giant pressed down. Niccolo was only just able to stop his bones from snapping, and he knew that he wouldn't be able to take another direct hit like that.

"Oh, c'mon! Don't just squash him!"

Ymir's voice reverberated through the air, which only made Niccolo angry. Pushing up with all his might, Niccolo forced the Nephilim's forearm back into the air and then threw it to the side, where it crashed into the dirt. Niccolo was about to swing Lux forward and cut through his first opponent's arm with concentrated energy, but then he was slammed from the side by a giant foot and was flung through the air.

"If this is what a devil is, I'm not impressed!" Ymir shouted above the grunts and bellows of the other giants, allowing Niccolo to focus.

Arresting his momentum by spreading his wings, Niccolo saw one of the giants rushing forward to swat him out of the air. After sending out a radiant arc of energy, Niccolo flew toward the Nephilim, pushing himself through the air ahead of the arm sweeping through his flight path.

The energy of Niccolo's attack splashed against the creature's eyes, cutting into his flesh and blinding him, but Niccolo was more focused on using it as a diversion. Once he landed on the Nephilim's

IN DEFIANCE OF HEAVEN

arm, he took a cue from Paimon's tactics and Niccolo dragged his black nails through the flesh. He shredded its muscles and tendons up to the elbow, and he would have gone further if it had not started flailing around.

Jumping off the creature's arm, Niccolo took his sword in both hands and then swung it across his body once he was within a foot of the blinded Nephilim's face. An eruption of light came out of his short sword and Niccolo used it to tear through the giant's head, cleaving off the top half of its skull, dead before it met the ground.

After that, Ymir was done with his taunts.

"And how was *that?*" Niccolo hoped to draw out a resigned grunt or cheer from his audience, but then he was grabbed out of the air by two strong hands. Only just able to see above the creature's fingers, Niccolo realized that he was completely at the Nephilim's mercy. It salivated as it looked down at him, its face twisted by a warped cleft palate.

"You part bird? You taste like bird?" it asked, the Nephilim's mind as warped as his face, and Niccolo realized he could not die like this. He couldn't ask for help, obviously, but he could *not* die like this. Straining against the Nephilim's grip, Niccolo tried to wriggle out of those fingers, but then the Nephilim clamped down further and shook his head.

"Not want break bones, ruin meat, but bird is dangerous." The giant compressed Niccolo's body further and further, every part of him creaking and bending under the enormous amount of pressure.

Panicking, Niccolo tried to think of any weapon he could use, but his arms were still pinned to his sides. He had to abandon his wings as the Nephilim squeezed further—he didn't want them to break—but his options decreased as time went on.

As a last resort, Niccolo screamed.

However, the Nephilim was not prepared for three voices in harmony to burst through the air around them, rupturing his ear drums, and he dropped the tiny man.

Feeling lucky more than anything, Niccolo still hit the ground hard and tried to push himself to his feet. He failed—realizing that a number of ribs must have broken while he was held in the Nephilim's grip—but he also knew he didn't have the option to stay there. He looked up to find the other Nephilim had come forward and raised its foot above him, ready to squash Niccolo. Thinking of little else, Niccolo instinctively created his bastard sword in his left hand, but he didn't have the strength to hold it when the Nephilim's foot came down to crush him. Niccolo barely escaped the blow as he dived out of the way.

A cry of pain went through the air, and Niccolo looked up to see the Nephilim lifting its leg back up and moaning, a green shimmer in the middle of its foot. Laughing at the absurdity, Niccolo realized the giant had stomped down on his sword and buried it in his foot like a massive splinter. For a moment, Niccolo just laughed and watched as the giant hopped around—every one of its jumps shaking him as he knelt there—and Niccolo almost forgot he was fighting for his life and an army.

Then, as a grin spread across his face, Niccolo realized what he needed to do.

Running forward and summoning his weapons of light, Niccolo let out his wings before he was underneath the Nephilim, who was gingerly setting his foot back on the ground. Willing his first sword to dissolve, Niccolo was rewarded with another scream of pain as the Nephilim lifted its leg back up to inspect why the bottom of its foot was burning. There was no way the creature could have known that Niccolo's bastard sword would dissolve into acid, but Niccolo was not in the business of fighting fair.

Niccolo jumped up to meet the bottom of the Nephilim's foot and flapped his wings to push further, which made the giant creature lose its balance. Soon enough, the Nephilim toppled over and onto its back, and Niccolo hovered in the air as he watched his giant victim. Gathering his energy, Niccolo flew higher into the sky before turning over and then spun forward in a fast tumble, Lux held vertical as he flipped over and over.

As he fell, Niccolo let loose two giant streams of radiant energy that slammed into the giant's splayed limbs, cutting deep into its arms and legs and hobbling the Nephilim. When he was able to recover himself and maintained his altitude fifty feet above the creature, Niccolo looked over his work and smiled. That Nephilim would no longer be bothering him.

However, he had forgotten about the Nephilim with the cleft palate, who had only suffered perforated ear drums. As Niccolo hovered in the air feeling pleased with himself, the giant came back around and slammed him out of the air with a hammer blow, causing him to plummet against the other Nephilim's rib cage.

"Bird make too much noise!"

Niccolo didn't know whether its shouting was because it was angry or because it could no longer hear. Picking himself up on the crippled Nephilim's chest, Niccolo realized that his diseased arm was broken and he wouldn't be able to use it, but he turned to face his enemy anyway. It leaned over and drooled, snapping at him once but then standing up straight.

"I'm not a bird, you idiot," Niccolo said weakly, but his wings were still stretched out behind him. He realized this as soon as the Nephilim lunged to grab his wings, and he shattered them into light rather than let himself be caught. When he tried to draw Lux into his hand, the sword was barely shining, which meant that Niccolo had stretched himself too thin. As it stood, Niccolo had no weapons left.

"This is what you get, devil, for using powers that aren't yours," Ymir stated, his voice somber and, more importantly, closer. When the last Nephilim opponent lunged forward, Niccolo rolled off the cripple's body and was able to see Ymir walking forward.

"They are mine, Nephilim. I earned them." Niccolo's voice shook despite his confidence, and the giant shook his head at the claim.

"Did you? Lucifer never earned them; Adonai gave them to him," Ymir said lazily before stopping twenty yards from Niccolo. "That green blade, that arm of yours, you *earn* those, too?"

"I..." Niccolo started, remembering his years of sacrifice and suffering, but then he remembered the source of his blight. It was *not* natural; it was *not* a product of chance. Sabrael as Innocenti had infected his arm to install Niccolo as the Horseman of Pestilence.

Sabrael had used that arm to kill Tamiel.

Remembering that he was still in the middle of a battle, Niccolo dove to the side and narrowly avoided getting bit in half. Rolling and recovering himself quickly, Niccolo turned to see the remaining Nephilim sprawled out, holding himself up with his hands like he was in the middle of pushing himself off the floor.

So furious about the depth of his manipulation, Niccolo had no fear as he ran toward the creature, his right arm cocked behind him.

What he did not notice before he threw his arm forward was the vibrant emerald fire that streamed out of his eyes and mouth, or the emerald aura that surrounded his right hand as it connected with the Nephilim's jaw. Niccolo only cared about one thing, and that was destroying his enemy.

And with a blow that was powerful enough to rocket the Nephilim's head to the side, Niccolo snapped its neck, completing Ymir's trial with nothing but his own power.

"You... *what?*"

Flustered, Ymir drew back from the display. He had thought the test was over, that Niccolo had failed, but the young human with an angel's powers had found a way to defeat three Nephilim by himself. Looking down at the remains of his warriors, Ymir saw a human standing triumphant.

"So... I guess..." Niccolo breathed heavily as he faced Ymir. "I guess that means I'm your devil, too."

"Not yet," Paimon said from behind him, and Niccolo turned to see her standing over the paralyzed Nephilim. Niccolo didn't understand how she had even gotten there, but he was more curious why she was there at all.

"It's done, Paimon. They're dead; that one is crippled," he argued, but Paimon crawled up to the middle of the Nephilim's ribcage before extending her fingers as far as they would go and then slashed into the creature, who screamed in pain. *"Paimon, stop it!"*

"You know... what you said... about mercy?" Paimon asked between slashes, tearing further and further through the bone until she was finally through the ribcage and looking at the soft flesh of the Nephilim's heart. When she saw her goal beating beneath her, Paimon turned to face Niccolo with scorn. "This is not the time to show it."

"Paimon!" Niccolo was shocked by her actions, but then she slammed her fingers into the Nephilim's heart and tore through it, sending out sprays of blood from the hole in its chest. Once the display was over, Paimon's golden skin was covered in streams of red. "What was the point of that?"

"They recognize strength, Nico," she said softly before turning around and approaching him, Ymir watching the whole display. "If this one was left alive, the agreement would be null and void."

"But—but you're the one who told me we don't have to kill them all! You're the one who came up with the fucking plan to join forces!" Niccolo pointed back at Ymir with his newly-healed demonic arm. "You're a fucking hypocrite!"

"No, Nico. I just know the Nephilim." Paimon walked past him until she could look up at Ymir in defiance. "You forget how old I am, how much I've seen. I was the one who put them *in* Purgatory, and I know exactly what they need to see. Just because I want to save them doesn't mean I won't make the tough calls when I need to."

"That's all bullshit, Paimon," Niccolo said, but when he looked up to Ymir, he knew he was on the wrong side of the argument.

"She's right. If you had left Filli alive, even crippled, I wouldn't have honored the agreement. She was very *violent* about it," he said, sneering at the demon king, "but that's the way of things. Blood for honor; death for promises. I can tell that she has changed, but *we* haven't."

"So, mercy only when it's convenient, then?" Niccolo didn't hide his condescension, but Paimon would not back down.

"No, Niccolo. Mercy when we can afford it." She let the gold creep away from her skin and looked at him with vacant eyes. "And the flip side of that coin is brutality when we can't."

"Sounds an awful lot like justifying your hypocrisy," he growled, but the demon king merely shrugged and walked away.

"Well, the good thing, Niccolo, is that I don't ever have to justify myself to you."

CHAPTER 7
A HAUNTING GROUND FOR MEMORIES

"Staying *behind*? You can't be serious." Niccolo pointed at the Nephilim standing behind him. "This bastard is just making excuses!"

"I ain't making anything, devil," Ymir said, and Niccolo turned to glare at him. "I sent out my messengers a couple hours ago, but it's gonna take a day before I can gather the Nephilim. We ain't too fast and we're spread out all over Purgatory. If you aren't waiting for us, we need someone to lead us to your trail."

"So you're taking one of my strongest warriors to do it?"

"Two, you jackass," Astaroth grumbled, surprising Niccolo. "What, you didn't really think I was going to leave Paimon here all alone, did you?"

"I didn't think we were going to leave Paimon *at all*. It doesn't make sense for *either* of you to stay!" Niccolo shouted, but Paimon set one hand on her hip before motioning to the gathered Nephilim with her other hand.

"It makes *a lot* of sense if you're paying attention. The Nephilim are only going to follow someone they respect—which is *me* in this case—and you're not sticking around to wait for them. We'll catch up, I swear."

"And you're going to steal Astaroth to do it?" Niccolo asked, but Paimon sneered at the choice of words.

"I'm not *stealing* anything. He could go with you and I'd still be fine, but that's not up to me."

"No, it's not," Astaroth agreed with a grunt, staring Niccolo down. "I make my own decisions. And right now, that decision is to stick around Paimon to make sure she has someone who can travel a great deal of distance in a short time, just in case we need to send a message."

"Since Buer needs to go with you and Crocell is crippled to the point of being *useless*," he added with scorn, "that means I'm the only candidate."

"Oh, that's the only reason?" Niccolo replied, and Astaroth accepted the implied challenge.

"Why do I need to have just one reason, monkey? How about I just don't want to be around your traitorous, selfish ass for—"

"That's enough, Astaroth," Buer interrupted, causing them to fall away from each other.

"I don't know, it was just getting good." Ymir chuckled at his own humor, but he stopped Buer glared at him over his spectacles. Under his gaze, even a Nephilim decided it was better to back down.

"We need to keep going, and wasting a day waiting for the Nephilim does not help our cause," Buer stated after turning away from Ymir and looking to Paimon and Astaroth. "While regrettable, I do believe it is in our best interest to let my brother and sister stay behind. Although you won your duel, Niccolo, you have more important errands. Paimon is the logical choice for your surrogate."

"Yeah, but—" Niccolo started, but Paimon cleared her throat and stopped him from going further.

"It's my choice, Nico. It will probably be better if we split up." She nodded at Ymir before continuing. "According to our new friend, there's a pretty nasty god waiting for you, and Astaroth and I would probably get in the way."

"And how is that?" Niccolo asked, drawing a scoff from Astaroth.

"Because apparently this Baphomet feeds on your past and your crimes," he said, smiling at his violent memories. "Paimon and I have millions of years of war and crimes behind us, and there are some horrors you monkeys aren't meant to see."

"Yeah, well..." Niccolo tried to reply, but his tongue wasn't cooperating. Giving up on Astaroth, Niccolo tried to grab Paimon by the shoulder before she drew away. "How do we know you'll even get back to us?"

"Ymir will get us to the gate, don't worry. They know how to get out, they just can't get past the guardian."

"Guardian," the Leviathan whispered from outside the group. "It is not such an appropriate word for Baphomet..."

"And what is?" Niccolo asked, and the Leviathan turned to him and cocked its mask to the side.

"Keeper. It keeps everything." The deep rumble of its voice dominated the statement, and then it turned away and shuffled into the mists.

"Because *that's* not cryptic." Seere sighed from his place on Fury's saddle before sitting straight up and pointing at the departing creature. "Wait, are we leaving?"

"Probably should," Ymir said with a yawn, waving lazily at the Leviathan's back. "He's going the right direction, anyhow."

"Goddamn creature..." Niccolo stomped after the Leviathan, but he hesitated just a few steps into his march. Turning back, he saw Astaroth and Paimon looking after him, each of them crossing their arms. He wanted to say more to them, try to persuade them to come along, but he could see their determination.

More importantly, he saw their disappointment.

Turning his back on them, Niccolo growled as he ran forward, but it didn't take long before he realized it made more sense to fly. Letting wings out from his back, Niccolo jumped into the air, keeping close enough to the ground so he would not lose his companions in the mists.

It only took a few moments before he was flying high above them, about to descend, but then he realized there was no point in joining them on the ground. They would not welcome his company nor enjoy his conversation. At this point, with all of the barbaric and terrible things he had done, Niccolo didn't have any friends left. There was the Leviathan, of course, but Niccolo had no desire to call such a monstrosity a friend.

So, instead of descending, Niccolo maintained his altitude and soared in the air of Purgatory, becoming lost in his own thoughts. It seemed like those thoughts were the only thing he had left, since he had destroyed his family and his friendships in such a short time. Over the last year, he had seen himself do terrible things in the name of vengeance, but he always assumed there were lines he would not cross.

Since coming to Purgatory, he had not only crossed them, he had destroyed the very ground where they had been drawn.

As Niccolo thought about his decisions, a flash of Cadmus hanging from the ledge came to his mind. Although he realized that he should have regretted the act, the very sight of his friend made him frustrated and angry. Cadmus was never supposed to be in that position; he was never supposed to push Niccolo into fighting him. They were friends, brothers, and Cadmus had personally betrayed him.

"So you intend to be separate from everyone, is that it?"

Niccolo turned to see Crocell flying beside him. As his dark wings trailed black feathers, Niccolo could see them melt into water and then join the clouds around them.

"That's the idea, Crocell. I would think you would understand." Niccolo hoped his snide tone would deter the fallen angel, but it had the opposite effect.

"I do, that's why I'm here," he said, another powerful flap of his wings sending a cool breeze at Niccolo and misting his face with water droplets.

"Would you mind? You're getting me wet," Niccolo said with annoyance.

"You are lucky Seere cannot fly, or he would make you pay for that comment." The odd joke shocked Niccolo into laughter.

"You ever think I'm up here to avoid that?"

"No, you are up here because you feel different from them," Crocell answered simply, not waiting for Niccolo to agree. "And you are right. You *are* different."

"With deductive skills like that, Crocell, it's no wonder you were the Slayer of Dis," Niccolo tried to tease, but there was no smile on the demon's face.

"Do you know *why* I became the Slayer of Dis, Niccolo?" he asked, turning his face to look at Niccolo. A crack of lightning spread across his dark eyes, and it was enough for Niccolo to become mesmerized. "I was told you encountered Lucifer's memories. Was that one there for you to see?"

"It's... yeah," Niccolo muttered, breaking eye contact. "I saw you kneeling in the courtyard. All of it."

"Then that makes explaining this much easier," Crocell replied before looking ahead and flapping his wings again. "I failed, and I spent the next millennium or so trying to make up for it before you made your appearance. You were there to witness my second failure, where I gave up my vengeance in Ronove's hovel.

"Between my first and second failure, I was not part of Hell," Crocell said, turning back to his young companion. "I was not part of Dis. I was not a fallen angel. I was a being entirely motivated by vengeance, by what I thought was justice. I was a slayer, *the Slayer*, and as such I was separate from everyone. I never slept, I never stopped; I never gave up. I had resolved to be the blade that would cut down the Shroud at all costs.

"But you know the end of *that* story, Niccolo. You were there to see me finally give up. You were there to see me give into my fear and fatigue, and you were there to see me become another fallen angel living in Hell," Crocell concluded, radiant tears streaming down his cheeks as the wind broke against his face.

Niccolo bit his lip, waiting for Crocell to continue, but it seemed like that was the end of his story. Looking down at the odd group below them, Niccolo desperately tried to understand the moral of the story. However, as he watched the ants beneath them, Niccolo surrendered and looked back at Crocell with a frown on his face.

"I'm sorry, Crocell, but what's your point?"

"Was it not obvious?" Crocell frowned at Niccolo before sighing. "No, I suppose it's not. I'm *showing* you what happens to those who willingly separate themselves from their friends and family. What you see is the product of a thousand years of vengeance, isolation and ignorance. I was obsessed with redemption, and when it came time for me to claim it, I faltered. I failed, and a young pup shamed me by taking that vengeance in my stead."

"That's not—"

"That is *exactly*," Crocell interrupted him, electricity coursing through his body and making him shine brighter. "I am not saying you will not claim your vengeance; I am not saying you will fail. What I am saying is that the price may not be worth it. I am a hollow shell of the angel I used to be, Niccolo, and it was entirely by my own actions. I pushed everyone and everything away, devoted to one single purpose. Now that my one purpose has been achieved by someone else, I have... nothing."

"You don't have nothing," Niccolo replied flippantly, but when Crocell looked at him, he saw the pain lurking there.

"I *do*, Niccolo. I am on this suicide mission because my very reason for existence is beyond me—whether by my hand or not—and I have no friends or family to make me want to continue. That is why I jumped through the portal and jeopardized everything. That is why I do not care that my wounds no longer heal the same way.

"I'm a fallen angel without purpose," he said, tears falling away from him just as rain started to fall from above. "I am immortal and my life means nothing."

"I don't know what to say..." Niccolo replied, his heart aching for Crocell. He didn't even mind the rain the angel had forced upon them.

"I want none of your words, Niccolo. I am merely warning you. If you continue down this path, if you continue to throw away your friends and your loved ones, your purpose will be the only thing left," he said before breathing in deep and closing his eyes. "I warn you because you are immortal, and no purpose lasts forever."

With those last words, Crocell dropped from the sky and circled down to the travelers below, taking the rain with him and leaving Niccolo dry after just a moment of flight.

Thinking about his warning, Niccolo's first reaction was to rebel. It seemed like Crocell was trying to make up for his past failures, failures Niccolo had rectified. Niccolo had been the one to kill Azazel; *he* had been the one to destroy the Shroud.

But then he remembered that scene from Lucifer's memories; he remembered seeing Crocell weeping while his hands were covered in blood. As Niccolo recalled the slayer's confession, he finally understood why Crocell had come to join him. It was only moments after seeing that memory that Niccolo had been kneeling over Plague, just hours before Tamiel's insides were torn apart by Niccolo's traitorous hand. Crocell knew exactly what kind of anger had driven Niccolo to start an apocalypse and a war against God. Lucifer had been there to see Crocell's bloody promises, and Niccolo had been there to see him fail.

However, Niccolo could not heed the slayer's warning. As well-intentioned as it was, Niccolo had a greater responsibility—a stronger *desire*—to see his vengeance fulfilled. Adonai had taken everything from him, manipulated him from the start, and Niccolo had already gone too far to stop now. Even as he looked down at his companions, even as he remembered the golden demon king he had left behind, Niccolo knew that his purpose was greater than all of them. Unlike Crocell, he would remain separate and defiant.

With a heavy heart, Niccolo continued forward, away from the bonds of his past.

GABRIEL SLAMMED his staff into the ground and watched as the serpents uncoiled themselves and stretched out, rejoining their mouths and creating a window that would normally allow Gabriel to communicate with his brother in Hell. However, he had not been able to establish a line between dimensions since he had come to Purgatory, and this time was no exception. No matter how deliberately he traced sigils into the air, the space between the serpents only showed him the empty mists.

Sighing, Gabriel retrieved his staff as the serpents resolved into their usual formation. His situation was dire; he knew someone would be coming for him eventually, and hope was a difficult prospect. He had bought some time by asking Michael to leave without him, but it wasn't enough for Gabriel to consider stopping for long. With a huff, the archangel walked forward and considered his options.

The truth was that he didn't really have any. Without a method to speak to Buné or a way to defend himself against whomever Adonai sent against him, Gabriel could only wander around Purgatory and hope he found the Horsemen or the others from Hell. Eons ago, Gabriel had flown around this realm, but it had been too long and he had forgotten too much.

Although he had come from the hidden entrance to Heaven, Gabriel's recollections of the surrounding landscape were completely obsolete. In his absence, Purgatory had rearranged itself, and Gabriel had been forced to find his own way.

Cursing, Gabriel paced in a circle before kicking at the dirt, resentful that he had been found out so soon. If Kushiel had not been so inquisitive, if Michael had minded his own business and stayed out of his apartment, Gabriel would not be in this situation. He would not be on the run; he would not be lost in a land devoted to *being* lost.

Even though a voice in Gabriel's head reminded him that this was partially his fault, the archangel grumbled and argued with himself, raising a finger to the empty air and turning his nose up at the silent suggestion. Breathing deep, still frustrated, Gabriel slammed his staff back into the ground and tried to contact Buné again, tapping his foot as the serpents slowly created a window he could use.

Again, he started to draw sigils in the air, but then he saw a dark figure solidifying through the golden ring made by his serpents. Instantly wary, Gabriel reclaimed his staff and held it in front of him, the serpents flattening until their bodies were sharp edges.

"Back! Stay back!" he shouted, foolishly hoping such a tactic would work. If it was an angel, they would likely press forward with the knowledge that they had found their prey. If it was a soul of Purgatory, they would probably see Gabriel as nothing more than a weakling.

Still, Gabriel had to try.

"I do not mean any harm, whoever you are," a stern voice came from the fog, but the figure remained in shadow as it approached. "Unless, of course, you intend to harm me."

"I don't intend it, but I am more formidable than you might think. Purgatory has its own tricks!" Gabriel's voice wavered even as he tried to sound more imposing. He was met with a light scoff and —once he was finally able to see the other person—Gabriel could see why.

Stepping out of the mists was a blood-covered warrior, splatters of gore covering her arms and grieves and blood staining what little clothing could be seen underneath her armor. On her face was an almost apathetic expression, but her eyes pierced right through

Gabriel. Whoever this was, she had been lost in the mists for a long time.

"I am well aware of Purgatory's tricks. You do not seem to be one of them." She planted the end of her weapon into the ground, a hooked spear that Gabriel did not recognize.

"Nor do you," Gabriel replied, lowering his blade and cowering slightly as she walked forward. "However, I will not hesitate to kill you, trick or otherwise. Just because you are real does not make you my friend."

"Wise words. You should put that down." She came to a stop three yards from him, motioning to Gabriel's staff with her own weapon. "It seems more likely that it will do more harm to its owner."

"I'll put it down when I'm ready." Gabriel raised his staff and held it with determination. "Who are you?"

"Who are *you*?" she replied quickly, the archangel shaking his head before shouting again.

"I asked you first!"

"I asked you second," she countered, but then she grunted and looked to her right. "My name is Hippolyta, but those in Hell know me as Cimeries."

"Cimeries..." Gabriel replied, but then he realized how foolish he had been. The weapon in her hand was clearly not developed on Earth—it had to be from either Heaven or Hell—and Gabriel remembered the briefing Buné had given him. Smiling, Gabriel dropped his weapon and rushed forward, his paranoia abandoned. "You have no idea how glad I am to see you—"

"I did not give you permission to come closer," she interrupted him, quickly dropping her pike to his throat. Even though she was still looking away, Gabriel obviously did not require her full attention. "Answer my question."

"Wha—what question..." he started to ask, but when the Amazon scowled, Gabriel realized his mistake. "Oh, I'm Gabriel! I'm the archangel! I'm—I'm the one Buné and Lucifer have been talking to all these years!"

"Prove it," Cimeries said, flicking her gaze so she could look at him out of the corner of her eye.

"H—how?"

"If you're the archangel, you would know how," she stated simply, throwing Gabriel's mind into a panic.

Backing away from the warrior, Gabriel tried to find some sort of display that would make Cimeries trust him. Failing to think up anything else, Gabriel let out his yellow wings and transformed his staff back into its usual shape.

"I—well, I can show I'm an angel!" he blurted out, worrying the staff with both hands before realizing his divinity would only make his death come sooner. Offering his weapon forward, Gabriel pointed out the snakes circling the main staff. "Oh, and this is my staff! This is what allows me to create windows into the different dimensions and talk to Buné."

"Can you show me this window?" she asked, and Gabriel balked and let his wings recede into his back.

"Well, no... I can't do it in Purgatory. There's too much residual energy..." he excused himself, but he knew Cimeries was unconvinced. Sighing, Gabriel shrugged before looking back up at the warrior. "Since you're Greek, you know Hermes, correct?"

"I know *of* him," Cimeries replied gruffly, dropping the blunt end of her pike back to the ground.

"I... this is his staff." The fight emptied out of Gabriel as he gave up trying to convince her. "The myth of Hermes was really based on me, since I'm the messenger of God and everything. I... nevermind. You don't believe me..."

"I do," Cimeries replied, and Gabriel lifted his head in confusion.

"But... why?"

"You might be a timid thing, but you are not lying. No one is that terrible on purpose," she said, drawing closer and inspecting him. "The question is: why are you in Purgatory?"

"I—well, I..." Gabriel stammered, looking down and biting his lip. "I got found out."

"Do I need to know why?" Cimeries asked, causing Gabriel to shake his head as he ground his feet against the dirt.

"No. No, the why doesn't matter. I messed up, but I didn't hurt the cause by doing so. I'm just not undercover anymore," he said, wincing at the woman. "And they're coming to get me."

"*Who* is coming to get you?" she asked, causing Gabriel to worry his staff with both hands.

"Best guess would be Uriel. I don't know what you know..."

"He killed Tamiel. He has killed many others." Cimeries walked past him and brought her pike to bear.

Gabriel turned in a panic and saw a figure approaching from the mist, absolutely certain that Uriel had found him. However, once the man stumbled forward, Gabriel realized it was just another human soul carrying a sword.

"That's... that's right," Gabriel muttered as he watched Cimeries advance on the spirit, thrusting through his heart before he could even speak. Cimeries withdrew her pike and turned as the figure dissolved into shadows and seeped into the ground, stunning Gabriel. "How did you know that was an illusion?"

"I did not know." She clenched and extended the fingers of her left hand. "If it had been the real man, I would have killed him anyway."

"That's..."

"Purgatory, Gabriel," she interrupted. "This place is filled with past enemies and friends, tricks and illusions mixing in with all of them. If you are not prepared to rid yourselves of the souls who would wish you harm, you have no business surviving in this realm."

"Have you met many friends here?" Gabriel asked, but he looked over the flecks of blood decorating her armor.

"The friends I care for are still alive, even if it seems like days have passed since I first came to this realm." Cimeries straightened her posture. "Have you seen any of my companions?"

"N—no," Gabriel replied, looking around trying to figure out their next step. "I've only been here for half a day and I came from the back entrance of Heaven. I sincerely doubt your friends have stumbled onto this pathway."

"Back entrance of Heaven?" Cimeries asked, and Gabriel felt instant shame for divulging his secret. Then he smacked himself in the forehead as he realized that this woman was one of his allies. After shaking his head at his idiocy, Gabriel turned to the woman and nodded in excitement.

"Yes! There is a back entrance buried deep within the walls of the Capitol. I assume that Niccolo and the others will try to force their way through the main portal for Purgatory, but for us—wait." Gabriel dropped his head in shame once he remembered their situation. "I didn't mean to get your hopes up. We can't use it."

"And why is that?"

"Like I said, I'm being followed. I'm sure Uriel and his cronies would be between us and the entrance," he said, but then he felt Cimeries' hand on his shoulder.

"And could these be your pursuers?" she asked quietly, jerking Gabriel around so he could look in the same direction. Seeing two shadows still obscured by the mist, Gabriel gave into fear, but then he realized his mistake.

"No," he whispered, leaning up so he could speak even softer into her ear. "Uriel and his angels would be flying. They don't much care for laying low."

"So this is another memory come to haunt us," Cimeries replied, holding her pike ready in front of her.

Once he realized her intent, Gabriel joined her efforts and transformed his staff back into a weapon. He doubted he could do nearly as much as the warrior woman—he had heard what she had done to Beleth—but Gabriel also knew he could not disappoint her. Something about Cimeries gave him hope, gave him courage. That humans like this existed was enough to justify Gabriel's commitment to the cause.

Cimeries was the kind of person who was supposed to live.

Gabriel gripped his staff tighter as the figures grew more distinct, taking their time even as they drew closer and closer. Fear filtered into Gabriel's veins once more, but just as the figures were about to break through the mists, Cimeries lowered her weapon and gazed at the new arrivals in satisfaction. It was enough to throw Gabriel into confusion, but she laughed at his reaction and nodded at his staff.

"Put that away. You have no reason to fear these reapers."

WILLIAM WAS SITTING on Buer's back, keeping his mouth closed as he looked at their surroundings. For the first few miles he had kept his bow in hand, but there was never anything to shoot, so eventually he put it away and instead watched his companions.

On his right was the last Horseman, who seemed to be having a conversation with himself. William hoped Seere was telepathically speaking to Fury, but he knew better than to put anything past the strange man. On their left, Phenex was flying along and keeping to himself, just out of earshot for casual conversation, and Crocell mirrored him on the other side.

In contrast, the Leviathan shifted his position along the group, clambering off in random directions before returning and overtaking the group, stopping whenever he felt like it. To William, it seemed like a dog being let outside for the first time in days, but he somehow doubted there was much innocence left in that monster. Just like the man flying above them, William didn't trust the Leviathan for anything but brutality and violence.

"Hey Buer," William spoke up, and the centaur turned his head to hear him better, "I have a question for you."

"Not surprising, William. Go ahead and ask. I may even have the ability to give a satisfying answer."

"Well, it's just that some of the names we heard from the

Nephilim," William said, squinting as he looked off into the distance. "They seemed familiar, like I've heard them before."

"Familiar? Hmm..." Buer grunted before turning away, taking a moment to stroke his beard. "Which ones?"

"Well, Ymir, for starters. And Jotunheim... I don't know, it just seems like I've heard the names before."

"Hmm, well, Ymir has always been the leader of the Nephilim. His legend goes back a long way... oh!" Buer yelped before turning back with scholarly excitement. "You come from around Stonehenge, correct? Northern part of Europe?"

"I... yes?"

"Ah, well that explains it. It's your mythology, William. Well, the mythology of one of your ancestors, perhaps," Buer explained, taking a deep breath before his lecture. "I believe it was the Norsemen—you may know them as Vikings or Normans—they had a deep and rich history that was... well, it took some liberties."

"Wait, yeah," William said, nodding at Buer's theory. "Yeah, I remember some of the bards singing about giants and... and one that got all cut up and they made the world out of him? Is that right?"

"You have the correct myth, but obviously it's not *right*," Buer replied, his voice smug. "The giant they supposedly sacrificed was Ymir, and you've seen for yourself that he's only missing an eye."

"Yeah, I guess they got that part wrong..." William trailed off, choosing not to get buried in the details. "But, how did that story get written? The Nephilim were exiled before humans existed, right?"

"Correct again, young man!" Buer was excited to have another student. "However, the *world* remembers. Whispers come from the Void and from the nexus points, and eventually someone hears those whispers. Most of your human creation mythology has vague ties to reality, even if you must take them with a grain of salt."

"From the Void? Nexus points?" William asked, almost biting his lip before remembering that he was on, essentially, a galloping horse. "I'm sorry, but you lost me."

"Well, you lasted longer than some of our more brutish

companions would have." Buer winked at him and let out a soft chuckle. "The Void is the space between the dimensions; we briefly traveled through it before coming to Earth. If we could have remained conscious, we would have seen it again when we came to Purgatory."

"So, that was that place with all the lights and crazy monsters?"

"If that is what you saw, most likely. Even the slightest change in perception brings about a different experience. I, for instance, merely saw a star exploding," Buer commented, causing William to let out a snicker.

"*Merely*, huh?"

"It may have been a poor choice of words," Buer said with a bashful smile, clearing his throat and shaking away his embarrassment. "But yes, the Void is the space between. The nexus points are where we can—for lack of a better term—access the Void. From there, we can travel to other dimensions."

"So Stonehenge was a nexus point?" William asked, earning an excited nod from Buer.

"Exactly! Stonehenge, the Overlook, the Gates of Heaven, these are all nexus points. There are dozens scattered around the world, but even *I* don't know where they all are. With the continents shifting on me, I haven't had a chance to find them again." Buer had started with enthusiasm, but then resentment had filtered into his tone.

"You will, Buer. Sounds like a good plan after we win this thing," William said with a light chuckle, and he was surprised to see Buer look back at him with hope. After a moment of appreciation, the centaur turned back around

"It may sound selfish, but I think I would enjoy it," he said, and William hoped the centaur would live to find these nexus points. Looking up and forward, the smile departed from William's face as thoughts of mythology and other dimensions quickly disappeared. They were quickly replaced by fear and apprehension, and it only took a moment for him to whip his bow around and nock an arrow against the string, even if it would do little good.

Ahead of them, sixty feet tall, was a massive creature that had somehow been hidden by the mist, but a giant plume of flames had burst from the center horn on its head and illuminated the entire monster.

As it burned the air, William was able to see every detail of the creature, who seemed like a man with a goat's head covered in black fur. It sat cross-legged, loose black rags covering its upper thighs, and giant black wings spread out from its back. It almost seemed bored as William's hellish companions came to a stop, brandishing their weapons and preparing for conflict.

"You have... taken your time," a wheezing voice leaked into the air. "I was getting so bored... waiting for you."

"We're here now, Baphomet," Niccolo declared once he joined his friends on the ground.

"You do have some grasp... of the obvious, Niccolo Vespucci... da Firenze." The massive goat head tilted to look directly at the tiny human.

"That's not my name anymore." Niccolo scowled, drawing a long, slow chuckle from the creature.

"It will... always be your name. Your past... never ceases to be *your* past," Baphomet stated, turning to gaze at each member of the group and holding out his hands in welcome. "All of your pasts... your memories... you do not appreciate them."

"Are you sure about that?" Seere asked, twirling the axe in his hands. "I can remember some pretty decent nights here or there."

"You remember... what you want to remember." Baphomet flicked his finger toward Seere and let out a red flame that rocketed toward the Horseman. None of them could react before the light consumed their companion, leaving nothing but a scorch mark where Fury had been standing.

"You bastard!" Niccolo sent an arc of energy at Baphomet before rushing forward, determined to kill the creature who had somehow destroyed his companion.

Groaning, the creature's head swayed as Niccolo's energy splashed against it, but Baphomet was otherwise no worse for wear. Turning back to the approaching devil, Baphomet lazily swatted his hand in front of him and sent another red fireball directly at Niccolo. Since he was rushing forward, Niccolo was only able to bring up his shield to defend himself, but it was no help.

After the flames splashed around Niccolo and dissipated, there was nothing left in the air.

"No!" Phenex shouted, fire bursting out of him as he flew forward without thinking. William assumed Phenex thought his flames would defend him, but they could only watch as Baphomet attacked with a spout of ethereal flames. Phenex sent out a huge wave of fire to intercept it, but it did nothing to stop Baphomet's attack, and soon Phenex disappeared just like Niccolo and Seere before him.

"Do they... understand yet?" Baphomet asked, tilting its head and staring straight into William's soul. He tried to figure out what they could do against such a monster, what kind of tactic would defeat this otherworldly deity, but he was spared the mental anguish. After he slid off Buer's back, the scholar turned to look at his remaining companions.

"They..." Buer started, gulping down empty air. "They're not dead. Not yet, at least. Baphomet is a creature of trials. That is why he guards the entrance to Heaven from Purgatory. They have merely been... transported."

"So... he's like his own nexus point?" William let his bow string back now that it was obvious that he could not harm this creature. Buer tilted his head to the side, opening his mouth for a moment in shock, but then he nodded toward their opponent.

"In a way, yes. In fact, I'm not quite sure that *is* Baphomet. Rest assured, our companions are not dead. They have merely been thrown into their own personal trials. Just like we will be thrown into ours, very shortly," Buer explained, at which point Crocell had heard enough.

Stepping forward, he raised his spear, light bursting from it and leaving behind a trident after it dissipated. Looking up at the giant creature, Crocell showed no fear as he planted the end of his weapon against the ground.

"If I must pass a trial, then I will face a trial," he stated, drawing out a prolonged chuckle from the ancient creature. After Baphomet flicked its hand in a quick movement, another fireball plummeted toward Crocell and broke against him, leaving nothing but a scorch mark in the dirt.

"I wish he had not done that." Buer slumped over, despite his considerable height. "I would have liked to warn him that Baphomet would mine our deepest and darkest regrets. With someone like Crocell..."

"Shit, well, can we help him?" William asked, keeping an eye on the giant creature, who seemed to be listening out of curiosity. "And what about the Leviathan?"

"You are a funny human," twin voices said, causing William to jump and turn in the same motion, since he had not yet realized the Leviathan had crept up to stand above them. As the monster continued, the Leviathan lowered its mask so its eyes were level with William. "This one has no hold over me. I stay only to see who will come out of the trials alive."

"Well, I guess you can be there for... moral support," William said, unnerved by the creature's display. After giving a deliberate nod, the Leviathan drew back and then sank into itself, watching as William turned back to Buer. "So, that answers my question about him. Can we help any of them?"

"I—I assume after our trials are completed, that we may have a chance to... coach our companions through their own encounters," Buer mused, but a low grunt made the air heavier. They turned to see Baphomet shake its head slowly, the movement of its head enough to cause a breeze.

"You have... no trials."

"What do you mean we don't have trials? I thought that was the whole point," William asked, Buer setting a hand on his shoulder while he spoke.

"Yes, why would the two of us go without trials?"

"You have... done nothing to deserve... trials. Buer... your heart is pure... a warrior of great honor... a scholar of great duty... you have no crimes... for which... to atone," Baphomet explained, each word drawn out far longer than necessary. Although Buer pondered the answer, William stepped forward and forgot he was talking to an ancient creature who might just unmake him.

"What about me? I've sinned plenty! I have my regrets, too!" he shouted, indignant as his thoughts retreated to darker times. A loud boom echoed through the air and sent a gust toward them, sending William's cloak out behind him, but the young human stood defiant. He could tell that Baphomet was just laughing at him.

"Too young... William Combe. The others... their sins are... delicious... *aged*. You... you are not worth... a trial," it said in a somewhat lighter tone, and William almost considered sending an arrow at this other god. He was in the process of grabbing his bow when he felt Buer's hand stop him, and he looked up to see the centaur shaking his head.

"No, there is no point in that, William. We can use all of this to our advantage," he explained before turning back to face Baphomet. "Since we have no trials, great Baphomet, is there any way we might assist our companions? May we intervene on their behalf?"

"Hmmm... how interesting," Baphomet mused, lifting a hand to his chin and stroking his beard. "I suppose I... could allow it. Only... to speak, however. You may not... fight for them."

"Words are all we need, great Baphomet," Buer declared, bowing in reverence. With a hearty chuckle, Baphomet raised its hands and four red orbs appeared over the ground between them.

"Very well. Choose the allies... you do not believe... will pass."

"I swear, if there's a second afterlife, that's just bullshit."

Seere groaned as he pushed up from the ground, every one of his joints aching. Deciding it was not worth the effort to stand, the Horseman leaned back and sat on his knees so he could look at his surroundings. It seemed just like every other inch of Purgatory; cracks in the floor and mist all around him.

"You're kidding, right?" Seere asked to the clouds above, slapping his fists against his thighs in protest. "It's the *same* thing every time and it's getting old! You're trying to make us insane, aren't you? *Aren't you?*"

There was no answer, but that was alright. Seere had stopped expecting answers from the sky during his first life.

"Motherfucker," Seere growled as he rolled forward, pushing with his hands so he could get to his feet. "Fury, get out here, already. I'm bored, and even your complaining ass will be good company."

Seere waited for a moment before realizing that his horse was not answering him, and after searching in his mind, the Horseman found that he was alone. The mental link had not been severed and he felt no sense of loss, but something was blocking him from communicating with the angry beast. Furrowing his brow, Seere looked around and tried to find some reason for it all.

All he found was more of the same.

"...crap," Seere muttered before grabbing the hammer from his back and holding it in both hands, wandering through the mists without any sort of purpose. As much as he wanted to kill enemies or figure out why he was here, there was no clue. Just endless cracks and thick fog.

"C'mon," he whined, pouting and setting the head of his weapon against the ground. "This is *stupid*! I am *not* patient and without someone to kill I get *antsy*!"

"Seere?" a weak voice called out to him, and the Horseman jerked around, trying to find the source. He hadn't heard the voice for some time, but he could never forget that slight linger on the tongue.

"Sitri? Sitri! Where are you?"

"This way... hurry," the feminine voice replied, and that was all Seere needed to find her. Rushing headlong toward the source, Seere stopped paying attention to the cracks on the ground or the impenetrable fog. He needed to reach her, needed to find out how Sitri had gotten into Purgatory.

"Where are you, you bitch?" he asked, playfully cursing the demon before he finally started to see something else in the fog. Sprinting toward the shape, Seere didn't realize what it was until he was just a few yards. Upon hearing Sitri's voice, he had been so excited that he did not consider what could be waiting for him.

However, once he could see the machine, he wished he had prepared himself. Strapped to a vertical rack, Sitri's limbs had all been pulled out of their sockets, her body hanging loose by the skin attaching her torso to her arms. The demon was completely nude; mangled breasts exposed to the air and maimed by what Seere could only assume were teeth, and the horror beneath her waist was worse than anything he'd ever seen in Hell. After taking a sharp breath and forcing the worst of the image to the back of his mind, Seere approached his lover and set his fingers against the side of her face.

"Why? What the fuck happened?" he asked, trembling at the sight of his on-again, off-again partner in lust. Before the wounded demon could answer him, Seere looked at her restraints and withdrew a knife from his belt.

"If you take the creature... from its restraints... you will be lost here." Baphomet's voice echoed around him, forcing Seere to stop just as his blade touched the leather strap keeping Sitri's arm in place. Keeping the knife steady, Seere looked down and gazed hard into an empty place on the rack in front of him.

"Is that how we're playing it? If I don't kill her, I don't get to move on and attack Heaven?" Seere drew back the knife before looking up into empty air. "That it? I have to kill the person who shares my bed?"

"No. You can spare her, or him... whatever they are. However... you must listen to their... confession."

"Confession..." Seere muttered, turning to face his wounded friend. "What confession is that?"

"You... already know," Baphomet's voice echoed once more, but Seere was still looking at the tortured demon still hanging from dismantled limbs.

"Seere," Sitri said, no glimmers of her mischief in her voice, "I did something bad."

"You slept with other people?" Seere suggested, crossing his arms in skepticism. "Because you know that's only bad if you don't invite me."

"I—I betrayed you; I betrayed all of you. When Azazel was planning to destroy Hell... he found me... he turned me and... and I'm responsible for—for so much," she squeaked out, her chin trembling from the cold and her guilt. Seere looked at her for a moment before letting out a disgusted sigh and looking up.

"You expect me to believe this? This is just sad, Baphomet," Seere claimed before pointing up at his invisible tormentor. "You're playing me! This is all about *confronting my past*, right?"

"This isn't Baphomet, sweetness," Sitri argued, painfully swallowing before taking a few frantic breaths. "I did it. I'm not lying."

"Oh, I *know* you did it," Seere replied quickly, glaring down at the tormented soul. "But I also know that you aren't *you*. Sitri isn't here; she's down in Hell doing whatever the fuck she wants. Maybe fucking whatever she wants, it doesn't really matter."

"Seere..." Sitri looked up at the Horseman in pain. "It's me. I was sucked into the spell when Crocell interrupted. I fell into the Void and... and Baphomet found me."

"Bullshit," Seere muttered, but he was starting to lose confidence. Although this Sitri looked far more damaged than anything he had ever seen, the likeness was uncanny. Baphomet had clearly taken the time to recreate Sitri's body down to the smallest detail, even if the shapeshifter had a new body whenever she got bored.

"No shit involved, darling." Sitri stifled a soft moan before sniffing and looking at her feet in shame. "I am paying for my crimes, for the death I caused."

"Look..." Seere said defiantly, tears forming in his eyes as he focused on the skies.

"I don't believe—I *don't* believe this. I *know* Sitri betrayed everyone. I found out a month after Azazel fucked up everything, but she doesn't deserve to *die*. Nobody would get anything from her death. So I'm not even going to kill her illusion, Baphomet!" he shouted, shaking his head and sending his tears to the ground. "Not going to do it."

"Then you... get to stay... and watch it suffer... until I kill it," Baphomet replied, causing Seere to sweep his hammer across his body in anger.

"Hey! That wasn't the deal! That's not what you said!"

"I... lied. Either you kill the traitor... or I do. This... is your trial. Will you continue... to bear her sins... or will you claim... your own?" Baphomet asked, clearly enjoying the plight of his captive. Seere was fuming with anger, he vividly imagined cutting off the goat's massive head, but his fantasies would likely stay fantasies.

"It's not her, you fucking goat. It's not even her," Seere claimed again, but doubt seeped through the words.

"Then... it should not matter... to you." Baphomet chuckled again as the machine ground to life, the leather straps pulling in different directions and stretching Sitri's body even further. When she cried, Seere stepped forward in concern, but he stopped when Sitri lifted her head to make eye contact with him.

"Please! Make it stop! Just—just..." she pleaded, but then the pain was too much and she opened her mouth in a silent scream, her body swaying as the machine did its work.

230

"You're not real!" Seere shouted, closing the distance until he was just a foot away. "You're not real, and even if you were, I wouldn't kill you!"

"P—ple... Seere..." Sitri squeaked out, lowering her head enough for her to stare straight into the Horseman's eyes, and he knew he could take no more.

Hyperventilating as he retrieved one of the daggers from his belt, Seere tried to convince himself that it was all an illusion, that Sitri's body would dissolve into a black puddle that would seep into the very same cracks scattered throughout Purgatory. He tried to remind himself that Sitri had never made it to Purgatory, that the whole story about coming through the Void was just a lie. However, when he looked into Sitri's black eyes, he saw the same person who made the last two thousand years just a little more pleasurable.

Pushing forward with his blade—without realizing it was wreathed in the red aura he usually kept hidden—Seere cut straight through the demon's ribcage and crushed her heart, drawing the knife down so he would cut it in half. Seeing the light depart from her eyes, Seere backed away and waited for the shade to fade from this world.

Except that Sitri's broken and maimed body continued to hang there, blood pouring out of the wound he had given her.

"Well done... Horseman. Your trial... is over. I will bring you back... soon," Baphomet stated, satisfaction dancing around the syllables. Huffing out and still trying to deny what he saw in front of him, Seere looked up and shook with anger.

"Why is she not disappearing, Baphomet? Why the fuck is she still in that rack?" he asked, and Baphomet was kind enough to answer him.

"Because, Seere. We were not... lying. I rescued Sitri from the Void. I placed her here... for you."

"No," he muttered, stepping closer to the person he had killed. "There's no way. Sitri's still alive. She can't be dead."

"See... for yourself," Baphomet teased just as wisps of energy leaked out of Sitri's body, dark purple and gold tendrils wrapping around each other. Seere was flatfooted as the energy found its new home, lunging toward him before he could react. As he saw the memories flit by, as he recalled events from two perspectives, Seere could not stop the tears springing to his eyes. There was no way to deny it now, and the mighty Horseman fell to his knees.

And as Baphomet laughed in some other plane, Seere roared to the sky and erupted with dark red energy, his misery and rage enough to make Purgatory tremble.

WHEN CROCELL WOKE, he opened his eyes to total darkness. Once he realized that was part of his trial, Crocell flexed his muscles and let lightning flow through his arms, giving a small amount of ambient light to his surroundings. He found his feet on solid darkness; cool to the touch but without any sort of texture to counteract his disorientation. It would have been unnerving if Crocell had not spent millions of years in the dark, in places other souls would not dare venture.

Crocell was still analyzing his surroundings when he saw something move just beyond his perception, and he brought his trident to bear immediately, gritting his teeth as he waited for the something to strike. Instead, he could only hear it shuffling beyond the light coming from his arms, and within a few seconds Crocell tired of the game. Releasing light from his trident and letting a crackle of electricity flow through his body, he increased his visibility by a few yards and gasped at what he saw.

Six feet away from the prongs of his trident was a small creature with a crow's head, clutching its talons to the gaping hole in its chest and weeping silently as tears streamed down through its feathers. However, once Crocell increased the ambient light coming from his body, the creature noticed that it had company and squawked, a small burst of green fire coming from its beak. Shying away at first, the creature tentatively looked back at Crocell before it recognized the slayer.

"You... you killed me," the bird said, and Crocell was at once overcome with guilt. Dropping his trident low, he tried to approach his dead brother, but Crocell never got the chance. Once he made it within a few feet of the creature, green flames swarmed around it and it screamed, its pain enough for Crocell to raise his hands to his ears and drop his trident entirely.

And within only a moment, the creature had burned away and left Crocell alone.

"That wasn't my fault," Crocell muttered, but then he heard something scoff from the edge of his vision. Looking up, Crocell watched as another small creature joined him, hopping forward on spindly legs until he was just a couple yards away. Then it ruffled its feathers and looked at him with large eyes set in an owl's face.

"Really, Crocell? Seems to me that if you had killed the Shroud when you had a chance, Räum would never have gone mad." The owl hooted in punctuation and then hopped forward to inspect Crocell's trident. "Funny, it looks so harmless when it's not buried in my heart."

"Andras, why are you here?" Crocell asked as his hands dropped from his ears, caution clearly abandoned in his guilt. Looking up at him in shock, the owl jerked his head quickly before standing straight and defiant.

"You heard what Baphomet said, of course! I'm here—we're *all* here—because this is your past. These are your sins! If you had bothered to fight Azazel at the beginning, we would have survived." Andras raised his left wing and pecked at the feathers with his beak, exposing three bleeding wounds in his torso in the process.

"I tried, Andras. I never wanted anybody to die," Crocell said softly, but Andras didn't entertain the notion. After lowering his wing, the small demon hopped forward so his face was inches from Crocell.

"Good deal that does any of *us*. I was trying to save Hell, Crocell, the Devil himself, too! I was minding my own business before Sitri let Azazel know exactly where I was going to be. A lot of good men and women died because of your mistakes," Andras replied, his usual light tone completely absent. Crocell's eyes filled with bright tears as the owl continued, but then he realized they were not alone.

"You... you said *us...*" Crocell said under his breath, finally realizing the extent of Baphomet's trial. Turning his head, he saw a number of huddled shadows just beyond the small circle of light and so he let out a crack of lightning, trying to see just who was waiting for him.

However, when the electricity illuminated his surroundings, Crocell's guilt became overwhelming. Standing around them were hundreds of demons—some of them partially changed into animals —and Crocell recognized every single one. Every creature huddled in the shadows was someone Azazel had turned feral; someone Crocell had killed with the weapon at his feet.

"I did, *slayer*. I did say *us*." Andras chirped as he picked up the trident with the talons of his feet, tossing it at Crocell expectantly. When the weapon bounced off of Crocell's torso, the Fallen doing nothing to catch it, Andras let out a hoot of laughter. "Every half-formed monster here was run through with that miserable thing."

"I did... what I had to do." Crocell dropped his gaze, but Andras brought up his chin with a wing.

"You did what you *wanted* to do. You wanted to slay, and it's obvious from this gathering of friends that you got your fill. It's a pretty weapon, this trident of yours; especially when you reveal it in such a grand fashion." Andras drew back and picked up the trident with his right foot, swinging it around in admiration and turning his back on Crocell. "Why is it so bright when the rest of you is so dark?"

"I tried to give you mercy," Crocell muttered, his words muddled as he drowned in guilt. "There was no way to bring you back."

"*Was* there?" Andras replied, turning his neck around completely before following with the rest of his body. "Did you ever bother to try? When you killed *me*, you didn't hesitate at all. Did you even talk to me, Crocell?"

"I..."

"Did you even utter a *word?*" Andras interrupted, hopping back and slapping Crocell's arm with the trident. "I'll answer for you! You did *not*. You saw me—a great big owl screaming its head off—and you just assumed I was a monster."

"Andras, you were too far gone," Crocell tried to explain, but the demon was not having it. Stabbing the trident into the ground, Andras hopped closer and slashed across Crocell's stomach with a talon, drawing dark blood.

"I was *not*, you bastard! I was alive, and I could *think*. I wanted to stop, but Azazel's hex was keeping me from getting complete control. If you had just restrained me, gotten Buer or one of the other scholars to take a look at me, I could still be alive! I could still be alive instead of a ghost haunting you in Purgatory! How does it feel, huh, to have my talon cut into your flesh? It didn't feel too good when you cut open *my* belly."

"Andras..."

"I didn't *deserve* this!" Andras screamed, growing larger with every word. "What did I do to deserve such a shameful death? I may have owed a few dozen demons a fair amount of coin, but I was going to pay them back! I may not have been the best spy in Astaroth's resistance, but I was still useful!"

"I didn't kill you because I wanted to!" Crocell yelled back, his composure forgotten as he pleaded with his victim. "I didn't kill *any of you* because I wanted to! I did it because I was guilty in the first place! I did it because I was making up for my mistakes!"

"No, *slayer*, you cannot make up for those mistakes by killing your friends," Andras said as he grew larger, towering over Crocell as his wingspan doubled, as four new, scaled arms burst out of his torso to support his heavier frame. His face widened until a new ridge appeared in the center of his face, a calcified extension bursting out in a spray of blood and revealing a new horn that extended up from his beak. Andras screamed as he opened his mouth far wider than normal, revealing two rows of teeth lining the inside of his mouth.

After his transformation, Andras looked down at Crocell in contempt.

"Look, Crocell. This is what you let me become," Andras said as he stood on his legs and one set of arms, sweeping the other set out to include the rest of Crocell's victims. "This is what we all became because on that day, when it really mattered, you refused to kill another fallen angel! Because you did not want to kill one of your precious brothers, you let hundreds of humans suffer and die!"

"You let us die," the crowd of demons chanted around them, swaying and transforming into their feral forms as Crocell turned to watch all of them. He could see a man he used to know turn into a giant pig, his tusks becoming so heavy his head could not support them. As they repeated the mantra, Crocell saw a woman scream as mandibles burst out of her mouth, as her eyes divided and became compound and broke the surrounding bones. Crocell's breath caught in his throat as he watched a young boy bend over backward and the legs of a crustacean burst out of his sides, supporting him as he cried in anguish and his hands became pincers.

"Actually, *my mistake*," Andras said, even as demons changed and chanted all around them. Crocell looked up to see blood flowing from the giant owl's eyes and the now-gaping wounds in his chest. "You did not *let* us die. You *participated*. You *killed* us. Look down at your hands, Crocell, and just try to say you were helping."

He looked down and saw just what he had feared. Staining his blue skin was dark blood, and suddenly Crocell was back in the palace courtyard, the loss of his friends threatening to tear his mind from reality. Without meaning to, his soul called out for rain and thunderclouds gathered in the darkness, weaving spiderwebs of lightning through the air as rain poured around him.

However, this time, the blood did not leave his hands. The deluge did nothing to wash away his sins.

"This is what you always do, Crocell. You run away. You find some way to justify what you've done." Andras seemed even more menacing as lightning forced most of him into a silhouette. "You can't run from your guilt this time. You killed us, and now it's time for us to return the favor. *That* is the only sacrifice we'll accept from you."

"Crocell," another voice joined them, and it was enough for Crocell to look up from his hands. As the creature walked forward, Crocell thought it was another one of his victims—some sort of man fused with a horse—but when lightning flashed around them, he finally saw the skull helmet. With his fused bone armor and a long sword in his hand, Buer was somehow more imposing than all of the terrors around them.

"No," Crocell muttered. "No, you're not dead. I didn't kill you."

"No, you did not kill me." Buer came to a stop two yards away from his kneeling brother, sheets of rain crashing into him, but seemingly to no effect. "I am here to help you through this pain."

"Oh, the scholar comes to join us." Andras turned to face the centaur in anger, his great wings spread out behind him. "Have you come to relieve Crocell of his burden? To take away some of his guilt? To convince him that our blood was going to be spilled anyway?"

"Why would I do such a thing?" Buer asked, walking over to his brother and setting his hand on Crocell's shoulder. "He is the Slayer of Dis. It was his duty to provide mercy to feral demons."

"Mercy? You call what he did *mercy*?" Andras shrieked, his beak snapping with each word. "He killed us without so much as a word!"

"Of course, he did," Buer replied, stepping closer to the giant creature without fear. "His pain would have been so much more if he had tried to reason with every infected soul. Crocell took a great burden upon himself, and the only reward was that he was able to maintain *your* dignity."

"My *dignity*?" Andras yelled before rearing back on his feet and flapping his wings, sending a torrent of rain and wind at the resolute centaur. "He *took* from us our dignity! He allowed us to become these creatures!"

"He allowed you peace after you had given into weakness. He stopped you before you could kill any of your fellow demons, before you could tarnish your names further," Buer said before looking down at Crocell at his side. "You had a burden greater than any of us, brother. That you feel such tremendous guilt is only a mark of your character."

"This is bullshit!" Andras roared as he settled back on all six limbs, but Buer would not let him continue and stamped his foot.

"What is... *bullshit*... is that you pretend to be Andras! You are nothing but an illusion created by Baphomet, and that is quite clear," Buer stated before looking up into the darkness, past the storm clouds summoned by Crocell's guilt. "You are informed by your captives, Baphomet, and that is your downfall."

"What are you talking about?" Crocell asked, drawing a scoff from the great centaur beside him. Buer lazily gestured toward Andras before explaining.

"If you had known the insufferable creature better, Crocell, you would have known Andras would not blame anyone for his death or his own misfortune. Even at his darkest, the owl would just laugh and hop around." Turning back to face the six-armed creature, Buer sighed. "This thing is clearly just a construct to inspire guilt, and you should ignore it."

"He's... not real. All of them are not real," Crocell repeated, becoming angry with himself for not seeing it sooner. Gritting his teeth, the Fallen breathed in deep and regained his determination.

"You foul little angel," Andras said, but his voice was much deeper and his words were drawn out. "You were just... supposed to watch. Why must you... ruin the trial?"

"Because Crocell has proven himself thousands of times, and he does not need to lower himself to *your* standards," Buer replied coldly, nodding toward his brother's discarded trident. "And if he bothers to pick up his weapon, you will see why we entrusted him to be the Slayer of Dis."

238

"And why... is that? Because he is heartless... because he can... ignore his conscience?"

Baphomet wheezed out of Andras' mouth, but Crocell was far past being manipulated.

As Buer faded from his trial and left him alone with the shades of his victims, Crocell picked up his trident and let out dark wings, electricity surging through his limbs. Even though Andras was gazing at him with interest—looking even more menacing as he approached—Crocell was uninterested as he raised his weapon to the sky and was engulfed in a column of electricity from above. After collecting enough energy to make his dark body glow with blue light, Crocell looked back at the giant creature.

"I do not ignore my conscience, Baphomet," he declared before slamming his trident into the ground and sending out a shockwave that paralyzed every creature in a hundred-yard radius. After a moment to catch his breath, Crocell calmly walked forward until he was standing underneath Andras, whose entire body was rigid from shock. Thrusting forward, Crocell sank his trident deep into Andras' heart, creating another set of entry wounds.

"I am the Slayer of Dis because I failed them," he added softly before sending a bolt of lightning along the weapon, causing the creature's body to glow momentarily before it exploded in a flash of light. Crocell merely stood there as the lightning gathered around him, as the rain poured upon the cruel recreations of his victims. After a moment of silence, Crocell pumped his wings and rose into the air, an electric storm surrounding his body.

"And I would not fail them again, because even the nightmares deserve their rest."

PHENEX HAD NOT experienced heat like this for centuries. Everything about this desert was disorienting and called back to the days of his first life, but Phenex knew this was all an illusion; it had to be. Even as he dug his fingers into the sand and let it fall between them, even as the grains got stuck underneath his fingernails, Phenex was able to keep his grasp of reality intact. However, that tenuous hold on sanity departed once he realized he was not alone.

There were eleven dark-haired men standing in a semicircle in front of him.

"Yeshua," the man in the middle growled, kneeling down and setting an arm on his knee. "This is what you've become."

"My name is not Yeshua anymore," Phenex said, trying to come to grips with seeing the man again after so much time. "And you are not Peter."

"Of course, I am, Yeshua," the familiar stranger replied, tilting his head slightly and sneering at Phenex. "I had to pick up the pieces of your revolution when Judas ratted you out. I was the one who had to salvage what I could for our people."

"You're not him. He's in Heaven," Phenex argued, but the man struck him with the back of his hand.

"Don't you give me that ridiculous story. You've never been to Heaven; you don't know what's up there waiting for you. For all you know, I never even had a soul," Peter explained, drawing a laugh from one of the smaller men at the edge of the semi-circle.

"I'm surprised *Yeshua* even had one," he said with a grin, causing his neighbor to groan and shake his head.

"Of course, Thomas, it always has to be you," the neighbor commented. At the snide tone, Thomas shrugged and looked away from the man.

"I'm just saying he was never one for a fight. Charismatic, I won't argue, but Yeshua never stood up for himself," he explained, earning a grunt from Peter as he grabbed Phenex's chin and scowled.

"That's for sure. Judas always fought his battles. Little Yeshua, always going to cry to the man who would do his dirty work for him," Peter said. At the mention of Judas, the apostles all broke into light laughter.

"You know, even though he basically killed me, too, I kinda love that he gave up Yeshua first. Serves him right for staying back and making sure we did all the heavy lifting," one of the taller apostles said as he cracked his neck.

"Screw that, Judas gave us up for nothing but a bag of silver. Just because he killed himself afterward doesn't make up for it," Thomas replied, crossing his arms and rolling his eyes. "Won't blame him for getting out when he could, but he could have at least made it worth it. That silver could have bought enough rope for all of us."

"Hah, like you would hang yourself," his neighbor said as he turned and shoved a finger into Thomas' shoulder. "I'm surprised you didn't betray us first."

"Who says he didn't?" Peter interrupted, demanding their attention. "I never saw the bastard after Yeshua got crucified. I built the religion that immortalized us and Thomas just fucked off to India."

"Hey, I had my doubts about the whole thing, and you should have, too! Can't blame me because they pinned you upside down."

"No, that I can't blame you for." Peter said as he turned back to Yeshua, whose chin was still held between his fingers. "That blame goes to Yeshua and Judas."

"You—you aren't them." Phenex's lip twitched in frustration, but Peter was undeterred.

"You *really* that confident about it? You really know for sure that we're not the apostles of *Jesus Christ?* We made you a god, and what did we get for it?"

"We got sold out, is what we got," another apostle yelled in response, and the rest murmured along in agreement.

"Just because you got greedy," Peter said, drawing closer to Phenex's face. "Just because you got impatient, and just because Judas decided we weren't worth a damn."

"I told you, that's not my name," Phenex said, the temperature around him rising. As he looked up at Peter with white-hot eyes, the saliva evaporated off his face. "And you *don't* get to speak about him."

"Who, *Judas*? Our *betrayer*? The one who gave you up to the Romans? How are you going to get so indignant about him when he was the one who was too much of a coward to stick it out?" Peter asked, letting go of Phenex's face and shaking his head.

"He was my friend," Phenex said as he stood up, flames coiling around his legs and melting the sand beneath him. "And he more than made up for his failure."

"He was your friend, huh?" Peter asked, placing his hands on his hips. "So *we* weren't? The name of a man who turned himself into a dog in shame is worth more than *us*? You haven't even bothered to apologize yet, you know that?"

"Because you're not real," Phenex said as he gathered flames into the palms of his hands. Seeing those antics, Peter shook his head and nodded past Phenex with a smile on his face.

"How about you tell that to *him*?" he asked, raising an eyebrow, and Phenex was forced to turn around to see who the illusion was talking about. Once he could, the flames abandoned Phenex and his jaw dropped.

There, hanging from the branch of a dead tree, was Judas Iscariot, his rigid body swaying slightly.

"He at least had the decency to kill himself after it all fell apart, I'll give him that," Peter said, stepping forward until he was standing by Phenex's side. "If only he had stayed dead, killed himself again once he fell down to Hell with you."

"It can't be him..." Phenex muttered, but Peter clapped him on the back and threw his arm around his shoulders.

"Oh, it is. This is what he does here in Purgatory. This is his punishment. Because deep down in that black heart of yours, Yeshua, you still haven't forgiven him. Even though he gave up his afterlife for you, you *still* haven't forgiven him."

"What are you talking about?"

"Do you really not get it? This whole *demon thing* you got going for you now, it's cute. Really. But denying that you're human, refusing to go by your name, it only reinforces the point that you're ashamed of the time you spent on Earth."

"And you should be!" Thomas shouted.

"See, you're ashamed of it, getting crucified and leading a failure of a rebellion, and that's good!" Peter crossed his arms and stepped closer to Judas' tree. "And you're ashamed of him, which is *also* good. He could never atone completely—he could never be *forgiven*—because he screwed up *that* bad. Just because he died for you this time around doesn't give him a free pass, at least in your head."

"No, I'm responsible," Phenex argued, grinding the heel of his hand against his temple. "He wouldn't have turned feral; he wouldn't have died if he wasn't protecting me. I have to make up for failing him."

"Please, that's not what this is about!" Peter exclaimed, gesturing toward the hanging body with his left hand. "You never accepted him as your *friend*. He was always just your servant who had to do what you said because he had to make it up to you. By dying like he did, you got confronted with the truth that he might *actually* be a better person than you. A scumbag who sold out *all* of us was still better than *you*. So you run away from your real name, you run away from your past, wash your hands of it, and all of a sudden you're some big, bad fireball of justice."

"That's not..."

"You don't have to convince *me*, Yeshua. According to you, I'm not even real. So, in a way, the only reason I'm saying this is because this is how *you* think. This is how *you* feel about it."

"So," Peter said as he walked forward, a smug grin on his face. "What's your goddamn name?"

"My name is Phenex," he said in denial, but the apostle rolled his eyes.

"Try again, Mister Messiah. We all died for your rebellion, the least you could do is man up and tell us the truth."

"My name is *Phenex*," he urged again, flames wrapping around him as his stubborn nature came to the surface, but he was distracted when the rope holding Judas in the air snapped and sent his body crashing to the ground. As Phenex watched in horror, his friend's body picked itself up and lifted its head, showing him a rotten face with its eyes pecked out.

"What is your name?" Judas asked, crawling forward on emaciated arms and legs. "Don't disgrace me, coward."

"No, you're not real, either." Phenex backed away from the approaching corpse, but his back hit something solid. Turning around, Phenex found that he was surrounded by his apostles, all of them looking down at him with hatred.

"What's your name?" they asked, each of them repeating it as they pushed him around their little huddle, and Phenex panicked. That panic led to fear, which led to frustration, which led to anger.

That anger finally caused Phenex to cry out, an inferno bursting out of him and burning everything around him to ashes.

After the anger left him, only his sorrow and guilt remained. Dropping to his knees and shattering newly-made glass—which cut into his legs in a dozen places—Phenex sobbed and tried to forget his pain. There was nothing he could do about it now, and there was no possible way he would be able to forgive himself. All of those men had depended on him, yet they were forced to deal with his failures even after his death.

"What is your name?"

The question hung on the air, but then Phenex realized someone was actually speaking. Turning to face the source of the noise, Phenex opened his eyes wide as he realized that he had not destroyed all of his friends.

Still crawling toward him even though his flesh had been burned away, Judas remained, the exposed bones of his fingertips cracking through the glass beneath him.

"No, I can't," Phenex whined, watching as the corpse drew closer.

"You can run, but I will always be with you, *inside of you*. You harvested my soul, Yeshua," Judas said, his lips burned away and showing charred teeth that made him even more menacing. "You will carry the shame of killing Judas Iscariot to your grave."

"My name is Phenex," he argued, slamming his fists into the ground beside him and cutting the skin between his knuckles, but Judas was not the one to respond.

"No, Yeshua, that's not your name," someone said behind him, causing Phenex to turn around in desperation. At first, he was confused—this person had no business being here—but then his confusion turned to anger when he realized that William Combe was standing above him.

"I told you—"

"And I told *you*," William said as he knelt down, "that running away won't solve anything."

"What do you..." Phenex muttered, but William's scowl was enough to halt the question.

"It doesn't matter what I know. What matters is that this guilt is eating you alive. Why else would your trial be about your apostles blaming you for their deaths, for the corpse of your best friend to be crawling toward you demanding you speak your name? You are denying the very fact that you are human, that you still feel, and no amount of running will fix that."

"I am a demon." Despite his belief, Phenex's voice wavered, and William narrowed his gaze at the audacity.

"And I'm Jesus fucking Christ," he said with a sneer. "Just because I say something doesn't make it *true*. You have to confront this."

"No, I don't," Phenex replied, but then he heard a rasp behind him and turned to see Judas only a yard away.

"Yes, you do," William urged as Phenex watched the delusion approach. "Because your name is Phenex just as much as *that* is your friend. It's just an illusion, a mask for you to hide behind. That thing right there is not Judas. That is Baphomet preying on your insecurity and your weakness."

"My weakness?" Phenex asked as Judas gingerly placed a gnarled, burnt hand on his knee.

"Who are you?" William asked. "And who is that?"

"I..." Phenex hesitated, only watching as Judas crawled up further, the perpetually-open mouth getting closer and closer to his face. "I—my name..."

"Who are you?" William repeated softly, and this time he heard what he wanted.

"My name is Yeshua," the man stated with tears in his eyes, but his pupils had returned to him.

"And who is that?"

"No one," Yeshua muttered, letting his flames envelop the illusion on top of him and sending the shade to oblivion. After the flames died down, Yeshua turned to look up at William with a forced smile.

"Judas... Judas had awful teeth, anyway. It couldn't have been him."

"*You* are joking around? I got here *way* too late if they messed up your head like that," William said in shock, watching as his companion picked himself up and breathed deep. Though he could not feel it, while Yeshua stared at the dead tree where the corpse had been hanging, the scars from his burning tears started to heal.

"It couldn't have been him," Yeshua repeated, a sad smile on his face as he placed his hand on his heart. "If the real Judas wanted to kill me, I would be dead."

"I... guess that's a way to look at it," William mused as he looked up at the false sun above them. "My friends and I weren't so casual about killing each other, but whatever works for you."

"He wasn't my friend, Will," Yeshua replied as he closed his eyes, feeling the light on his skin and feeling like a new man.

"He was my brother, and I will not disgrace him further."

"NICCOLO," a voice came from a shadow in the mist, and it was hard for the new devil to resist sending an arc of energy at the mystery figure. Realizing he should probably avoid his usual reckless behavior, Niccolo held onto his weapon and trudged forward, more annoyed than anything.

"And who the fuck are you?" he asked, almost snarling as he got closer to the figure, but then a nagging sensation ate away at his anger.

"I see you after how long and you talk to me like this?" the figure answered him, and that was enough for Niccolo to realize who had come to meet him.

Sighing, Niccolo let his weapons disappear as he walked forward, cracking the knuckles of his hands before letting them swing by his sides.

"So are you the real Marco, or am I killing another illusion?" Niccolo asked in annoyance, not surprised as the mist departed and revealed his friend sitting on a small stone wall.

"Nah, it's me. I'm Baphomet's trial for you," Marco explained, appearing exactly as he had the last time Niccolo had seen him in that market square. Noticing his friend looking him over, Marco waved his hand at the stone wall underneath him. "Yeah, he's not exactly creative. If we had a silver tin, we could recreate the whole scene."

"Not quite, my hand got a little bit more gruesome, and I'm not really in the mood for begging."

"Eh, you're fine. I'd just as soon forget the whole thing. I don't have any coin for you to refuse, anyway," he said, somehow drawing a smile out of Niccolo.

"I don't need it, Marco. I'm about to go kill a god. A few pieces of metal aren't really going to help me."

"No, I suppose they won't. Sit down, rest a little. We can catch up," he suggested with a soft pat on the rock wall, but Niccolo shifted on his feet and crossed his arms.

"Is that my trial, or can I kill you and be done with it? This is getting tiresome."

He was surprised to see Marco glare at him in disappointment. No fear, no hesitation; just disappointment.

"Don't skip to the end, Nico. It's Purgatory. Let me at least *try* to atone," Marco said as he crossed his legs. Niccolo approached the soul—more curious than anything—and stopped a few feet away before sitting down.

"*You* want to atone? I would think my trial would be about *my* atonement." Niccolo raised an eyebrow at the man, but Marco waved off the idea with an absent-minded flick of his wrist.

"Oh, c'mon, we both know I'm the hero of our story." Marco chuckled for a moment before staring into the mists. "I'm supposed to guilt you. That's why I'm here. Baphomet is all about getting the real souls when he can, but you already killed your father, so I was the only one left in Purgatory for him to show off."

"So when are you going to start guilting me? You're doing a pretty lousy job so far," Niccolo teased, both of them laughing at the comment.

"Baphomet doesn't know how much I like you, and he apparently doesn't realize that *I* was the one who ruined our friendship." Marco sniffed as he remembered his part in Niccolo's downfall. "Hell, he chose this spot even though this was where I admitted I fucked up."

"Why isn't he stopping you, then? He's not watching this?"

"Oh, he's distracted. Your friends are already finishing their trials, so he's exerting some effort just to keep them captive. Especially that Seere guy."

"How are they almost done? I just got here!"

"Time's messed up in Purgatory, Nico. You should know that by now. This conversation could take five minutes, but it would be all of ten seconds on the outside," he said with a shrug before swinging his feet against the stone wall. "So you're gonna fight God, huh?"

"That's the plan. I've already—" Niccolo paused as he remembered his crimes, but he shook his head and brought up his knee, holding it close to his chest. "I've already gone too far to stop now."

"You're gonna have to kill me, too, you know? Just in case you *didn't* want to." Marco yawned, as if he was apathetic about his part in that tragedy. "Especially if you're going up against God."

"This place is ridiculous..." Niccolo muttered, but Marco grunted and forced his friend to look at him.

"It is, but it's not Purgatory that needs my death. You're cutting ties to your humanity and... well, I'm one of those ties. Baphomet picked me because he thought I would manipulate you and get you lost in Purgatory, but it honestly saves you a lot of leg work," Marco explained, pursing his lips. "When you kill me, you'll be closer to your goal."

"Thanks for telling me, though I'm curious how you know that," Niccolo replied, breaking eye contact and looking down at his demonic arm.

"Hey, that's what friends are for," Marco said with a laugh that turned into a sigh. "I wasn't a good enough friend in life, so I'm willing to let you do it. And being dead has its own perks, you know. I've gotten a lot of insight about souls and monsters since being here."

"Seems to be a common thread... And just so *you* know, you're not going to *let* me do anything," Niccolo teased, but he was rewarded with Marco slapping him on the shoulder.

"Hey, let a miserable drunk keep some sense of pride!" he said in mock annoyance, but Niccolo could see the smile on his face. "I could probably get in *one* punch to your face."

"Hah, alright, if that's what you think." Niccolo shook his head before looking at the ground in the middle distance, the mist swirling and breaking apart on one of the exposed crags. "I have a question for you."

"Yes?"

"That day—*this* day," Niccolo said, biting his lip. "Did you know it was me?"

"Ah, *that* day," Marco repeated, knocking his feet against the stone wall for a hesitant moment. "No, not the whole time. Only about halfway through when your jackass nature started to shine through."

"You're calling *me* a jackass?" Niccolo asked, pointing at himself with a diseased finger.

"Only because it's true! Not saying I didn't *outshine* you from time to time, of course, but that's just how it is. Jackasses herd together."

"Yeah, that we do," Niccolo replied softly, remembering happier times in Firenze. They were silent until Niccolo's curiosity got the better of him, and he turned back with a sigh. "What did you do after I was gone?"

"A lot of homely girls," Marco said, keeping a straight face for only a second before they both broke into laughter. After it subsided, Marco shook his head and rubbed his knee. "I didn't last much longer than you did, Nico. When I heard you died in that duel, that fucking coward stabbing you in the back..."

"You killed yourself?" Niccolo asked in shock, but his friend sat up straight and shook his head violently.

"No! No, I would never!" he said, holding out his hands, but then he tilted his head to the side. "Well, kinda. I didn't *mean* to, it just sorta happened because I got drunk and I thought this guy was a lot smaller than he was and... I didn't know he had friends... or that he was connected to the Simonettis..."

"You didn't," Niccolo muttered, but Marco's anguished face was enough for him to know the truth even before he spoke.

"I *did*. I insulted the dead son of a nobleman and, well," Marco admitted as he brought his hand behind his neck. "I paid the price."

"Damnit, Marco," Niccolo said, breathing out in dismay. "You shouldn't have died like that."

"Didn't mean to, you ass," Marco said, standing up and motioning for Niccolo to join him. "Get up. I want to do this right."

"Do *what* right?" Niccolo asked, already rising to meet him.

"Apologize, for real," Marco said before breathing in deep and shaking his arms to rid himself of anxiety. After a few hops from side to side, Marco settled down and opened his eyes. "Niccolo Vespucci da Firenze, I am sorry."

"I already know, Marco," he replied, but Marco put out his finger.

"I needed to say it, though. I should have been there for you, and I shouldn't have thrown you away. It wasn't your fault."

"Marco—"

"It *wasn't* your fault," Marco interrupted him, placing his hands on Niccolo's shoulders. "You got a raw deal, but look at you now. You're about to go up against God, you son of a bitch."

"You say that like it's a good thing," Niccolo said in dismay, but Marco replied with a warm smile.

"I do, because it is. Because there isn't any way I'd support a god that would do what he did to my best friend," Marco said before patting Niccolo's shoulders and drawing back. "Now kill me, you scourge of humanity, you."

"Marco," Niccolo protested, shaking his head at his friend's audacity. "You can't be serious."

"Never am, and I certainly won't let Purgatory stop me!" Marco bounced with glee for a moment, but when he settled down, he looked to the ground to avoid the seriousness of the moment. "You better kill me soon, otherwise I'm gonna get scared and have cold feet."

"I'm sick of this..." Niccolo was about to argue with his friend, but then he saw the flicker of sorrow in Marco's eyes. It was enough to change the entire tone of the conversation.

"So am I. I've been here two hundred years, Nico, and there haven't even been any homely girls to comfort me," Marco said before grabbing Niccolo's left arm and bringing it up to his chest. "I finally got to apologize and see you again after all this time, and my death is far more important than another five minutes of verbal sparring."

"Marco, you don't deserve to die," Niccolo said weakly, but his friend just tilted his head and frowned.

"It's not about what we deserve, Nico. It never is. I want this and you *need* this. I'm only holding you back from becoming the devil you need to be," he said before letting go of Niccolo's hand.

"Marco," Niccolo repeated, but Lux had already manifested in his hand. Seeing the grief on his face, Marco nodded, which was all Niccolo needed to walk forward and shove the short sword through his heart. Although he grunted in pain, Marco made eye contact with his friend and seemed relieved.

"I wish I could have been a better friend, Nico," he said before the power of Lucifer's sword blazed through him, burning him to ashes and setting him free. Niccolo could tell that Marco had wanted it, that he had been right all along, but it didn't make the pain any less. Trying to convince himself that Marco's sacrifice was necessary, Niccolo sniffed back his tears and looked away from the stone wall.

"Me too, Marco. Me, too," Niccolo said to himself before light burst all around him, the ground disappearing beneath his feet as he was torn away from the pocket dimension and back to Purgatory.

It was disorienting at first and drove him to his knees, but eventually Niccolo was able to look around.

Once he did, Niccolo realized he was the last one to arrive; his friends had all returned from their trials and were all kneeling or sitting on the ground in front of Baphomet. Crocell looked much worse for wear, scratches and bruises covered his arms and torso, but he was alive. In contrast, Phenex looked much better after his ordeal—even the scars on his cheeks had disappeared—and Niccolo momentarily felt relief for his tormented friend.

However, once he looked up at Baphomet and remembered Marco, Niccolo suddenly felt very angry. He stood up, ready to manifest his weapons and attack the gatekeeper, but he was interrupted by a war cry from his left side.

Turning to face the noise, Niccolo saw that Seere had stood up and was breathing so hard that his entire frame shuddered from the effort. What was even more surprising was the scarlet energy covering every inch of him, ebbing in and out with every breath. Although Niccolo tried to speak, he was unable to react as Seere let out another painful roar and ran forward, brandishing his hammer as he got closer to Baphomet.

"Foolish..." the entity said before flicking its wrist and sending out a wave of red flames. To everyone's surprise, Seere burst straight through the energy and continued forward, roaring his heart out the whole time. When he jumped up and brought his hammer above his head, no one could have expected what came next.

"Show yourself!" Seere yelled as his hammer met the ground, causing the entire realm to shake underneath the force of his blow. However impressive that was, Niccolo's eyes widened as the force tore a giant rent into the ground leading to Baphomet's seated position, forcing boulders into the air as a yawning chasm opened in front of him.

It was enough cause for the giant creature's eyes to open wide— his seat disappearing beneath him—and they all watched as Baphomet picked himself up and stood, even more massive once he got to his feet. Strangely, the rocks Seere had forced into the air remained hanging there as if gravity had no hold on them, and the Horseman realized quickly how he could use those boulders to his advantage.

"I said *show yourself!*" Seere commanded as he launched himself into the air, landing on one of the airborne boulders before pushing off and using the suspended rocks as a bridge, eventually landing on Baphomet's black arm and digging his axe into flesh. As the creature moaned in pain, Seere grabbed a tuft of its hair before loosing his weapon and setting it on his back, taking another handful of fur with his other hand.

And as they all watched in amazement, Seere scaled Baphomet's arm, leaping ten feet at a time as he pulled himself up and foaming at the mouth. Niccolo had to wonder what had happened during Seere's trial, but then he heard the pain in his screams and anger. Although Niccolo did not who, it was clear that Seere had lost someone. Niccolo had felt that pain far too often.

"I will not say it again, monster," Seere growled as he landed on the creature's shoulder, retrieving his weapon from his back as Baphomet turned its massive head in fear.

"Just... who..."

"Wrong fucking answer!" Seere roared before slamming his hammer down on the creature's collar bone, the resulting crack loud enough that his companions could hear it from hundreds of feet away. Although Baphomet wailed loud enough to shake their surroundings, Seere rushed forward and brought his axe behind him, determined to cut through the creature's throat.

However, it was at this point that Baphomet gave up the illusion, and Seere was left without a target and in freefall once Baphomet's body disappeared. Clenching his jaw hard enough to shatter another's bones, Seere fumed with anger until he saw what had happened. On the ground a hundred feet below him was a creature trying to crawl away from the chasm Seere had formed with his axe. And as he fell closer, Seere realized that it was a miniature version of Baphomet, that this was the real creature behind the illusion.

With a cruel smile, Seere realized what he was about to do and prepared himself for the impact.

Before the true form of Baphomet could escape, Seere landed directly on the creature's legs and crushed them entirely, his weight and velocity enough to destroy another man. However—brimming with red energy—Seere was healthy and whole after crashing to the ground, his joints creaking only slightly as he moved. He stood up and carried his weapon with one hand, watching as Baphomet turned to him in fear.

"How... how could someone like you..." it wheezed in a panic, but Seere didn't bother with an answer. He just stepped forward and set his foot on the creature's shoulder before throwing his axe into

Baphomet's unguarded wing. It screamed as blood sprayed out of the wound, not giving Seere nearly enough satisfaction.

"Open the portal," Seere commanded, but the creature only moaned and shook its head.

"I won't. Not for..." he started, but then Seere used his axe to cut through the other wing and then leaned down to dominate Baphomet's vision.

"*Now*. I'm not playing. This isn't a trial. This is your chance to make sure you don't suffer."

Seere's tone was more than enough to convince the entity. Baphomet quickly looked away and made a sign in the air, causing a rip in space and time to form over the middle of the new chasm. If not for Seere's antics, the portal would have been a marvel, but nothing could compare to the Horseman's fury.

"Just go... just go," Baphomet muttered weakly, but Seere had no intention of leaving yet.

"So what do you want to lose first, monster," he growled, waiting for Baphomet to look at him in terror. "Your left arm or your right?"

"I opened the portal... you ape," it wheezed, but Seere shook his head.

"I didn't say you were going to live, I said it was your chance to make sure you don't suffer." Then Seere leaned down and grabbed hold of one of Baphomet's arms by the shoulder. "And you fucked that up by speaking again."

"Seere!" Buer shouted, putting out his hand just as the Horseman tore Baphomet's arm from its socket and lazily tossed it into the chasm to his side. "Seere, don't! We might need him!"

"You don't get to command me, Buer," Seere replied, not watching as Baphomet tried to turn toward the open portal and close it with his other arm. Although the others were about to warn him, it seemed like Seere already knew what the creature was attempting. He had already wrapped his fingers around Baphomet's frail forearm and clenched his fist hard enough to break bone before repeating the process by tearing away Baphomet's forearm away at the elbow.

"Seere..." Niccolo muttered, all of them drawing closer to the Horseman and hoping to stop this display of brutality. However, when Seere stood up and turned to face them, Niccolo could see there was no hope for compromise.

He had chosen this specific path.

"My trial was Sitri, Nico. He tortured her, pulled her arms and legs out of their sockets," Seere said as he walked away from the writing, moaning creature. "He cut open her body, split her... her— he forced pain on her that we would *never* allow in Hell."

"I—that's horrible," William said, stepping forward and drawing the Horseman's attention. "But this is too much. Just kill him and be done with it."

"No, I *won't* just kill him, and I'll forgive you, Will—because I like you—but don't you *dare* tell me what to do again," he said before turning to face Niccolo with tears in his eyes. "What would you do if that had been Paimon?"

"I—she wouldn't..." Niccolo started, but Seere lifted his foot and crashed it into the ground, destroying any possible argument.

"What if he had tortured her to the point that she could never recover, and then he forced you to *kill* her," he said, stepping forward until he was just a foot away. Seeing the tears in his eyes, hearing his words, Niccolo finally realized what had happened.

"Sitri's..." Niccolo muttered, but he could not give life to the words.

"Yeah, that *thing*," Seere replied, pointing back at the monster rolling about without arms, "made me kill the lover of my many lifetimes."

"My God," Yeshua uttered, wanting to offer his sympathies, but Seere stomped back to the creature who had forced them through their trials.

"All of you will go through the portal. You will make all the preparations you need." Seere leaned down and grabbed Baphomet's chin, forcing it to look up at him. "I will follow when I have finished."

"Seere—"

"Don't fight me on this, Nico. You've had your grudge matches. This one is mine," Seere said before pointing at the portal hanging in midair. "So go on, jump on through. I'll be there in a minute."

"We cannot wait for you forever, Seere," Buer said as their companions followed his orders, unable to fight a barbarian in the throes of grief. Although Buer stayed behind to speak, each hellish warrior jumped through the portal and disappeared from Purgatory, leaving the two of them alone with Baphomet and the Leviathan, who had been watching from a safe distance. "Eventually we will have to move on, with or without you, and we do not know if the portal will stay open long. Is this creature's torture... worth the risk?"

"I don't need forever, centaur," Seere stated plainly, squeezing Baphomet's jaw almost to the point of breaking. "But if that portal closes behind you, I will not have any regrets. There are just some things that need doing."

"I hope it does not cost you more, my friend," Buer said before continuing on, halting at the edge of the chasm and breathing in deep.

"It already cost me Sitri, Buer. I have to get something in return," Seere replied, his voice trembling as emotion overtook him.

"Good luck, Horseman. And you," Buer replied before looking at the Leviathan, but he could see the greed in its eyes. "Are you..."

"This one knows how to prepare a meal. I will keep him company," the Leviathan said in a whisper, turning its drooling mask to watch Seere in his efforts. The Horseman did not seem to notice, but Buer knew that any warning or comment would be unwelcome.

Seere was beyond caring.

Buer sighed before turning back to the shimmering portal and leaping through, leaving Seere alone with two minor gods devoted to suffering and pain. As he was just about to crack Baphomet's jaw between his fingers, it struggled out one last question.

"You're just... a human. How are you so... powerful?" Baphomet asked, his insolence enough to cause scarlet energy to warp the space around his tormentor.

"I am no human. I am the Horseman of War, and you are my enemy," Seere explained before pinching his fingers and crushing Baphomet's jaw. As the creature squealed in pain, Seere forced it to look into his eyes.

"If gods *have* gods, now would be the time for you to pray."

CHAPTER 8
THE TRUE NATURE OF THINGS

"Where is everyone else?" Cimeries asked immediately, giving Cadmus no time to adjust to their reunion. Although Cadmus looked over her golden-haired companion, her question reminded Cadmus of Niccolo's betrayal, and all the emotion lying dormant broke through the surface.

"I..." Cadmus started as it truly sank in. After hundreds of years, his best friend had turned into a monster, betrayed him and left him for dead. They were never supposed to fight; they were never supposed to care about who was stronger or better, but this Apocalypse had forced them to claim dominance. Purgatory's retreat into his memories had been enough to delay his pain, but now Cadmus was confronted with a very real possibility.

Niccolo truly was a devil, and Cadmus had failed to kill him.

"There was a confrontation," Solomon volunteered, stepping forward before appraising the small man in yellow clothing, who regarded him with suspicion. "It finally became clear that Niccolo had lost his grasp on humanity, and Cadmus tried to bring him back from the edge. Unfortunately, Niccolo proved to be beyond reason. He—"

"Niccolo threw me into the abyss," Cadmus interrupted, forcing himself to breathe normally. "I didn't kill him when I had the chance, and Solomon was dragged into the abyss with me when I fell."

"Solomon, huh?" Gabriel asked, allowing Cadmus to finally remember that he was in the presence of a stranger. He was about to speak up when Solomon stepped forward and set the end of his scythe into the ground.

"That is correct. In my life—" he started, but Gabriel put out his hand to stop him.

"I know who you were, reaper, don't get me wrong. I just didn't expect to see you here," he replied, at which point Cadmus could no longer hold back.

"Just who are you? Cimeries, why are you traveling with him?" he asked, but she only shrugged before nodding at the small man.

"The enemy of our enemy," she hinted, gesturing toward the man so he could introduce himself.

"My name is Gabriel, the archangel, but don't worry!" he shouted, putting out his hands in protest and ready to defend himself, but Cadmus proved it was unnecessary.

"I'm not worrying, Gabriel, I know exactly what you've been doing. Buné was my teacher, after all, even if he didn't tell us what was going on until we were already on Earth." Cadmus ended the explanation with a forced smile and tried to forget the pain Niccolo had caused. "But what are you doing down here? Shouldn't you be in Heaven and preparing for the battle?"

"I was discovered when I was talking to Buné, actually," Gabriel said before looking at his sandaled feet. "I wanted to let him know that you had all gotten through the portal—that you had beaten back Michael—but I wasn't careful enough. I'm sorry, I screwed up."

"We all screw up sometimes." Despite his consolation, Cadmus bit his lip and broke eye contact. "I'd be a hypocrite if I judged you for that."

"Indeed, reaper," Cimeries added, taking their attention from each other. "But there is no time to dwell on our mistakes. We must act soon. If Niccolo is this dangerous, it is imperative we get back to the rendezvous point and warn the others."

"How are we supposed to do that?" Cadmus asked, his tone conveying more than just despair. "I'm not even sure how Solomon and I are even alive after falling through the abyss, and I'm not sure we can find our way to the exit in time."

"Luckily we have another path." Cimeries set her hand on Gabriel's small shoulder, surprising the archangel. "Gabriel knows of a back way into Heaven, and if we are careful, we may arrive before Niccolo and the others establish the portal to Hell."

"What, no, we can't use that!" Gabriel protested, drawing away from her grip, but the reapers could not let go of the possibility.

"You know of a back way, archangel?" Solomon asked, and Gabriel turned to him with a mix of annoyance and frustration.

"I—yes, I know of another way in, but we can't *go there!*" he shouted, tapping his staff against the ground for emphasis. "I had to run away as fast as I could because they're following me!"

"Just who would be following you, Gabriel?" Cadmus asked, but he could sense a change in the atmosphere and turned to see Solomon looking past Cimeries and Gabriel, his face even more somber than usual.

"It seems we are about to find out," Solomon muttered, all of them turning to watch at least twelve angels flying toward them. They were wearing golden armor and holding weapons just as radiant. Already, Cadmus and his companions could hear their war cry, but he was more focused on the angel leading the charge.

In the lead was an archangel with long brown hair and a shining, golden spear, and the last time Cadmus had seen him was just after he had murdered Tamiel.

"Gabriel!" Uriel shouted as he came within twenty yards of them, arresting his momentum completely and hovering in the air as he flapped his powerful wings. He was soon joined by his escort, whose efforts to stay in the air were enough to scatter the mists of

Purgatory for fifty yards. "Traitor and coward, I am here to bring you to Adonai's justice!"

"What justice?" Gabriel summoned false bravado as he let out his own wings and the serpents of his staff become blades once again. "Adonai has no sense of justice! He is a cruel tyrant and I will not help him anymore!"

"It is not your place to judge God, brother!" Uriel sneered at his fellow archangel as he directed his spear toward him. "If it were up to me, I would kill you right where you stand, shove this spear through your entire body and let you suffer as your essence faded away. It is only by Adonai's mercy that you are denied that fate."

"You will not claim him, Uriel," Cadmus declared, causing the archangel to look at him in confusion. It was only at this point that Uriel even noticed that Gabriel had company, and the long-haired angel scowled before his eyes fell on Solomon.

"My God, what are you doing here?" Uriel asked, looking directly at the old man and descending until his feet met the ground. "It has been centuries since we last heard from you, reaper."

"And I had planned to stay away far longer," Solomon replied before dropping his scythe into a ready stance. "I have no wish to reminisce or speak with you. I am here to help Cadmus on his path."

"You are here..." Uriel started, dumbfounded for the first time in Gabriel's memory. "You are here to help a *human* on his *path*? What ludicrous notion is this? You do not belong here."

"I never belonged anywhere, Uriel. I have been alone my entire life," Solomon said gravely before bringing his scythe behind him and narrowing his eyes to slits. "Now you will retreat, Uriel, or we will be forced to kill you."

"To kill me?" Uriel asked, his wings stretching out behind him as he shook with anger. "To kill *me*? Reaper, I will not tolerate such words or ridiculous ideas. I have come to take our brother to Adonai, and he will kill the traitor in front of Michael—in front of the *Host*— as an *example*."

"You will have to go through us, first." Cadmus was worried

about Solomon's apparent relationship with Uriel, but he had no time to focus on the reaper's past. With a glare, Uriel pushed himself into the air and raised his hand to signal his escort.

"You speak as if that will be a problem, Horseman."

Then he threw down his hand, signaling his guard to swarm down from above.

With just that motion, everything turned to chaos and Cadmus summoned Mercy from his mind, the horse swirling into existence before a pair of angels came down to crush him with blunt weapons. Focusing on the present, Cadmus slowed time so Mercy could carry him out from under their attack, and they were jerked back into the normal flow just as an angel with a heavy mace cracked the ground where Cadmus had been standing.

Turning his mount swiftly, Cadmus brought back his scythe and sliced up and under the angel's armpit, cleaving the warrior's arm from his shoulder and sending spurts of blood onto cracked ground. Cadmus was about to look around the battlefield for his next target when he noticed another angel descending from above, a lance aimed directly at his heart.

Cursing and urging Mercy to dissolve, Cadmus fell through the collapsing dust of his horse just in time for the lance to miss its mark, but he wasn't going to let the angel make another pass at him. As soon as his feet met the ground, Cadmus brought his scythe up behind him in a half moon arc, the point of his scythe sinking into the angel's back and dragging through her pelvis, taking her from the fight.

Although he was glad that he had already crippled two angels, he knew Uriel was no stranger to pragmatism and would willingly sacrifice his troops to get what he wanted. As Cadmus turned and dug in his heels to stop his forward momentum, he tried to find Gabriel amid the chaos. All he wanted was to see some hint of the short angel, to see his golden wings carrying him out of danger.

However, when Cadmus looked around the small battlefield, all he could see were other golden wings and blood sprays; his companions were doing their part to drive back Uriel's forces. As Mercy formed beneath him, Cadmus watched as Cimeries jumped off the shoulders of one angel before slamming her pike through the heart of a woman wielding a sword and shield, only to recover and drive forward so she could roll underneath the powerful downward strike of another angel's axe. Solomon was likewise carving his way through the enemy, taking his blade through the unguarded flesh behind an angel's knee before forcing the point of his scythe into the soft meat of his enemy's throat.

It does not help that Gabriel is quite small, Mercy's voice entered his head, and Cadmus found it hard to disagree. Without any clear sign of the short angel, Cadmus was left with only one option: riding through the battlefield and looking for some hint that their ally was still alive. Urging Mercy forward and preparing himself to slow down time, Cadmus breathed deep and readied his scythe.

Except that he had not accounted for Uriel, who had been waiting for this opportunity. He slammed into Cadmus' back from above and forced his spear through the reaper's ribcage, missing his heart by inches.

"It appears that I have gone *through* you, Horseman," Uriel said after he drove Cadmus from Mercy's saddle and slammed him into the ground. Once he retrieved his spear, he walked forward at a slow pace. "You really must improve, Cadmus, or the final battle will not entertain Adonai at all."

"No..." Cadmus croaked, feeling his blood pouring out of him, but the most he could do was pick himself on his forearms and watch as Uriel stalked the battlefield. When he saw Mercy galloping at the archangel, determined to avenge his master, Cadmus was at first relieved. His relief turned to fear as he remembered Niccolo's pain and how he had lost Plague and—just as Mercy was about to slam into Uriel—Cadmus urged the horse to dissolve.

It was just in time, as Uriel had noticed Mercy's approach and had turned to plunge his spear into the horse's heart. Once the dust scattered against the point of his spear, Uriel turned to look at Cadmus with a malicious grin.

"Clever, reaper. No one can deny that." His grin became even wider as he turned back to the battlefield. Although Cimeries and Solomon were still holding their ground, it was obvious that Uriel did not care about his troops. He merely walked forward—his path somehow clearing ahead of him—and Cadmus noticed that Gabriel was on the other side of the fray, his back to the approaching archangel.

"Gabriel, turn around!" Cadmus shouted once his wounds healed enough for him to breathe, but it was too late to warn the treasonous angel.

Gabriel turned around in time to see Uriel standing just a yard away. He tried to stop Uriel, used his staff to swipe at his neck, but the taller angel merely ducked out of the way and then swatted the weapon from Gabriel's hands.

"I told you all," Uriel said as his hand closed around Gabriel's throat and he rose into the air, turning to face the others still on the ground. "I came for my brother, and you will not stop me."

"Uriel," Solomon protested, pulling his blade out of the last standing angel. "Your god will *not* take you with him. Adonai intends to go alone to this new dimension. You must know that!"

"I know nothing except what Father tells us!" Uriel hovered in the air, his brother helpless in his grip. He didn't even care that Cimeries had finished off her opponents and was readying her pike to throw at his position. "I obey because that is what I was created to do! And I will not listen to an angel who chooses to spend his time among the animals!"

"An..." Cadmus murmured, his every thought a blur as he pushed himself to his feet. Looking at Solomon, who was still staring at the angels hanging in the air, Cadmus could not comprehend Uriel's claim. "An angel? Solomon, what is he talking about?"

"Solomon?" Uriel asked, disgust evident on his face as he turned to look at Cadmus. "What nonsense are you going on about, Horseman? Why do you call him Solomon?"

"That's—that's his name. He's the first human reaper," Cadmus answered, his jaw shaking as his body continued to heal, but he still lacked the strength to keep stable. "What are you..."

"*That* is not Solomon!" Uriel laughed raucously as he looked at each warrior on the ground. "Solomon exists, I assure you, but that is not him!"

"If he is not Solomon..." Cimeries turned to face the old reaper and dropped her pike to a ready stance. "Then who is he?"

"Oh, this is just *delicious*." Uriel smiled as he looked down at Solomon and shook his head. "How long have you been traveling with them, leading them, and you haven't told them the truth? Tell me, was this all part of Father's plan? If so, I must commend the two of you."

"Solomon..." Cadmus brought up his scythe and watched the old man turn to him, sorrow in his pale eyes. "What is going on?"

"Horseman, Amazon." Uriel flapped his wings and chuckled softly as he delayed the tantalizing moment. "Allow me to introduce my brother Azrael. During the Rebellion, he was known as the Angelic Reaper, but it seems he's taken to pretending to be an ancient king."

"*What?*" Cadmus asked, his eyes going wide.

"Oh, I do wish to stay and enjoy this, but I must return. Azrael, I really am proud of you. This was masterful," Uriel said before laughing and flapping his wings, sending a gust of wind around them. Within just a few seconds, Uriel was soaring away, the doomed archangel in his grip barely holding onto consciousness.

However, that was the least of their concerns. Cadmus and Cimeries turned to face the old reaper, hoping Uriel had been lying, but the truth was evident. Solomon stood straight up, set his scythe against the ground and turned to look directly at Cadmus.

And as his student stared at him in horror, six black wings spread out from behind the reaper's back, stretching out to their full span before curling back down into a relaxed state.

"The deception is over, Horseman. My true name is Azrael, the Angelic Reaper, and I have no excuse to give you."

———

"This is… Heaven?" Niccolo asked to no one in particular, standing on what seemed to be a solid cloud. Countless spheres hung in the sky, bathing every inch of the dimension in golden light, and it was difficult for Niccolo to fully comprehend that they were finally at the end of their quest. Purgatory was behind them, but some part of Niccolo did not trust it. Some part of him thought it was another trick.

"It is, Niccolo. This is where Adonai and his Heavenly Host dwell, this is the site of our final battle," Buer stated, breathing in deep the air of his former home. A smile was on the centaur's face and his eyes were closed, and Niccolo assumed the fallen angel was taking a moment to forget his past and just enjoy the warmth.

However, the moment was over within just a second and—once Buer's eyes opened—he started to retrieve a number of objects from the satchel on his belt. The portal to Purgatory shimmered behind them, promising a trip across the Void, but the centaur was more focused on drawing symbols into the ground beside it. Deciding it would be best to leave the fallen angel to his work, Niccolo turned to look toward the massive capitol, the sheer size of Adonai's home causing him to gape in wonder.

"He was never one for moderation, Adonai," Crocell commented as he sidled up to Niccolo, dark blood weakly pulsing over the hand he had pressed against the deep cut on his torso. "He created a mountain just to set his own capitol on top, and as the city grew, he chose to build it higher and higher into the sky."

"It's incredible." Niccolo had forgotten his anger for the moment, but Crocell scoffed beside him.

"It is gaudy and pretentious. Luckily, we have wings, so it will not take much time to retrieve his head," Crocell said before turning and walking away, leaving Niccolo to stand by himself.

However, he was not alone for long; Yeshua and William came to join him in staring at their destination.

"So this is where I would have ended up if I was a good little boy, huh?" William asked, not waiting for Niccolo to reply with a snide answer. "Honestly, I'm glad I fell. The Pestilence Quarter reminded me of home, this is just... too much."

"There is a province in Hell that reminds me of home, too," Yeshua commented, his calm demeanor stunning Niccolo enough to turn and face him. As he spoke, Niccolo realized that the man's pupils had returned, and he had trouble listening as Yeshua continued. "I spent some time there, but *home* loses its appeal after a few decades in Hell."

"Phenex..." Niccolo muttered, causing Yeshua to turn to him without hostility.

"Yes, Nico? What is it?"

"Your eyes, they aren't... on fire anymore. Just what happened to you in there?" Niccolo asked, causing his friend to look down sheepishly.

"I... well, I'm not running away anymore. With William's help, I realized just what I was doing, and what I saw..." Yeshua said, sniffing back a tear before looking back up with a forced smile. "I'm not going to say I'm innocent, I'm not going to say that I have forgiven myself, but I have started on that path. Please... call me Yeshua from now on."

"Yeshua? You..." Niccolo started, becoming flustered as he realized his friend was no longer an agent of vengeance and endless anger, leaving him alone on that path. "So Marchosias, you're not going to..."

"Oh, believe me, I haven't forgotten about him and I... I still wish that things had turned out differently," Yeshua admitted, looking toward the capitol and refusing to give into anger. "I will still fight for him, Niccolo. You have not lost your ally."

"He might even be better, actually," William teased, causing them to look at him with skepticism. It was enough for William to try and escape their attention, turning to look back at their goal, but what he saw caused him to grab the bow from his back. Almost immediately his friends turned to join him—Niccolo letting out his wings and forming his weapons, Yeshua wreathing himself in fire—and they prepared themselves for the worst.

There were ten figures running along the ground, most of them wielding spears.

"Who goes there?" one of the figures asked as soon as they were within twenty yards, his voice sounding hollow because of the faceplate of his helmet. In his right hand was a great staff with a head larger than his torso, and in his left was a round shield three feet in diameter.

"Keep away," Niccolo cautioned, letting out a burst of light from his shield. "We've already gone too far and lost too much to lose to you."

"Really, Niccolo, try to stall them, at the very least," Buné urged from his place by the portal. "I need more time!"

"We will be sure to give it to you," Yeshua replied, at which point the soldier with the giant staff stepped forward in alarm. Raising his left arm and lifting his faceplate, the angel looked at him in shock.

"Y—Yeshua? Yeshua!" he shouted, his voice filled with joy. "My god, Yeshua, you're finally here!"

"Do you know this guy?" William asked, drawing back the arrow in his hand and ready to send it through any angel who dared approach, but the gatekeeper seemed to have forgotten the danger and looked like he would run to greet them.

"Of course, he does! Yeshua, it's me! It's Peter!" the angel shouted, and at once Yeshua realized this was the true apostle. This was not another trick from Purgatory; this was the friend who had created an entire religion off of his revolution.

That was all Yeshua needed to abandon the flames wrapping around his hands, and he stepped forward in shock.

"Peter... it's really you, isn't it?"

The angel enthusiastically nodded before sighing in relief.

"Oh, you have no idea how glad I am to see you. That you may have ended up in Hell or in Purgatory was too much for me to bear. I thought that you and your friends, that you..." Peter hesitated once he looked over Niccolo and William, as he saw the centaur continuing to draw sigils near the rippling entrance to Purgatory. "Yeshua, where did you come from?"

"You knew him back in the old days. You should know," William said, earning a smirk from Niccolo, but Yeshua was not so entertained. Ignoring his young companion, Yeshua stepped forward and offered his palms out in a show of peace.

"Peter, I am not here to fight on Heaven's side. My friends and I have traveled a long way, we have sacrificed too much, and we have come to stop Adonai," he explained, preparing himself for the worst.

"Yeshua, how could you?" Peter asked as he drew back, a scowl on his face. "I created a religion for you, we promised to bring light to the world, and now you fight against our god? You would throw everything away for—what, *vengeance*? Do you hate God so much for damning you to Hell?"

"God did not damn me to Hell!" Yeshua replied, white-hot flames covering his eyes. "I fell because Adonai has no say whether or not people go to Hell or Heaven or even Purgatory! He is a cruel tyrant, using us as playthings, and I am *glad* that I do not serve him."

"What is this blasphemy?" Peter motioned to his troops to fan out and hopefully flank their outnumbered enemies. It was obvious that he did not know the full extent of their capabilities. "He is *God*, my friend, and that should mean something even to you! Your mind is twisted, Yeshua, and I can only blame Judas and his betrayal for such pitiful circumstances."

"You do *not* get to blame Judas!" Flames crawled along Yeshua's arms and legs, wings of fire sprouting behind him. "He may have betrayed us in life, but that man was my friend."

"He was my friend as well until he threw you to the Romans," Peter growled, stepping forward and holding his staff to his side. "Do you have any idea how hard it was for us to carry on after your death? *You* were the politician; *you* were the one with the golden name and reputation. I was killed in your name."

"And I am sorry for that—"

"But still you defend him. Still you hold Judas above us. Do you know that he gave you up for a mere bag of silver?" Peter asked as his angels stopped moving, arranged in a semi-circle just as the apostles had been during Baphomet's trial. "That coward killed himself soon after that, probably because he realized he could have gotten gold, instead."

"He was no coward," Yeshua replied, every inch of his body covered in fire before he started to float in the air. At the sight, Peter grunted and shook his head.

"And you were no *messiah*. We should have known." Peter growled before slamming the head of his staff against his shield, giving his soldiers the signal to attack.

Unfortunately for him, he had underestimated the strength of his enemies.

Before William could react, Yeshua and Niccolo rushed through the air and took out angels on either side of Peter; Yeshua bathing two warriors in flames as he flew past them, Niccolo sending out an arc of energy at the angel on the far right before slamming his blade down against an angel who guarded himself with the handle of his spear.

However, while he would have liked to count on them or even Crocell to take out the remaining angels, William could see that three of Peter's guards were flying forward, ready to impale him on their weapons.

Cursing, William loosed his arrow, not bothering to watch as it flew right past the middle angel. Instead, William drew out the long sword on his blade with his right hand, dropped the bow from his left, and grabbed a dagger as soon as he could. Noticing two of the angels were circling around to his sides and likely intended to flank him, William ran forward to meet the angel he had missed with the arrow.

Just after he knocked away the spearhead of the angel with his sword, William tried to plunge his dagger into the man's chest plate. However, he was rewarded with the angel slamming into him and carrying him through the air before they both fell to the ground in a heap, expending their momentum only after a few seconds of tumbling over each other.

Smiling, William realized that he had been able to force his dagger through the chain metal just above the angel's collarbone, but from his groaning, William knew the man was still alive. Pushing the angel's body off him and retrieving his dagger in the same movement, William quickly climbed on top and stabbed him again, this time through the neck, and drew the blade across.

After he slit the angel's throat, William scrambled over to his sword, picked it up and turned just in time for a spear to sink into his lower gut, driving him from the angel's corpse and pushing him along the ground.

"Insolent wretch!" the owner of the spear shouted as he stood above William, his long beard moving with every word. It was the only thing visible underneath his half-helm—the rest of the angel was covered in gold and silver armor—and it almost made William laugh even as a spear was buried in his gut. "Charles guarded these gates for two *centuries.*"

"Guess his shift is over," William said with a smirk as he pulled on the handle of the spear and dragged himself along the shaft so he could thrust his sword forward. Because William had pulled on the spear, the angel lost his balance and fell to meet him, the blade shearing through the man's chest plate and cutting into his heart.

"What—how? My armor..." the angel weakly protested, but William shrugged despite the overwhelming pain from his gut.

"Someone should have told you that gold and silver make worthless armor," he said before turning over and forcing the angel's body to the side. He was just about to pull the spear out of his belly when he noticed Buer still writing runes in the ground, oblivious to the two angels preparing to dive at him with their spears.

"Buer!" William shouted as he yanked out the spear in his belly and picked himself up. As Buer lifted his head and realized that he was not alone by the portal, William brought back his arm and threw the spear that was drenched in his own blood.

It was done out of desperation—William never had any real training with spears or in throwing them—but it flew through the air and covered the ground between them in less than a second. Even more surprisingly, William had somehow aimed well, and before the angels had any time to react, one of them was skewered through the sides with a golden spear and fell out of the air.

Seeing that he was alone against the centaur, the remaining angel attacked anyway, but Buer would not be outdone by a mere human. After summoning a lance, Buer merely reared back and then waited for the diving enemy, who was unable to stop her momentum and fell directly onto the centaur's weapon.

"I told you that you would make a difference, William," Buer declared before tossing away the foolish angel. "However, I have much more work to do. Please keep them away from now on."

"I'll... try," William said, groaning as he crouched down to pick up his weapons.

As he lowered himself, William was surprised to feel his insides rearranging themselves and his skin starting to reform, and he laughed at the absurdity of it all. He would have marveled at it for much longer, but when William lifted his head, his jaw dropped and whatever hope that remained abandoned him. A hundred angels were descending from the sky, their cries filling his ears.

Peter had called for reinforcements.

"So this is what you've become, Yeshua?"

Peter swung down his heavy mace, the weapon crashing against the ground and dispersing the white clouds underfoot, and Yeshua had to dive out of the way to avoid it. However, he had no time to focus on his surroundings; Peter was almost salivating from his anger, and he was the least of Yeshua's worries. A minute into their confrontation, Peter sent a flare high into the Heavens, and Yeshua could see reinforcements gathering in the distance.

"I became what I *needed* to become," Yeshua replied as he sent a fireball at his old friend, who brought up his shield to defend himself. Although it splashed against the metal harmlessly, Yeshua could tell that Peter still felt the heat of it. "Thirteen centuries in Hell has taught me much more than all my years on Earth."

"Oh? What have they taught you?" Peter said as he advanced and swept his mace in front of him, which Yeshua hopped over. "Have they taught you cowardice and betrayal and evil?

"Actually, my mistake!" he shouted as he continued his momentum and brought his mace up and over, intent on squashing his airborne enemy. Although Yeshua avoided it, Peter was already settled in a forward guard position before he could counter. "You would not have landed in Hell if you were not already corrupted."

"That has nothing to do with it," Yeshua said, the flames growing and spiraling around his limbs. "Although there are scoundrels in every part of the universe, I have met noble souls in Hell who would never have made it to Heaven. I have traveled with men and women who were far better than me, far better than any of our revolutionaries, and they certainly do not need to bow to your god."

"Bow to *my* god? He is your god, too!" Peter lifted his mace and pointed at him. "Adonai is the only reason you exist, Yeshua!"

"No, that is a *lie!*" Yeshua's flames grew in intensity before solidifying into an infernal armor, burning swords extending from both arms. "Adonai created the angels, he created so much of this world, but he did not create humanity! I *exist* because of Lucifer, because of my friends, because of... Judas. That man is the only reason I am alive today."

"Then he is guilty of another crime," Peter said as he slammed down the faceplate of his helmet, and Yeshua knew there would be no further conversation.

It was just as well, as the swarm of angels had come to greet them and throw the battlefield into complete chaos. Before he could pursue Peter, his old friend had jumped into the air to join his fellow warriors, leaving Yeshua to contend with a dozen angels circling above him. With a wary breath, Yeshua jumped into the air and created a ring of fire that completely immolated four of the closest angels, turning them into cinders.

"Come back, Peter, and I will not be forced to kill your subordinates." Yeshua was calm even as a dozen angels hovered around him and held spears at the ready. After a moment, two of the spearmen parted to reveal Yeshua's former colleague, his mace shining in the limitless light of Heaven.

"They are the Heavenly Host, Yeshua, and I am *Saint* Peter. Hundreds of them would die for me, and there would still be thousands left to sacrifice themselves after them. Christianity may have been founded on your poor example, but it was I who built it up. It was I who started your faith and our religious empire."

"Our religious *empire*?" Yeshua growled, his eyes burning even hotter. "That was not what we were trying to do! We were trying to save our people!"

"At the expense of others, coward. Don't speak to me like you didn't understand our purpose. When you died, we were given a martyr, a way to manipulate the masses. Really, when it comes down to it, Yeshua, the best thing you ever did for our revolution was *die for it*," Peter said, his smug nature coming to the fore. In disgust, Yeshua let the flaming armor around him disperse.

"I wanted you to come to your senses, Peter, but it seems like you never had any. I wanted you to come over to our side, to be on the *righteous* side, but everything you're saying... I don't recognize you."

Yeshua shook his head and clenched his fists. "You're even worse than the shade I encountered in Purgatory."

"As Hell has taught you much in thirteen centuries, Heaven has allowed me to see the light. Why would I fight against a God who could bring me to his new dimension? Why would I resist when told that I would have real power?"

"You do not have real power." Yeshua's flames grew once more, but he smiled once he felt rain splash and evaporate on his cheek. Looking up to see storm clouds gathering, Yeshua realized just what was about to happen. "And you will not make it to Adonai's new home."

"And how do you know that?"

"Because I have a friend who would like a word with you." Yeshua smiled before he abandoned his flames and dived to the cloud-covered ground of Heaven, leaving his enemies to hover in confusion.

However, as soon as Yeshua's feet touched the ground, a large column of electricity cracked through the sky and sent tendrils of deadly current out to the exposed angels in metal armor.

It would have been beautiful if it was not such a brutal display of violence. Blue arcs of electricity connected all of the angels like a malicious spiderweb as a torrent of wind and rain flowed around them, causing them to drift through the air. Yeshua only gaped in wonder until he was able to pick out the blue demon with the shining trident, his arms and weapon making him stand out from the storm around him.

And just as soon as it started, it was over, dozens of corpses falling out of the sky, their bodies burnt-out husks inside metal shells. Yeshua was pleased by the sudden turn in their chances, but then he saw that Crocell was also falling; his strength had abandoned him once the storm departed.

Running forward and praying out of habit, Yeshua pushed off the ground and rushed through the air, hoping to catch Crocell before he met the ground. He was forced to avoid falling angels as he flew—an errant leg actually caught him full on the back—but he was able to make it to Crocell within just a few seconds, and he dropped to the ground with the fallen angel in his arms.

"Crocell, open your eyes!" Yeshua demanded, noticing immediately that the slayer wasn't breathing. His torso was still covered from wounds he had suffered in Purgatory, along with a few new gaping holes that must have come from the Heavenly Host. Shaking him, his wings breaking apart and turning to water, Yeshua tried to convince himself that he would not lose another friend. There had been too much death in the last year, and he could not forgive himself if Crocell was added to that list before the final confrontation.

However, he was given hope when the fallen angel sputtered back to consciousness, his eyelids fluttering open to reveal dark eyes still in pain. Smiling, Yeshua wiped the tear from his cheek and gave a nervous laugh.

"You had me worried there for a moment," he said, causing Crocell to turn the head Yeshua had propped up on his lap. "Thought you were going to die."

"I will. You have only... delayed the inevitable," Crocell said, every word tinged with pain as he tried to sit up and failed. "Stopping the Host, even for just a moment, seemed like a worthy sacrifice. I am content with this death."

"You're not going to die!" Yeshua forced Crocell to wince from the volume. "You're conscious and you still have your heart and your brain. You're going to heal."

"I will not. That is the issue," Crocell replied, his breath halting at the end of the sentence. "I no longer heal and I have suffered too many wounds, pushed myself too far. I will bleed out... soon."

"You'll bleed out," Yeshua muttered as he looked at Crocell's torso and saw the holes scattered along his skin. "What if I cauterized the wounds?"

"I... had not considered that." Crocell hesitated as he realized what Yeshua was suggesting, but then he looked up at his companion and nodded. "Delay my end further and I will search for a better grave."

"Stop being so depressing."

After removing Crocell's head from his lap and then kneeling over the slayer, Yeshua let his hands brim with well-intentioned flames. "Are you ready?"

"I would rather not lose more blood. Continue," Crocell urged as he prepared himself for Yeshua's efforts.

Placing his hands against the Fallen's wounds—blue skin searing underneath his touch—Yeshua forced himself not to watch Crocell's reactions. Although he grunted in pain and took sharp breaths, his body lay still and in complete control as Yeshua melted flesh and formed scars along his body. Once Yeshua closed up the wounds on his abdomen, he urged Crocell to turn over and let him repeat the process with the exit wounds.

After a few moments, Yeshua leaned back on his knees and watched as Crocell sat up and shakily rose to his feet. Rising up to meet him, Yeshua threw Crocell's arm over his shoulder and supported the fallen angel, who grunted and looked away in shame.

"Thank you, Phenex," he said, almost too soft to hear, and it brought a warm smile to Yeshua's face.

"You're welcome. You're not dying yet, not if I can help it." Feeling one act closer to redemption, Yeshua helped Crocell back through the battlefield, dead and dying angels all along the ground. "And... I'm going by Yeshua again, just so you know."

"Yeshua..." Crocell repeated, turning to look at his companion before standing up on his own and lifting his arm from Yeshua's shoulders. "So the act is over, then?"

"I—yes," Yeshua replied, Crocell's direct nature enough to shame him. "I'm just a man. I should not pretend to be a fallen angel or use his name. It's not... right."

"Right and wrong have no bearing on that name or how you used it," Crocell said, water ebbing out from his back before solidifying into dark wings. "Phenex would have been touched if he knew what you have done in his honor."

"What are you doing? Conserve your strength," Yeshua urged, his hand closing around Crocell's upper arm, but the slayer grunted before pointing back at the portal with his trident. Turning to look where he was pointing, Yeshua's heart filled with despair. He had thought all of their enemies dead, dying or broken; he had thought Crocell's lightning storm had destroyed the host.

However, while William was doing his best to give Buer more time, he stood alone with his weapons drawn as twenty angels prepared to descend upon him. And commanding them from twenty yards back was Peter holding a heavy mace, his wings showing scorch marks where Crocell's lightning had burned through him. In desperation, Yeshua looked around for Niccolo and found him in the air a mile away—too far to help—and when he turned back to see Peter give the signal to attack, he realized an awful truth.

They were too far to help.

———

"What do you expect to accomplish here?" Peter asked from ten feet in the air, his wings flapping lazily. Half of his face seemed to be flaking off—Crocell's lightning storm had ruined the skin underneath his helmet and he had discarded the ruined armor soon after—and whatever mercy the apostle had in life had long since given way.

As Peter hovered in the air, his elite guard flanking him on both sides, he smirked and looked down on William Combe.

"Oh, you know, I'm just stalling," William replied, hoping the light-hearted statement would make the angel reconsider attacking. Instead, Peter chuckled and shook his head before pointing at Buer, still furiously scribbling on the ground behind William.

"That I will believe, young man. I'm more curious as to your friend over there. It seems like even the threat of my soldiers is not enough to stop him in his task. Just what is he doing?" Peter asked, parts of his face healing as he spoke.

If he had not just recovered from the hole in his gut, William would have thought it unfair.

"Oh, Buer likes to draw. Didn't you know? We're actually here to just bring more color to the place. Gold and silver was *so* last millennium," William teased, his voice only faltering toward the end.

Even if Buer turned around and fought with him, there was no way they could take on all those angels at once. The more powerful members of their group were too far to make a difference, and this was the one occasion where William wished that Niccolo was fighting by his side. Since William hadn't had that option, he had made his peace and now stood his ground.

"I like you, young man," Peter said, the smile on his face enough to crack his skin again. "If you just back away from this... Buer... I will speak highly of you to Adonai. Perhaps you could even join us at our new home."

"Nah, I think I like the old one." William gulped down his fear and shrugged as he held his sword and dagger in his hands. "And after traveling through so many dimensions in the last three days, I feel like I need a break."

"William, I need more time. If death is the price we pay, I am sorry," Buer whispered as chalk cracked between his fingers, but Peter could tell what he was saying. As Buer scrambled to find another piece in his satchel, the lead angel turned to face William again.

"More time for what, William? What is it that you're stalling for?" Peter asked, abandoning the smile and replacing it with a stern expression. Motioning to his troops by raising his mace, Peter waited for his answer.

"I... screw it." William's heart sank once he realized there would be no more stalling, no more jokes. Standing up straighter, William prepared himself for death. "Buer is summoning the legions of Hell, and I will die before letting you stop him."

"Well said, even if it proves you are a fool," Peter said before swinging down his mace. Almost immediately ten angels dove out of the air toward William—the others heading toward Buer as he continued to scrawl runes on the ground—and he was left with no options. Preparing for a world of pain, William silently promised to kill at least one of them, even if his death was guaranteed in trade.

However, before any of the warriors came within a few yards of William, a giant hand filled his vision and protected him from the onslaught by slamming down just a few feet away. Stupefied, William turned around to see a giant arm coming out of the portal from Purgatory and wondered just what creature had followed them. That wonder stopped quickly once the creature pulled itself out from the nether realm, revealing an ancient face with a metal plate covering his missing eye.

"What creature is this?" Peter asked in shock, about to fly forward and strike, but the Nephilim lifted its one-eyed gaze and smiled.

"Well, I'll be damned, more flying monkeys," Ymir said before jumping forward and swiping five angels out of the air. Once he got his bearings, Ymir threw them at Peter, who rolled out of the way before watching the Nephilim stand up to his full height.

"No matter! I am Saint Peter, the Guardian of the Gates, and I will not turn craven when a monster invades Heaven!"

That bravado made Ymir give into shock before laughing heartily, doubling over even as a swarm of angels flew around him. When he stopped laughing, Ymir pointed back at the portal with his thumb.

"I ain't a monster, little chimp. *That* is."

Right on cue, the Leviathan screamed out of the Void, eight sprawling limbs crawling forward and its vertical mouth revealing long teeth, three tongues flailing about and trying to grab whatever angel was closest. Once it shoved a man into its gullet, the angel's face joined the countless others on its torso, and the Leviathan let out a deep scream once it came to a stop ten yards away from Ymir.

When it looked back down—its terrible mouth still hanging open—William could tell that the flames of its eyes burned a little brighter.

"I was so... hungry," it whispered, causing Peter's jaw to quiver in fear, but he soon breathed in deep and gathered his courage.

He was about to speak again, proclaim more meaningless titles about his position in Heaven, but then a huddled mass on the Leviathan's back broke away and heaved itself into the air, slamming into the former apostle and causing him to dip a few feet.

"You dare—" Peter started, but then the brute slammed his fist into Peter's face and then wrestled him all the way to the ground.

Picking himself up and jumping away, Peter tried to ignore the blood pouring out of his nose, but then he realized that it was just another man that had attacked him. Black hair hung about his face, crude armor covered his massive left arm, and there was an axe holstered to his back.

When he turned to look at Peter, the gatekeeper thought him more beast than man.

"You talk too much. Fight me," Seere commanded as he stomped forward, refusing to draw his weapon. Peter laughed at his behavior and dropped his shield into a ready position.

"Draw your weapon and we will be on equal terms." Peter was smug, but the warrior continued forward and shook his head.

"We will *never* be on equal terms," Seere replied, coming within striking distance of Peter's mace and raising his fists. Scoffing at the statement, Peter swung his mace across his body, knowing with certainty that the blow would shatter the man's arms.

Instead, Seere threw his fist into the head of the mace and almost forced it out of Peter's hand, forcing him to spin around just to keep hold of his weapon. When he turned back to face Seere, Peter trembled at his raw power.

"How... you're just a..."

"No. *You* are *just a. I* am Seere, the Horseman of War, Scourge of the Black Plains, Champion of the Shattered Skull, and I need no horse or weapon to strike *you* down."

282

Then the Horseman rushed forward, his right arm poised for a haymaker. Lifting up his shield and hoping to deflect the blow, Peter prepared to swing his mace into the man's skull, but he never had the chance. When Seere's knuckles struck the shimmering metal, Peter's shield shattered apart and his left arm broke from the stress, sending him backward.

"*You can't do that!*" Peter screamed, throwing away the remnants of his shield and allowing his left arm to heal. Jumping into the air, Peter pointed down with his mace and bristled with anger. "I don't care who you are! I am Saint Peter and I will guard these gates!"

"Then you have already failed," Seere stated before leaping into a midair collision, forcing Peter to flap his wings harder just to stay airborne.

Before he could fully react, Peter felt hands close around the bones where his wings met his shoulders. In a panic, Peter's eyes widened in horror as Seere pulled, separating wings from body and forcing both of them to the ground.

When Peter opened his eyes, it was only because he felt a blow across his cheek, and what he saw removed any trace of confidence. One last man from his force of a hundred angels was still airborne, but Peter watched as the Leviathan plucked him out of the air and dragged him halfway into his mouth. In a spray of blood and gore, the monster's mouth clamped shut and the bottom half of the angel fell to the clouds underneath, leaving Peter alone with demons, giants and terrors.

And more Nephilim continued to crawl out of the portal to join them.

"You will not win." Even if he had been defeated and left broken and kneeling, Peter could at least be stubborn about being on the right side. "Adonai will tear you apart, even if the Host does not."

"Do you not have the courage to look at us, Peter?" Yeshua asked, and that was enough for Peter to look back in defiance at his old friend.

"I have all the courage I need to face death, *Messiah*. Feed me to

283

your pet, let that monster tear me apart limb from limb, I do not care! I will face my second death with no regrets!" Peter shouted, picking himself up despite being completely outmatched. Even with that display meant to inspire anger, Yeshua looked at him with sorrow.

Peter's words meant little to him, now.

"I don't want your death. It's pointless. If you come over to—"

"Come over to your side?" Peter interrupted, his ruined face crackling as he scoffed. "I would rather die than spend another minute by *your* side! If you had not turned to trickery and summoned these monsters, my forces would have killed all of you! You never had a chance, Yeshua! You *don't* have a chance!"

"Denial is not a good look for you, Pete," William commented, gaining the apostle's anger as he whipped around to snarl. With a shrug, William lazily tossed his dagger at Peter, who caught it with his right hand. "Yeshua is more than enough to handle you, but if you don't think so..."

"Peter," Yeshua said, shaking his head as his former friend turned to face him. "Don't. I don't want to hurt you."

However, his words fell on deaf ears. Peter was already rushing forward, William's dagger in his hand.

It almost seemed like he would succeed—the point of the dagger was only inches away from Yeshua's unarmored chest—but the blade melted before it came any closer. In shock, his eyes widening as the knife dripped away, Peter followed after his strike and barely noticed the flames building around Yeshua until it was far too late.

When his arm came into contact with Yeshua's chest, it burst into flames and his bracer melted along with his skin, and Peter was already going too fast for him to stop his momentum. His entire body crashed against Yeshua like a wave against a cliff, and no part of Peter remained intact. Metal poured down in front of Yeshua, ashes scattered against him, and all without a scream of pain.

And just like that, Saint Peter was turned into a heap of molten metal and ashes.

"I... did not expect that," William said in shock, looking at what remained of the biblical figure, but then he felt a hand settle on his shoulder. Turning to look at its owner, William found Niccolo had leaned in to whisper in his ear.

"Just stay quiet."

They watched as Yeshua looked down at what remained of his friend. They were silent for a moment—they didn't entirely know what kind of reaction Yeshua would want—but eventually he looked up at them and took a deep breath. Once he let out that lungful of air, Yeshua nodded and turned away from the ashes.

"Yeshua, it wasn't your fault, he was—" William started, ignoring Niccolo's advice, but he stopped talking once Yeshua turned to him with tear-brimmed eyes.

"Saint Peter, the Guardian of the Gates. I was foolish to think I could change his mind," he replied, sniffing back the tears and breathing shakily. "Some people just aren't meant to be saved."

"It wasn't your fault," William repeated, and that was enough for Yeshua to offer him a sad smile.

"Maybe, William. Maybe. I'd *like* to think that, but the truth of the matter is..." he said, looking down at his feet and clenching his fists. "There never would have been a Saint Peter if there wasn't a Jesus Christ. I am guilty for one, if not *both*, of his deaths, and I will not deny my responsibility for that."

"He was my friend, William, as stubborn and corrupted as he was. Please, permit me my grief," Yeshua said weakly, turning around to hide the tears he could no longer hold back.

As he walked away—even knowing he was on the right side, even knowing how corrupted Peter had become—Yeshua felt the heartache that only comes from loss. This was his lot in life; watching as his friends died for him. Peter had been his last chance for redemption, his last chance to make sure one of his apostles did not die for him, and Yeshua had failed.

His last friend from life was now just a pile of ashes, and Yeshua grieved for them all.

MICHAEL KICKED OPEN THE DOOR, his fury enough to cause his sword to flare even as it was stowed on his hip, and he found exactly what he expected. Sprinting forward and using his wings to propel himself even faster, Michael made it to the other end of the throne room within seconds, his breath measured and exact. When he finally got to Gabriel's side, Adonai, Uriel and Sabrael watched him with interest.

"Stop this *now*," Michael commanded as he brandished his sword, ready to fight Uriel and Sabrael if it meant saving his brother.

Setting the end of his spear against the ground, Uriel looked at him with a raised eyebrow.

"Stop what? We're just talking," he replied, at which point Sabrael stepped forward, hands buried in his sleeves.

"Yes, in fact, we were waiting for you. We would not kill this traitor without you in the audience, Michael. You should know that," he said, causing Michael to return his weapon to his belt and look down at their sniveling brother.

Uriel had already done a number on Gabriel. Just on one side of his face, open gashes ran along his cheekbones and he had a black eye. From the swollen skin near his jaw, Michael guessed that it had already been broken and mended.

"Don't do *that*, Mikey," Adonai said, sitting forward before pushing himself to his feet. When he descended the small set of stairs, Michael tried to understand what his god intended. "Take out your sword and let it breathe."

"Why? What is the point of all this?' Michael asked, but Adonai responded with a light chuckle as he stood over his treasonous angel.

"Well, surely you had your sword out because you wanted to kill the traitor. I mean, c'mon, we all know that you wouldn't fight any of *us*." Adonai turned to leer at Michael, a mischievous glint in his eye. "So? Go ahead and draw your sword."

"It was a mistake, Father," Michael argued, motioning to the brother kneeling by his feet. "Gabriel was tempted, tricked into joining them. There is no need for bloodshed."

"I was not... tricked," Gabriel added weakly, causing all four members of his family to look down at him in surprise. When Gabriel lifted his head, Michael could see that his other eye was swollen shut. "I knew what I was doing."

"Signing your death warrant?" Uriel teased, smirking even as Gabriel looked at him in defiance.

"The *right thing*, you disgusting creature. How many of your soldiers died when you came to get me?" His voice trembled with each word, but Michael was amazed that anyone could speak like this in front of their father.

"I don't know, and I don't particularly care, traitor," Uriel answered, almost bored, but then Gabriel slammed his fist against the ground.

"It was *all of them*! You sacrificed *all of those angels* just to bring me back and kill me. For what? For *what*, you bastard? I can't *fight*. I'm not going to change the outcome of this war! When you kill me, it will be for your own twisted satisfaction, and that's *all it is*. All of this is because you're all so mentally deranged that the only thing you enjoy is hurting other people!"

Gabriel's anger was enough to warp some of his speech, but he was understood. Although Uriel was about to respond, Adonai put out a hand before kneeling down and placing a finger underneath Gabriel's chin.

"What's your point?"

"*This* is *why*," Gabriel said, staring hard into Adonai's eyes, but his words meant for someone else. "This is why I stood up and I betrayed Heaven. Because the true demons have been by our side since the *beginning*. If humanity has even the slightest chance, I would gladly give up my life a thousand times for their cause. I have no need for excuses."

"Just as well. We would not listen to them even if you did," Sabrael commented as he turned to face Michael. "To strive against

God is already a terrible crime, one without defense. One that must be punished accordingly."

"Let him live," Michael asked weakly, looking down at the favored brother who had forced himself into such an awful position. Michael finally understood—he *sympathized*—but Gabriel was being foolish. If he would have just come to Michael, all of this could have been avoided.

"That's not going to happen, Mikey," Adonai said, sighing as he dropped his hand from Gabriel's chin and then picked himself up. Michael looked at his creator and saw him shrug as if this was all just a chore. "Gabriel has to die."

"And quickly, we need not waste time on this vermin." Uriel clucked his tongue in disgust, and Michael almost wanted to slash him apart for that insolence.

"If you hurt him..." Michael started, his voice dropping to a low growl, but Uriel laughed at him before turning to their father. After Uriel nodded back at him, Michael quickly realized there was something more sinister at work. His hand drifted to his sword, and his anxiety only increased once Adonai crossed his arms and stared down at him.

"I told you to draw your sword, Michael," Adonai said, and Michael understood exactly what they wanted. Grabbing the hilt at his belt hard enough to make his skin creak, Michael shook his head.

"Don't make me."

"Michael. My *son*." Adonai stepped forward until he towered over the archangel. "I already told you that you are nothing. Nothing if not my servant. And since that is the case, you have to do what I command."

"Father—"

"*Whatever* I command, Michael," Adonai interrupted, his voice echoing throughout the open chamber. "Draw. Your. Sword."

"Please," Michael muttered, but he had already taken the hilt from his belt so the flames could grow and become the blade that had already taken the lives of thousands of angels. "He's my brother."

"And he is my son just the same," Adonai said, stepping back so Gabriel was between them. Using his foot—yawning as he did so—Adonai pushed Gabriel's entire body around so that he was facing Michael. "You don't see *me* complaining."

"Gabriel," Michael whined, causing the small angel to look at him with a tear in his eye. Gathering what little strength remained, Gabriel sat up straight and gulped down air.

"Don't grieve for me. I've been prepared for this." His lip quivered slightly as he tried to face death after all these eons. "That it's you... makes it easier to handle."

"Gabe..." Michael said, tears streaming down his cheeks now that it was finally certain. "I don't... I can't..."

"You must, and you will," Gabriel said before making eye contact one last time. "You always do the right thing eventually."

"I'm getting impatient," Adonai grumbled, which caused Michael to force back his tears and prepare himself. Readjusting his grip and looking down at his brother, Michael wondered if he could fight all of them—*save* Gabriel—but he could see the pain and determination on the small archangel's face.

When Gabriel nodded and closed his eyes, Michael realized he had no choice.

Closing his own eyes, Michael brought his blade across Gabriel's neck and tried to remember another lifetime. He tried to remember the days before the rebellion; back when Lucifer, Tamiel, Gabriel and all of his other siblings could work and live in peace. With his eyes closed like that, it was so easy to see their smiles, their joy, to see the lives that Adonai had denied them.

When Gabriel's head hit the ground and rolled into his foot, Michael was forced to live in the present and forget that happiness.

"About time. For being known as Adonai's sword of justice, you certainly know how to keep company with traitors," Uriel commented, his snide tone enough for Michael's mind to devolve into chaos. Before Uriel could react, Michael's burning blade was already at his throat.

"You will stop there," Michael declared, standing up slowly and brimming with so much fury that the inferno almost leaked out of his skin. Uriel stepped back, his lip twitching in anger, and brought his spear to bear.

"You *dare* raise arms against me? Have you not seen for yourself how we deal with *traitors?*" he asked, but Michael would not back down. He stepped forward and let out his wings, the flames along his crimson blade growing even hotter.

"I am not betraying Adonai, *brother*. You will not speak further because I will kill *you* if you say another *word*. *Nod* if you understand," Michael commanded, causing Uriel to shake with anger. However, he did not speak and just looked up at Adonai, expecting their creator to side with him.

Contrary to what Uriel expected, Adonai smiled in satisfaction.

"It's been so long since you've spoken like that, Mikey, I *missed* it. Not since the rebellion have you been so... I don't know, so *intimidating*," Adonai said, shivering in appreciation. "I should get you to kill more of your brothers if that's the trigger. It's just so much fun to—"

God himself was interrupted as a large explosion rocked Heaven, shaking Adonai's throne room and forcing all of them to stagger. Once he recovered, Adonai snarled and rushed through the air to the double doors of his throne room, throwing them open with his mind and looking into the distance once he stepped past the threshold.

When he realized what had happened, Adonai let out a roar that shook the heavens.

"*What* was *that?*" Uriel asked in surprise, letting out his wings and flying to join Adonai's side, hovering in the air once he got past the doors. Michael squinted as his brother dropped his spear, and he turned to see that Sabrael was walking to the doorway in no hurry. The stout archangel hesitated once he noticed Michael's attention, but shrugged once he regained his poise.

"It was inevitable. I have no need for the spectacle, but you may want to watch," Sabrael said cryptically before continuing on his path. Michael followed after, staying silent, and he watched as Sabrael headed toward his laboratory.

Scowling and remembering just what horrors the angel had created with Adonai's permission, Michael put the archangel out of his mind and joined Uriel in the air, curious as to what had rocked Heaven to its very core.

It was almost impossible to comprehend, and Michael dropped his weapon to his side.

Just past the Gates of Heaven was a towering column of shining energy, pulsing with chaotic energy from the Void. Pouring out of it were the legions of Hell, hundreds and thousands of demons circling the portal and flying around it, giants and monsters spreading out along the ground and likely clamoring for justice and revenge. In a sudden, horrible moment, Michael realized his brother may have been right all along—that these people might actually have a chance to defeat Adonai—but that realization came far too late.

Hell had come to Heaven, and Michael was the archangel at Adonai's side.

CHAPTER 9
TWILIGHT FOR A GOD

"You're a fucking angel?" Cadmus shouted, his entire world falling down around him. Just seconds ago, the kindly old man had been his erstwhile mentor, but the moment six wings spread from his back, Solomon had become the enemy. He was Azrael, the Angelic Reaper—Buné's counterpart—and for all Cadmus knew, he was still loyal to Adonai.

"I'm sorry, Cadmus, truly," Azrael said, his weathered hands folded over his scythe, his wings fanned out behind him. "You are a good man—a *great* man—and deceiving you was regrettable."

"What was the point of it all? Why did you do this? How did you even hide... Are you... are you..." Cadmus tried to ask, but his thoughts were muddled, conflicting feelings clashing against each other.

What made it worse was that Azrael still looked at him the same way, with the same amount of compassion.

"I was sent to mislead you, I was here to delay and keep you from the final battle. Why else would one of Adonai's servants stay by your side for this long year?" Azrael's gaze did not waver even as a gust of wind set his robes fluttering about him.

"So you are an enemy after all," Cimeries interrupted, drawing the angel's attention. "If I strike you down now, Adonai's plans would be thwarted."

"No, Amazon, the plan has already succeeded. I suspect that Niccolo and your other companions have already made it to Heaven, that they are facing our God without the benefit of Hell's greatest hope," he explained before turning back to look at Cadmus. "In any case, Cimeries, you will not strike me down."

"And why are you so certain of this, reaper?"

"Because you know this is *his* fight. You are a noble warrior, and you will not deny Cadmus his righteous vengeance. Need I explain further?" Azrael looked back at her out of the corner of his eye, and Cimeries obliged.

Setting the end of her weapon against the dirt, Cimeries stood back and waited for the start of their duel.

"You won't get away with this, Azrael," Cadmus said, abandoning his confusion and gripping his scythe tighter. "I will kill you, harvest your soul and then I will reunite with Hell's forces before the battle starts."

"I think not, Cadmus. You are very far from that goal." Azrael picked up his scythe and held the blade to his side. "Do you know how long I kept you in that illusion? Do you know how long I kept you caged in those memories of Rome?"

"You—you *what*?" Cadmus shouted, his teeth clattering in anger. "*You* were behind that?"

"Of course. Did you really accept my explanation? That Purgatory itself was testing you? You are not so foolish." A sly smile crept across Azrael's face. "You only wanted to believe that, to believe that your sister had come back to see you once more. Really, you are somewhat easy to manipulate."

"You had no right!" Cadmus shouted, running forward and aiming his scythe at the angel's neck. Almost as if he was dealing with a child, Azrael met the blow with his own weapon and knocked Cadmus back. "Have you no decency?"

"Decency has no place in the life of a reaper. *That* is a lesson I should have taught you, that Buné should have given you a long, long time ago," Azrael said before twirling his scythe and settling back into position. "Death has no friends, no enemies, and there is no dignity in escaping this mortal coil. As the Angelic Reaper, I simply do what I must."

"What you must..." Cadmus muttered, shaking from his fury. "Then as a Horseman of the Apocalypse, so must I."

His emotions were still raging about, memories and prophecies still swirled in his head, and as a result he had forgotten the soul tied to him. Finally calling out to his horse, Cadmus tried to settle himself, to find the focus necessary for stopping time. If anyone could help him, it would be Mercy.

However, Mercy did not respond.

"You cannot reach your horse, can you?"

"What have you done, Azrael?" Cadmus asked, his anger enough to make his eyes flare with blue energy. Chuckling softly, Azrael held still and smiled at the Horseman.

"Only enough to make sure we are alone in this fight. Reaper to reaper, no allies or horses involved. I've also made sure you cannot use your time manipulation, as well," Azrael explained, digging into the soil with his feet.

"How? How are you able to do all this?" Cadmus asked, gritting his teeth and trying to hold himself back from recklessly attacking.

"The angels all had gifts, Cadmus, and I was given more than a few because of my position. Essentially, in order to best destroy my brothers and sisters, I was given the ability to suspend their powers," Azrael said, stalking forward a step at a time. "That applied to Räum and Amon, and it seems that this control affects you, as well. A twist of fortune, really, but I will not deny my feelings of relief."

"This—this is not fair! You have your wings and I..."

"Will do what you can, I understand. I will not judge you for fighting poorly."

Azrael seemingly drew in power from the air around him before flapping his wings and letting out a gust of wind that almost knocked Cadmus off his feet. He had to close his eyes briefly, and when he opened them, Cadmus saw Azrael looking at him with a stone face.

"Now, Cadmus, we will finish this."

Azrael rushed forward, using his wings to propel him even faster than Cadmus had expected. If it had been someone else, Azrael's scythe would have carved through them, the razor-sharp blade making quick work of the spine and ending their life. Unfortunately for Azrael, his enemy was the Horseman of Death.

And he had never seen Cadmus truly angry.

Throwing his scythe against Azrael's blade, Cadmus knocked away the strike and sent blue sparks flying out in a brilliant arc that seemed to hang onto the moment. Then he brought his scythe back and down to the ground at their feet, hoping to bring it up into Azrael's gut. Anticipating this, Azrael jumped into the air and avoided the strike before falling beside the weapon, hoping to carve through Cadmus' shoulder as he did.

Reacting quickly, Cadmus turned his blade to the side and caught the crest of Azrael's scythe before dragging it down, redirecting its momentum so that it sank into the ground and left Azrael open. After twirling his scythe over, Cadmus prepared to cut horizontally through Azrael's midsection, but the angel flapped his wings again and sent Cadmus back along the ground. The Horseman could only dig his heels into the dirt as Azrael recovered his weapon.

"Good, Cadmus, very good. If you ever were to make it to that battlefield, I expect you would have a great harvest," Azrael mused before he stood to his full height. "It is a shame that I must end you now. For all my deception, I do respect you."

"I cannot say the same for you." Cadmus gritted his teeth, his scythe wrapped in tendrils of blue energy beyond his notice. After letting out an appreciative grunt, Azrael crouched into a ready position.

"Perhaps I may be able to persuade you otherwise," he said before his approach, his scythe somehow gleaming in the twilight of Purgatory. As Cadmus prepared for whatever the angel would attempt, Azrael jumped high into the air and then settled into a deadly spin, his own blade creating a whirlwind of destruction that descended on Cadmus.

Hoping to intercept Azrael's body with his scythe, Cadmus held on tight to the handle and waited, anxiety gnawing at his nerves. He had just started to sweep the blade in front of him when Azrael's wings flared out and caught him in the air, halting the angel's momentum and allowing him to fall directly to the ground.

Cadmus cursed as he had already committed to the swing and could not stop, and he knew Azrael was rushing forward, his scythe intent on cutting Cadmus from his left shoulder to his right hip. Breathing in deep and hoping that this would not be the end of his life, Cadmus continued his spin, trying to hit Azrael with his second rotation.

It was too late, he knew it, but then something happened neither of them had expected. A wave of energy followed after his spinning blade and slammed into Azrael, stunning him enough to stop his assault and guard his face with his left arm. After stopping his spin and seeing Azrael still held his eyes closed, Cadmus realized that this would be his only real opportunity.

He leapt forward, ready to carve through his would-be mentor.

Just as Azrael lowered his arm and opened his eyes, he felt a sharp pain in his upper chest. Looking down, he found that Cadmus had sunk his blade into the notch between his first and second ribs, and he only had enough time to look back at the reaper's shining blue eyes before Cadmus pulled down, breaking through Azrael's ribcage and cutting halfway into his ancient heart.

"You—you were still able to use your power against me," Azrael said weakly, his long life finally at an end.

"You will not stop me, Azrael. No one will ever stop me. I will save humanity, I will end this war, and Adonai can do nothing to change that," Cadmus stated calmly, hate flowing through his words along with determination. He was hoping to give fear to the ancient reaper, to make him wish he had never met Cadmus or tried to deceive him.

Instead, Azrael smiled.

"I know, Cadmus. I know. This... this is why we trusted you with so much," Azrael said before gripping the handle of Cadmus' scythe. He somehow held himself up even as blood leaked out of the corner of his mouth. "I am so proud of you."

"What—what are you talking about?" Cadmus was completely stunned by the change in the old reaper's expression. Shaking, his life fading even as he spoke, Azrael swallowed down blood before replying.

"This was your last test. I did not... I did not want to be revealed so soon, but it was necessary. You must stop them all, Cadmus." Azrael rushed through the explanation, his eyes losing focus and his eyelids flickering as he tried to keep them open. "Niccolo—he cannot kill Adonai because... because..."

"Because..." Cadmus repeated under his breath, completely forgetting that he was responsible for this angel's coming death. When Azrael looked back up, the light of his eyes was already fading.

"Adonai's life keeps—keeps this universe safe. It keeps it constant. You must stop him. The world must live, but he must stay alive," Azrael concluded with a wet cough, blood spraying onto the scythe buried in his heart.

"How—what is..." Cadmus muttered. When Azrael placed his hand on his shoulder to steady himself, Cadmus did not notice.

"You can stop him, Cadmus. You must stop him. You must stop Niccolo. You are the one we have been waiting for," Azrael said before weakly lifting his head, his eyelids already heavier. "And I am so sorry I did this to you. I am so sorry I must give you this burden."

"What burden?" Cadmus asked, his thoughts becoming more frantic. When Azrael dropped his head and sagged against his chest,

Cadmus thought it was already over, but then Azrael fell back, standing only because of the weapon halfway through his heart.

"You had to harvest my soul. You had to kill me, to reap me..." Azrael said, his voice barely above a whisper, but he gathered his remaining strength just so Cadmus could hear his last words. "You had to reap me and the thousands of angelic souls I have collected for two million years. I am sorry, Cadmus, but I will force you to abandon your humanity... to best serve it."

Before Cadmus could react, Azrael dragged the Horseman's scythe through the rest of his heart, dead before he hit the ground.

Panic tore through Cadmus' mind; he couldn't comprehend what was happening, but Azrael had seemed sincere. Backing away slowly from the angel's corpse—completely forgetting that Cimeries even existed—Cadmus could only wonder what the reaper had meant. The words seemed familiar and he had no doubt that they made sense to someone, but there was too much information in too little time.

Master, Mercy's voice came to him—his presence more than just welcome—and Cadmus almost thought he would escape from this ordeal without harm. However, before he could respond, wisps of blue energy started to rise out of the wound in Azrael's chest. Breathing in deep and preparing himself for the usual onslaught of memories, Cadmus tried to focus on staying conscious.

That goal was proven impossible once a volcanic burst of energy exploded out of Azrael's body, a column of pure, unrestrained destruction climbing higher than Cadmus could perceive. Lowering his scythe and staring up at the spectacle, Cadmus watched as the energy broke against some sort of invisible ceiling and spread out, banishing the mists and covering every inch of sky for miles before starting to arc back down to the ground. Feeling the pain of thousands of souls breaking against his mind, Cadmus stood by as the column of energy grew wider, new pulses and tendrils of chaotic potential swirling around.

Then, in horror, Cadmus realized that the energy had only stalled in the air for a moment before every little bit of it started heading straight for him.

"Mercy..." he uttered—unaware he said anything at all—and then the torrent of energy had found a new home.

Slamming into him harder than anything he could comprehend, Cadmus was thrown directly into the mindset of thousands of dead angels, most of them dying during the Rebellion. Cadmus could feel their emotions, their pain—experienced every single one of their memories—understood and empathized with all of their decisions, and he lost himself among the first of Adonai's children.

Rising into the air—his consciousness completely detached from the present—Cadmus screamed and light and energy poured into his mouth as Azrael's torturous gift removed him further and further from humanity. His soul was lost—he had become a legion of immortal creatures—and it was difficult to pinpoint just which life belonged to which angel.

Cadmus was literally in a million different points of time as the energy drowned him, forcing him to live as creatures he could not possibly understand. Hope, desire, happiness, despair, every human emotion was denied him; his entire existence had been erased and he could not even choose death. It seemed hopeless that he could ever be sane again, that he could ever be conscious again, but then something miraculous happened.

All of the memories and lives vanished, and Cadmus was in the middle of a white room with no floor, no walls, no ceiling. It was just him and the nothing.

Until Tamiel and Azrael appeared in front of him. With a heavy sigh, Tamiel lifted his hand to the back of his neck and shook his head. Once he was able to make eye contact, he dropped the hand and cleared his throat.

"I don't expect you to understand why we did this," he said, forcing Cadmus to the realization that he knew these two people.

Opening up his mouth to speak, he found that he had forgotten how. He lifted his hand to his jaw and tried to make it move, but no sound came out. Confused, he looked back at Tamiel and tilted his head.

"Shit, we broke him, didn't we?" Tamiel turned to Azrael, who shook his head and folded his hands in front of him.

"He will recover. Cadmus is stronger than any of us. He was able to break through my hold. In time, he will remember himself," Azrael explained, turning back to face Cadmus with a smile filled with sorrow. "Again, I cannot express how sorry I am for this."

"Cad... mus..." he repeated, wondering at the sound of this name. He didn't exactly know what the syllables meant, but it seemed familiar.

"Adonai will be so scared," Tamiel said under his breath as he crossed his arms. "Can you try to remember who you are, Cadmus? You're the Grim Reaper, the Pale Rider, the Horseman of the Apocalypse. *Death* himself. Does *any* of that ring a bell?"

"Death..." Cadmus looked down at his hands and found his fingers curled around the handle of a scythe. "I... am Death."

"Yes, you're... getting there, at least." Tamiel dropped his arms and floated through the sterile nothingness. "You are Cadmus; a doomed Christian in life, a reaper in death. You cannot stay here long."

"Where is here? I don't remember."

"You would not remember, because you have never been *here*. This place is beyond your world, any of the dimensions that you know," Azrael explained, drawing closer and setting his hand on Cadmus' shoulder. "You are here because your soul has been lost in the chaos you inherited from me."

"What did you give me, Azrael?" Cadmus almost shouted, the fury of thousands of angels flowing from his soul and burning through him. He hadn't even known the angel's name. It had been others to speak for him.

"I was the Angelic Reaper, Cadmus. I was the being tasked with collecting the souls of my thousands of siblings who died fighting each other over the fate of humanity. However," Azrael said as he backed away, fearing Cadmus' wrath even after death. "Like all angels, I was limited. I could only hold onto their souls and let their existence latch onto mine. Although their thoughts constantly tore at me, it was a burden I held without complaint."

"You gave me their souls."

"You needed them," Tamiel interrupted, drawing his gaze. "Niccolo—as strong as he is—can't beat Adonai. As soon as I saw what Lucifer had done to that kid, I knew we needed to make a plan of our own. You were always supposed to be the one, Cadmus."

"Every moment I spent with you has been a test, a way to see if you were worthy of the souls I held," Azrael added, offering Cadmus a warm smile. "And every day it became more evident that you would be my successor. You would be the champion humanity would need in these dark days."

"They are your responsibility now," Tamiel declared, staring straight into Cadmus' soul. "When you leave this place, you will be back in Purgatory. It won't even have been enough time for the energy to have been absorbed into your soul. It's going to continue, and it's going to hurt."

"More than you can possibly imagine. However, you must stay strong, you must remain yourself," Azrael urged. "You cannot fail."

"I..." Cadmus said, looking down at his feet and finding nothing underneath. Finally remembering his mission, his friends—the very reason he had risen from Hell in the first place—Cadmus looked back at Azrael and nodded. "I already said that no one will stop me."

"Then follow through with that promise."

No sooner had Azrael said the words than Cadmus was back in his own body, energy swarming around and trying to find its new home in his soul. However, this time he was prepared and clenched his fists, bit his cheek and his tongue, tried to force his eyes closed and bear with the pain; anything to remind himself that he was real, that he was the one in control. All of the energy drowning him was nothing more than the residual presence of thousands of angels, creatures that had been wrapped around their brother's heart like parasites. If he only lasted through this anguish and torture, Cadmus would be able to accomplish his own goals.

Except that when he tried to remember, Cadmus forgot what his own goals really were. Suddenly, all thoughts of rising against Adonai were replaced with millions of desires; chasing after the short angel with the long brown hair and throwing her down in a sunlit meadow, clashing blades against the champion of the arena, flying high above the newly-made mountains of Earth. It all seemed so nice, it all seemed like it was *his* life; as if he could only remember vaguely that it was out of place.

When he lowered his head, it was almost impossible to see beyond the storm of cascading energy surrounding him. Cadmus didn't even know why he tried to look, or where he was, but then he was able to see a small shadow between the ebb and flow of chaos.

Focusing on the shape, Cadmus squinted until a small space appeared in between the waves, and he could finally see there was a woman kneeling there on the ground. Floating forward—not even realizing that he was floating forward—Cadmus got closer to the woman before realizing she was holding onto a stick buried in the ground, only just barely able to keep her feet touching the cracked soil beneath her.

That was when Cadmus realized that it was not Earth beneath her; it was the ground of Purgatory. That was not just a woman; that was Hippolyta, the warrior queen who had taken the name Cimeries once she had fallen to Hell. Trying to remember why he would know this, Cadmus remembered that he had spent centuries knowing Cimeries as an acquaintance before traveling with her for a year on Earth.

Once the thought of traveling on Earth broke into his consciousness, Cadmus remembered that he was not an angel. He was nothing but a human who had gotten himself involved in the plans of fallen angels, devils and gods. There was a war going on, and it was his duty to stop it. Even through the pain and the chaos, Cadmus remembered just who he was.

Shouting in defiance, Cadmus raised his scythe to the heavens and absorbed the remaining maelstrom, harvesting Azrael's gift as the torrent of energy rushed into him.

When Cimeries realized the storm had finally stopped, she opened her eyes and looked at the trail she had left during the incident. Once she climbed to her feet, Cimeries used her pike to steady herself and saw she had been pushed back twenty yards from where she had dug her weapon in the soil. Although she hoped she was not alone, Cimeries looked up to see something she could never have expected.

Standing there triumphant—blue energy leaking out of every pore—was Cadmus. However, this was not the same reaper Cimeries had known all these years. Standing straighter, taller, he looked at her with piercing blue eyes. It was distracting enough that Cimeries almost didn't notice that the reaper's hair had turned white, even the scruff on his face turning to snow. When he spoke, it was almost as if there were dozens of soft voices echoing his words.

"It's me, Cim," Cadmus stated, looking at her, through her, as if he could see her sins and her soul just in those few seconds.

Determined and unafraid, Cimeries slowly approached the Horseman until she was just a few feet away, outside the reach of his scythe.

"And who is *me*?" Cimeries was rewarded with a disgusted look from Cadmus, instantly making an answer unnecessary.

"I'm glad you didn't get hurt after all of that." Cadmus motioned out with his hand and waited for dust to collect into the form of his oldest friend. "Both of you."

"I am not accustomed to being shoved into the corner of someone's mind, Master." Mercy rattled in annoyance, but among the thousands of souls that now dwelled inside his soul, Cadmus could still feel relief from the stallion tethered to him. "The next time you do battle with an archangel, you will not be allowed to attack so recklessly."

"I won't let that happen again, old friend." Cadmus traced his fingers through the fine hair of his horse before turning to face Cimeries.

"Did you need such power, reaper? It will come with consequences." From the flicker in his expression, Cimeries could tell that her words rang more truly than she had thought.

"It already has. What I felt when Beleth summoned all those chimera... that was nothing. What I am now—it's... chaos. Pure, unbridled random chaos and pain. I'm not so entirely sure I'm myself anymore." Cadmus looked to her, and she could swear that she saw an instant of grey before his eyes turned back to their now-permanent blue color. "But this is my burden. This is what I was meant to become. I *am* Death."

"And you think this is enough to stop Adonai?"

"It will. More importantly, it will be enough to stop Niccolo."

"THIS IS NOT the time to turn back, to turn craven," Michael declared, looking out on the thousands of angels that had gathered, all of them covered with gleaming gold and silver armor. Thousands of faces were hidden behind masks that would not protect them once the monsters of Hell came forward to devour them all. Hundreds of them would die within the first clash, before Michael or any of his troops could even hope to beat back the waves of gnashing teeth and wicked blades.

But it would do them no good for Michael to admit it. Instead, he was tasked with deluding these thousands of angels into thinking they could survive against the hell-forged army.

"We will beat them back, my brothers in arms!" Michael let his sword burn brighter to emphasize the statement. "These are merely monsters come to our door, and we will show them the way back!"

They all cheered at what the archangel said, but Michael knew it was hollow. He knew that the only reason the legions of Hell would be killed was if Adonai stepped in and used his infinite might. Out of all the angels present, Michael was one of the few who could even meet the strength of the group he had encountered back at Stonehenge.

Then there was his vanguard, the ten creatures standing by his side in the battle line. Even as they stood just a few feet away from him, determined to stop the onslaught of the demonic army, Michael knew they were no friends. Looking to his right, he found Camilla, that poor woman destined to fight a man she used to love. Seeing her standing there resolute—crimson and gold armor wrapped tightly around her frame—Michael was reminded of his more majestic sisters, those who already given up their lives in the pursuit of justice.

Turning and raising his sword and seeing the towering portal to Hell on the other side of the gates, Michael tried to muster his own courage. These fools standing behind him had no concept of what they would face; they thought they were fighting a just war. They had no idea that the fallen angels and men and women who had gathered on the other side of those gates were just as noble, just as resolute, perhaps just as or more than deserving of achieving victory. Gabriel had seen it that way, and in his last moments had shaken Michael's faith.

But it would do his troops no good if Michael confessed before the final battle.

"They stand there, massed, poised to strike at the heart of Heaven. They think themselves righteous!" Michael's voice carried above the din and shouts of the army at his back, piercing through their cheers.

"They would see the world burn if they would be the masters of it. They fight against God himself! They must not be allowed to trespass further into our home! They must not be allowed to desecrate this beautiful utopia," Michael hesitated, knowing just how far from a utopia Heaven really was. "Today, we fight for Heaven, for our home, for our almighty God, and we *will* win!"

Thousands of angels cheered, yelled, hooped and hollered, beat their shields, stamped their feet, did everything an army should. They all held hope to follow Adonai to his new home, to beat back these hellish invaders and be rewarded with an eternity of a new and better paradise.

Michael knew that was all a lie. He knew that maybe one or two souls might find their way to a new world—if that—and he knew none of this army would be considered. If anybody was to follow Adonai, it was likely Uriel and Sabrael, the most sadistic and cruel of all his siblings.

But it would do Michael's army no good to know how terrible their God could be.

"You are troubled, archangel."

Camilla had interrupted his thoughts, and Michael turned to look at the beautiful woman. There was so much pain in that voice, in those eyes, but he could see her measured stance, every thought, action and word considered. This was a subject, a servant of Sabrael and Adonai, no matter who she had been before.

"Are you not convinced by your own words?" she asked, patient during his moment of scrutiny.

"I was never one for public speaking." Michael looked back at the legion of monsters setting up tents and creating infantry lines. They were better organized than his own army of flying weaklings. "It would take a better tongue than mine to make me believe such pretty lies."

"And if I were to say those words, Michael, would you believe them?" A light smile was on Camilla's face, and it was almost enough to make Michael forget the horror he had seen in Sabrael's laboratory. "I do believe we will win this fight."

"I am certain we will win, Camilla, but it is not because of this army. Even the weakest of Hell's legions will cut through them."

"Then you believe it is up to Adonai's champions to turn the tide," she assumed, crossing her arms as she stared out at the creatures beyond their reach. Michael wondered if she was looking for Niccolo, trying to find him now so she could chase him down during the battle. "You think it will only be because of you and your vanguard that Heaven will win this day."

"No, I don't think any of us will matter when the day is over," Michael admitted, joining her in watching the forces of Hell prepare for battle. "I think we will win only because we have a god on our side."

"A god?" a deep voice rumbled from his other side, and Michael looked up to see a towering individual about ten feet high, entirely covered in brown and viridian plate mail but with no weapon in sight. He had been another one of Sabrael's experiments, but even Michael did not know what powers lay dormant inside his body. The rumbling of his voice as he continued reinforced that mystery. "You speak as if there is more than one."

"That would be blasphemy, Gregorious," Camilla responded, leaning forward so she could look at the giant directly. "Michael is the Burning Sword, the general of our army. He would not stoop so low as to entertain *other* gods."

"Why not?" Michael said as he crossed his arms and shrugged. "I've seen other ones."

"You *what?*" Camilla asked in shock, and Michael turned to her with a raised eyebrow. "Other *gods?*"

"You might have the misfortune of meeting one. I saw the Leviathan at Stonehenge, and I am fairly certain he would have made it through Purgatory." Michael didn't bother looking at either member of his vanguard. "Adonai is not the only one with such power. He is just the most powerful that has ever existed in this dimension."

"I don't... I don't know what to say," Camilla said, looking down in doubt. Although Michael immediately wanted to take back what he had said and give her back that confidence, he realized it was better this way. It was cruel to take away hope, but he knew the dangers of misplaced faith.

Gabriel had taught him that.

"Then say nothing," Michael said quietly, ending the

conversation and forcing Camilla to retreat from his side. The giant nearby regarded him with a fair amount of hostility for a moment—Michael almost thought he would have to deal with whatever terror Gregorious was hiding beneath all that armor—but then he likewise retreated.

Looking down the line of his vanguard, Michael knew that every one of them was a monster; a human corrupted by the faith they had held for Adonai. He knew that every one of them had likely been a good person, devoted to justice and righteousness, but they did not have the right perspective. They did not know they were serving a cruel and insane deity. Until recently, Michael had also been deprived of that perspective.

And as he looked out at the massing army, Michael knew that perspective would also do them no good.

"Asmodeus, that doesn't make any *sense*."

Astaroth almost spat out the words as they leaned across the battle plans. Buer had drawn them up back in the Infernal Library, but he had not anticipated the introduction of the Nephilim into their ranks, so Astaroth was trying to find a place suited for them in the battle lines. However, Asmodeus was not helping. The Fallen king had taken on more aspects of the dragon since they had failed to stop Azazel and Beleth, and he was almost clattering around in his intricate, emerald-green armor.

"And why the fuck not?" Asmodeus asked, his eyes burning at the intense question. "If we make each end heavy with Nephilim, we could push through and then flank their front ranks, surrounding them and taking them out quickly. Then we can get our heavy hitters to focus on the soldiers that *actually* matter." He slammed his scaled hand against the table so hard that it caused a nearby crate to fall over and spill scrolls across their makeshift headquarters.

"Do you even know what we're up against?" Astaroth replied

with a scoff. "First off, this is the end of the world to those bastards, so getting surrounded is only going to make them fight harder. Second, you *child*, Adonai is all about sacrificing his units. I wouldn't be surprised if he would want us to surround his men just so he could use them as suicide bombers. It would only make us *vulnerable*."

"You're fucking kidding, right?" Asmodeus stood up and crossed his arms before turning to face Niccolo, who had been trying to stay out of the argument. "Nico, weigh in on this."

"Oh, like he would fucking know what he's talking about..." After a loud sigh, Astaroth waved his hand as a sign of permission. "Screw it. He might actually have some sense."

"Why do you think it'd be better to have them scattered around?" Niccolo earned Astaroth's gaze before supplying his own answer. "Because they might get in their own way if they're fighting next to each other?"

"Yes, actually. Didn't think you were paying attention," Astaroth replied before turning back to Asmodeus. "His way, we'd be wasting all of their strength on their flanks when we could be pushing through and breaking their lines completely."

"That's fucking bullshit, they wouldn't—"

"You weren't fucking *there*, Asmodeus. You and Amdusias weren't even born when we fought against the Nephilim. Trust me, they'll trip over themselves more likely than not." Astaroth did not mean offense, but Asmodeus' eyes turned from green to red at the mention of his lost brother, the scales on his hands doing the same.

"That makes no difference. And don't you fucking dare speak his name."

"Amdusias? I'll say it as many times as I want, kid. You think you're the only one who misses your twin? He was cold as fucking ice, for sure, but he was my brother, too," Astaroth said, but it seemed to make no difference to Asmodeus. He had stepped around the table and was ready to throw a haymaker into Astaroth's face before he was interrupted by a tired voice.

"Niccolo," Barbas said, causing the leper to turn around and face him. The old Fallen saw a glimpse of that boy who had fell to the Pestilence Quarter, the same archer who had wavered and suffered for years before finally becoming a Horseman. Even when Niccolo recovered himself and regained his posture as a new devil, Barbas still saw the boy who had been practically family.

"You don't have to fight, Barbas, if that's what this is about," Niccolo said as he turned back to the battle plans, but neither Astaroth nor Asmodeus made moves to save him from Barbas.

"It's not about the fight, Niccolo," Buné broke into the conversation, taking his place at Barbas' side. Once Niccolo recognized his tone, he knew they were not concerned with the Nephilim's placement in the battle lines. As if on cue, Eligos and Ronové joined their brothers, the giant warrior standing next to the squat, fat, scholar.

"This is about your actions in Purgatory," Ronové added.

Crossing his arms, Niccolo stared hard at these leaders of Dis, and awaited their judgment.

"Did you kill him, Nico?" Barbas asked, his voice faltering with emotion for their lost Horseman. "Did you kill Cadmus?"

"I... maybe."

All of them flinched as if struck. Eligos roared as he slammed his fist into the ground, a spiked ball and chain forming in his hand.

"You fucking idiot! Do you know what this means? Do you know what you've done?"

"I *know*, Eligos!" Niccolo shouted back, his wings forming unintentionally. "Lucifer gave me his memories. I know what Cadmus was to you! Just a way to get back at Adonai!"

"Niccolo," Buné's voice came suddenly and quietly. When Niccolo faced Buné's silver gaze, he saw the cold stare of a grieving parent. "You look at me and say that again."

"It's... not what I meant," Niccolo said, looking down at his feet to avoid their staring. "I just know what your plan was. I saw you coming up with it in his bedroom, of all places. I know *Cadmus* was supposed to be the leader of this army."

"And you killed him for that?" Disgust was evident in Eligos' tone.

At the accusation, Niccolo stared at the brute, walking forward until he could poke at his chest with a diseased finger.

"I didn't *kill* him, even if... even if I tried a little bit. He pushed me and I pushed back. He just happened to have the abyss behind him."

"He fell into *the abyss*?" Barbas asked, causing Niccolo to look back at him, and he immediately wished he had not. The disappointment on the old demon's face was enough for Niccolo to regret every decision he had made in the last year. Although Niccolo had thought he would be able to take it, Barbas still had a special place in his heart.

"Along with Solomon, the reaper who guided us on Earth and through Purgatory," Niccolo explained, at which point Astaroth cleared his throat.

"That wasn't Solomon, Niccolo," he said with a grudge. "That was Azrael, the Angelic Reaper."

"That was... That was *who*? Why didn't you *say* anything?" Niccolo had completely forgotten about the others in the room. When Astaroth stood up and shrugged, the viper on his arm flicked its tongue in mild disinterest.

"Hate to break it to you, Nico, but we couldn't trust you to know there was an angel in our midst. Only reason *I* didn't kill him is because Paimon told me that he was part of this whole mess," Astaroth said before turning his attention back to the battle plans. "If Tamiel trusted him, let Azrael *reap* him, then I didn't really have an option."

"You're kidding me..." Niccolo muttered. Astaroth rolled up the plans on the table and stood up straight, his armor clinking against chainmail as he looked down on his replacement devil.

"No, I'm not, but let's not forget how much you fucked up. Cadmus is gone, maybe dead, and instead of *two* almost-gods, we only have *one. You.* And I don't particularly trust that you can go up against Adonai." Astaroth watched as Niccolo bristled with anger. "But it's time, and we can't wait for Cadmus to appear out of nowhere. I'm going to go on ahead and get these plans to Zagan, Ymir and the others. We don't have the luxury of arguing like this."

"I didn't ask for you to do that, I didn't ask for this," Niccolo said, but Astaroth shook his head and stared at him with Lucifer's eyes.

"Yes, you did, Nico. You wanted an Apocalypse, and now you have one. And since you're our last chance, it's my job to make sure you get to Adonai. Now," he said, pushing past Niccolo and pointing at the mass of creatures beyond their headquarters, hundreds upon thousands of demons milling about and waiting for some sign. "You need to go out there, convince them you're the Devil, and start this battle. At least do *that* right."

Before Niccolo could argue against him, Astaroth was already flying away with Asmodeus, leaving him alone with four angry fallen angels. Turning back to them, Niccolo tried to think up a suitable excuse, but then he saw the pain on Barbas' face and the anguish hiding behind Buné's eyes.

"I'm sorry. I didn't really want to kill him," Niccolo admitted, clenching his fists and remembering his friend. It seemed like it had been a week since Cadmus had fallen off that cliff, and all the anger he had held for the reaper had evaporated in that time. Now all he felt was sorrow—the same sorrow these angels were feeling—but he was also responsible for it.

"Cadmus is strong, Niccolo." Buné's voice brought him out of his thoughts, but once Niccolo lifted his head to look at him, he found no sympathy. "It's possible that he would have survived the abyss, and Azrael could have helped him do that."

"However," he continued, his voice wavering before he swallowed down his emotion and forced himself to be analytical. "Since we cannot anticipate if he will ever join us, if he is even... alive, we have to deal with the current situation. *You* are here. *You* are Lucifer's heir. If anybody is to lead this army, it has to be you, even if it's just as a symbol. Your goal is to destroy Adonai, but you *must* be the hero, the champion that humanity deserves."

"I'm... I am, Buné. I know it. I know that this is what I'm supposed to—"

"Don't you dare tell me what you're supposed to be, Niccolo. I've been manipulating your life for centuries and you know it," Buné snapped, glaring hard at him. "You went off the plan and Cadmus suffered for it. I lost *my* heir, and it's because of you. Can you imagine what I'm feeling right now?"

"Buné—" Barbas started, but the armored demon put out a hand before he could say another word.

"I am doing this for *them*, Nico. I am doing this for my brothers and sisters, for your race, for this planet, but do not think I forgive you for what you have done. You have my support and guidance, but you have lost my sympathy. Do this, lead your people, and you may regain my respect, but that is all," he explained before turning and walking away. "To think... I used to think of you as a nephew."

"Buné," Niccolo muttered, but it was obvious that the conversation was over. Giving one last grunt of disapproval, Eligos turned and walked after his armored brother before Ronové joined him, leaving Niccolo alone with Barbas. Realizing that he could not face the old Fallen directly, Niccolo bit his lip and stared at the demons gathered below their small hill.

"He pushed me, Barbas." Niccolo had tried to excuse himself, but he could tell from Barbas' silence that it was a poor one. "He wouldn't let us know the prophecies he was getting from Räum and Amon."

"And that was enough to kill him, Nico?" he asked, and at once, Niccolo's argument fell apart.

"No, it wasn't. I'm—I've lost myself, old man." Niccolo turned and saw Barbas' face filled with compassion and pain. "This last year, I thought I was in control... I've been letting myself go further and further down this path and I—I can't stop now."

"This path..." Barbas said, setting his aged hand on Niccolo's shoulder. "Is this the path you think will let you overcome Adonai?"

"Yes." Niccolo paused, remembering the Leviathan's words, the pleasure from its fiery eyes. He remembered the power he had momentarily harnessed when he fought the Nephilim, and wondered at its source. "I'm losing my humanity the further I go, but I'm—I'm more powerful for it."

"Are you sure it's power? You sure it's because you're letting go of your humanity at all?" Barbas asked, and Niccolo collapsed into his mentor, holding his arms around the frail body as hard as he could. It surprised Barbas, but he let an arm wrap around his young student in return.

"I don't know," Niccolo admitted, his voice squeaking slightly, and Barbas was overcome with emotion. This man had possibly killed his best friend—possibly ruined all of their plans for destroying their god and winning this apocalypse—but Barbas could not help but feel for the poor boy. His entire life had been pain, and this was just the latest agony added to his story.

"I believe in you, Nico," Barbas said softly, knowing Niccolo would hear it. When the leper drew back and looked down at him, Barbas realized he had to do this. Even if it was wrong, even if he didn't believe a word coming out of his mouth, Barbas would not make the boy feel this much pain.

"If this is your path, if you believe that it will help you, you have to do it. We will grieve for Cadmus, since it was a mistake. And since there's nothing more to do for it, we'll just have to believe in you. For me, well, for me, it's not a change at all. I've always believed in you."

"Barbas, what are you—"

"The day you fell, Nico. The day you fell wreathed in fire and falling out of the sky, crashing into my courtyard even as that twisted arm broke and turned into something even more hideous," Barbas said, looking at the gnarled appendage on Niccolo's left side. "I knew you were something special, kid. You've proven it every day since I met you. And if this is the way you've chosen, I know you're just going to prove everybody wrong all over again."

"We planned on Cadmus because we could." Barbas raised his hands and placed them on either side of Niccolo's face. "You were always more than a plan. That's why I believe in you. That's why Scratch believed in you."

"That's why," Barbas said before turning and pointing at the demons and giants surrounding them, "that's why all of *them* believe in you."

"We're hurting, Nico. We love Cadmus and so did you, but don't let that change anything about what you have to do. Adonai has to pay, and this is the army that's going to do it." Barbas turned back to face Niccolo and set his knobby staff in front of him. "So you go out there, you lead them. You tell them there is hope. You tell them that you're the Devil and that you're going to avenge Lucifer. You tell them whatever you need to say."

"Barbas, I'm..."

"You're Niccolo. That's all it is. Now get," Barbas said before slapping his staff against Niccolo's shin and causing him to jump backward. "Use those fancy wings from Scratch and fly to the head of this army. Tell them we're going to war. Don't waste more time on an old man."

Niccolo opened his mouth to argue, but he could tell that Barbas was on the verge of tears, and a single syllable out of Niccolo's mouth would cause them to come pouring out. Closing his mouth and nodding, Niccolo jumped into the air and left Barbas to his misery and pain, knowing that the old Fallen did not want a witness if or when he collapsed into grief. Niccolo ached for him, wanted to spend more time with the mentor who had raised him from the depths, but he knew that Barbas had already used up all his courage.

Flying over his army, Niccolo actually marveled at the size of it. Even in his wildest dreams, he couldn't have expected the thousands of souls that had come to his aid, so many of them victims of the Black Death he and Cadmus had created. Momentarily, Niccolo felt guilty for it, but then he realized that this had been the purpose all along. These people had been sacrificed so Niccolo could have this chance against Adonai and his legions of devoted and misguided followers.

Soaring higher in the light of Heaven, Niccolo resolved to create a better future, to be a better devil for these people. They had suffered for him, died for him, and all of the demons who had risen from Hell were here for one purpose; to defend humanity and defy a cruel tyrant. They deserved a better leader, a shining, radiant example of righteousness. They deserved the kind of leader who could make Lucifer proud.

Letting out a flare of magnificent light and forming Lux and Morningstar in his hands, Niccolo silently promised to his lost father that he would try.

"Everyone!" he shouted, descending from the clouds just in front of the first line of infantrymen. He must have been a glorious sight for all of those men—most of them covered in black lesions from Niccolo's plague—but Niccolo was more focused on what he could say to these people. "My name is Niccolo!"

"We know who you are," Paimon's voice came from behind the lines, and he watched as the crowd parted for her. She walked straight up to him, annoyance evident from her scowl. "What's all this?"

"Paimon," he said, his tongue failing him, but she seemed to read his mind. As soon as Paimon saw his expression, heard the shift in his tone, she furrowed her brow and looked at him with concern.

"Niccolo, what's wrong?" she asked, her voice much softer as she looked him over, but then Niccolo regained himself.

"Everything," Niccolo whispered, licking his lips before looking at the army in front of him. "But I'm trying to make up for it. I need —I need to be someone they can believe in, even if I don't."

"Niccolo, just... just what happened?"

"Too much; not enough. But *they* need me, and it's time. This is it, Paimon," Niccolo said, and he could tell that she understood.

"So there's no turning back, huh?"

"There never was, sweetie," he said, borrowing her usual term of endearment. "I'm sorry for what I did to you, what Scratch did to you. You deserved so much better than us."

"Of course, I did, but I could say the same for you." Paimon laughed off the statement, but Niccolo's smile disappeared once she looked back at him. "Hey, don't give me that."

"Stronger and better, and I can't tell you how awful I feel for mistreating you. Promise me you'll try to live through this," Niccolo said, and Paimon almost thought he was joking. However, there was no glint of mischief in his eye, no slight tugging at the corner of his lips. Abandoning her smile, Paimon nodded at him.

"Only if you do the same."

"*I* can't."

"Then we're at an impasse, *sweetie*." Paimon crossed her arms and tried to smile, but she couldn't keep up the act for long. "So this is how it ends?"

"Seems like. When you walk away from here and let me say my speech, the battle starts. I actually become the Devil instead of just saying it. I'll be waging a war against God."

"It's our war, Nico." Paimon was half-offended, but she abandoned her disdain and shook her head. "Even if you fail, it's more than anybody has done since Lucifer started the first rebellion."

"I'll try not to fail."

"You better, Nico. You better," Paimon said before turning and walking away, trying to hide the tears in her eyes. As much as she wanted to hate him for what he had done, she couldn't bring herself to do it. He was still the same sweet kid haunted by Lucifer's memories; he always would be. If she had the chance to remember anything after this battle, this was how she would choose to remember the Horseman of Pestilence.

However, as Niccolo looked out on his army, he was no longer the Horseman of Pestilence; he was the leader of Hell's legions.

"Men and women, angels and demons, Nephilim and monsters,"

he shouted in three harmonious voices, rising into the air so the masses could see him and his shining weapons. "We are here today to avenge Lucifer, to fight a cruel tyrant who thinks himself a god! We are here to take back our lives and our independence!

"But more importantly, we are fighting for humanity! We are fighting for the people who are *not* on this battlefield! We are fighting for the people yet to come! If Adonai wins this battle, if we are not victorious, the world will end. If we fail, there will be no home to go back to!

"Many of us will die! Hundreds, thousands of us will die! And I tell you now that every death will be *worth* it. Our backs are against the wall, and this is our last chance to take back our world! We will defy Heaven, we will defy Adonai, and in doing so we will achieve something that no one thought possible. We will become the leaders of our own *destiny*!

"There is every possibility that we will fall," Niccolo faltered, losing steam in his own speech, but then he looked out on the creatures staring up at him. He saw fear, of course; he saw apprehension, but among so many others he saw something amazing.

He saw hope. So many of the people gathered below him looked up to him as a real champion, as a general worth following. At that moment, Niccolo knew there was no retreat, no *reason* for retreat. With their hope holding up his spirits, Niccolo turned and pointed Lux at the capitol of Heaven, Adonai's army waiting for them beyond the gate.

"There is every possibility that we will fall, but there is *also* a possibility where we succeed! And imagine if we did!" he exclaimed, a smile on his ruined face. "Imagine a future where humanity is no longer enslaved by this tyrant of a god who forces his subjects to fight each other for his amusement. Imagine a world where we are not forced to live in the dirt while a monster lives in the clouds...

"Imagine that world, my friends. Imagine that world as you fight. Imagine the world we will leave behind, even if we die today,"

Niccolo said as the smile disappeared, as he furrowed his brow and breathed in deep.

"Today, we fight for humanity. Today, we fight for our fallen friends, and the families we left behind. Today is the beginning of the Apocalypse!" he declared before swinging his blade and sending an arc of radiant light toward the Gates of Heaven. When it met the shining door, it exploded and blew the gates apart, leaving no obstacle between the two armies.

"Today, we wage war against God."

CHAPTER 10
THE BEST LAID PLANS

Seere carved through the midsection of a foolish angel, sweeping his axe through the stomach and out the side in a spray of brilliant gore, but Fury was galloping too fast for him to stop and appreciate his work.

Instead, Seere brought around his hammer to the other side and crushed another angel's skull where he stood on the ground. There was blood and carnage everywhere; every four or five strides, the Horseman ended another life.

After what he had gone through in Purgatory, it was quite cathartic.

"C'mon, you cowards! Give me more than this!" He crashed through a woman's shoulder before Fury trampled her body, another corpse left in the clouds behind them.

"Do you truly expect them to give you a challenge?"

The apathetic voice came from beside him, and Seere looked to his left to see a scrawny man with long, scraggly hair on top of a withered horse. In his left hand was a circular hoplon shield, and in his right was a spear currently embedded in another angel.

"By the gods... Diogenes? I never expected you to actually make it up here."

Even distracted, Seere still slammed his hammer into the chest of another faceless angel and sent his body crashing through a crowd of other soldiers, and after taking out his spear and urging his horse to stop, the Horseman of Famine looked back at him with mild interest.

"I must fulfill my role in this play. At the very least, it breaks up the monotony," Diogenes said while his horse ran forward and he plunged his spear through the helmet of another angel. "However, I will admit they don't provide much of a challenge."

"Not yet, it seems, but there's a lot of them. Can't say I don't mind the bloodshed," Seere replied before turning his attention on another angel flying down from above. Throwing his weapon forward, it turned end over end before the axe head sunk into the angel's groin, at which point Seere jumped up to meet him.

After riding the warrior down, Seere crushed the man's head with his heel and looked back at his horse in disapproval.

"Come on, then. You should have been here to catch me," he chided his horse as he pointed at the ground, and Seere could tell Fury wasn't pleased even before he spoke.

"If you stop doing idiotic things in the middle of battle, maybe I *would* be," Fury screamed before galloping straight at his rider, and Seere grinned in anticipation. He jumped and then claimed his seat in the saddle as the horse ran beneath him, grabbing onto the reins with his left hand as they looked for more enemies.

"He will never stop his pursuit of idiocy, Fury. Seere does not exactly care for tactics," Diogenes said before he used his shield to bash another angel out of the air and then slammed his spear into his opponent's heart, withdrawing it in a spray of blood. "If he is able to get up close and personal, he will. It is the way of brutes."

"Oh, don't you talk down to me, you bastard," Seere said as he wagged his finger at the philosopher. "My way gets me through the day."

"Don't misunderstand me. You abide your nature, which should be commended."

Diogenes then leapt off his horse and ran forward on bare feet, plunging his spear through the hearts of five men and women before a single one of them fell. Once they were all dead or dying, smoke billowed out from beneath Diogenes until it solidified into his emaciated horse.

"If only the rest of the Horsemen had followed your example, Seere, we would not be half our number."

"Hey, they did what they needed to do." Seere supported the handle of his weapon on his shoulder as Fury turned to face the other Horseman. "We'll just pick up the slack. It's not like we're anything to scoff at."

"Really?" Niccolo yelled above them, and Seere looked up to find the leper descending from the sky, four angelic corpses crashing into the ground before he landed. "Because you didn't even notice you were about to get attacked by these guys."

"I believe we would have been fine," Diogenes commented. "Every member of the Heavenly Host seems to be made out of paper."

"Adonai sent out the weakest first, to gauge our strength. There are stronger out there," Niccolo said, noticing that Diogenes was scowling at him. Assuming it had something to do with Cadmus, Niccolo turned to the other Horseman. "Don't do anything stupid, Seere. It's not going to bring back anyone."

"Nico. *Buddy.*" Seere growled as he leaned down, his face inches away from Niccolo's maimed skin. "*Go away.* Diogenes and I will be just fine, and you better not bring up *anyone* again."

"Seere—"

"Go! I'm serious," Seere said as he sat back up in his saddle. "You're not a Horseman anymore, so you don't owe us anything. You have better things to do than slum it with us."

"It's not *slumming*, Seere." Niccolo glowered. "I was one of you."

"And now you're *not*. Now go before *we* fight. I can't just *stop* on the last battlefield, Nico," Seere said with a wink as he tapped his heels against Fury's flanks, causing the crimson horse to scream in anger. Before Niccolo could say anything else, Fury carried his rider out of earshot.

"He's alive, Niccolo," Diogenes said, almost too soft to hear over the din of battle, but Niccolo whipped around as if he had yelled.

"*Who's* alive?"

"Cadmus, obviously. Who else would I speak about?" Diogenes asked, not bothering to wait for Niccolo to recover from the statement. "If Mercy was dead, Despair would already know."

"Wait, but Fury..."

"Is fire and noise. Despair listens, and she hears everything. The white horse is alive, and he would not suffer life without his master. Do not fret for the Pale Rider," Diogenes explained before turning his horse to follow after Seere. "If Plague was still alive, he could have told you the same thing."

"If Plague..." Niccolo started, but Despair was already running to join her brother and carrying Diogenes with her. Niccolo was left with a revelation he had not expected to hear, and he struggled to realize what it meant.

However, that realization was delayed by the echoes of Diogenes' comment about Plague, tearing away the scar that had been left by the horse's absence. He once again felt the pain of Plague's soul being ripped away from him, of being left alone.

Seere and Diogenes were right, after all. He was no longer a Horseman.

His mind swamped by grief, Niccolo launched himself into the air and then rushed toward the capitol, flying past the battle lines and sweeping Lux across his body to destroy columns of the enemy. These troops were all too weak to face him directly or indirectly, and he could feel the power of their weak souls joining his. Still, the pain of Plague's loss tore away at him, and it was all he could do to keep flying, to keep moving even as tears flowed out of both healthy and ruined eyes. When the grief became too much, he closed his eyes and drifted through the air.

And was immediately rewarded with a great blow that slammed him into the ground.

"Niccolo," a feminine voice snarled at him, and the leper had a difficult time reconciling that name, that voice and that tone.

Pushing himself out of the crater he had made on the cobblestone street, Niccolo wavered from side to side before he mustered enough strength to sit up on his knees. Looking ahead of him, he saw a flickering shadow retreat into a small woman fifteen yards away, but something seemed very familiar about this angel in red and gold armor.

When she stood up, Niccolo saw olive skin and dark hair, and as she lifted her head, Niccolo recognized her eyes, her cheekbones, and the lips he had kissed so many times. In this last war, Niccolo looked down this street in Heaven and saw a miracle. After two centuries, they were finally reunited.

"Camilla..." he uttered, a smile momentarily appearing on his face as he looked at the woman he loved. However, he could see the hate in her eyes. She walked forward, taking in and letting out harsh breaths, and Niccolo realized Camilla was not happy to see him. As he watched the shadows massing around her hands, as dark lines spread over her face and along her arms, Niccolo realized that this was not a reunion.

It was just another cruel joke.

MICHAEL FELL out of the sky, burning corpses surrounding him, and he realized that he had not missed that smell. There were at least six demons who had died rushing at him—intent on making the archangel their next meal—and those six demons would be no more than ash within a moment. In the heat of battle, Michael had forgotten the nature of his enemies, but he wondered how many of them had been fallen angels or noble humans who deserved to live.

Then a giant hand slammed him out of the air, forcing him into the ground and creating a wake of marble as his body crashed through Heaven.

Cursing, Michael pushed off with one hand and became airborne, using his wings to stabilize himself so he could face the Nephilim. It was certainly one of the bigger giants—his fist was about the size of Michael's entire body—and his face was disfigured by an unsightly tumor. In preparation for his next brutality, Michael let himself drop to the ground and drew his sword behind him, readying his body so he could burst straight through the Nephilim's chest. When he pushed off the ground and flapped his wings, Michael thought he would destroy this creature without difficulty.

Of course, he had not expected a radiant fist to slam into his face when he was only halfway through the air.

Tumbling head over heels, Michael was dazed for a moment before he righted himself and looked for his new enemy, but another golden fist slammed into his gut before their shin met his temple and made Michael's body crash back to the ground.

He had almost recovered before someone landed beneath him and threw another fist into his back, forcing him to go sprawling through the air again.

Deciding that he had had enough of these games, Michael threw himself into a spin with his blade and created a maelstrom of fire he hoped would deter any further strikes. Once he was able to stop his spin and gather his breath, Michael realized he had done the right thing, but then he also saw the angel hovering in the air just ten yards from him.

"I should have known it was you," Michael said, watching Astaroth for any further attacks. Instead, Lucifer's twin shook his head and clenched his fists.

"You're lucky I gave you warning shots. With the way that Nephilim was distracting you, I could have killed you, Mike."

The archangel swung his blade across his body, letting out a short wave of flames.

"Why *didn't* you? After all these years, after two rebellions, why didn't you just *end it*?" Michael shouted, the rage from the first betrayal rising up from his memories. "You and Lucifer gave up *paradise* for them."

"And we would do it again, and you can see that. I *know* you can see that," Astaroth said, mimicking Michael's sweeping motion and letting out a wave of energy. "Gabriel, your *favorite*, came over to our side. You know that, right?"

"I know that," Michael admitted, looking down as he shook with anger. "I was the one who had to execute him."

"Y—you killed him?" Astaroth's voice was shrill enough to cause Michael to look back at him. He could see the pain on his face and hear his breaths coming in halting motions. "You killed *Gabe*?"

"I didn't have a choice..."

"*You killed Gabriel?*" Waves of energy flowed away from Astaroth's body, the snake on his arm hissing and spitting along with his master. "How *could* you? He was our *brother*, Mike!"

"You are my brother, too, and we will be forced to kill each other," Michael responded, but he had lost resolve by the time he saw the pain in Astaroth's eyes.

"He was *Gabriel*, Michael!" Just that simple statement was already a more potent argument. "He was the *innocent one*! He was the one we all looked out for! He was our *little brother*!"

"Asta—"

"He looked *up* to you, Michael! Gabriel *worshipped* you! You were the good one, the best one, and Gabriel was our little brother!" Astaroth shouted, his rage enough that he blasted streams of energy out with every yell. Michael watched as Astaroth gave into his fury, unafraid.

Unafraid because this was how *Michael* was supposed to react to Gabriel's death. Instead of being part of his murder and execution, he should have been side by side with Astaroth in grief.

He had no defense for anything Astaroth would say.

"Did he suffer?"

The question was barely above a whisper, but Michael heard it all the same. Looking at Astaroth, it seemed as if he had already been beaten to his last breath, but Michael knew this was merely a lull in his chaos. It would only be moments before Astaroth was all rage and justice once more.

"No," Michael replied, his sword arm at his side. "One blow. He said that he... that it was better that it was me. He told me that... I would do the right thing eventually."

"And what is the right thing, Michael?" Cold murder seeped through Astaroth's words, and Michael knew the conversation was over.

Lifting his head and bringing up his sword, Michael prepared himself as Astaroth rushed forward, but then something hit him hard from his left and he tore through the air, much faster than he had ever flown. Once he hit the ground, Michael, *the* Archangel, fell unconscious.

When he woke back up, Michael threw his arms forward and pushed himself directly into the air, holding his sword to his side and ready for any enemy.

However, there was no enemy intent on killing him; they were all busy killing each other. There were dozens of them—demons and angels alike—and it was more than just chaos. Astaroth himself was now fighting a legion on his own and would not be able to follow, and the way things stood, Michael would never be able to reunite with any of his vanguard. Before he turned around, Michael thought he was relatively safe.

When he did turn around, Michael finally noticed that Eligos and Buné were waiting for him, their weapons drawn. On Eligos' hands were two massive gauntlets shaped like the mouths of terrors from the Void; in Buné's grip was a long, silver broadsword. Each of those weapons, especially Eligos' shifting weapon, had claimed hundreds of lives during the rebellion.

"How is this going to play out?" Michael asked, holding his burning blade in both hands as he waited for the fallen angels to strike. Instead of rushing forward, Eligos and Buné circled around in opposite directions, intent on flanking the archangel.

"You will likely kill us. I never could match you in swordplay," Buné commented, his gaze unwavering. Instead of agreeing, Eligos let out a guffaw before slamming against the ground with both of his gauntlets.

"The reaper speaks for himself. Me? I think I'll be tearing your head off soon."

"In any case, we have to try. We have to do *something* for our brother's memory," Buné added, and Michael made eye contact with him. After slightly lowering his sword, Michael breathed in deep.

"You know about Gabriel," he said, met with a roar from Eligos.

"Of course, we know, you burning *bastard*! He was supposed to check in with Buné every few days, and they were talking to each other when that other angel barged in. It makes sense, even if it's goddamn *awful*," Eligos said, flexing his muscles and squatting into a crouched position.

"I didn't have a choice."

It sounded hollow even to Michael.

"You always had a choice, brother," Buné replied. "You just never had any imagination."

"I'm sorry it has to end this way." Michael sighed, but he brought up his brand and tried to anticipate their attacks.

"We're not," Eligos said before leaping forward, his right arm held behind him and ready to slam into Michael.

The archangel brought his weapon to the side, ready to lop off Eligos' hand, but then the gauntlet shifted and transformed into a ball and chain now poised to wrap around Michael's blade. As soon as the chain wrapped around once, Michael pulled forward just as the ball was about to slam into his head. That made Eligos lurch forward—off balance—and Michael used the opportunity to slash at the giant's exposed neck.

However, that attempt was met with the clash of silver as Buné entered the fray, saving his brother and then landing on Eligos' shoulder before redirecting his momentum so he could dive down with another attack. Leaping away from the attack and sliding his weapon out of the chain, Michael flapped his wings to gain even more distance from his brothers.

"That was nice, Buné," Michael said as he adopted a forward stance, but the reaper was not amused. He just stared analytically at his angelic brother as Eligos picked himself up and created a heavy lance from the remnants of the ball and chain.

"You and I both know that I am not *nice*. Prepare yourself."

"Out of respect for you, I will." Michael swept his blade in a diagonal arc from left to right, creating a wake of fire heading toward the fallen angels. After jumping high into the air and using his wings to redirect his momentum to the right, Michael fell on their left side and rushed forward, trying to use the flames to mask his movement.

It seemed that Buné had noticed the feint and had turned to face him, but Eligos always had a terrible time adapting to anything more than pure martial skill. Sweeping his blade again, Michael sent a wall of fire at the brute that slammed into his back, crackling skin and forcing Eligos to cry out in pain. Buné jumped forward to slash at Michael, but the archangel parried the blow before kicking behind him, sending Buné sprawling.

With a roar, Eligos threw the lance in his hand, but Michael evaded with a twist of his torso, and it only just missed impaling Buné behind him. Stunned by the revelation, Eligos was almost unable to react as Michael rushed forward, but the giant Fallen created a sword from the hilt that remained in his hand and met Michael's blade head on.

Michael did not feel pride in this situation—he knew that Eligos was a much better warrior than this—but his shifting weapon could not match the direct strength of Michael's blade and both of them knew it. Using his colossal might, Michael forced his blade through Eligos' sword and shattered the weapon, sending splinters of steel into the air before tearing into the fallen angel's chest, cutting through his heart and then out his other side.

"I'm sorry, Eligos." True sorrow colored Michael's apology, but the warrior's face was content.

"I'm not. What's that... say about you?" Eligos asked as he fell to his knees. He stalled there for a moment, basking in the light of heaven before his body crumpled to the ground. Michael grieved for him—Eligos had always been a good brother—but he could not ignore reality; he was not alone.

Turning to face Buné, Michael found the fallen angel standing there with his silver blade, eyes cold and resolute.

"You can retreat, Buné. I won't stop you," Michael said, but the flicker of Buné's eyelids was all the answer he needed. "Of course. That was inappropriate. I did not mean to offend."

"What were Gabriel's last words to you, Michael?" Buné asked, shocking him out of the moment and back to Adonai's throne room. At the time, he had been more focused on the bruises and broken bones, but in his memories, Gabriel's determined face dominated his vision. Michael was still recalling the memory when he felt a sharp pain in his side.

Looking down, he saw that Buné's sword had pierced through his right side, doing negligible damage to a body that would eventually heal.

Seeing that it had all been a ruse—a way for Buné to distract him —Michael was instantly angry. He would have chopped off the reaper's head right then and there if he had not seen the cause of Buné's horrible aim.

Buried in his back was the spear of another angel, his brother-in-arms still floating a few feet above the ground.

"Are you alright, sir?"

Michael was instantly filled with an even greater fury. This nameless individual had killed a fallen angel who was worth a thousand of these armored souls. Although Michael was about to avenge his fallen brother, Buné slumped down to the ground, his breathing already staggered. Michael's anger abandoned him, and he fell down to kneel with his brother, forgetting the two million years they had been apart. At this moment, he could only feel sorrow and grief for his dying sibling.

"Leave us," Michael said, and his tone was enough for the angel to leap into the air after pulling out his spear from Buné's back. The sloppy retrieval was enough for the reaper to cry out in pain, but he grabbed Michael's shoulder and pulled himself up so he could look the archangel in the eye.

"Why? Why would you attack me like that?" Michael asked in shock, but then he saw something even more surprising. Looking up at him with half-shut eyes, Buné smiled.

"If anybody was going to kill me... I wanted it to be you," he said, chuckling softly. "Same with Eligos."

"This was... this was assisted suicide?" Michael asked, indignant and horrified at the same time. Buné shook his head at that, but he lost his strength soon afterward, forcing Michael to take his head into his lap.

"Well, yes and... no. If we won, that probably would have been better, but once you got Eligos, I knew it was over. Figured—figured it would be the best way to go."

"But why?"

"It's the *end*, Michael. Eligos and I... our role in this is over. We trained our Horsemen, and they are doing us proud. Well... they did us proud," Buné trailed off, turning his head to look back to the portal to Purgatory. "I hope—I... he..."

"Don't speak," Michael urged, but Buné shook his head weakly.

"What did Gabriel say, Michael?" Buné closed his eyes, but Michael tried to shake him out of it.

"Stop asking that. It doesn't matter." Sorrow overcame Michael, and it was almost too much for him to keep his composure. Michael waited for a moment before realizing that his brother was not responding, so he shook him again. "Stay with me, Buné."

Then Michael realized his brother wasn't breathing.

"Buné?" Michael asked, shaking him even harder, but his brother's eyes remained closed. "Buné! Buné, don't you dare! Don't you dare die because some bastard stabbed you in the back. Don't you dare!"

Michael shook his brother's body every time he shouted, but it had no effect. No matter what he did, Michael's brother did not respond. After a moment of fervent shaking and pleading, Michael realized the truth

Buné would never ask him about Gabriel's last words ever again.

Michael took a moment to lay Buné's head on the ground before setting his hands over his chest, trying to make it seem like he was at rest. He had not been prepared to grieve for *these* lost brothers and sisters. Michael had thought that if he was on the righteous side, on Adonai's side, it would hurt less. It was supposed to hurt less if he was doing the right thing. And perhaps it was just Buné's taunt, but Gabriel's last words came back to Michael in that moment.

Knowing that he was not doing the right thing anymore, Michael collapsed to his knees and wept for his fallen brothers.

It was all he could do for them now.

"CAMILLA, WHAT HAPPENED TO YOU?"

Niccolo struggled to his feet, ignoring whatever physical pain he felt at that moment. Seeing the hatred in Camilla's eyes was too much to fully comprehend. The last he had seen her, she had still felt something for him.

Before she even spoke a word, Niccolo wished that she had forgotten him instead of this.

"*You*, Nico. *You* happened to me. You could have just stayed away, sinned against God without dragging me into it." She snarled, her armor clinking as she shook uncontrollably and dark tendrils of corruption swirled around her arms. "Instead, you ruined my life."

"My love—"

"*You ruined my life!*" The shadows on Camilla's arms flared out, faces appearing in the darkness. "You stole my husband from me, stole my ability to live! I was forced to become a nun, Niccolo! I had no options after what you did to me!"

"Camilla, stop! It wasn't supposed to be like that! I wasn't supposed to die and leave you alone!" Niccolo abandoned his weapons and his wings as he pleaded with the woman, but she drew back and scoffed at him.

"You weren't supposed to *die*, Nico? You were *always* supposed to die! The corruption in your heart, your defiance against *God* gave you that monstrous arm! The moment you turned against him was the moment you started the clock that would end your life. And I? I would *never* have gone with you," Camilla stated, her tone frigid.

"Giovanni may have killed you, but even if you had lived through your duel, I would never have stooped so low as to spend my life with a *leper*."

"I won that duel. That *snake* did not beat me," he growled back. It had been her distraction that had allowed Giovanni the chance to stab him in the back, and her words were enough to fill him with resentment.

"He lived and you died, Niccolo. Just because you were a coward and used poison does not mean you were the victor." Camilla spat before rising to her full height and starting forward, dark masses collecting at the end of her fists.

"I am not a coward!" Niccolo's wings flared out in pure reaction. "I lived for four years covered in that blight, and every day I thought about returning to you, beating back the world and giving you the life you deserved!"

"The life I deserved, Nico?" Camilla asked, setting her hand on her hip and flourishing with the other. "Do you see the life you gave me? After you died and left me alone and without social status, I gave up every earthly possession. I suffered for thirty long years before God took pity on me and let me die."

"Took pity on you? Adonai does not have pity!" Niccolo shouted back, but he was met with bitter laughter.

"Oh, but he *does*. Because I was given *this* chance, Niccolo Vespucci. He gave me this chance to tear out your cowardly heart, to end your life and take your future." Camilla' skin stretched tighter as she grew and expanded, the metal of her armor creaking as she changed. "In these final days, I was given the chance to return to you the pain you gave me."

"What have they done to you?" Niccolo asked, watching as the love of his life changed in front of him. He could tell that it would only be moments before he saw the terror waiting for him.

"Sabrael—he has..." she struggled to say, her teeth growing longer, the skin around her lips and eyes cracking and starting to breathe, "Sabrael has given me power, Niccolo. When I am... done with... you, you will regret..."

"I already regret. Don't make me kill you," Niccolo urged softly, his arms hanging by his sides as he waited for Sabrael's cruelty. Before she let herself fall apart, Camilla looked at him once more, a twisted smile on her scarred face.

"Don't make me laugh. It makes my face hurt," she said before screaming and arching backward, Sabrael's magic wreaking havoc on her body.

Her armor cracked open to reveal a body covered in those same black lines, but that was nothing compared to the dark masses flowing out of her body, leaving bloody, gaping wounds. Her limbs bent and broke, reforming with the support of those dark shadows, and her arms extended to three times their normal size, ending with vicious, dark claws formed of blood, shadow and bone. Four tendrils of dark shadows burst out of her midsection and four from the small of her back, supporting her like a spider even as her own blood poured around her.

Niccolo could have recovered from that—the Leviathan was just as much a monster—but her transformation was not complete. As she howled up into the sky, her bottom jaw split along her chin and flared out, rows of teeth lining the inside of her mouth. Niccolo dropped Lux as he watched her horrifying turn; her hair growing longer, the gaping wounds left by the dark masses now lined with teeth, puckering and gasping in air. By the time Sabrael's magic ran its course, there was almost nothing left of the woman he had loved.

Even her eyes were different, clouded by cataracts, and Niccolo realized she had truly been blinded by her anger.

"Do you see what you've done to me, *my love*?" Camilla spat out, her upper torso only barely supported by the rest of her massive body. "This is what the love of Niccolo Vespucci da Firenze does to people. All that you touch—all that you care about becomes corrupt!"

"I did not do this to you," Niccolo muttered as he broke eye contact. He knew there was no other option now; there was no way to save this woman. "This is just another of Adonai's crimes. This is just another cruelty."

"*You* would know cruelty, Niccolo. You have so much *experience*!" Camilla lunged forward with two dagger sharp claws, her every limb propelling her forward and digging up cobblestones in the process. Niccolo was prepared for the attack and dived out of the way so he could slash through the air and unleash an arc of energy, hoping to cut through her dark legs.

However, Camilla had anticipated the attack and leapt over the energy, her legs easily strong enough to send her high into the air. Niccolo could only watch as her giant, twisted body seemed to float upward, becoming little more than a silhouette before crashing back down to the ground with deadly appendages aimed at Niccolo. Realizing his mistake at the last second, Niccolo rolled forward— narrowly avoiding five bone claws that landed on both sides of him —and tried to run out from under her body.

Unfortunately, he didn't anticipate the coil of dark energy that burst out of her stomach and wrapped around him so Camilla could bring him up and dangle him in front of her terrible face.

"You're making this too easy, Niccolo. I was watching you,

making sure you didn't have any surprises for me." Her many teeth gnashed together as she spoke, and the smile on her face was something out of a nightmare. "Where is *that* Devil, I wonder? Are you keeping that monster at bay because you're fighting someone you care about?"

"No," Niccolo uttered, the dark tendril squeezing him tighter and making speech difficult, "I just didn't anticipate this... power."

"It is nice, isn't it? Sabrael gave this to me, and I could not be happier with it," Camilla said as another tendril rose into the air, gasping mouths writhing in the darkness. "Souls at my command; souls I can use to make Adonai's enemies suffer."

"Do you even... hear yourself?" Niccolo struggled to make eye contact with Camilla, looking over her body in disgust. "What kind of god would imprison souls just for you to have a weapon?"

"They are guilty souls, sinners all," she claimed, but Niccolo laughed at the absurdity.

"I doubt that. Tell me, Camilla, when would he get those guilty souls? This is the first time any souls from Hell have ever come to Heaven, and Adonai hasn't left his capitol in millions of years. Where *exactly* did he get those souls?"

"Before they fell, obviously," Camilla argued, but he could tell from her slackening grip that she hadn't fully considered how Sabrael had given these powers.

"Please, Adonai didn't even know about Hell when Lucifer led the Fallen there. Hell is for the defiant. Those souls you're using right now," Niccolo said, leaning forward even as she held him in her dark grip, "they are people who made it to Heaven only to be given pain and torture, to be turned into a monster's weapon."

"You liar, you treacherous, conniving, yo—you..." Camilla stammered, her fury and confusion blending together and causing her to squeeze Niccolo tighter.

"Listen to their voices and their screams, Camilla. Really *listen*," Niccolo said, and tears formed in her eyes, flowing down cheeks marred by black lines. For a moment, he could tell that guilt attacked her from all sides, but then she turned back to him in anger.

"I don't need to listen to *you*." She sneered before bringing up one of her dark legs and stabbing at Niccolo, intending to skewer him.

Feeling the tendril slacken just a little, Niccolo used that opportunity to summon his considerable strength and let out a harmonious shout, light bursting out and banishing the dark tendril around his body. When Camilla's claw came down at him, Niccolo parried it with his shield before dropping down and slashing across his body, cutting off the closest of Camilla's legs.

She screamed from the pain, but Niccolo looked up to see that she was already attacking him with her other front leg. Refusing to back down, Niccolo threw his blade forward and met the claw head on, cracking through the bone and splitting the leg in two.

"I will *tear you apart*," Camilla promised as he jumped away with her remaining legs, and Niccolo's heart dropped once he saw what she intended. More blood and darkness poured out her, wrapping around her wounded leg and mending it, and her other leg was soon reformed in the same way. Crouching down with all of her legs and preparing to lunge forward, Camilla cackled at him. "Just look, *my love*. You cannot cut any part of me that I cannot repair."

"You ask *me* to look? Look at *yourself*!" Niccolo shouted back, pointing at her with a demonic finger. "You were a good person—the best woman I ever knew—and look what your god and archangel have done to you! Gaping mouths lined with horrible teeth, tendrils of darkness made out of imprisoned, tortured souls, and I *know* you're in pain! You never wanted to kill *anybody*!"

"I will *not* listen to you!" Camilla crawled forward on powerful legs, reaching Niccolo within a few seconds. She swiped three of her legs at him from both directions; Niccolo knocked away one with his shield, countered the other with Lux, and then leapt over the one aimed at his feet. She thrust two more claws at him while he was in midair, but Niccolo flapped his wings and avoided the strikes before flying up and over her next attack, twisting his body so he could slice off the four legs that had sprouted out of her back.

From her screams and the outpouring of blood, Niccolo knew his assault was successful, but he could already see her trying to reform the limbs. With sadness, he could see that she was having difficulty —the flow of her blood was weak already—and Niccolo realized that Sabrael had never intended for Camilla to kill him. This was all just another mind game.

"Camilla..." Once he landed and walked forward, Niccolo watched as the giant terror spun around to greet him, her jaw flapping out to the sides as she glared at him. "I can end this pain."

"You can end... nothing," she protested, hacking up darkness from her throat. "I will end *you!*"

Camilla screamed again, sending out twin tendrils of darkness that Niccolo banished with a flare from his shield. When that failed, Camilla ran forward and tried to slam her front arms onto Niccolo's body, but he merely sidestepped the attack and then stomped on the closest arm with his boot, shattering the bone.

"I hurt you, Camilla. I know, and I'm sorry," Niccolo said as she rose two of her left legs to attack him, but he sent out a slash of light which severed them both at the elbow joint. "I never wanted to cause you pain; I never meant for any of this. I love you, and my entire life on Earth was *for* you."

"Niccolo, you—you..." she tried to say, but her voice faltered as more darkness poured out of the gaping wounds on her torso, outside of her control. As Niccolo had predicted, there was no more blood to support them. "My legs, my darkness..."

"Is *mine*. You're right, Camilla, I *did* corrupt you," Niccolo admitted as he advanced, knocking away another attack from her right with his shield.

With that last effort, Camilla collapsed in front of him, her upper body supported by what was left of her arms. She looked up at him in defiance, like she wanted to tear out his heart, but Niccolo knelt down in front of her so they could see eye to eye.

"You ruined my life, Niccolo," Camilla said again, but the tears in her eyes gave the statement an all-new meaning. "I fell in love with you and it ruined my life. When you left Firenze, you were supposed to stay gone," her voice squeaked out. "I could have been at peace if you had never come back to fight Giovanni. I could have been... I could have been content knowing you were still out there. I loved you, Niccolo, and then I had to see you die."

"I'm sorry, my love. I was trying to save you."

"Then save me, Nico. Save me from all of this." Camilla lifted her right hand to Niccolo's face, all violence abandoned. "We were supposed to be together, but fate drove us apart. I'm actually—I'm actually glad... I'm glad that at the end of the world, that we met once more. It's... poetic, if you think about it."

"Camilla..." Niccolo had to swallow back his pain, tears streaming down his face. Moments ago, this woman had fully intended to kill him. Now, as she looked up at him—even with those lines covering her face and her lower jaw still split down the middle —Niccolo was not afraid. All he could see was the merchant's daughter from Firenze, the woman he had lived for, had died for, and whose entire life had been destroyed by him.

"You saved me once," Niccolo said, lifting her chin with his diseased thumb. "It's my turn to finally save you." Then he lowered his head and kissed her on her ruined, blackened lips.

She met that kiss with equal warmth, knowing that it would be their last embrace, and for a moment they were once again children with their whole lives in front of them. However, the moment could not last forever, and so Niccolo ended their embrace and withdrew his lips, staring into Camilla's eyes as they both wept.

With his human hand wreathed in green energy, Niccolo reached into her chest and grabbed her twisted heart, crushing it without hesitation. And even though she had been prepared for it, Camilla still screamed right into his face, the pain and misery so much greater in that last moment. Niccolo did her the courtesy of staying with her, holding her with his other hand as her spirit departed from her body, but he could not help being overwhelmed by emotion and pain.

When her scream ended, when he could see the cataracts depart and her dark eyes glass over, Niccolo almost did not react at all. He laid down her body, closed her open eyelids with his hands, and then stepped back to look at the monster Sabrael had created.

This had been the woman he had loved, placed in his path just to cause him pain. Niccolo had failed her, and that pain was second only to her loss. Sabrael had done this, manipulated her into throwing her life away and becoming a twisted horror, and Niccolo could only assume it was because it amused the sadistic archangel. And as he looked back at the palace beyond the streets of the capitol, knowing that Adonai and Sabrael were waiting for him, Niccolo promised that they would pay for those crimes.

If nothing else, they would pay for Camilla's pain.

CHAPTER 11
A WAR FOR MONSTERS

With a flick of his wrist, Yeshua sent four more angels to oblivion. Once the fireball burned itself out, leaving charred corpses inside golden armor, Yeshua looked out at the rest of the battlefield and found death and destruction as far as he could see. From his vantage point in the air, Yeshua couldn't even tell friend from foe. The only obvious allies were the Nephilim raging about the blood-stained fields and the Leviathan ravaging the battle lines.

Dropping down to half his altitude, Yeshua flew among the angelic and demonic troops and tried to find some familiar face, some friend in all the chaos. Every few yards, he would see someone who may have visited Astaroth on occasion, but then they would be swarmed by angels. Too often Yeshua was coming to the aid of dead soldiers, but he made sure to avenge them, at the very least.

In comparison, the souls that Niccolo had sent down to Hell with his black plague seemed to be holding their own, banding together in groups of two or three and destroying the angelic soldiers who came against them. However, he did not know these people, and as a result they were just as foreign as the giants they had recruited from Purgatory.

As he flew on alone, Yeshua remembered Judas and how, if he had not doubted his old friend, they would still be together.

Yeshua's heart was pulled in different directions as he recalled his grief, but he mustered his resolve and looked around for his next enemy. The whole point of this war—the whole reason he was still fighting—was for his friend's honor, to save humanity, and giving into grief and becoming distracted would help no one. Once Yeshua saw a group of angels circling a wounded Nephilim, he sent out a ring of flames above them that burned their wings and sent them crashing to the ground.

"Not too shabby, Yeshua!" William's voice came from below, and Yeshua stopped flying long enough to look around for his companion.

He found William on a small outcropping fending off a pair of wingless angels, sending out arrows that glanced off their armor, were knocked away, or were avoided entirely. Grunting loud enough for Yeshua to hear, William set his bow onto his back and retrieved his blades before leaping between the warriors, forcing his short sword into the biggest angel's armpit and then rolling forward so he could wait for the other angel's attack.

Before the warrior could advance toward William, Yeshua created a pillar of flames that turned the angel into a molten pile of silver and ash.

"I will never get used to that," William said as he picked himself up and Yeshua dropped down to join him. "The smell alone..."

"I don't enjoy it myself," Yeshua replied, keeping flames coiled around his arms and legs. "I'm sure they're in quite a bit of pain, but... it's a quick death. It's the only mercy I can afford."

"Better than they would give you, I guess," William said before looking around the battlefield. "Have you seen any of the others? I lost everybody within the first few minutes since, you know, you're all ridiculously fast or can *fly*."

"You've been alone this entire time?" Yeshua asked, and William frowned as if insulted.

"I can handle myself. Well," he paused as he looked at Yeshua's handiwork, "most of the time anyway."

"There's no shame in asking for help."

"Oh, man, to hear that coming from you. A couple days ago you would have gagged on those words," William said with a laugh, and instantly Yeshua felt guilty for how he had treated this companion.

However, before he could say any words to that effect, a large slab of marble landed a few yards away from them and sent shards of rock clattering along the ground. Turning to face their new enemy, William and Yeshua watched as the clouds departed and they saw a huge man covered in brown and green armor.

"I gagged *for* him, demon," the brute said as he drew closer, the green of his armor reflecting light from the floating suns above them. "The battlefield is no place for levity or laughter."

"I'm human, you bastard!" William crouched down slightly, ready to dive out of the way of the brute's next attack. "Sometimes we have to laugh just to keep ourselves from crying!"

"Then as I crush your arms and legs, laugh all you want."

Then the giant set his fists against the ground, the impact enough to shake William and Yeshua where they stood. Once they were able to recover, they saw vines starting to grow and cling to the joints in the brute's armor.

"You do not know who you are facing, angel," Yeshua declared as he let fire wrap around every inch of his body, covering him in blazing armor. "If you leave now, I will not end your life."

"You have no place to threaten Gregorious, *False Messiah*," another voice shouted out, and they looked up just in time to see a creature descend from the sky, at least twelve feet tall.

Once it landed gracefully, Yeshua saw what appeared to be an elongated woman, twice as tall but disproportionate, with ice and frost covering her torso and the ends of her legs and arms. Pure white hair fell down to her hips and—as she grinned—most of that hair started to wrap around the length of her pale, blue arms.

"Gregorious, huh?" William asked as he stared up at the woman. "And just who are you?"

"You want to know the name of the witch who kills you, human?" she asked, chuckling softly as her hair collected at the end of her hands, creating claws she reinforced with ice. "How amusing. You may call me Freyja, if you wish."

"Oh, like *Hell* you're a goddess." William sneered, shaking his head before turning to look at Yeshua. "What is it with you people taking the names of mythological creatures?"

"Who's to say I'm not?" the woman asked, but William scoffed and pointed at the wounded Nephilim still kneeling a hundred yards away.

"Please, that giant over there is more legendary than you could ever be, and I don't even know his *name*. And—really—you have control over ice, which would be more impressive if Yeshua wasn't entirely wrapped in *fire*," William said as he lazily motioned toward his companion. "I'm not scared."

"You should be," she replied, her tone as frigid as her the ice surrounding her, but William rolled his eyes and pointed his long sword at her.

"No! No, this isn't going to be one of those stupid moments! I'm *not* fucking scared. I've seen horrors and bullshit in the last week that would drive a normal person *crazy*, and a tall woman who looks like she spent too much time in a blizzard *isn't* going to intimidate me!"

"You're a fun one," a whisper answered him, and blood spewed out of the ground between them before collecting into a large puddle. William and Yeshua watched the puddle retreat as a figure rose from the center, solidifying into a blood-covered human after just a moment, his arms crossed in front of him. When the creature opened his black eyes and looked up at them, a twisted grin on his face, William found that he could not speak.

"Why must you antagonize the angels trying to kill us?" Yeshua asked, and the bloody figure spread out his arms and cackled into the air, bat wings stretching out from his back as blood flowed back into his body. When he breathed in deep and looked at William and Yeshua, he was just a pale, bald man with pronounced features, form-fitting black and red clothing covering everything but his head.

"We are no angels," the newcomer replied, stretching long fingers that cracked as he curled them. "Our lord Sabrael gave us so much more than that."

"Vladimir is correct," Freyja added, stepping forward and somehow banishing the heat Yeshua had created. "We are not the pitiful creatures you have massacred so far. We are as gods to them."

"Well, I guess that's good," William said, mustering misplaced confidence. "Because I have one part of the Holy Trinity standing next to me."

"Hah, that creature pales in comparison to Adonai, just as *you*," Gregorious said, finally looking up from his position, "pale in comparison to us. Prepare yourselves."

As soon as the giant finished the statement, the ground they were standing on shook violently, and Yeshua realized that William would not be able to stay there without harm. Banishing his flames for the moment and collecting his companion, Yeshua flew a short distance through the air before turning back to watch Gregorious and whatever he was attempting. What he saw was enough for Yeshua to realize they were outmatched.

Gregorious' armor seemed to explode out from his body, but Yeshua watched as green vines connected the various pieces before they went too far, and it was only a few moments before Yeshua realized what power was hiding inside that armor. Gregorious had already been massive—considering his human nature—but Sabrael's experiments had transformed his soul into something even more immense.

By the time the encroaching vines and growth connected the boulder-sized pieces of his armor, Gregorious was standing at sixty feet tall and looking down at Yeshua and the human held in his arms.

"Do you understand now?" he rumbled, flashes of green coming from the eye sockets of his helmet. "You are an insect against titans, and I could crush *you* as easily as you would crush a cockroach."

"And I would steal the warmth from your bones," Freyja said from their left.

"Only after I take the blood from their veins," Vladimir added from the other side, staying aloft with his powerful batwings. As they floated there surrounded by these angelic monsters, Yeshua almost gave into despair. With creatures this powerful fighting against them, even his flames would not be enough. He couldn't even consider what William would be able to do in these circumstances.

However, before Yeshua could give up hope, Gregorious staggered to his side with a shout of surprise, the wounded Nephilim taking his place as he shoved the angelic golem to the ground. Yeshua was about to say something to the Nephilim—the wounds covering his body would end his life soon even if Gregorious did not crush him—but William grabbed his shoulder and stole Yeshua's focus.

"Hey, throw me at the bloody whatever he is," William said, only serving to confuse his companion. With a loud sigh, William pushed hard on Yeshua's shoulder before turning back to face the blood-covered angel. "Never mind, I'll do it myself."

With a great push of his legs—which caused Phenex to dip a few feet in the air—William jumped off his friend and flew toward Vladimir, who was so shocked by the action that he didn't even try to avoid it. His blades at the ready, William slammed into him and they began wrestling in mid-air, dragging the creature down with him to the ground. After a second of marveling at William, Yeshua realized he had his own opponent to face and he turned back to Freyja, who was still glowering.

"I can still take your life without the aid of my fellow titans."

Ice built around her like an exoskeleton, but Yeshua was not

348

scared of the witch. Letting flames cover him once more, Yeshua let his rage solidify and become even more intense.

"You forget your place," he said, fire pouring out of his back and becoming wings ten feet across. It was purely ornamental, but he could see the fear in the angel's eyes. "You are just human—no matter what Sabrael did to you—and I will show you the anger of the righteous."

With a snarl, Freyja sent out a trio of ice spears aimed at Yeshua's midsection. Throwing out a tendril of flames, Yeshua expected to melt them easily, but the missiles continued on their path and Yeshua was forced to roll to the side in order to avoid them.

"They are colder than your flames can counter, *False Messiah*," she repeated the taunt, forming five more icicles above her head before she sent them forward with a lazy gesture of her hand. "I was created to destroy you."

"How terrible that must be," Yeshua replied before sending out concentrated fireballs at each spear, causing each to wither away before evaporating completely. As he continued, Yeshua could see the frustration on her long face. "That you were given the wrong tools to do so."

"That was only the first attack!" Freyja shouted as she flew toward him, her claws poised to tear him apart.

Yeshua waited for her approach, wondering what other tricks she had in store, and when she swiped at him, he merely dropped a few feet and looked up to see that he had been right. Some of the hair coiled around her arms had become loose and bristled with icy spikes, spikes that would have ensnared him if he had not been careful.

"If that was the second, I should be just fine," Yeshua gloated before letting out an inferno that stretched for twenty yards in every direction. Although the woman was not destroyed—she had created an icy shield in front of her—Yeshua could tell that Freyja was losing confidence.

"You will be destroyed, *Messiah*. This is your punishment for claiming yourself an equal to God!"

Yeshua recalled the friends who had helped him come this far; his fellow revolutionaries who would become his apostles, Judas and their hellish companions. He wondered for an instant what they might think of him, if they would say the same thing as this ice witch. However, when he looked down to see William struggling in his fight against the vampire, Yeshua realized that none of that mattered.

"I never claimed to be a god," Yeshua said as he turned back to face the witch still staggered by his last attack. "I was only a shepherd."

"You will die the same," Freyja spat out, but Yeshua only smiled at the remark.

"I hope so." Wreathed in flames, Yeshua rushed forward and slammed his fist against her chest—through the ice armor she had tried to form in that last moment—and he looked into her eyes with undeserved compassion. "Be at peace, Freyja."

Before she could bring up her claws to tear out his eyes, Yeshua covered his fist in flames hotter than any of the lava in Hell, more intense than the miniature suns floating around them, and then pushed his hand through the woman's torso.

While Freyja screamed, Yeshua let the flames grow around his arm and burned the ice witch from the inside, her skin crackling and burning away in moments. Soon enough, the woman could not stay airborne and fell away from Yeshua, a massive hole in the center of her torso. As Freyja fell, her body further covered itself in ice, and once she hit the ground, her body shattered into pieces.

Even considering the disdain and hatred she felt for him, Yeshua still felt sorrow eating away at him for her death. None of this was necessary; none of this needed to happen. All of this pain and misery on this battlefield was caused by a cruel god who wanted nothing more than to see bloodshed and death in the most spectacular fashion. Resolving that he would help end all of it,

Yeshua turned his attention to William and his opponent far below him.

Vladimir was suffering from a few wounds, it seemed, but William was far worse for wear. Open gashes ran along his arms and his chest and—from what Yeshua could tell—droplets of William's lifeblood flowed through the air and into the monster's mouth. Breathing in deep, Yeshua dove toward the two combatants, determined to save his friend, but he could not make it to William's side.

Before he was twenty yards from the pair, something slammed into him from above and he crashed into the solid clouds below.

Turning over even as he felt all of that pain, Yeshua realized his mistake. Towering above him was Gregorious, the giant creature completely unharmed after his duel with the Nephilim. Already knowing the result, Yeshua looked to the creature anyway and found that Gregorious had crushed its skull to a pulp. Feeling pain for that death as well, Yeshua choked down the bile in his throat and looked at the golem looming over him.

"You may have killed the witch, but I am more than enough to destroy you, Jesus. To think, I used to worship you, thinking you were one of Heaven's elite," Gregorious rumbled, leaning down so his shadow completely covered Yeshua. "Then I find out that you became just another demon."

"Maybe I used to be," Yeshua said as he picked himself up, aches and pains all over his body. He could tell that his pinky was broken, but that was of no concern; the giant intended to break much more than that. "But I'm not lying about that anymore."

"I don't care if you lie. Your life is what I want," Gregorious said as he slowly lowered his right hand, but something small darted through the air before landing in his eye socket, causing the giant to stand back up with a roar of pain.

"Still not scared... you bastard!" William shouted, and Yeshua turned to see the man was barely conscious and weakly holding his bow. He was rewarded for the attack by Vladimir jumping onto his back and then sinking his teeth into his neck, at which point Yeshua lost all control.

Forgetting the giant still intending to crush him, Yeshua tore through the air and closed the fifty yards between him and his friend within just a few seconds. The vampiric angel was only just able to stop slurping blood out of his victim and liquefy as Yeshua threw a blazing fist into the blood Vladimir left behind. He reformed fifteen feet away with a chuckle, wiping William's blood off his lips with the back of his hand.

"Don't you know it's rude to interrupt someone in the middle of a meal?" Vladimir asked with a malevolent grin, and Yeshua had to force himself to stay where he was standing. His pupils disappeared as rage flowed through his veins, and Yeshua lifted his arm in front of William in a gesture of protection.

"He is not a *meal*. William is my friend and you will not hurt him again," Yeshua declared. The vampire shook his head and laughed once more, setting the heel of his palm against his forehead.

"You humans... always looking for excuses to die. What makes you think you can destroy the likes of me? Every time you strike me, I only need to turn to blood," Vladimir stated, bowing deeply before making eye contact with Yeshua. "Your *friend* knows this well, and his blood has already been added to mine."

"Be careful..." William said weakly from the ground, and Yeshua looked down to see the defiant human pallid and curled in on himself. "Every time I stabbed him, he just... laughed."

"That's right, Jesus, what makes you think you can destroy a monster like me?" Vladimir said as he liquefied into a puddle and rushed toward them, rising out of the ground at the last second to strike at Yeshua with sharp claws. Yeshua evaded the strike and countered with a wall of flames, but Vladimir dropped away and only his head was visible from another puddle. "See? I only have to wait for you to make a mistake."

"It is unfortunate for you, then," Yeshua said as he let flames build in his palms, looking down at the angelic monster in fury. "That you are too stupid to realize your own."

"Oh, and what is my mistake?" Vladimir said, still smiling as half his torso rose from the ground.

"Blood is made out of water, you idiot," Yeshua said before launching the spheres of flames he had been building in his hands. Realizing what Yeshua intended, Vladimir retreated in his puddle and avoided the blast, but Yeshua had already created a circle of flames that trapped Vladimir within a ten-foot radius. Solidifying completely and letting out his bat wings, Vladimir sneered at his opponent.

"And I can *fly*! Who's the idiot now?" the vampire asked as he jumped into the air, but William replied with a weak laugh.

"It's still you."

Then Yeshua raised his arms and let the circle of flames climb higher and faster than Vladimir could outrun. Tapering the flames together a hundred feet in the air, Yeshua could see the shadow of Vladimir attempting to find some escape, but he was truly captured now. Letting the flames grow even more intense, Yeshua collapsed the blazing tower into a true inferno to mar the heavens, and Vladimir's resulting shriek echoed above the din of combat surrounding them.

"I should have... taken the giant."

William's joke obviously came with a struggle, so Yeshua knelt down to look over the friend at his feet. Yeshua was about to offer words of sympathy when another boulder crashed into the ground just a few feet away from them, forcing him to turn his back to the shrapnel so he could shield William from harm. Even that was not enough—the force of the impact caused both of them to go tumbling along the ground—but Yeshua was soon on his feet and standing between William and the behemoth bearing down on them.

"You would have had even worse chances, human," Gregorious said, his every footstep shaking the heavens as that boulder was dragged back to rejoin his arm. Although Gregorious was still far from defeated, Yeshua could see that one of his green eyes had stopped shining. "I admit, I did not expect you to hit me with such a small stick—let alone take my eye—but I will have it back soon enough."

"There is no need for this, Gregorious," Yeshua started, but the pain from the shards peppering his back was too much for him to continue.

"No, there is no need," the giant agreed, coming to a stop outside Yeshua's range, but well within his own. "There is no need for this final battle; no need for this display of destruction or death."

"Then why? Why are you doing this?" William asked, his voice barely above a whisper, but Gregorious heard him all the same.

"I was created for *this purpose*. If I deny that purpose, what right do I have to exist at all?" he asked, not expecting an answer. Then Gregorious brought down his fist to crush them both, knowing they were too wounded to avoid him again.

Closing his eyes, Yeshua held William close and hoped this death would be quick. His companion had already suffered so much in such a short time.

Except that death did not come, and a thud as loud as an explosion rocked through their ears. Opening his eyes in a flash, Yeshua looked up to see a centaur in demonic armor with his left hand held aloft, a great shield covering his arm. In his right hand was a glory hammer and—with a great heave of the weapon—the centaur knocked away Gregorious' fist and then stood ready to defend his companions.

"Your purpose is denied, monster!" Buer shouted, and Yeshua's face broke into a smile at the sight. Standing up straighter, Yeshua watched as another Fallen joined them, lightning flaring out along the upper clouds before he slammed down on the stone goliath and shocked him into staggering backward.

"Just what trickery is this?" Gregorious roared as he dug his heel into the ground, sending out a wake of stone and dissipating clouds.

"No tricks," Crocell said from the air, his wings flapping with purpose as he readied himself for his next attack. "You simply have new opponents."

"Buer," Yeshua started, trying to stand up, but the centaur looked over his shoulder and pointed away from Gregorious with his hammer.

"Go, Yeshua, and take William with you!" Buer commanded before turning his attention back to the monster. "We will not be able to focus on this creature if you are underfoot."

"I can still fight!" Yeshua protested, even as the shards in his back tore at his mind, but Buer kept his eye on the gigantic angel.

"I know this well, Yeshua, but William cannot. He will not be able to escape on his own," he said before turning back to face Yeshua again. "Save him, my friend. He does not deserve this death."

"Don't you worry... about me," William mumbled, but it was difficult enough for him to keep his eyes open. Looking down at the poor soul, Yeshua realized that Buer was correct. Gathering William in his arms, seeming lighter than a child, Yeshua nodded at the centaur.

"I will return to help, soon."

"It will not be needed," Crocell said, at which point Yeshua could finally see the wounds covering the slayer's body. No amount of cauterizing would help him now, and Yeshua realized that he was intruding on the swan song of a fallen angel. Jumping into the air, Yeshua flew away from the demons and the giant monster that should have destroyed him moments before.

He was greeted with the sight of a legion of angels bearing down on them from the west, but that just meant Yeshua had to fly faster and push harder. Even as the swarm of angels sent out a downpour of arrows—four of them sinking into the flesh of Yeshua's back—he pushed away the pain.

Buer and Crocell were risking their lives to save them; the boy in his arms had attacked a giant even as a vampire lunged at his neck. At this moment, Yeshua finally understood Judas' final smile and words, the love that drove him to take his best friend's death. Flying through the air and his enemies swarming all around him, Yeshua promised to himself that he would save the man in his arms.

He had to save at least one of his friends.

CADMUS ALREADY KNEW he was too late to join the start of the battle; the visions in his head were clear on that, at the very least. However, he could not help himself from worrying that he would not make it in time to stop Adonai or Niccolo. Every detail after their meeting was cloudy—as if the universe did not exist after their battle—and Cadmus knew that was a bad sign. Gripping Mercy's reins even tighter, Cadmus urged his horse to go faster.

You know that I cannot, Master. It is already hard enough to find my footing, Mercy thought back, and Cadmus realized that he may have been asking too much.

Along their journey to the secret portal, Purgatory itself seemed to have rebelled against them; no true path existed. Although Cadmus knew they were going in the right direction, Mercy was only able to continue by jumping onto floating islands in the mist, and it was a marvel that he was able to keep up any semblance of galloping.

With another powerful push, the white horse launched them up to the next floating rock.

I'm sorry, Mercy, it's just that everything is on the line. If Niccolo reaches Adonai before I can, I might have to—I might have to... he thought, unable to say the words even in his mind.

Yes, you may have to kill him. I am well aware that he is your friend and that you may not want to end his life, Mercy said as he jumped to the next island, clearing the thirty-foot gap and sending pebbles along the cracked ground once he landed. *However, the universe itself is at stake. If Adonai's life is truly what keeps this dimension intact, you may not have a choice.*

The entire reason we were doing this was to end Adonai's reign! If I leave him alive, all of this will be for nothing! All of the death, all of our pain, it will be nothing more than a tyrant's memory once he leaves to go make a new universe.

You will find a way, Cadmus. You must trust your instincts. Your doubt comes from a place of good intention, but it will not help you when you face Niccolo.

How do we even know that Azrael was right? It may have been another trick, Cadmus suggested as Mercy ran along a narrow peninsula, but he felt disappointment flow through their bond.

You already know better than I that the reaper was not a servant of Adonai. Whatever the case may be, Azrael truly believed that Adonai's life was tied to these lands. And let us not forget your visions, Master. Although I only see a fraction of what you witness, it is obvious that a future after Adonai's death is... chaotic, at best.

That... that could be just because my future sight was given to Räum and Amon **from** *Adonai. My visions themselves might just be tied to his life.*

A possibility, certainly, but is that something you would want to risk? Would you want to risk the entire world, all of these dimensions, on the possibility that your gift for prophecy only extends to the limits of a god's life?

I... no, Cadmus admitted, looking down at the abyss beneath them. He hadn't even noticed that Mercy had jumped again.

Then you know what you must do, Master. Any further speech on the subject will only serve to undermine your resolve, and you will need it soon. The portal is ahead.

Cadmus looked ahead of them to find a shining rift only a hundred yards ahead of them, golden light pulsing through the mists of Purgatory. A smile crept onto his face and Cadmus leaned forward and readied himself to join the battle, momentarily forgetting how dire their circumstances really were.

That was until he saw that the ground fell away from them fifty feet away from the portal.

"Can you make that leap, Mercy?" Cimeries asked, and the reaper felt guilty that he only just remembered her presence.

"It is... possible," Mercy responded, his rasp weaker than normal due to his exertion. "It would be a gamble."

"It would take too long to find the other portal," Cimeries stated, and both horse and rider realized what she was truly saying.

"I believe in you, Mercy," Cadmus whispered, and a clattering of invisible teeth filled the air. Having almost forgotten the sound, Cadmus took a second to realize the stallion was laughing.

"I need no one's belief."

Then Mercy galloped even faster, the wind tearing around Cadmus and Cimeries to the extent that hearing another word was impossible. Closing the distance to the cliff's edge within just a few seconds, Cadmus took a sharp breath once Mercy jumped, the ground falling away from them and promising an eternal drop into the abyss if they missed the portal.

Cadmus's heart was in his throat as they drifted through the air, the wind resistance slowing their advance and gravity doing its part to drag them down. After the first hundred feet, Cadmus almost thought they would not make it, but Mercy continued to sail through the air, his last, powerful leap driving them toward their destination and then through the dimensional passage.

Once they made their way through the portal, they found themselves deep within the shimmering capitol of Heaven, the chaos of war echoing around them.

"As you can see, your belief was unnecessary," Mercy said as he slowed down from his gallop, and Cadmus shook his head and ran fingers through his stallion's mane.

"You don't have to be an ass about it."

He had smiled during that simple moment, but then a dozen visions tore at him. Every instant was filled with agonizing pain, the dead eyes of hundreds of friends and demons, the chaos that would come with the final battle for all of humanity. Cadmus was almost able to bring himself back from the visions when one distracted him entirely.

In his mind, Cadmus watched as the Leviathan devoured Astaroth, gulping him down in three vicious bites.

You cannot, Mercy urged, but Cadmus could not shake this responsibility.

*I can't **not,*** he thought back before turning to look at Cimeries over his shoulder.

"The Leviathan—" Cadmus started, his words coming out with echoes of the fallen angel's pain. "He's going to kill Astaroth."

"The monster turns on us?" Cimeries scowled. "I cannot say I'm surprised, but I do wish he had better timing."

"I have to save him, Cim. Once this is all over," Cadmus explained, remembering the lives of Tamiel and Azrael, "Astaroth is the only one who could lead Hell. He's the only..."

"Then I will save him," Cimeries said simply as she jumped off Mercy's saddle, but Cadmus shook his head.

"No, you won't make it. It's only—it's only moments at this point. It'll take you an hour to get to him. I could make it there and —" he said, but Cimeries slammed the end of her pike against the street.

"You have much greater responsibilities!" She furrowed her brow and glared up at him. "Above all, you must stop Niccolo."

"I know that!" Cadmus shouted, losing his temper and regretting it. All of the conflicting emotions and memories in his head were getting to him, and he brought a hand to his temple in an attempt to focus. "But if Astaroth falls, Hell falls with him. And the Leviathan... Astaroth won't be his last meal unless I stop it."

"So you must go. That is what you are saying to me. You do not have enough time for this, reaper," she argued, Cadmus surprising her with a bark of laughter.

"Of course, I do, Cim. I'm the *master* of time." His smile abandoned as soon as he saw her frown. "Niccolo hasn't met Adonai yet. I can do both..."

"Then it is decided," Cimeries said before walking up the street and toward the audacious palace towering over the rest of the capitol. "Go save the fallen angel and then return to stop our Devil."

"Where are you going?"

"To intercept Niccolo. If you are not going to stop him, it is my responsibility to stall him for you," she said, picking up speed as she started to jog.

"Cimeries, don't. We can go together!" Cadmus shouted after her, at which point she finally stopped, turned and pointed back at the palace with her pike.

"No. This is where our paths diverge, reaper. I will attempt to stop the monster Niccolo has become, and you must kill the monster we brought from the depths. This is the way it has to be."

"Cimeries..." Cadmus started, but then a handful of prophetic deaths flashed across his mind. Looking at her one last time, he nodded. "It was an honor to fight with you."

"Likewise, Cadmus. For a man, you are worth something."

She gave a bittersweet smile at her companion before turning and running up the street. Cadmus thought about joking back at her, trying to keep some sort of levity, but the end of the world was too close and it was up to them to stop it. After turning Mercy around, Cadmus headed toward the gates of Heaven, focusing on the current moment and forcing time to stand still.

And even with all that power at his disposal, Cadmus knew he did not have enough time to save them all.

ASTAROTH SENT out another burst of radiant energy toward the ground, his arms shaking from the effort, but it had the desired effect. The screams of eight angels tore through the air as the energy slammed into the surface, creating an impact crater thirty feet across. Once he let the energy disperse, Astaroth allowed himself to take a breath before looking for his next enemies, hoping to find someone more powerful to destroy.

Looking to his right, he spotted Paimon fighting alongside Ymir, climbing up his massive frame as he attacked a creature that seemed entirely made out of yellow tentacles, rotten teeth showing between the gaps as it tried to capture demonic infantrymen. Diving down to join them, Astaroth watched as Paimon leapt off Ymir's back in a terrible spin, using her extended claws to slash through the creature and lop off three tentacles.

When Ymir picked up the shrieking horror, ready to slam it into the ground, Astaroth landed beneath him and caught the giant's attention.

"No! Into the air!"

After giving him a skeptical look, the Nephilim obliged. Once Ymir launched the monster high into the clouds—an errant tentacle burning away as it touched one of the small suns peppering the aerial battlefield—Astaroth rushed underneath the monster's shadow and then collected as much power as he could.

Light gathered between his fingers, threatening to break out of his control, and even Astaroth's wings disappeared to join the energy. Finally satisfied by what he had at his disposal, Astaroth lifted both of his arms and let the radiance flow out of him, a column of destruction rising up to greet the falling creature.

Seeing that the screaming terror was still able to keep its form as energy collided into it, Astaroth furrowed his brow and pushed with all of his might, his armor collapsing into his body and transforming into energy he could use to increase the intensity of his attack. With a furious cry, feeling the frustration of millions of years of exile, Astaroth focused the potential energy and narrowed the column until it was only just barely wider than the monster he was attacking. Astaroth had to abandon his assault after a few seconds and dropped to his knees, but he was rewarded when he looked up and realized the monster no longer existed.

"Holy shit, Roth, I haven't seen you do something like that

since..." Paimon paused, actually forgetting the last time she had seen such fury, but the Nephilim standing nearby finished the statement for her.

"The Plains of Jotunheim. I remember losing forty of my strongest to that power," Ymir said, grief and resentment filling his voice. For a moment, as Astaroth's armor started to reform from the aura surrounding him, the fallen angel considered that he may have a new opponent.

"I will not apologize for my actions in war," Astaroth declared, receiving a glare from Paimon in the process, but Ymir was unoffended.

"I never asked you to. You get the respect you're due, angel."

"Haven't been one of those for a long time, Ymir," Astaroth said as he picked himself up, looking around the battlefield for more creatures like the one he had destroyed. Instead, he found thousands of humans clashing against each other and trading lives. "What the hell *was* that, anyway?"

"Human, if you believe it," Paimon replied, crossing her arms as ashes floated down from above. "Sabrael apparently got free license from Adonai to twist their souls into nightmares."

"I do believe it," Astaroth growled, the viper on his arm spitting out in sympathy. Turning around as if the squat archangel could be nearby, Astaroth let out his wings and prepared to launch himself in the air. "Someone needs to kill that bastard and it might as well be me. Do we know where he is?"

"Probably hiding somewhere in the capitol," Paimon said as she approached him and set a hand on his shoulder, causing Astaroth to turn back and face her. "Someone will get him eventually, Roth. We'll make sure of it."

"*I'll* make sure of it," he said before gesturing at his chest with a thumb. "He killed Tamiel, Paimon. It may have been the kid's arm and Uriel's spear, but he needs to pay."

"Hey!" she barked, slapping him on the arm. "You aren't the only one with a grudge, but you know for a fact you're more useful

362

out here. We can go find that snake once we control the battlefield."

"Control?" Astaroth scoffed at the idea before sweeping out his arms. "There's no *control* here, Paimon. This is chaos, and I can just barely tell our humans from theirs!"

"You think *you* have a problem, angel?" Ymir interrupted with a deep bellow of a laugh. "You all look like rats to me."

"Watch it." Astaroth pointed up at the Nephilim, the snake on his arm rearing back and poised to strike. "The Fallen existed before those things even evolved."

"Hungry..." dual voices interrupted them, and they turned to find the Leviathan crawling toward them, the top half of an angelic corpse wrapped up in one of its tongues and another corpse hidden behind grey fingers. It had grown larger since they had last seen it; the creature's feast had somehow made it even more immense and terrifying.

As Astaroth looked at the crawling monstrosity, he could see that dozens—maybe even hundreds—of faces had joined the others on its disgusting torso.

"The Leviathan..." Paimon muttered before turning to face the creature, who was twenty feet from Ymir. "If you're hungry, there are plenty of angels to eat."

"Not enough—no... *sustenance*." The whisper dominated the last word. With a whip of its tongue, the torso it held was thrown into its gullet and they watched as another face appeared along its too-long neck. "Need more..."

"Then turn the fuck around and find it," Astaroth said, walking forward and gathering power in his hands. He could tell something was wrong; he could hear the hunger in the beast's words, the desire burning in its blue eyes. "There are more than enough humans serving Adonai. Just eat more than one."

"*Did that*, angel," the Leviathan shouted in its deep voice, slamming three of its hands against the ground and sending slivers of marble into the air. "Had to find better ones. Tastier ones."

"Tastier ones," Paimon repeated, watching as the Leviathan brought up the body in its hand, its three tongues wrapping around the man and retrieving him from its fingers. Once Paimon was able to see the man's panic-stricken face, covered in boils from Niccolo's plague, she understood what had happened. Covering her mouth, Paimon watched as the monster ate one of their own.

"You *bastard*!" Astaroth shouted, realizing the truth and focusing the light in his hands. "He was from *Hell*! You're eating your allies!"

"Gods do not have allies," the Leviathan replied in both voices, looking at the three of them with interest. "Just food that is not prepared yet."

"Back away."

Ymir clenched his fists as he approached the creature from the depths, but the Leviathan only saw it as an invitation. Turning swiftly, the Leviathan dragged its massive body along the ground until it was in front of Ymir, lurching up and onto the Nephilim's chest before any of them could react. Roaring in two voices, the Leviathan knocked the giant over and brought its horrific mouth up to Ymir's face, the Nephilim only just able to grab its throat and push it away.

"No! Don't you dare!"

Paimon extended her nails as she ran forward, but Astaroth had already leapt into action. Rushing through the air, Astaroth drew his arm back and was about to throw a blast at the monster, but one of its eight hands flew out and grabbed him by the leg. Taking in a sharp breath, Astaroth tried to attack even while in its grip, but the Leviathan whipped him around and slammed him into the ground before throwing him aside.

Dazed momentarily, Astaroth regained his balance and stopped himself in the air, but it wasn't nearly quick enough to help the giant.

Paimon and Astaroth watched as the Leviathan's mask snapped down on Ymir's head, leaving only the back of his skull intact. Astaroth had difficulty keeping bile from rising in his throat as the Leviathan raised up its bloody mask before lunging forward again, eating the rest of the Nephilim's head before swallowing and pushing itself to its full height. Once it raised its head and howled in twin voices, Astaroth could see a one-eyed face join the others on the Leviathan's torso.

All thoughts were abandoned as Astaroth tore through the air; he couldn't even hear his own voice as he shouted in rage for the fallen Nephilim. As he flew, Astaroth let out multiple streams of energy at the monster, knocking the Leviathan off of Ymir's body and forcing it back. By the time he was within striking distance of the monster, Astaroth collected his fury into his right fist and threw it into the Leviathan's torso.

The radiant blow would have destroyed a lesser creature—any angel or demon—but all it did was push the Leviathan along the ground for ten yards, its eight limbs scrambling for something to halt its momentum. Seeing that the creature was still alive, Astaroth rushed forward even as Paimon yelled after him. If he could have listened to reason, her words might have stopped him.

Because when Astaroth leapt into the air, intent on slamming both of his fists into the Leviathan's body with a hammer blow, the creature was ready for him. It grabbed him with five hands, one for each of his limbs and his torso.

"The giant... delicious... but lacking." The Leviathan stood up with its remaining arms, his massive body somehow supported by the lanky extensions. A low murmur filled the air as the monster laughed, and eventually the Leviathan's mask opened and a three-pronged tongue delicately touched Astaroth's face. "I can *smell* the power on you."

The viper on his arm sank its fangs into the grey fingers pinning it to his body, but Astaroth realized there was very little he could do. This was his last mistake—Moloch had even warned him before they had left Hell—and the Leviathan was clearly stronger than he had thought. Although Astaroth snapped his teeth at the tongue as it continued to taste his skin, he knew it was nothing more than a defiant, futile act.

"I hope I give you indigestion," he spat out, hoping to anger his killer in the end, but the Leviathan only laughed.

However, just as the creature was about to withdraw his tongues and swallow him whole, golden claws slashed through Astaroth's vision and the Leviathan's tongue fell to the ground, the severed appendage spraying black blood all around them. The pain was enough for the creature to release its hold on Astaroth, who fell to the ground and rolled out of the way, recovering just in time to avoid the Leviathan's temper tantrum.

Once he was able to gather his senses and stand back up, Astaroth could see Paimon continuing her assault on the terrible creature, using her claws and talons to tear great rents in its grey skin. Flying forward to join her as she dug her claws into the Leviathan's back, Astaroth intended to strike from the other side and distract it, but then the monster leapt into the air and Astaroth flew past harmlessly. After flapping his wings to halt his momentum, Astaroth watched the Leviathan plummet through the air, Paimon still clambering over its torso, and he once again marveled at his sister's strength.

Except that when the Leviathan landed, it had twisted in the air so that Paimon was beneath it, and the impact sent out a cloud of dust that obscured Astaroth's view.

"No!" Astaroth shouted, tearing forward and gathering energy between his fingers, but he only made it halfway toward their landing site before a golden object flew toward him and they collided midair, forcing him from consciousness.

After opening his eyes, Astaroth panicked and jumped to his feet, realizing quickly that the Leviathan had thrown Paimon at him. Once he was able to see the battlefield once more, Astaroth saw that Paimon had recovered first and was already fighting the monster again.

He was at first relieved, but then Astaroth saw that only half of Paimon's body was covered in armor and scarlet ran down her arms, and he knew that she was in trouble. When she tried to roll out from under the Leviathan's next strike, two of its other arms caught her and picked her up, holding her in front of its gruesome mask.

When he heard the creature laughing in that grim display, Astaroth could take no more.

"Get," he began, running faster than humanly possible and using his wings to push himself even harder, "your dirty... *fucking* hands..." He closed the distance and jumped through the air before crashing into the Leviathan's shoulder, grabbing tightly onto the slick surface of its armpit. "*Off my sister!*"

And before the Leviathan could do much more than turn and give him a curious look, Astaroth tore the monster's arm off its body, covering himself in dark ichor before he dropped to the ground and then jumped toward the other arm holding Paimon. Gathering fury into his right hand, Astaroth swung down at the Leviathan's elbow, all doubt abandoned, and he was rewarded with a sickening snap and pop as the monster's joint gave way.

"Forget about me, Roth!" Paimon shouted as she fell to the ground, still unable to move in her weakened state, but Astaroth had no intention of abandoning her now in this final battle.

Turning around as the Leviathan roared at him, Astaroth could see the monster stamping its remaining six hands in anger and snapping its jaws wildly before lunging at him. However, the fallen angel was not afraid. Astaroth only dug his heels into the ground and set both of his hands in front of him.

Screaming so loud that his throat was in agony, Astaroth let out a tidal wave of radiance from his outstretched arms, claiming all of the energy his martial soul possessed. The Leviathan's form was drowned in light, but Astaroth could still hear its twin roars, so he pushed even harder. His armor and his wings collapsed into his body, even the viper along his arm withered away and joined his

KEVIN KAUFFMANN

attack, and Astaroth almost felt his own body fading from reality. By the time his attack was finished, the fallen angel was naked, barely conscious, and he had collapsed to his knees, but once he was able to lift his head and see the result of his fury, Astaroth had to laugh at the absurdity of it all.

He had used everything in those last moments, but the Leviathan stood there looking at him with a mix of hunger and enmity.

"Almost... almost, angel," the Leviathan whispered, its words staggered as it recovered from the assault. Using its remaining legs, the monster approached the kneeling warrior until it was only a few feet away. "No cause for shame. It will be an honor to taste one like you."

"I tried, Paimon," Astaroth said, turning to face his sister before the end. He could see a tear rolling down her cheek, but he did not judge her for that. "I just wasn't strong enough."

"Roth, you can still leave," she said, trying to stand up and failing. With a heavy breath, he could see that Paimon had been hobbled by the Leviathan crushing her body. "I can't, but you can still run."

"I don't run, Paimon. Even... even when I'm defeated." He turned back to face the Leviathan and felt its remaining tongues gingerly wrapping around his torso. "I will never back down."

"It will make you taste that much better," the Leviathan replied, the glint of its eyes showing the creature's satisfaction. Gritting his teeth as the Leviathan grabbed his arms with grey hands, Astaroth tried to keep his iron will and stared straight into the monster's fiery eyes. "Be grateful, angel. After all this time, death has come for you."

Astaroth was ready for this—he had written his own fate by bringing the monster with them—but the Leviathan had only started to drag Astaroth's body toward his mouth when a blue aura filled his field of view and he felt himself yanked backward. In his confusion, Astaroth watched as the remains of the monster's tongues spurted and sprayed everywhere, but then he realized that he was also five yards away from the creature. Looking up, Astaroth found the one thing he had never expected to find.

Sitting atop a white horse was a cloaked man with white hair and shining blue eyes, and he crackled with slight charges of electricity. In his hand was an ornate scythe with a skull on the crest of the blade, which was the only reason Astaroth recognized him. After millions of years, Astaroth finally saw something that made his jaw drop.

"Cadmus..." Paimon squeaked, but the reaper ignored her and kept his gaze on the Leviathan, who had recovered from its pain and was looking at the new arrival in anger.

"Death has not come for *them*, monster," Cadmus declared, his voice echoed by a handful of others. With a steady hand, he pointed his weapon at the creature bristling with hate. "My friends will not die this day."

"Reaper!" the Leviathan shouted, the whisper drowned out by its deep counterpart. "*Why*? You are one of *us*! You are beyond these creatures!"

"I am not like *you*," Cadmus spat out, sweeping his blade across his body and causing a typhoon of blue energy. "*You* led my friend astray. *You* ate hundreds of human souls, angel and demon alike. *You* are a monster."

"As are *you*," the Leviathan replied, gathering strength in its six legs. "You are not human, Cadmus. You returned from the abyss as one of *us*."

"I may have returned from the abyss," Cadmus said, "but I am not one of you. I care for these people—*my* people—and I will not let you harm them."

"Then you will join the rest of my feast!" the Leviathan screamed, pushing forward on its six hands and hitting the ground with such force that it tore out clumps of stone as it crawled.

Astaroth and Paimon watched as it approached Cadmus, who merely sat in Mercy's saddle, and they almost thought the Leviathan would make good on its promise. When the Leviathan towered above Cadmus, poised to swallow him whole inside its terrible mask, Astaroth thought it was all over.

However, their struggle was far from over. In that last instant, when the Leviathan's head was only inches away from Cadmus' skull, blood and gore filled the air as a hurricane of blue energy dispersed around the monster. Astaroth almost could not believe it as all six of the Leviathan's arms fell away from its torso—all of them severed cleanly by the shoulder joint—and the monster's body collapsed to the ground, unable to do anything but squirm.

"Like I said, I am not one of *you*." Cadmus' voice rose above the creature's howls of anguish, silencing the Leviathan as it turned to see him. Cadmus had dismounted and slowly walked to the Leviathan's head, stopping just a yard away from its dangerous jaws. "There has never been anything like me."

"They do not deserve your protection," the Leviathan said weakly, squirming so it could look up at Cadmus. "They *will* fail you."

"You say that like I don't expect it," Cadmus replied, and he almost didn't notice the flicker in the Leviathan's eyes. After the last word, the Leviathan whipped out its maimed tongues in one last attempt to drag Cadmus into his mouth, but the reaper would not allow it and caught each one with a deft movement.

After coiling all three of them along his right arm, Cadmus planted his foot against the edge of the Leviathan's mouth and pulled, tearing the Leviathan's tongues out from the root before throwing them aside. Even though it screamed in twin voices, Cadmus had no intention of listening.

"You will not be missed."

Cadmus then brought down his scythe, letting out a spatial distortion that tore through the Leviathan's body and bisected its terrible torso. When the two halves of its mask fell to different sides of its corpse, Cadmus turned back to face the fallen angels he had saved. Paimon was the first to recover, pushing herself to her feet on shaky, newly-healed legs.

"Cadmus... how? How did you make it back?"

Although she staggered toward him, Astaroth remained kneeling. Cadmus turned to face her, setting his scythe against the ground, and they could see the disappointment in his eyes.

"Azrael saved me. We're going to have a conversation about that, by the way," Cadmus said, looking at both of them. "You let me get tutored by an angel for a year and didn't tell me."

"I—he... Tamiel," Paimon stammered, but Cadmus put out a hand to stop her.

"It's fine. It all turned out according to their plan. It just would have been nice to know." Cadmus took a deep breath before looking at Astaroth, who was rising to his feet. The fallen angel avoided eye contact as he approached, but once he was close, he looked up at Cadmus with golden eyes.

"Did you kill him?"

"He made me. When Uriel revealed his identity, Azrael... pretended to betray me so that I would kill him and harvest his soul."

"And all of the souls from the rebellion," Paimon muttered, earning a nod from the reaper. When Cadmus looked back at her, she could see the pain and sadness haunting his new eyes.

"I can handle it. I don't have the option to fail. I have to stop Niccolo," he said, confusing both of his companions. "Azrael didn't tell you..."

"Didn't tell us what?" Paimon responded, which was enough cause for Cadmus to massage his forehead in frustration.

"Adonai's life is pretty much the only thing holding the universe together," he said, already noticing the skepticism on Astaroth's face. "I wouldn't trust that blindly, of course, but my visions... they don't go past Niccolo and Adonai fighting."

"So you have to stop Niccolo, and this whole war means nothing." Resentment tinged Astaroth's words, but Cadmus shocked him by slamming his scythe against the ground.

"I'm going to stop both of them!" he shouted, looking back at the palace over his shoulder. "I can't... it can't all mean nothing."

"Then what are you doing down here?" Paimon asked in surprise. When Cadmus paused and glanced at Astaroth, he understood immediately.

"Saving me," Astaroth muttered, Paimon looking at him in shock before realizing the truth. Both of the Fallen looked at Cadmus expectantly, making him feel like a child due for a scolding.

"I had to," he excused himself, turning and gesturing at the battlefield with his scythe. "I had to save you. I have to save all of them. You're important and I'm not going to just let you die."

"You're being selfish!" Astaroth shouted, grabbing Cadmus by the shoulder and whipping him around. "All of creation is at stake and you waste time saving a jackass like me? What's *wrong* with you?"

"You're *welcome!*" Cadmus replied, turning and somehow standing over the defiant Fallen. "Maybe you don't realize this, but you're the next leader of Hell, you ass! If you died, there wouldn't be a home to go back to."

"Oh, you insufferable piece of shi—"

"Enough!" Paimon interrupted, slapping both of them and grabbing them by their necks. "He wasted his time, but he saved you. Water under the goddamned bridge!"

"Now you," she said, focusing on Cadmus. "You have to go stop Niccolo, and I don't want to hear any excuses."

"There are more to save, Paimon," Cadmus said, and Paimon almost scared him, she looked so furious.

"You don't have the time to do it!"

"Yes, I do!" Cadmus shouted back, breaking her hold on his throat and crackling with electricity. "I control time itself! I can save all of them and be at the palace before you take another breath."

"Don't you *dare* waste your power on us any more than you have! Did you forget what your time manipulation does to you? It takes too much of your energy to do it," she said, stepping forward and extending a golden claw up to his face.

"You may be a god now, Cadmus, but you are *not* infinite. If you waste your power down here with us, how do you know that you'll be strong enough to face Niccolo, Adonai or *both* of them? How can you be certain that you will be able to save us *and* the world?"

"Paimon..."

"You *can't*," she said, removing her hand and pointing at the palace. "And don't argue. You know I'm right. You have to go, Cadmus, and you have to go now."

"I can't let them die," Cadmus tried to argue, and Paimon's hardened expression melted. Turning her claws back to fingers, Paimon placed her hand against his face and offered him sympathy.

"You can't save them all. You might not even be able to save the world," she said, hesitating at their dire circumstances, "but you're our best chance."

"Time to go, Horseman," Astaroth added, causing Paimon to withdraw and stand back with him. "Stop them."

"I..." Cadmus started, but he could tell that any further argument would be a waste of time they did not have. After summoning Mercy in his mind, the white stallion was by his side within a moment. Wordlessly, Cadmus climbed into the saddle before turning back to look at his Fallen companions.

"Just go, and try not to use your powers on the way. You'll need all of them when you get there," Paimon said, Astaroth nodding in agreement. Cadmus bit his lip at the notion, but he nodded at them before Mercy turned and headed toward the palace.

Once they were alone, Astaroth turned to Paimon and was surprised when she threw her arms around him and buried her head in his chest.

"What the fuck are you doing?" he asked, but that only caused his sister to hold him tighter.

"You're such an idiot sometimes, you know that?" Paimon released him and stepped back, avoiding eye contact with a shake of her head. "You could have gotten away from the Leviathan so many times, but you kept on throwing yourself at it. You almost died because of me."

"Yeah, well, you didn't have to rescue me, either. No one was asking you to do that."

"Of course, no one was *asking*. You *never* asked for help in millions of years, even though I'm always bailing you out," Paimon replied, causing Astaroth to bristle with anger.

After a moment, however, Astaroth lowered his head and started to laugh. Paimon was confused at first, but then she joined him once she realized what was so funny.

"Millions of years and things never change," she commented, and Astaroth finally realized the purpose of this war. Once he was able to stop laughing, Astaroth lifted his head and turned to watch the departing Horseman, letting himself hope for the first time since the rebellion.

"Maybe this time," he said under this breath. "Maybe this time they will."

PUTTING one foot in front of the other, Michael could not bother himself with the rest of the battlefield. Instead, he just stared down at the ground beneath him, trying to ignore the heaps of gore and the blood splatters in his path. Michael could not help but think of earlier times, happier times, when a war like this was beyond his imagination. Before all of the human empires, the tribal squabbles, the rise of the Nephilim.

As he walked through the plains of Heaven, Michael tried to remember those days before the rebellion.

It had seemed absurd all those years ago; that any angels would even *want* to rise up against Adonai. Their creator was not the most *noble* of beings—they had seen him give into childish malice before —but Michael couldn't comprehend that any of his servants would rise up against their god. What had made it all the more painful was the source of that rebellion: his brother Lucifer.

Stepping over the disembodied head of an angel, Michael recalled that first pain, the first realization that Lucifer was leading the charge against Adonai. Michael had felt betrayed; he remembered so many afternoons spent on sunny meadows, Lucifer and Gabriel by his side. In those visions, Paimon and Lilith and Tamiel were also there, the future exile continually making eyes at Sathariel and trying to hide it from Lucifer. Remembering the watcher's boyish affection, Michael had to laugh, even as he walked along the bodies of dead angels.

However, that laughter abandoned him when he remembered the present. In their own way, all of those angels had betrayed him, betrayed Adonai, and they had destroyed the utopia they had created. None of them had bothered to stay with Michael, abandoning him and forcing him to keep awful siblings like Uriel and Sabrael in his company. They had left Michael alone, forsaken their god, and he had been forced to fight them.

Except that now, with all of this bloodshed around him and knowing Adonai as he did, Michael finally understood that they had not abandoned him. They had simply realized that Adonai was not a god worth worshipping, that it was better to strive against him than blindly follow orders. Their defiant acts had nothing to do with Michael at all. They simply wished to be on the right side of a terrible war.

And even though he knew Adonai could destroy him in an instant, Michael wished desperately that he had joined them all those years ago. This pain was too much; this guilt was overwhelming. They had all been so noble. Lucifer and his shining weapons, Tamiel and his golden wings, and Buné and Eligos were two of the most righteous and honorable creatures Michael ever had the pleasure of knowing.

All of them had suffered at Michael's hand, but Gabriel's words haunted him. His poor brother—the one he had sworn to *protect*—

375

had died with the hope that Michael would do the right thing, that he would be worthy of his trust and affection. In this war, Michael had betrayed that hope, had not proven himself worthy at all, but it was too late.

It wouldn't be much longer before this battle was over—once Adonai would join the field—and Michael knew of no power that could face *him*. Even if Michael wanted to join his forsaken brothers, they would die just the same.

Sickened by the carnage surrounding him, Michael let out his wings and jumped into the air, hoping to distance himself from the sight and the smell. When he was fifty feet above the ground—the cool air refreshing him and taking the stench of war from his nostrils —Michael was finally able to look out on the plains of Heaven, and what he saw amazed him.

The Heavenly Host was outnumbered, outmatched, and demonic forces were pushing them back into the city. Although there were plenty of corpses on both sides, powerful demons and Nephilim were holding their own and taking down more angels every second. From what he could see, even Michael's horrific vanguard was not able to stand up to the legions of Hell; only two of them remained. Gregorious had transformed into his giant form and was fighting two black specks, and the other monster—Michael did not even know her name—was skittering along the battlefield like a giant beetle.

Michael did not feel pride as those two wreaked havoc and destroyed their enemies. However noble their souls had been in life, Sabrael had twisted them, and Michael did not know if they could be considered human anymore. When a giant green dragon with six wings fell from the sky and landed on Michael's insect subordinate, he did not feel sympathy for the creature. All he wondered was where the dragon had come from and who it might have been, but then he recognized the power leaking from the giant creature.

"My god... Asmodeus," Michael breathed out, realizing that his infernal brother had forged himself into the shape of that magnificent, terrible lizard. There was no turning back at that point of transformation, no matter what kind of magic they had at their disposal. After this battle, Asmodeus would forever be a feral creature destined to be put down, but Michael could only assume that the demon king had decided it was worth it in this final battle. That without his twin, his life held no meaning.

Choking down grief for his insane brother, Michael turned from the battlefield and flew toward the palace. With the end of the fight close at hand, there was no reason to delay it further. It was time for Adonai to join the battle, end this war and this world and all this suffering. Michael didn't care if he would be punished for his impatience or impertinence; he would not allow any further cruelty.

Halfway through his journey, however, Michael found something curious far below on the streets of the capitol. One lone black speck was fighting its way through a column of angelic troops, dismantling them quickly and efficiently, and Michael realized that without any resistance this demonic warrior would eventually make their way to Adonai's throne. Sighing, Michael realized that he had one last duty in this war and he fell out of the air, determined to intercept the demon.

Landing ten yards behind his own troops, Michael brandished his sword and let it burn to life, waiting for the demon to rush through the rest of the human warriors. It was only seconds before their corpses were thrown aside, a spear complemented by a curved hook carving through them, and Michael realized this was no fallen angel.

Standing there triumphant, covered in blood and analyzing him intently, was a woman in light armor, her weapon held confidently in both hands.

"I am the archangel Michael, and I cannot allow you to go further." Michael hoped the woman would turn back, but she stared at him without fear.

"I am Cimeries, Knight of Hell, and I cannot allow you to stop me," she said, and Michael realized there was no arguing with this woman.

Taking his sword in hand, Michael bowed to this obviously regal warrior before standing back up and holding his blade in a comfortable stance. Seeing the respect offered her, the woman returned the bow before gripping her pike even tighter.

As they rushed toward each other, they both knew only one of them would leave those blood-soaked streets alive.

CHAPTER 12
ΛRCHANGELS AND DEMONS

Lifting up his blade, Michael diverted Cimeries' thrust and knocked it away so he could throw a fist into her unguarded face. However, the woman dropped down—underneath his arm—and pivoted to launch her foot into his midsection. Already overextended, Michael had no choice but to take the hit and stagger back, reclaiming his stance just in time to throw his sword against the curved blade of her weapon and stop the spear point from piercing his neck.

"Good. At least you are not a fool."

Cimeries' gaze was unwavering as they pushed their weapons against each other. Their strength seemed to be evenly matched and when she withdrew her weapon and jumped back, Michael did the same, keeping his burning blade in a forward guard.

"Just who are you?" he asked, circling to the right and seeing her mirror the action. "Cimeries was my brother's name, a noble warrior in Lucifer's ranks. I somehow doubt you would have been given that name on Earth."

"I was not given this name, archangel. I claimed it," Cimeries said before stepping forward and thrusting three times in rapid succession, trying to find some flaw in Michael's defenses. After knocking away all three strikes, Michael had to wonder if she had found any, but she continued speaking after a satisfied grunt. "My true title shamed me at the time of my fall, and so I rid myself of it."

"As is your right." Michael rushed forward into a sweeping strike and let out a wave of flames as he did. When she saw the fire coming from his weapon, Cimeries jumped to the side and sliced through the air with her curved blade, which Michael avoided before slashing vertically at her position. She evaded it easily, but it did give him the opportunity to ask another question. "But I ask merely out of respect. An opponent like you deserves their own name, and so I ask again. Who are you?"

"You are stubborn, archangel," Cimeries replied in a weary tone before lunging forward, past Michael's blade.

Michael brought up his arm—ready to catch the shaft of her weapon—but then she jumped up and over him, determined to plant her weapon into his back. Turning and dropping away, Michael slashed through the air in an attempt to swat her weapon away from him, but then Cimeries landed and twisted, shoving the butt of her pike into his stomach. Instead of backing away, Michael grabbed at the handle and gripped it tight to keep the woman from retreating.

"Please. Do me this courtesy," he urged, and Cimeries could see the sincerity in his eyes.

"Hippolyta. Once, I was Queen of the Amazons. Does it please you to know the truth?" she replied, scowling as she looked away briefly, but Michael only gazed at her with respect. Letting go of her weapon, Michael allowed her to jump back and ready for her next assault.

"I know that name. It suits you better," Michael said in a lighter tone, but he could see her pike waver slightly. It only took him a second to realize that it was from anger.

"Because it is not a noble angel's soul? Because it is merely the name of a beaten, defeated woman?" Cimeries swept her pike across, trying to attack Michael with the curved blade, but Michael caught the weapon with his sword and redirected the strike. When she spun around—twisting the pike above her so she could mirror the strike against his other side—Michael put out his hand and caught the weapon just below the head.

"Because it is the name of a glorious queen who led her own people, and who never gave in, even when crippled," Michael said, shocking her into silence. "I know your story, Hippolyta, and it brings you no shame. Fighting you here, now, makes me see just how noble, righteous and powerful you really are. It is my distinct *honor* to fight a warrior like you when I am surrounded by fools and cowards."

"Fools and cowards," Cimeries mused as she backed away, recovering quickly from the archangel's knowledge of her life. "You speak as if you have lost faith in your cause."

"It was not faith that led me to this path, Hippolyta." Michael held his sword to his right side, the blade pointed behind him as he settled into his next stance. "When one side of a war has a *god*, it is foolish to fight for the other. It is futile to fight against Adonai."

"How amusing..." Cimeries crouched so she could counter Michael's attack. "You think Adonai is the only god on this battlefield."

"There is another?" Michael asked, not believing it for a second, but then he saw the confidence in her smirk.

"More than one. Perhaps you will meet them," she said, beckoning him with a curled finger.

Grunting in dissatisfaction, Michael used his wings to propel himself forward—his feet only an inch off the ground—but Cimeries was not impressed. When he swept his blade across his body and let out a crescent of intense flames, she rolled out of the way. Unfortunately, that had been what Michael had intended, so when he used his wings to redirect his momentum and attack again— letting out a burst of flames along the ground—Cimeries found that she had little options.

Surprising the archangel, Cimeries thrust against the ground with her weapon and flung herself into the air, trying to twist her body so she could strike at him once she landed. Once he saw that opportunity, Michael ran forward and tried to slam his sword on her from above, but she met the blow with the crest of her pike. Michael used his considerable might to push down on the weapon, driving the woman to her knee, but then she astounded him. Grabbing the burning blade of his sword, Cimeries pushed him and his strike to the side, retrieving her weapon before jumping to a safe distance and leaving Michael to slam his sword into the ground.

After picking up his weapon, Michael considered that she must be resistant to fire, but then he saw her blackened hand. Michael gaped in wonder at this human warrior who more than lived up to the legends.

"Your hand... why would you do such a thing?"

"It was necessary. What other reason would I need?" she replied with disgust, and Michael had to shake his head in disbelief.

"Those flames are more intense than anything on Earth. They are worse than anything you could have encountered in Hell..."

"I was burned alive once. Your brother, Beleth, tied me to a cross after crippling my limbs and let the flames devour me," Cimeries said before gripping her pike, the skin of her burnt hand crackling with the effort. "I shoved my pike through his head for the insult. Do I need to go further?"

"No. I understand," Michael said, regaining his resolve and holding his sword with both hands. "I will not disrespect you like that again."

"That is appreciated," Cimeries said with a smile, but it disappeared when she lunged forward.

Refusing to use his flames against such a strong opponent, Michael knocked away the strike but was surprised to see her leap up. Lifting his left arm to guard his face, it did little to take away the force of her flying knee, but it was enough that he could pivot his body and heave her to the side. When she swiftly turned and brought her pike around his knee, hoping to pull back and cut through the unguarded flesh, Michael lifted his leg out of danger and threw his elbow against her jaw.

Although she was staggered from the blow, she crouched down before thrusting up at his chest, which he only avoided by leaning back. Using his wings to regain his balance and drag him out of danger, Michael then jumped forward just in time to see Cimeries stabbing down at him.

All thoughts abandoned, Michael threw out his left arm and grabbed at the shaft, pulling it down so that it sank into the ground. In the same movement, Michael stepped forward and dragged his blade across her upper arm, and he only realized what he had done when she let out a yelp.

Once she jumped back, Michael saw that her left arm had been cut through between her shoulder and elbow, dangling by a small amount of flesh he had not severed with the blow. Hating himself for crippling her like that, Michael let the point of his blade fall to the ground.

"I am sorry, Hippolyta. I did not mean for that to happen, but the fight is over," he stated, but that just earned a scoff from the warrior.

"The fight is over when only one of us draws breath," Cimeries replied, and Michael watched her slice through the tissue connecting her arm to her body. When it dropped with a soft thud, Cimeries didn't even flinch and instead settled into a balanced stance, holding her spear to her side and poised to strike.

"You fight on even crippled..." Michael muttered, and he could see the woman's nostrils twitch.

"I fight on until I cannot. That is the way of a true warrior," Cimeries said before hopping forward, thrusting and slashing the air with her weapon once she was in range. Ducking out of the way of her thrusts and parrying the slashes, Michael could only look at this woman in wonder. That she was on the opposite side was no surprise, but her fierce nature and resilience even against insurmountable odds was nothing short of awesome.

Michael hated himself for what he was about to do.

"Then I must again ask your forgiveness for doubting you," Michael said before launching into his own strikes, slashing and burning the field around them. Whenever he thought the woman was cornered, she leapt out of the way or used her pike to propel herself out of danger. In spite of himself, Michael was enjoying this turn, this worthy enemy, but he knew that this battle could not go on indefinitely. They both had their limits.

And when she was finally unable to jump out of the way, Michael sank his sword deep into her left side.

"You are forgiven for your doubts," Cimeries said after a moment, struggling with every word but still looking him in the eye. "But I cannot let you stop me."

"Even *now*? Even as my blade runs through you?" Michael became frustrated at the situation, but he could see the determination in her eyes.

"In *spite* of it."

Cimeries pulled the blade out of her as she juked to the side, trying to plant her own weapon into Michael's armpit. After knocking the weapon out of her hand, Michael watched as she scrambled across the ground and tried to regain her balance.

"Just stop it!" Michael shouted, seeing the blood pour out of her wounded side. Still, she looked up at him defiantly, propped up by her remaining arm. "Is it worth this pain? Is it worth it to die like this?"

"It is *only* worth it to die like this!" Cimeries shouted back, her voice breaking and surprising him as she climbed to her feet. She swayed slightly, but he could feel her defiance from a few feet away. "I was deprived a glorious death in my first life, archangel. When Lucifer was killed, it gave me another purpose, but that purpose was achieved when I claimed vengeance. With the end of the universe so close, there are no more opportunities for a warrior's death. Either I will stop these madmen, or I will die in that struggle."

"A warrior's death..." Michael mused, dropping his weapon slightly. At last he understood this Amazon; he understood why she would not give up even when outmatched. Even in failure, this woman would succeed. When Cimeries lunged forward, determined to tear him apart with her nails and teeth, Michael finally did something right.

Shoving his sword through her heart and ending the fight quickly, Michael caught the woman as she fell.

"I could not let you pass, noble Hippolyta, but I can give you this," he said, holding her face with his left hand. Michael expected frustration, he expected pain, but he could see the satisfaction in her eyes even as her lip quivered.

"A gift I cannot repay," she said, placing her hand behind his neck and pulling herself up. "I wish you luck on finding your own."

"Thank you, Hippolyta. Truly," Michael said, drawing a nod from the woman just before she coughed up blood. Shaking her head as he tried to ease her pain, the woman merely opened her eyes and nodded to the palace behind them.

"You must stop them, Michael. It is your duty," Cimeries said, making Michael balk.

"Stop them? My duty…" he said, but the look she gave him forced the words from his mind. It was obvious Cimeries didn't have much longer, so he allowed her to speak.

"Your god, Niccolo… the two of them will destroy this universe," she stated, flinching as pain tore at her every fiber. After a moment of shaking, Cimeries resumed eye contact and gripped Michael's neck fiercely. "Cadmus is the only one who can save us."

"Cadmus?"

"The Pale Rider," she choked out. "Niccolo would destroy this world if it meant destroying Adonai, but Cadmus… he would save us all."

"What are you talking about?" Michael asked, but then the woman closed her eyes. Shaking her, the archangel panicked, and her eyelids fluttered open for the briefest moment.

"You will do the right thing, Michael. Gabriel believed you would," she said, throwing Michael's mind and heart into chaos. He would have demanded more answers from her, but it was already too late.

Hippolyta, the mighty Amazon queen, was dead.

Setting her head onto the ground and retrieving his blade from her heart, Michael did what he could to make her look at peace even though she had taken that possibility from him. When he stood back up, Michael realized that he had no options left.

It had taken the death of a noble warrior, but he finally saw the truth, finally realized just where he stood. He did not want this world to end; he did not want to see Adonai and his Heavenly Host triumphant. If there was even one other human soul like Hippolyta, if there was even a handful of brave souls within Hell's legions, Michael had another duty entirely.

Letting out his wings and setting his sword ablaze, Michael promised to himself that he would save the world Adonai would destroy, even if it meant his own death.

EVEN THOUGH HE tried to ignore them all, Cadmus could still hear the thousands of angelic voices in his skull, Azrael's gift almost causing more harm than good. It did not help that the enhanced power and energy threw his prophetic visions into overdrive, which in turn caused dozens of death scenes to flit across his mind every few seconds. If he didn't think it would waste his reserve of power, Cadmus would have stopped time just so he could make it to Adonai and Niccolo that much sooner.

He wondered what he would say to Niccolo once he arrived, how their interaction would unfold. Although Niccolo had tried to kill him and throw him into the abyss, Cadmus still felt the centuries of their friendship weighing on him. On the cracked fields of Purgatory, Cadmus had the opportunity to kill Niccolo and couldn't go through with it, and even now he wondered if he had the ability to stop his friend. Whatever grudge he felt toward Niccolo was completely overshadowed by the affection and kinship he held for him, and it would make this final confrontation even more difficult.

Especially since that kinship was overshadowed by his duty to the universe.

Seeing a pair of angels descending on a demonic warrior to his right, Cadmus diverted his course slightly so he could sweep his scythe through their bodies. He would not stop time to save the man, obviously, but he didn't see the harm in helping the souls along the way.

There is no point to it, Mercy rasped, and Cadmus briefly thought up an argument to the contrary. Before he could relay it, Mercy read his mind and sent him thoughts of disapproval. *A universe it at stake, Master. One human soul is nothing.*

Then why did we start the Black Death in the first place? Cadmus snapped back, but he instantly felt ashamed of himself. *I'm sorry, that doesn't—it didn't have anything to do with you.*

You speak as if I do not know that. However, their role in this war is over. There are only three people who matter, and that soul is not one of them.

When did you become heartless? Cadmus asked, causing the white horse to face him with a blank eye.

I speak this way because I wish to avoid as much pain as possible. If you do not understand that by now, then I cannot help you, Mercy replied, causing Cadmus to realize what he had just said. However, before he could seek forgiveness, Cadmus was distracted by the battle occurring in front of him.

After sending a mental apology, he drew his scythe and directed the stallion into the middle of the chaos.

Even though Mercy did not approve, he carried his master along the edge of the circle, allowing Cadmus to drag his blade through unsuspecting angels, relieving them of limbs, wings and cutting others in half. After just a few seconds of this, the Heavenly Host caught on and turned to face him, but that was exactly what Cadmus wanted.

Riding into the center of the massacre, Cadmus twirled his scythe above him fast enough that it drew in the airborne angels, acting like a meat thresher. By the time Cadmus was finished, only a few angels remained.

"Cadmus?" a deep voice asked, and Cadmus turned to find Seere gaping at him. The Horseman's armor had been partially dismantled during the battle and he suffered from a few minor wounds, but he seemed to be mostly intact. Even as he looked dumbfounded at his lost companion, Seere took his axe and slammed it into the side of an angel's head, killing him quickly. "By the gods, it's really you."

"Yeah, it's me," Cadmus replied before turning around, watching as four angels fled from the massacre. They only made it a few yards before they were swallowed in flames and Cadmus followed the trail of flames back to its source, finding Yeshua panting as he knelt on the ground.

His heart broke as he saw the dozens of wounds covering Yeshua's upper body, the arrows sticking out of his back, and he wondered why the man was so hurt. Once Cadmus saw William's unconscious body lying behind him, however, he realized the truth.

"So this is what has become of our fellow Horseman," another voice interrupted, and Cadmus quickly turned to find Diogenes hunched over on the ground, cradling his side. There was a gaping wound there, but Cadmus could tell that the philosopher was already healing. "You are somewhat late."

"Trust me, I got here as fast as I could," Cadmus said, looking at Diogenes in confusion. "Where are your horses?"

"Fury's hurt and he's a whiny bastard, so he's recovering right now," Seere coughed out, cracking his shoulder and looking away before considering his next words. "Despair is..."

"Her war is over," Diogenes interrupted. Instead of giving into sorrow, Diogenes turned to Cadmus with grim determination. "She fought well."

"Diogenes, I am so sorry," Cadmus started, but his fellow Horseman stood up straighter and used his spear to hold himself up.

"That is unnecessary, Pale Rider. You had no part in her death. Now, will you help us with this next wave?" he asked, nodding past Cadmus. Laughing in despair, Seere shook his head before setting the head of his weapon against the ground.

"Hah, seems like the Horseman of Death joined us just in time to reap our souls."

Looking over his shoulder, Cadmus saw something that made his heart sink. At first it seemed like a cloud, but then Cadmus realized that it was hundreds of angels descending upon them, intent on destroying the Horsemen of the Apocalypse. Turning back to face his companions, Cadmus realized the horrible truth. He wanted to fight, to stay here and help his comrades, but he could not allow himself to jeopardize everything.

Quickly, Cadmus. They will understand.

"I—I can't stay," he said, causing all three of his friends to look at him in shock. "The whole universe depends on me making it Niccolo before he gets to Adonai. I—I…"

"Go," Yeshua said weakly, forcing Cadmus to look at the ailing soul. Standing up even as blood poured out of his wounds, Yeshua made eye contact with Cadmus just before his pupils disappeared and flames covered his body. "We will hold them back."

"I can't ask you to do that. Just run—" Cadmus tried, but Seere let out a deep laugh and slammed his weapon against the ground.

"Like we're gonna *run*. We're the Horsemen of the Apocalypse, Cadmus, and that one over there was supposed to bring the Rapture." He slung his weapon onto his shoulder and nodded at the horde of angels. "*They* should be scared of *us*."

"Seere…"

"You were never one to waste time, Pale Rider," Diogenes said, the hole in his stomach finally healing. Pointing his spear at the palace rising above the capitol, Diogenes snorted and spat at his feet. "The end of the world is not a good time to start."

"You're all going to—" Cadmus started, but then he realized that it was pointless to argue. They all knew what was at stake, what it meant to lose him in this final battle. Facing insurmountable odds, they still made that choice, and Cadmus would not dishonor them by wasting their sacrifice. "I will be disappointed if those weaklings even scratch you, you know that?"

"If I break a sweat, I'll let you know," Seere said almost apathetically, winking at the end, and Cadmus surrendered a knowing smile before nodding at the other heroes. Once he had given his silent goodbyes, Cadmus urged Mercy along their path and the horse galloped onward, leaving the three maimed warriors to fight against an entire army by themselves.

"So," Seere said before turning to his companions, "you want to bet who will die last? Gentleman's wager, of course."

"You're no gentleman," Diogenes commented, drawing a weary smile from Seere before he took his weapon in both hands and prepared for the heavenly onslaught.

"Shit, guess we don't get to die, then." Seere wondered if he even believed his own bravado.

He hoped, at least, that it was possible.

"ENOUGH!" Gregorious declared before slamming down his massive gauntlet, sending a shockwave through the air that forced Buer to stop his forward assault.

Seeing his brother turning to avoid splinters of rock, Crocell fell out of the sky and let his dark wings catch the air so he could redirect his momentum toward their foe. As he saw the golem stand back up, Crocell let the current crackle around his trident before pointing the weapon at Gregorious, sending an arc of wild electricity at the angelic monster.

He hadn't expected to do much more than momentarily distract the giant—they had been trying to bring down Gregorious for a few minutes to no effect—but the stone golem merely looked up at Crocell with his remaining eye. Feeling the monster's gaze, Crocell flapped his wings to gain altitude, but Gregorious whipped around his stone arm, the vines of his joints letting him move faster than his size should allow.

Crocell continued upward—hoping to escape the colossal hand rushing toward him—but then a gigantic, scaled foot fell down from above and intercepted Gregorious' arm, causing Crocell to think he was safe for the moment. However, the sudden arrival of the foot and the huge body it belonged to caused gale-force winds that Crocell could not avoid, and he was swept along the current. Once Crocell was finally able to see what manner of creature had saved him, his arms dropped to his sides.

"Asmodeus," he muttered, the name swallowed up in the roar of wind crashing against him.

The great emerald dragon with six wings—what remained of the mischievous demon king—was grappling with Gregorious, and Crocell watched as Asmodeus knocked over his opponent, sending both of them to the ground with the feral dragon on top. Still airborne, Crocell let a tear roll down his face as he realized the sacrifice Asmodeus had made and the pain he must have felt for his twin's death. In another life, Crocell would have been the one responsible for providing a dignified death for his brother, but he knew he could not hope to best such a creature.

Crocell only watched as the dragon tried to clench its jaws down on Gregorious' helm and yelped once several of its teeth cracked, unable to pierce the angel's stone armor. Frustrated and furious, Asmodeus picked himself up before pouring liquid fire over Gregorious body, smoke rising from the vines connecting the armor as flames consumed organic matter. As awful a sight it was, Crocell understood that it was likely the only real way to subdue the golem.

"Crocell!" Buer's voice came from below, and the slayer turned his attention to his brother galloping beneath him. Buer waved at him before pointing away from the monsters struggling far too close for comfort. "Retreat! We cannot help him now!"

"This was supposed to be our fight," Crocell argued, too soft for the centaur to hear, and he looked back at the giants just as Buer ran out of range of their attacks. Asmodeus continued to breathe flames over the giant's body, but Gregorious realized what kind of danger he was in and wrapped his fingers around the dragon's neck, pulling him to the side and causing them to roll over nearby combatants as they continued to fight.

It was a marvelous thing to behold, however sorrowful it was, but Crocell realized the wisdom of Buer's words soon enough. Yet again, Crocell had been proven useless in this fight—he could never have beaten Gregorious alone—and the realization caused him to look down at his torso. A handful of long scratches ran along his skin, but most worrying were the three puncture wounds in his gut. All of them wept black blood, and Crocell knew it would not be much longer before they caused his death. It had been so long since a Fallen had died from blood loss, but it seemed like Crocell would be the next.

Looking back at his retreating brother and hoping to escort him in these last moments, Crocell's eyes widened in horror once he saw the airborne enemy pursing Buer. After folding in his wings and diving, Crocell only let his feathers catch the air once he had picked up enough speed, but he knew that he was already too late.

Redirecting his momentum and flying low along the ground, Crocell let surges of electricity flow from his arms and along his trident, gritting his teeth so he could suffer the pain his own powers caused him. When it became obvious that he would not intercept his brother, Crocell breathed in deep—ignoring the pain from his numerous wounds—and gambled that Buer would react well to his warning.

"Buer! From the air behind you!" Crocell shouted as loud as he could, and he saw that Buer had noticed the effort.

However, the centaur did exactly what Crocell did *not* want him to do and turned his head, pausing enough for his pursuer to impale him from above. Crocell did not waste his breath on shouting further —he had already failed—and instead tried to close the distance as

Uriel gracefully landed on Buer's back and drove his spear even further through the centaur's abdomen, causing his four legs to buckle beneath him.

"This is how it ends, brother?" Uriel asked as he rode Buer's body to a stop, a cruel smile on his face the entire time. Once the centaur's broken body stopped moving, Uriel twisted his spear and pulled it out of Buer's gut, the Fallen protesting weakly from the pain. "You would never have allowed yourself to be struck like that during the rebellion.

"And you," Uriel said before turning with his weapon and catching Crocell's oncoming trident between the tines, the sound of their impact echoing throughout the battlefield. As he gazed up at Crocell, Uriel chuckled and shook his head. "You know better."

"I had to try."

Crocell then used his wings to propel himself backward, just out of reach of Uriel's counterthrust. Still standing on Buer's body, Uriel used his free hand to pull his long hair behind his ear before hopping off the moaning centaur.

"It is always *trying* with you, Crocell. You try to lead a vanguard against the Heavenly Host, you try to kill the Shroud, you try to hitch a ride back to Earth, you *try* to redeem yourself," Uriel said before reclaiming his spear in both hands. "Have you *ever* succeeded?"

"Sometimes," Crocell said, staring down the archangel in contempt. Seeing his anger, Uriel grinned and stretched out his wings behind him.

"Just not when it counts, is that it?" Uriel swept his wings forward and slowly rose into the air, matching Crocell's altitude within a moment. "Azazel told us how you tried to find him, how you killed all of the humans he turned into feral beasts. Here's what confuses me. He said that you felt *guilt for them*. Why would you stoop so low as that?"

"I did not *stoop*," Crocell responded, his voice confident as he gathered electricity along his weapon. "They deserved my compassion and my mercy."

"Oh, they deserve *nothing*, brother. On the other hand, I believe our Asmodeus might deserve your *compassion*," Uriel said before nodding through the dust at the giant dragon still fighting Gregorious. "How despicable that he would *choose* to change into that form."

"Some things are beyond petty *existence*, Uriel." Crocell glared at his brother as they both floated higher into the air. "In these final days, Asmodeus found something in his soul that allowed him to live on, to fight even in his brother's absence."

"Spare me another lecture about *purpose*," Uriel said in his snide tone, jerking his head so that his hair swept around his shoulder. "With all those spectacular failures concerning your own, you have no ground to stand on."

"Perhaps that is why we have wings." Crocell gathered his fury and let dark skies gather above them before sparse rain started to fall. Crackles of electricity arced from cloud to cloud, but Uriel was unimpressed.

"Flashy, Crocell, but you must do better when facing an archangel. Tell me, throughout this entire conversation, those wounds of yours have continued to bleed. You must tell me the story behind that." Uriel wore a malicious smirk, but Crocell was not amused.

"I have no obligations to you," Crocell stated simply before rushing forward, pushing himself too hard and letting out a spurt of blood from a gash in his shoulder. Ignoring the pain, Crocell watched Uriel as he flew forward to meet him.

At the last second before their impact, Crocell withdrew his wings and dropped down ten feet in the air, raising his trident above him. Noticing his brother's attack after a split second, Uriel narrowly avoided the column of electricity that flowed down from the clouds to meet Crocell's weapon, sending a surge of energy through the Fallen. Although he tried to recover in time, Crocell lowered his trident too slow and was rewarded with a spearhead through his left shoulder.

"Not bad, Crocell, but I've seen that before," Uriel said.

Crocell brought up his legs and pushed hard against the archangel's chest, forcing the spear to slide out of his shoulder and allowing Crocell to dive backward.

Rolling over, Crocell tried to fly away from Uriel but found that the archangel had redirected his own flight path so he could intercept him. Crocell only had time to bring up his weapon with one hand, but he was able to muster enough strength to catch Uriel's spear in his trident.

"Are you running away again, brother?"

"There is nowhere to run, Uriel." Somehow, Crocell matched the archangel's strength with just his right arm. "I was just waiting for your mistake."

"My mistake?" Uriel asked, realizing the answer far too late. Letting the current surge along his weapon and, by contact, through Uriel's spear, Crocell electrified his brother before drawing his trident back. As Uriel fell toward the ground, Crocell lifted his trident to the sky and great columns of lightning arced through the storm clouds, all of them meeting at the single point.

Satisfied by the power held in his trident, Crocell hurled it down at Uriel's falling body so fast that it caused a sonic boom. For a moment he had thought himself foolish for letting go of his weapon, but Uriel's body met the ground almost at the same instant that his weapon crashed down, letting out an electrical shockwave that would have killed any normal souls within a fifty-foot radius. The great surge of energy let loose by his trident threatened to overwhelm even Crocell, but it dissipated before it reached him.

Unfortunately, once the dust settled, Crocell was able to see that his attack had failed. Almost before he could react, a gold spear flew up from the ground—aimed at his position in the air—and only by rolling to the left was Crocell able to avoid being impaled. Letting out his hand just as the spear reached him, Crocell grabbed hold of the weapon and let it shine magnificently before transforming it back into a trident.

"Well done, brother. I confess, I did not expect that from you."

Uriel's voice had come from the cloud of debris, which dispersed when the archangel used his wings to scatter the dust. Once Uriel jumped into the air and joined him a hundred feet above the ground, Crocell noticed the scorched pathway that had been burned into Uriel's cheek.

If nothing else, it gave the slayer some small satisfaction.

"What difference do your expectations make?" Crocell asked, bringing up his trident to bear. It was supposed to be intimidating, supposed to show that Crocell was still in this fight, but the weapon wavered in his grip. Suddenly, whatever strength he had received from the storm abandoned him, and Uriel noticed.

"You have always been an angel of few words." Uriel sneered as he brought up his spear. "Perhaps you should continue that behavior."

"I would not respond if you did not break the silence," Crocell countered, which made Uriel glare at him with even more hatred. In just that moment, Crocell realized that Uriel would no longer toy with him.

Murder danced in the archangel's eyes.

Before Crocell could take another breath, Uriel rushed forward with lethal intent, thrusting his spear so quickly that Crocell could only deflect two of the strikes, ducking and diving out of the way of the rest. When Crocell was forced to drop down two feet to avoid a thrust aimed at his throat, Uriel rolled through the air and attacked from the side.

Unprepared, Crocell couldn't avoid this strike and felt the spearhead sink into his flesh just beneath the ribcage, where it tore through his side and came out the other.

"How does it *feel*, Crocell? How does it feel to fail *again*?" Uriel asked, condescension dripping from each syllable. Ignoring the pain of the spear skewering his torso, Crocell looked up and held the shaft by the entrance wound.

"I will tell you if I fail," he said, gripping Uriel's spear tight as he thrust his trident at Uriel's unguarded midsection. The archangel noticed the attack, but he had not counted on the strength Crocell still held in his left arm, and so he was only able to pull out the spear a few inches and couldn't escape entirely. One of the prongs of Crocell's weapons punctured Uriel's stomach, the middle prong only grazing against his side, but it was enough to shock the archangel.

"You miserable—" he started, but he was so angry he could not finish the insult. Uriel slammed his hand against Crocell's face, forcing the slayer's body to the ground and freeing their weapons, and Crocell wondered if he would have the strength to stop his momentum before he crashed against the surface.

He didn't.

"You did it, you coward. You *failure*," Uriel spat out as Crocell regained his senses.

Once he was able to turn over and pick himself up from the ground, Crocell realized the blood loss would claim him soon and shock was starting to set in. Trying to force that into the back of his mind, Crocell looked around and noticed that his storm clouds had completely disappeared. It made sense; he no longer had the strength to keep them around, but he had hoped he could send one last bolt of lightning at his brother.

Remembering the archangel, Crocell turned his head just in time to have a boot rocket into his jaw, dislocating it and sending him rolling along the ground. When he coughed up blood and felt the pain spread along his face, the slayer realized there was almost no time left. Swallowing down the metal taste in his mouth, Crocell got to his knees and watched as Uriel approached.

"You wounded me, Crocell. After so many years, I almost have to thank you. No one has dared fight me, made me bleed in *millennia*," Uriel snarled, walking toward his broken brother without sympathy.

Realizing that the archangel was merely gloating before his kill, Crocell looked past his brother and saw Buer trying to stand on broken legs. It was no stretch of the imagination to consider that Uriel would turn his sights on him once he was finished with Crocell.

"I hup—" Crocell started before realizing that his dislocated jaw garbled the words. Setting his palm against the bone, Crocell shoved the bone back into place and looked back at Uriel once he could speak. "I hope you enjoy the pain."

"I never had much use for masochism, brother, however much you enjoy it. Do you have any last words before I tear open your chest?" Uriel asked while planting his foot against Crocell's left shoulder. With a wince, Crocell looked beyond the archangel to see Buer one last time. He had hoped to save the centaur from Uriel's sneak attack, but he had failed in that mission, as well.

Remembering his other mission, Crocell turned his head to see what had become of the great dragon that had saved them from Gregorious. If he had been healthy and whole, it would have been Crocell's duty to destroy that feral Asmodeus, but he would fail in that responsibility, too. His heart filled with despair as he looked for the pair of giants, but then Crocell saw something that brought a smile to his face.

"Last words... I could ask you the same," Crocell replied as he turned back to face his confused brother.

Uriel was still looking down at him when Crocell grabbed the archangel's foot and sent a surge of electricity through the limb. Already cursing Crocell for the weak attack, Uriel thrust his spear at Crocell's heart, but he did not notice what the slayer held in his right hand. Just as the archangel's weapon tore into Crocell's chest, a trident plunged deep into Uriel's gut.

"You fool." Uriel laughed weakly as he stared into Crocell's black eyes. "You *missed*. I stand just a foot away from you, my heart for the taking, and you *still* fail."

"I did not fail, brother," Crocell said cryptically, throwing Uriel's mind into a frenzy of thoughts. "I have succeeded in holding you *here*."

"What does that mean?" Uriel asked, but then he noticed the shadow that suddenly covered them in darkness.

Looking up, the archangel finally noticed that a great green dragon loomed over them and looked down in primal hunger. Once he saw the appetite in those eyes, Uriel tried to run, tried to pull free, but he could not move. As he looked back down, he found Crocell gazing up at him with a grim smile, his arms anchoring Uriel to that spot with the last of his strength.

"It means that I have finally found my purpose," Crocell declared as Uriel screamed obscenities, frantically trying to pull away from his sacrificial brother, but it was too late.

Asmodeus lowered his great maw down from above and snapped his jaws shut, his sharp teeth tearing both Fallen and archangel apart and taking them from this world. After swallowing them, Asmodeus lifted his head and roared, sending out a great burst of flame that dispersed once it devoured the oxygen around it.

Crippled, Buer watched as his feral brother lowered his head and gazed at him, but his thoughts were not about his own safety. In his current state, there would be no way for him to run, but Buer didn't particularly feel inclined to escape. Crocell had made his death count —Uriel was one of their greatest enemies—but Buer had lost his will to fight. The war was over for him, and if that meant becoming his brother's next meal, he would not fight it.

However, Asmodeus only looked at him for a moment before tilting his head, causing Buer to think that his lost brother might recognize him. Once the beast lost interest and turned away, Buer tried to rationalize that it did not consider him a viable source of food, but he could not shake the feeling that Asmodeus was still there, deep down. If he had time, access to more records, he may have thought about how he might drag the demon king back from the edge. However, since he did not have the time or the records, Buer simply waited for his legs to heal so he could rejoin the others.

Sinking further into grief for his fallen and corrupted brothers, Buer soon realized there may not be others to rejoin.

"I'll tell you this once!" Seere declared from the ground, twirling the axe in his hand as the swarm of angels came within earshot. "The first five angels are going down in one hit!"

"Your bragging would be more impressive if your allies weren't covered in their own blood," Diogenes added, and it seemed like the angels agreed with him. Three hundred angels had circled around them, waiting and analyzing their every move, but Seere stubbornly refused to abandon the smile on his face.

"*Please*, that was just a personal challenge," Seere replied, winking at Diogenes before catching sight of Yeshua pulling the last arrow from his back. He was tired, weak from blood loss, but Seere could still see the fire in his eyes. "You guys want to add to that number?"

"We're just here... to stop them, Seere," Yeshua said, gulping down a mixture of blood and spit before standing straight and letting intense flames build in his hands. Keeping his gaze skyward, Yeshua looked like a very different kind of messiah. "If I go airborne, would one of you be able to protect William?"

"No," Diogenes said abruptly, and Yeshua looked down in shock to see the man holding his spear and shield at the ready. "In this fight, we have no hope of protecting ourselves."

"I... then I guess it falls on me," Yeshua whispered, but Seere heard his despair and shook his head.

"It falls on *us*, Yeshua. We'll keep him alive. I swear it."

Yeshua was about to joke about how little Seere's promise meant, but then he saw the determination in his stare, the white of his knuckles as he gripped his weapon. Before Yeshua could give voice to his gratitude, the first angels descended from the sky, twelve spearmen determined to defeat the Horsemen of the Apocalypse.

"What did I *just* say?" Seere shouted as he launched himself into the air, spinning his body so he could slam his axe into the side of an outmatched angel.

Once the edge was buried into the man's torso, Seere continued his spin and used the angel's body to strike through four of the other attackers, collecting them before throwing them back to the ground along with his weapon. In just a few seconds, that first group of angels were reduced to almost half their number and stopped their attack as Seere plummeted back to the ground.

Although a foolish angel rushed through the air and somehow buried his spearhead into Seere's thigh, the Horseman grabbed the man's helmet and dragged him back down with him as he fell, crushing the angel's skull once he landed. Standing up and flinching slightly from the pain, Seere yanked out the spear before tossing it aside and limping back to the pile of angels near his discarded weapon. By the time he bent down to pick up his axe, the wound in his thigh had healed completely.

"Please, don't," one of the surviving angels said from the dogpile, but Seere frowned as he looked down at his opponent.

"Sorry, kid, I made a promise," he said before slamming his weapon back down and cutting through all five angels in an explosion of energy. When the dust cleared, Seere's audience saw the giant tear in the ground and numerous discarded body parts, but he was not surprised. Turning back to look at the angels hovering above him, Seere lifted both arms and bowed his head before letting a malicious grin twist his face.

"You have to try better than *that*, guys! I've been waiting for this fight for *thirteen centuries!*" he shouted, which was all the invitation the angels needed. Hundreds of war cries filled the air as the Heavenly Host descended, and Seere bit his lip in anticipation for the coming bloodshed.

Yeshua, on the other hand, would have preferred it if Seere would have been less antagonistic, but he knew his role in this. Letting the inferno cover him once more, Yeshua jumped into the air and through the gaps left between the angels falling all around him. Sending out streams of flames and throwing condensed fireballs at the angels closest to him, Yeshua could already smell the burning flesh of his enemies, but it was not enough.

Every time he sent an angel to their grave, three more flew right past him, ready to destroy his friends. After only a few seconds of flying through their ranks—incinerating the soldiers foolish enough to approach him—Yeshua realized that too many angels were heading straight toward Seere and an unconscious William. Cursing, he flipped back over and dove straight to the ground, maintaining a halo of flames that consumed anything that got too close.

Once he was within a few feet of the ground, Yeshua noticed an angel standing over William's body, poised to slam his sword through the young man's heart. Upon seeing the danger, Yeshua sent bursts of flames behind him to propel him further and then flipped over his body at the last moment, slamming both feet into the angel's ribcage and saving William from his fate.

As the angel recovered from the blow and hovered a few feet above the ground, Yeshua directed a plume of flame at him, melting his armor instantly and transformed him into a screaming pile of metal and burned flesh.

"Will never... get used to that," William's voice came from the ground, weak, but it caused Yeshua to look down at his friend. Color was starting to return to his cheeks, but it was clear that William would not be moving anytime soon.

Yeshua was about to kneel down and speak to the boy, but he felt a sharp pain in his back and looked down to see a bloody spearhead poking out through his stomach. In fury, Yeshua grabbed the shaft sticking out of his back and clenched his hand just as fire covered his skin, breaking it easily before turning to look at his enemy.

He could see the fear in her eyes, her trembling lips, but Yeshua could give her no mercy. After grabbing the woman's spearhead and yanking it out of his stomach—doing his best to ignore the suction pulling at his insides—Yeshua rushed forward and shoved the broken spear up through the woman's throat and into her brain. It was awful, but it was quick; more mercy than anybody could expect.

"Gross," William muttered, and Yeshua looked over to the see that William had turned over and was struggling to pick himself up. "And I thought burning people alive was violent."

"Don't move, William, we don't need your help," Yeshua said, but William laughed before nodding past him.

"Coulda... fooled me. Just look at Diogenes over there," he said, and Yeshua whipped around to find that the Horseman was standing in the middle of a pile of bodies, deflecting each strike with his shield before countering with his spear. Yeshua was about to argue that Diogenes was holding his own, but then he noticed the arrows sticking out of his legs and the gashes covering his back.

"I'll—he'll be fine."

"And what about you? You got a hole in your stomach, Yeshua," William said, his words coming easier now.

At the remark, Yeshua turned around to see that William was still on his knees, but the effort it took him to turn was enough to make Yeshua's vision cloud over. Collapsing to his knees, Yeshua brought his hand to his chest and felt the warmth of his own blood before realizing that the wound would not close. After all the damage he had taken during their escape from Gregorious, it seemed like Yeshua's body had finally reached its limit.

"I'm alright." His voice trembled through the lie, and William shook his head with a smile.

"No, you're not. And it's all my fault. You were protecting me," he said, at which point Yeshua crawled over and set his hand on William's shoulder, sending a lazy fireball to his left to intercept a pair of angels intent on killing them both.

"It's not your fault, William. None of this is your fault. You saved me, and I saved you. It was a fair trade," Yeshua said, hoping to convince the young man, but they were interrupted by Diogenes' voice.

"Arrows!" he shouted, louder than Yeshua thought possible, and they turned to see the former Horseman holding his shield above him. Looking up, Yeshua and William to see that hundreds of black sticks covered the sky, blocking out the light from dozens of miniature suns. It was such an amazing sight that neither of them could react, but once the whistling reached their ears, Yeshua finally realized what was about to happen.

"Keep down!" he shouted to William before standing up and letting an inferno spread from his outstretched hands. A blanket of fire instantly formed above them and stole the air from their lungs, but Yeshua could see through the chaos, the arrows falling into the blaze and burning away. At first, he was satisfied, but then he was able to see that only the shafts had been destroyed; the arrowheads continued to plummet toward them.

Yeshua was about to increase the intensity of his flames, but a whimper from his side forced him to remember the boy he was trying to save. If he made the inferno any hotter, he would destroy William in the process, and Yeshua could not accept that outcome. In that same instant, he also realized that he would not be able to escape with William in his arms; there were too many arrowheads to avoid.

Abandoning his flames, Yeshua jumped on top of William's body and hoped he would be strong enough to follow in Judas' footsteps.

"No! What are you doing?" William tried to shove him away, but Yeshua held the boy close as the arrowheads fell, sinking into his back and forcing him through agonizing pain. However, Yeshua kept his body still, grabbed hold of William's shirt as more and more arrowheads punctured his skin, and clenched his jaw tight to deal with each new blow.

"Stop it! Just stop it!" William's anger and frustration turned to whining, but Yeshua could not give into his demands. Finally, after the thirtieth arrowhead, Yeshua could not keep himself from hacking up blood onto William's face, but he kept his place on top of William's body. It made his companion sputter and blink away the residue, but Yeshua could not pay attention. He was barely conscious as the onslaught continued.

"You're going to die!" William shouted, and at that point Yeshua could no longer ignore him. Making eye contact one last time, Yeshua smiled at the young man he hoped he had saved, even as another arrowhead punctured his lower spine and stole the feeling from his legs.

"I know," Yeshua said, and instantaneously he was back on Earth, Judas holding him as a silver blade punctured his heart. In this last moment, as the last arrowhead fell to the ground, Yeshua finally understood his brother. When he closed his eyes one last time, he felt what it was like to give his life to save his friends.

Silently urging his friend to stay alive, Yeshua rolled off William's body and faded away, a smile on his face.

"Yeshua!" William screamed as he rolled over and knelt next to his savior, shaking the man by the shoulders and hoping there was some shred of life left in him. Tears fell down his cheeks, his throat ached from the screaming, but William could not accept this. He could not accept that Yeshua had given his life for him.

"Please, wake the fuck up, Yeshua. Please!" he urged, but no amount of shaking brought Yeshua back from the edge, no amount of pleading would stop the man's eyes from glassing over. After a few seconds, William surrendered to reality and buried his face in his hands, weeping for the man who had given himself to his people in life, and given himself to William in death.

The worst part of all was that William knew he was not worthy.

"Diogenes," William said abruptly, lifting his hands and looking back to the Horseman. On this last battlefield he did not have the luxury of grieving for anyone, no matter how important they were, so William brought out his sword, ready to defend Diogenes from the enemies surrounding him. However, he was far too late to help.

Still standing with his shield high above him, Diogenes was dead on his feet, a dozen spears and swords propping up his corpse. And although he was surrounded by dead or dying angels skewered by countless arrows, that small victory would not bring the Horseman back from the dead.

"They're all... they all died... for me," William muttered, his sword arm dropping as the fight emptied out of him, and it was almost too much for the man to bear. Only once shouts of victory rose from his left did William realize that he was still alive, and that murderers of noble heroes were cheering for their coward's victory. Immediately, William turned to face the remaining angels, half their original number, and he sheathed his sword quickly before taking the bow from his back.

"No. No, I *won't* let you fucking cheer." William drew a pair of arrows from his quiver and set them against the string. Pulling back, William wondered where he should aim, but he realized that it did not matter.

Wherever he aimed, he was sure to kill at least one angel.

"Let's see how you like it," William whispered before tilting his bow to the side and sending both arrows into the crowd of angels. He had intended for the arrows to strike two different targets, but he could not have anticipated the dull, moss-green energy that covered the arrows as they rocketed toward the angelic troops.

When they slammed into the front rank of angels, the arrows continued through their armor and bodies and into the next ranks as if they were nothing more than paper. William could only drop his bow and watch as the mystically-charged arrows continued through each rank, killing dozens of angels as they celebrated the death of Yeshua and Diogenes.

The cheers stopped.

"I... I'll do you proud, Yeshua."

William raised his bow back up and grabbed another pair of arrows, but the angels recovered from the attack quickly. Before William had a chance to repeat the devastating assault, angels swarmed into the air and scattered, filling the sky like a tidal wave ready to crash against him.

Even as the terrifying sight filled his vision, William stood his ground as he sent out another pair of arrows, each of them covered with green light. An angel fell with each arrow, but the swarm continued to approach, ready to destroy William as soon as he was within reach. Only after sending another thirty angels to their graves did William realize that he had run out of time, so he threw his bow to the side and grabbed his sword and dagger, ready to die with dignity.

"Come on then!" he shouted as the swarm of angels was about to crash down on him, but then he felt something yank him from behind and he was suddenly airborne and falling away from his enemies. Before he could do more than yelp in protest, William was shoved into a saddle behind a bloody giant with black sticks scattered along his arms and legs. It was disorienting at first, but William finally realized who had come to save him once he saw Fury's crimson body beneath him.

"Seere? I thought you were—"

"Dead? Please, I just haven't gotten around to pulling out all the arrows yet." Seere looked back with a grin, but a slight twitch in his eye told William that it was all an act.

"I... I'm so glad," William said before turning back to find that the swarm of angels was following them closely, the confident ones throwing their spears and javelins and missing only by a few feet. After stowing his dagger back in his belt, William wrapped his arm around Seere's bloody midsection and held his sword at the ready to deflect any lucky arrows. "If you didn't know... Yeshua and Diogenes—"

"Yeah, I know, kid! I can still see!" Seere shouted, as if the death of their allies was a minor issue, but a slight wavering in his voice gave him away. "They died the right way. They did it the best way."

"I—I don't know about that," William said as he knocked away an arrow that would have otherwise punctured Fury's backside. After a few tense seconds, William gulped down his fear and tried to figure out what they could do. "We have to stop them."

"We *are*, Will. We're leading them on a fucking chase," Seere replied just as he brought his hammer down on an unsuspecting angel that had the misfortune of being in their way. "We just have to make sure they don't go after Cadmus."

"Seere, we're going straight toward Adonai's palace," William said, at which point Fury wheeled about abruptly and Seere jumped off his horse, allowing William to see how much damage the Horseman had actually taken.

Seere had dozens of open gashes and tears in his skin, his right bracer had been torn off completely and a handful of arrowheads were sticking out. His right eye had been slashed open and blood weakly pulsed out of the wound; chunks of skin were missing around his ribs and made William gasp once he saw exposed bone. That Seere was still alive was a miracle. That he was now standing was impossible.

Yet, even with all of that pain and damage, Seere looked up at him with a smile and a wink.

"No, *you're* going straight toward Adonai's palace, because someone needs to stop them if I don't. But let's be serious. They *probably* won't get past me," Seere claimed before walking forward and gripping his axe tight.

"I'm not going to abandon you like this." William was about to jump out of Fury's saddle, but the horse balked and William had to grab onto the pommel just to avoid breaking his neck on the ground.

"I made a fucking *promise*, Will," Seere shouted abruptly, and William looked at the man's face and saw a tear mixing with the gore splattered on his face. "Yeshua asked me to keep you alive and I'm gonna make damn sure I do."

"Seere..." William muttered, but Seere abandoned his anger and sorrow for the moment and looked back at him fondly.

"You got a raw deal, kid. I'm doing my part to make up for it," he said before turning back around and waiting for the storm cloud of angels, which was almost within striking distance. William was about to leave, but then—surprising both of them—Fury turned his head and stamped his hoof against the ground.

"Hey, idiot!" Fury screamed, and Seere was shocked enough that he turned to his unwilling servant. With a nod of respect, the crimson horse neighed and shook his mane. "Don't die just because I'm not around."

"And here I thought you hated being my horse," Seere said, scoffing as he turned back to the swarm.

"I do, but I don't want to train another Horseman. Try to be smart for once," Fury said before turning around and then galloping away, taking William from the fight and leaving Seere to his own devices.

Thanks, Fury, Seere thought, his smile fading away as he made peace with his fate. *But I lied. No matter what he says, keep that kid away from the action. I'm not standing here just so he can die later.*

You're too obvious. If you die, do it right, Horseman.

Seere had to chuckle as he looked up at the hundred angels diving down to obliterate him.

It was at this time that Seere finally allowed himself to grieve for Yeshua, for Diogenes, for Sitri, for all the friends he had lost along the way, and he let that grief turn to hatred and anger. As the angels yelled their war cries and cascaded to the ground, confident that Seere would be nothing more than a corpse in just a moment, scarlet energy exploded out him as his own war cry deafened the angels closest to him.

With the end so close, Seere let his fury consume him and poured all his energy, all of his soul, into one last sweep of his axe. Pulling the blade across his body, Seere couldn't even see past the chaos of his unrestrained anger as his body twisted, as pain tore through every single one of his muscles and joints.

All he knew was that his friends were dead, that his enemies were in front of him, and it was up to him to wreak vengeance upon them.

Once Seere brought his axe across his body and let loose the critical mass of energy, he did not have the strength to hold onto the weapon and it flew away from him, clattering against the ground as he fell onto his side. He could feel blood pouring out of his sides, out of the holes in his arms, but Seere had just enough strength to pick up his head and open his eye to see if he had succeeded, if any angels had been killed by his last attack.

Although there were still twenty angels in the air, Seere could just barely understand that they were flying away, as if they were escaping. Only after looking at the battlefield did Seere understand, and a weak smile formed on his face as consciousness started to slip away from him.

At least thirty angels had been killed immediately after Seere had unleashed his fury, but he could see a hundred angels on the ground screaming, moaning, or calling out for parents and friends who would not save them. In his last-ditch effort, Seere had succeeded, but he knew it would only be a few moments before an errant angel realized that they only needed to strike him one last time, that the Horseman of War could no longer fight.

As his mind faded away and darkness crept into his vision, Seere thought he saw a giant green lizard walking to his right, toward the palace in the distance, but he put the thought out of his head. It was impossible—it had to be a hallucination from all his blood loss—but that was beyond Seere's ability to care. Closing his eyes, Seere wondered how it would feel to finally fade away, to sleep forever, and wondered what dreams he might see.

And in that last moment before he lost consciousness, Seere hoped he would meet Sitri on that other side.

Niccolo trudged up the abandoned street, breathing shakily as he went. It was difficult to place one foot in front of the other, but that had less to do with the physical effort than the pain in his soul. He had lost almost everything now; both fathers, both of the women he loved and so many of his dear friends. Even if Diogenes was telling the truth and Cadmus was still alive, that almost made it worse. That just meant that he had *tried* to kill Cadmus and failed, and his best friend might be coming to repay the favor.

As a foolish angel ran toward him with a spear, Niccolo almost wanted Cadmus to come and lop off his head right then and there.

However, rage filled him just as the angel was within striking distance, so Niccolo stepped aside and used his demonic arm to tear out the foolish soul's throat. Air gurgled out of the wound as the angel fell, but Niccolo didn't stay to watch him die. He just kept putting one foot in front of the other, each step bringing him closer and closer to his revenge.

Although Adonai had not directly caused the torment of Niccolo's life, he was definitely responsible. Without Adonai's permission, Sabrael would never have been given the chance to mutilate his arm and send him on this forsaken path. As soon as he saw the stout angel's face in his mind, Niccolo clenched his bloody fingers and imagined that he was crushing the man's throat. Sabrael had pretended to guide Niccolo, adopting the guise of Innocenti, that merchant, and he had taught Niccolo everything he knew about being an assassin.

"You used to have more finesse, young Vespucci."

Innocenti's voice came to him, and Niccolo was almost convinced that it was in his head. Only after he looked up from the ground and saw the purple robes and the bored expression on Sabrael's face did he realize that his enemy was in front of him.

Standing there with his staff, not worried at all, was the archangel responsible for ruining his entire life and afterlife.

"Finesse was always something *you* wanted," Niccolo spat out with a healthy dose of venom, summoning Lux into his hand and stalking toward the apathetic angel standing in the middle of the road. "I was always a fan of brutality and violence."

"That is not true and you know it. You took to your lessons with zeal," Sabrael argued, seemingly not bothered at all that his former student was intent on murdering him. When Niccolo came to a stop a few feet away, he merely looked up at him with mild interest. "You were a good student, even if you were quite brazen and, well, somewhat forgetful."

"Do you have any defense? Any words you want to spit out before I tear out your heart and shove this sword through your brain?"

Niccolo had already drew back his sword so he could plunge it underneath Sabrael's fat chin. Rolling his eyes as Niccolo brought his arm forward, Sabrael snapped his fingers and caused him to fall away, screaming at the sudden pain.

When Niccolo looked down, he found that his demonic arm had turned against him once more, the bones snapping and the muscles making it twist in grotesque fashion. Even the skin seemed to leak out more pus and blood as splinters of bone shoved their way to the surface, and it was all Niccolo could do to grab his wrist with his right hand as his arm writhed out of control.

"Like I said, Niccolo, you were somewhat forgetful. Did you not consider that I would manipulate your arm again? I would think such a painful lesson would have been burned into your memory, especially since it was your fault that Tamiel died at Uriel's hands," Sabrael said, drawing closer so he could inspect the arm that Niccolo was barely keeping under control. "I am quite proud of this one."

"You manipulated me from the start," Niccolo growled, taking a sharp breath to deal with the pain. His statement was met with a harsh laugh, and he looked at Sabrael with rage.

"*And?* Niccolo, I am an archangel—one of God's most trusted servants—and I have been manipulating thousands—*millions*—of lives over the course of just as many years. To be quite honest, I even played a part in arranging your lineage." Sabrael retreated a few feet and leaned on his staff. "*Some* part of you should be grateful."

"Forgive me, Sabrael," Niccolo said, gasping slightly as his elbow joint snapped and his arm rotated around completely. "But I don't see it that way."

"You do not have the proper perspective, so I understand."

"Do you?" Niccolo asked, facing the archangel with endless rage. His teeth were clattering as he considered his next words. "You stole from me my family. You stole from me the love of my life. You stole from me my *freedom* and my *happiness.*"

"And then!" he shouted, releasing his hold on the maimed arm and pointing at Sabrael. "Then you have the *gall* to corrupt and defile Camilla and make me kill her!"

"You most certainly did not have to kill her." Sabrael turned and shook his head as if offended. "You *chose* to kill her. If she had been allowed the time, if you had somehow—in some absurd situation—*defeated* Adonai, she could have recovered. That you decided to end her life is no fault of mine."

"No fault? No fucking *fault?*" Niccolo was so enraged that he swept his broken and twisted arm around and felt no pain. "You turned her into a monster! You turned that sweet, innocent girl into something hideous and deformed, forced her to live with damaged and tortured souls connected directly to her mind!"

"She did not have to listen. From what my informants told me, you forced that pain on her. And let's be honest, Nico," Sabrael said, clucking his tongue. "By making her a monster, I only made you a better match."

"I will kill you," Niccolo promised, but Sabrael scoffed at the words as he waved his left hand in the air, twenty angels in black clothing appearing from the shadows at the motion.

"I sincerely doubt that. Even if I did not control that arm, my personal guard would protect me. I have invested hundreds of souls into these specimens—" Sabrael explained, but then a massive crescent of light tore through two of the angels closest to them. Sabrael stopped speaking immediately, turning his head to find that one of the angels had been cut in half, but the other had avoided the strike. "Really, Niccolo, you must have more patience."

"You don't get to talk to me about *patience!*" Niccolo shouted, gripping Lux even tighter. "I have waited too long to kill the person responsible for my pain, and you have only made it worse in this last year. I promise you, Sabrael, I *will* kill you."

"Don't be absurd," Sabrael said as he snapped his fingers again, causing Niccolo to double over in pain as his arm curled back on itself, twisting and wrapping around his midsection as Niccolo felt the agony of every exposed nerve. "Your promises mean nothing in these last moments. Once you give up, I will take you to Adonai and he will decide what to do with you."

"I..." Niccolo struggled, ignoring the demonic arm squeezing his chest tighter, making eye contact with the angel all the while. "I... will... end you."

"*How*, Niccolo? Tell me that. I have you at a severe disadvantage and waving around Lucifer's sword does not gain my respect. He lost his rebellion and taking up his standard does not inspire confidence." Sabrael rested his hands on his staff and looked down his nose at Niccolo. "So how will you end one of the mightiest creatures to ever exist?"

"Like this!" Niccolo shouted, sending an arc of energy at Sabrael, but the angel did not move out of the way. He merely waited until the light was just about to hit him and then he lifted his staff, swatting away the deadly strike as if it was nothing.

"You see now why I am unimpressed," Sabrael said, sighing heavily. Lifting his left hand, Sabrael made a motion before turning around and walking toward the palace. "Subdue him and bring him to me after he is more cooperative."

As soon as Sabrael lowered his hand, a wave of angels leapt toward Niccolo in order to take him. Avoiding the vertical slash of one angel, Niccolo stepped out of the way just in time to get a knee to the face, which staggered him enough that he dropped to the ground, his twisted arm unwrapping from his chest at the impact. Holding himself up with the only hand which truly belonged to him, Niccolo was rewarded with a swift kick to his ribs before another foot hit him in the elbow, causing him to fall onto his face.

The elite angels continued to beat him while he was down, but Niccolo's mind retreated to his memories. Almost immediately, Niccolo felt like he was back on the streets of Firenze, Simonetti's thugs beating the life from him just before the noble decided to piss on him. Camilla had watched that cruelty, had sacrificed her happiness just so that he could live, and this was how that sacrifice had been rewarded.

Niccolo was once again crippled and broken on the ground as a malicious elite walked away.

When he opened his eye again, Niccolo's fury could not be contained. Brimming with emerald energy, Niccolo threw out his hand and grabbed at an angel's clothing, yanking hard and pulling him to the ground. Once they were on the same playing field, Niccolo clambered on top of the angel's body before raising his fist. Although his companions tried to wrestle Niccolo off the angel, he threw them away before slamming his fist into the angel's head, leaving just brain matter, skull and blood after just two strikes.

Bloodlust taking over every sense, Niccolo picked himself up before leaping at the next closest angel, grabbing the angel's hood and pulling his head to side before lunging forward with his head and sinking his teeth into the soft meat of his neck. After tearing out his throat and releasing an arterial spray, Niccolo turned to face two angels rushing at him with short swords. Spitting out the flesh in his mouth, Niccolo summoned Lux and swept it across his body, which the angels did not expect.

Within just a minute, Niccolo had killed four of Sabrael's guard.

"Impressive," Sabrael called out, and Niccolo turned to face the archangel. He had stopped in his tracks, but he still did not appear worried. Snapping his fingers again, he sent Niccolo's demonic arm into a frantic seizure meant to drive him mad. "But you forget—"

"I have forgotten *nothing*," Niccolo snarled, blood spraying out his mouth along with the words. He approached Sabrael without flinching, even as his arm spastically moved outside his control. "You destroyed my life, you gave me horrible pain, but there is one thing I cannot forgive."

"You ruined Camilla's life," Niccolo said, picking up speed before Sabrael put out his hand and looked at him with a clear sense of superiority.

"Niccolo, if you come one step further, I will make that arm of yours turn against you," he threatened, hoping to stop Niccolo in his tracks, but he was surprised to see Niccolo start laughing hysterically. Gripping his arm by the shoulder, Niccolo made eye contact with Sabrael and shook his head.

"*This thing*? Tell you *what*. You can have it back," Niccolo said before pulling hard, shocking everyone in his audience. Yelling as he did so, Niccolo pulled harder, gripped tighter, until the maimed skin by his shoulder stretched, until the bones of arm were dislocated with a loud pop. Sabrael could only look on in horror as Niccolo screamed and pulled down his right arm with all his strength.

When he did, he wrenched his own demonic arm from its socket.

"You—you fool!" Sabrael shouted in protest, but Niccolo only smiled up at him as blood poured out of the severed limb in his hand.

"I told you, Sabrael, I will kill you, and I will not let you stop me by any means," Niccolo said, walking forward even as blood gushed out of his ruined stump. Panicking slightly, Sabrael had no choice and tapped his staff against the street, causing two more angels to appear from the shadows. Noticing their appearance, Niccolo stopped in his tracks.

After all, he could not stop himself from staring at a battered and bruised Barbas, held captive by Sabrael's forces.

"I did not want to bring him out, but he was my insurance," Sabrael claimed, looking indignant at the leper who had torn out his own arm. "I have no ill feelings toward my brother, but I will end his life if it will stop you."

"Why would it stop me?" Niccolo replied too quickly, taking any further words from Sabrael's mind. "Why would that *matter*?"

"But he's... he brought you up..."

"*So*? Have you forgotten the lessons you taught me?" Niccolo asked, advancing on Sabrael and still carrying the treacherous arm with his remaining hand. As Niccolo approached, Sabrael noticed that blood had stopped pouring out of the arm socket and—to his wonder—green energy was coursing about and flowing freely from the self-inflicted wound.

"Have you forgotten the life you gave me?" Niccolo shouted, unaware of the power bursting from his body. "Whatever family I have, whatever connections I make, none of it matters. It will all be taken from me in the end. It will all just mean extra pain."

"So go ahead, you coward," Niccolo prompted, only ten feet away from Sabrael as he waved around his severed arm. "Go ahead, kill him. See if it fucking matters to me! All I want now, all I could *ever* want, is to see you die. To see *Adonai* die! All I want!"

Niccolo was just a few feet away from Sabrael now, the archangel unable to move as he looked at the insane human.

"*All I want*," he repeated, bringing the demonic arm up above his head and brimming with light. Niccolo paused there, the tension around them palpable, and then something happened that amazed them all.

The green energy pouring out of Niccolo's arm socket intensified until it became a climactic flare. Once the light disappeared, everyone was surprised to see that a healthy human arm had appeared where there had been nothing. Looking at his new arm with satisfaction, Niccolo turned back to Sabrael before grabbing the angel's jaw with his new left hand.

"All I want is to return your *gift*."

Then Niccolo forced the archangel's mouth open, crushing his jaw, and shoved his mutilated arm into Sabrael's mouth and through his heart.

After Niccolo let go, Sabrael stood unassisted for a moment as he gazed at the sky, but the stout archangel eventually collapsed, his eyes almost popping out of his skull. Refusing to even look at the other guards or the fallen angel who had mentored him, Niccolo stepped over Sabrael's body and continued on his path, determined to make his way to the palace and the god hiding there.

"Niccolo," Barbas said weakly, not strong enough to yell, but he already knew that he had lost the boy. The leper who had crashed to Hell with that maimed arm, that friendly archer Barbas had trained, the poor boy Lucifer had adopted and then manipulated, was gone.

The monster walking up the hill was a stranger, and Barbas wept for his lost student.

"I—" the angel to Barbas' left started, looking at his fellow guards for some clue. "What should we do? Should we go after him?"

"You're kidding, right?" asked an angel across the street. "That guy just tore off his own arm and shoved it down Sabrael's throat. Don't know about you, but I ain't exactly confident I can take down a devil."

"Well, shit, I mean," another voice joined them, "what should we do then? Should we kill this old man?"

"Why? It's not like that bastard cares."

"Yeah, but Sabrael made the threat. Shouldn't we follow through with it?"

"Why the fuck would we do *that*? He's not giving orders with an arm in his mouth."

"I don't know! Maybe Adonai would appreciate us taking initiative! He *is* a demon, after all."

"*So*? There are *tons* of those out there."

"Which means we should get rid of this one and then we can go kill the rest of them without having to worry."

"That's stupid, why would we do that?"

"Because maybe Adonai will take us with him! Goddamnit, man, are you not paying attention?"

"Enough of this!" shouted the angel holding Barbas. Drawing his sword, he stepped in front of Barbas and readied himself. "We'll kill him and then figure it out from there. Anything you want to say, demon?"

"What does it matter?" Barbas muttered, looking down at the ground and wishing he could join his brothers and sisters in death. He had been alive too long, and he had seen too much pain.

It seemed right to end it this way; in disgrace.

Except that the end did not come for him. As he stared at the bricks beneath him, he was surprised to see a shrouded head plop against the ground and roll away, leaving no trail of blood. As he felt intense heat around him, Barbas looked up just in time to see a firestorm raging about the street and the bodies of angels falling around him. He was confused at first, thinking that maybe Yeshua or Asmodeus had come to aid him, but then he saw his savior and his jaw dropped to the floor.

Floating down on brilliant wings, a blazing sword in his hand, was his brother Michael.

"What are you..."

"Saving you, brother," Michael stated, sorrow plain in his voice. "I'm sorry it took me so long to see reason."

"But...why? Why would you turn now? What are you—" Barbas asked, unable to comprehend how the general of Adonai's forces could possibly have such a change of heart, but then he saw the pain in Michael's eyes.

"I've seen too much pain, Barbas. Too much death, and it's clear. Anybody worth a damn is on your side, and I never should have fought against any of you. I'm sorry," Michael said, turning to see Sabrael's corpse and then looking further on down the road and noticing the leper stumbling toward the palace. "But we don't have time to keep talking. Is that Niccolo?"

"I... yes," Barbas said, looking at the forsaken soul before turning back to Michael. "Or at least he was."

"Then we have to stop him. If Niccolo kills Adonai, it means the end of the world, somehow. Between the two of us, we can probably —" he ventured, but he was interrupted by his brother's weary laughter. Looking back at the Fallen on his knees, Michael waited for Barbas to explain himself.

"Of all the—of course. Of course, we could never win," Barbas muttered before lifting his gaze to his magnificent brother. "The game was rigged from the start."

"Look, we can figure out what to do with Adonai later, but we need to stop Niccolo—"

"We *can't*," Barbas interrupted again, and his brother looked at him with skepticism. "That boy is beyond anything that has ever existed, Michael. If we tried to fight him, we would just make him more powerful. Sabrael died like he was *nothing*."

"Then... then how?" Michael asked, looking back at the human making his way up the street. He did not seem so powerful like this, but Michael had never known Barbas to lie.

"We only had one chance, one safe guard, and Niccolo killed him. Cadmus was the only one who could stand up to him."

Barbas stared at the street, but Michael whipped around as soon as he heard the name.

"He's here somewhere, Barbas, we can find him," he argued, causing Barbas to look up at him in dismay.

"He *died*, Michael. He fell into the abyss in Purgatory," he mumbled, but Michael pursed his lips and shook his head.

"Then he must have made it out, because the woman I fought told me that she came here with him. Her real name was Hippolyta, but she apparently took Cimeries' name," he explained, and Barbas shocked him by leaping to his feet and grabbing him by the collar.

"You met *Cimeries*? She said Cadmus was *alive*?" Barbas asked frantically, causing Michael to back away and nod nervously.

"Y—yeah, she said that she was clearing the way for him, that he was the only one who could save us all," Michael said, causing Barbas to grin and jump for joy.

"Gods, we could actually pull this off. Where is Cim? Did she go back to fight with the others?" he asked, causing Michael to break eye contact. It took Barbas a moment, but he realized exactly what that meant and backed away.

"She fought well, brother. Fiercely, with an inner strength I've never seen from a human. To say she helped me make this decision is..." Michael tried to explain, but he gave up the effort when Barbas put up a hand to stop him.

"We need to go find Cadmus. That's what matters. I'm... I'm sure Cimeries wouldn't blame you for what you did," Barbas said, but Michael already knew that was the case.

"How will we find him?" he asked, earning a snort from Barbas.

"It's the end of the world, Michael. Death will be easy to find."

420

CHAPTER 13
THE UNHOLY TRINITY

Niccolo approached the massive double doors in front of him and prepared himself for the monster on the other side. After all this time, after all this death and betrayal, it would finally be over. Adonai, in his cowardice, hid in that throne room and Niccolo would take great pleasure in dragging him kicking and screaming from his golden throne before killing him with as much brutality as possible. As he stood in front of the door, Niccolo had his doubts, but he quickly realized there was no option.

He would face a god, or that god would end the world.

Niccolo lifted his left hand to pull on the handle, but he hesitated when he saw the raw skin covering his arm. That limb had come out of nowhere, created from pure energy, and it scared Niccolo. If he could create a new limb from his rage, Niccolo had no real concept of his limits. Back on Earth, Azazel had stabbed him through the heart and it had not killed him. Tearing off his arm had only resulted in a new one springing from its socket. If his brain was destroyed, Niccolo had no way of knowing whether or not it would reform itself.

For the first time, Niccolo considered that he might be a god, himself.

However, there were more urgent matters at hand, so Niccolo mustered his nerves and lowered his arm, realizing that he wanted to make a more dramatic entrance. Kicking out with his foot, he almost surprised himself with the force he was able to generate; the door broke off its hinges and cartwheeled end over end before coming to a stop thirty yards into the room.

When he lowered his leg, Niccolo could see Adonai gazing at him from his throne a hundred yards away, and Niccolo's rage came back to him in that instant.

"Finally," Adonai said, lifting his head from his palm and leaning back in his chair. "I've been waiting a long time, Nico."

"A long time." Niccolo let out his wings and marched forward, closing the distance as he spoke. "You could have come out to greet me."

"Yeah, but what's the point of that? If you couldn't make it through the Heavenly Host, why would I bother giving you any of my time?" Adonai responded, offering a lopsided grin. Even sitting there on his throne, this god towered over the approaching devil.

"Your *time*? You owe me so much more than that after what you've done to me," Niccolo growled, his voice echoing through the chamber. He was halfway to the lounging god at this point, but he kept stomping forward. "You've manipulated me—manipulated *everything*—for some petty little game."

"Is that what you think it is?" Adonai asked, crossing his right leg over his left and laying massive arms on the cushioned armrests. "It's not a game, Nico. I mean, you can think of it like one, but that only makes it more complicated."

"Complicated..." Niccolo laughed in dismay. "If it's not a game, what is it? What was all of this for if it's not some childish display of power?"

"It was more a test than anything," Adonai said, cocking his head to the side and offering a warm smile. "And I think it was a pretty good one, actually."

"A test? Are you still offering that *bullshit*? That you're going to bring the worthy souls with you to the next universe?" Niccolo scowled as he came to a stop twenty yards from the divine monster. "You can't expect me to believe that."

"*You* were never supposed to, Nico. That was for all my loyal, insignificant followers," Adonai said with a shrug. After a short pause, he leaned forward and gave Niccolo a wide grin. "*You're* the one I was looking for."

"You were looking for *me*?" Niccolo crossed his arms, and almost to counter him, Adonai leaned back in his chair and uncrossed his legs.

"Of course! Or, well, someone of your strength and defiance. I've been watching you a long time, Nico. Really, *really* good job out there. The way you've transformed yourself over the centuries has been incredible," Adonai gushed, pushing himself off the throne and cracking his back as he stretched his arms high into the air. "You went from insignificant speck to *the Devil* in record time."

"Explain yourself," Niccolo demanded, causing Adonai to snicker at him.

"I'm a god, Nico. I don't give into ultimatums from mortals," he said as he lowered his arms and let them swing by his side. After stepping down from the raised platform, Adonai approached Niccolo until he could walk around the smaller man. "If you ask nicely..."

"How about you tell me before I slice you open?"

"Oh, fine," Adonai said, but he kept circling. "Being a god is pretty lonely, Nico. Seriously, just... boring stuff."

"So you cause apocalypses for shits and giggles."

"Hey, this is the first one, and it was more of a... call to action." Adonai came to a stop on the far side of his throne and looked past the broken door. "I want an equal, or at least a companion."

"A companion?" Niccolo asked, raising his eyebrow at Adonai as the god looked over his shoulder.

"Pretty much. And I found out pretty early on that any angels I created couldn't hold a candle to any of the creatures and monsters from back home," Adonai said before turning around to face Niccolo. "They were always limited, which—I mean, sometimes I have a lack of imagination. Half of the shit that happens in this universe was completely unintended."

"That doesn't surprise me." Narrowing his gaze, Adonai gave him a slight frown before continuing to circle around him.

"Yeah, well, that's just how it is. I'm sure your brain would run a little dry after billions of years of trying. Anyway," Adonai said before adopting another smile. "I actually have to thank Lucy for spurring you humans on. I was angry at the time, but I can't tell you how excited I was to see that you had *souls*."

"Get to the point," Niccolo urged, causing Adonai to sigh as he walked back up to his throne and sat down.

"I'm already there, ya jackass. What I noticed—what *Lucifer* noticed—was that you had unlimited potential, which *completely* changed the game. Now, my son had his plans for creating someone who could kill me, which is honestly pretty crazy, but he was on to something, alright." Adonai breathed deep and looked down at Niccolo with a smile.

"Here you stand before me, Niccolo. Someone who can travel with me through the Void."

"What are you talking about?" Niccolo clenched his jaw so hard that his teeth creaked. With a light chuckle, Adonai rested his cheek on his palm.

"This was all for you, Nico. All the manipulation—all the death and pain and terrible things I let Sabrael do to you—all of it was so that you would fight and become more powerful. To *rise* to the occasion and become someone like *me*."

"Like you? You wanted me to become like *you*?"

"Exactly, though you should probably work on that repeating thing," Adonai said, waving off the verbal regurgitation. "I *needed* you to be defiant, to rebel against all the systems. I needed you to become powerful enough to at least *approach* being a rival. Because *now* it's interesting. Because *now* when I remake the universe and start it all over, I'll be working with someone who can hold a decent conversation."

"Work with you?" Niccolo asked, his eyelid twitching at the concept. "After all this, you think I'll *work* with you? You think I'll go with you to a new universe *just to keep you company*?"

"Well, yeah," Adonai said with a shrug. "I mean, I'm sure you'd prefer that to *oblivion*."

"You're insane."

"I'm gonna let that slide—this is a lot of information after all—but you're starting to sound like you're not grateful," he said, acting surprised when Niccolo scoffed at the idea.

"You expect me to be *grateful* for ruining all of existence just so you have a friend when you decide to kick over your sandcastle?" Niccolo shook his head at Adonai's audacity as the god stood up. "I have one thing to say to that."

"This better be good, Nico. I've been waiting for this conversation for thousands of years."

"Well, here it is." Niccolo let out his wings and formed his weapons. "*Fuck you.*"

"Seems like you have a lack of imagination, too." Adonai gathered energy in his right hand until it became a staff as long as he was tall. "You have Lucifer's memories, right? That mean you know what happened when we fought?"

"Yeah, I saw that. I saw him *cut your face*," Niccolo taunted, defiantly looking up at Adonai as the god leaned down and dwarfed his opponent.

"Then you must have also seen how I tore Tamiel's wings off. You must have also seen how Lucifer and his entire army retreated just because they could not hope to beat me."

"Old fucking news, Adonai. You said yourself that I was like you now."

"You still got a long way to go." Adonai's tone became deeper as he gave into anger.

"Then how is this for a start?" Niccolo asked before bringing Lux forward and striking Adonai's cheek, letting out a flash of light that would have blinded another creature.

When Niccolo was able to see the result of the blow, Adonai merely looked disappointed, with a red mark on his face.

"I told you, Nico. A *long* fucking way."

Then Adonai threw his head forward and slammed it into Niccolo's body, sending him tumbling along the ground of the throne room. Although confused, Niccolo set his hand down and pushed hard, allowing him to recover with the aid of his wings. After taking a breath and gathering his senses midair, Niccolo looked at the god approaching him lazily, carrying his staff behind his neck and holding it with both hands.

"But how? Scratch cut you."

"Cut me once because I wasn't prepared. I toughened my skin a little after the rebellion. See, that's the thing, Nico," Adonai explained before bringing the staff up and over his neck, rolling his shoulder and letting it pop. "I have *unlimited* power in this dimension. You're *not* going to beat me, especially with Lucy's powers."

"We'll see."

Shaking off that revelation, Niccolo flew through the air, rushing directly toward Adonai's face. When Adonai flicked up his staff in order to intercept his flight path, Niccolo rolled over the weapon and ran along its surface so he could jump off the end. Adonai gave him a slight smile, but then Niccolo let out a flare from his shield and blinded him momentarily. And though Niccolo redirected his momentum with a flap of his wings and tried to attack from the side, Adonai slapped him out of the air.

"Try, try again," Adonai muttered, his words muddled as he yawned and turned to where Niccolo had landed on the ground. The human was panting there, feeling his ribs healing after they had been cracked, and it was hard for Niccolo to control his rage.

"*How*? I blinded you!"

That caused Adonai to bury his face in his hand and laugh. When he raised his head, Adonai looked at Niccolo like a pleased parent.

"You think I need *eyes* to see you, Niccolo? You're *outmatched*, kid. When you're done, though, just let me know and we'll stop all this. We'll have plenty of time to spar in the next universe."

"I will *never* go with you! I'd rather die!" At the childish display, Adonai rolled his eyes and set the end of his staff against the ground.

"I mean, that's the other option, but that's such a *waste*. I've been grooming you for so long, and you've suffered so much just to get to this point. After all this time, erasing you from existence would be such a letdown," Adonai said, crossing his arms over the top of his weapon. "I'm starting to think you're not completely in control of your emotions here."

"Not in control of my emotions? What makes you think that, Adonai? What makes you think that my rage and frustration aren't *completely fucking justified*?" Niccolo shouted, sending out an arc of energy with each emphasized word. Adonai merely flicked each of them away with his fingers before letting out a deep breath.

"Because your soul isn't entirely yours right now. You got that parasite just *sucking* the life out of you, and I'm starting to think it's affecting your judgment," Adonai suggested, nodding along with his own comment. When he noticed Niccolo's confusion, Adonai leaned down to inspect his opponent. "Oh... *you don't know*."

"I don't know *what*?" Niccolo asked, his temper already long gone. Contrary to what he expected from a cruel god, Adonai slapped his hand against his forehead and sighed while lifting his head to the sky he had created.

"Lucy, you piece of work. So fucking spiteful," Adonai said before looking down and setting a hand on his hip. "Come here, Nico."

"Why?"

"Just come here," Adonai said, beckoning Niccolo to come closer with a flippant curl of his fingers. Instead, Niccolo brought his shield forward and prepared to attack.

"Only way I'm coming over there is to end your life," Niccolo spat out, causing Adonai to look at him in resignation.

"Ugh, fine, then do that," Adonai said impatiently, which was enough for Niccolo to lose all semblance of reason. Jumping forward and flapping his wings, Niccolo settled into a direct assault and gathered all of his strength into his right arm, determined to let loose a powerful arc of energy.

However, before Niccolo could react, Adonai quickly hopped forward and slapped Niccolo out of the air, sending him directly to the ground and breaking bones. Humiliated, he promised to the universe that he would get his revenge, but he saw something earth-shattering once he picked himself up. His lip quivering, his eyes watering, Niccolo could not comprehend the sight in front of him.

There was no way it was possible; no way this living ghost could be standing there.

"Don't know where you got that cruel streak, Lucy," Adonai said, smug, and it forced the point home. Sitting on his knees, Niccolo could only stare as Lucifer turned to face him, looking at him with those same golden eyes. His face was a mix of sorrow and relief, but it was like he had never died.

"It's good to see you again, Nico. Even if it's at the end of the world."

CADMUS WAS SURROUNDED BY DEATH, every soul in his immediate vicinity seemed to be cut down as soon as he passed, and part of him wondered if it was because of his presence. Although he could sense Mercy trying to argue against those feelings, the stallion's thoughts were drowned out in all the excess noise coming from the souls dwelling inside him. Cadmus considered for a moment if there was some way to rid himself of those distractions, but he immediately put the thought aside. There was no way he could waste even a single ounce of this newfound power, especially if he would find himself facing a battle between God and the Devil.

Out of the corner of his eye, Cadmus noticed a great demon with horns coming out of his head, and he realized quickly that it was Zagan in the midst of battle. He would have smiled and called out to the demon king, but then he watched the friendly monster overrun by angels and other beasts—saw his blood spraying out in great spurts—and Cadmus had to look away in order to stop himself from becoming sick. Over these centuries he had obviously seen worse, but he had known Zagan. He had appreciated the demon king's company, and now he was gone.

As much as he hated the idea, Cadmus knew that he had to look ahead. Whoever would be lost in these final moments was merely collateral damage. If he didn't stop Niccolo, they would die anyway, but that did not stop the guilt. It tore at him; added to the already abundant guilt he had inherited from Azrael and the others. Once this apocalypse was over—if he could even stop it—Cadmus had to wonder if he could survive a future burdened by insurmountable guilt.

Cadmus.

If it had been anyone else, Cadmus would have continued to ride, but even Mercy knew the reaper's limits. At the familiar voice of his mentor, Cadmus was forced to stop and look around for some sign of Buné. It was difficult through all the smoke and the chaos of battle, but Cadmus knew something was wrong. Something about his voice was off, told Cadmus that he would not find the armored Fallen standing around with other demons. Once Mercy turned back to face the palace, Cadmus was able to see why.

Standing above his own corpse was Buné's spirit, a blue shade of what he used to be.

"No," Cadmus muttered as Mercy carried him forward, but his mentor nodded at him slowly.

I'm afraid so, Cadmus.

"How? Who killed you?" he asked as he dismounted, only for the shade to shake its head, the edges of its form flitting about.

Someone who deserved that privilege. This is no cause for anger.

"I could have stopped this," Cadmus said as he looked down, but a blue wisp of a hand settled onto his knee. He found Buné's spirit shaking his head, a slight smile on his lips.

No. It was before you escaped from Purgatory. Do not grieve.

"How do you expect me not to grieve for *you*?" Cadmus asked, tears falling from his eyes. Buné's soul reached out to wipe them away, but the form broke against his skin. Chuckling through the ether, Buné withdrew his hand and sighed.

You would think I would know how that works after all this time, he said before looking back at his student. *You should not grieve because I have waited for death far too long. My existence was a burden, Cadmus; a trial. I existed merely to give rise to you.*

"Buné..."

When I heard that you had fallen into the abyss, I thought all was lost, but to see you now... Buné said, smiling warmly from the beyond. *I am glad that I existed long enough to see you achieve your potential. You are humanity's guardian, Cadmus, and I am so proud of you.*

"I don't know... I have to stop Niccolo and I don't... know if I can," Cadmus said, causing Buné's spirit to laugh at him.

*And you think **I** know? You'll think of something.*

"I can't kill him, Buné." Cadmus looked his mentor in the eye, but the shade had little to offer him.

You may not have to. If it makes you feel better, I know you'll make the right choice.

"Buné, my god," a stranger's voice interrupted them, and Cadmus turned his attention to the angel falling from the sky. Recognizing Michael from the battle at Stonehenge, Cadmus let power surge through his muscles and prepared for a fight with an archangel. However, Michael ignored him almost entirely and approached Buné's ghost. "I didn't..."

I know, Michael. It's fine. I knew you would come around eventually.

Sorry for using Gabe's memory like that, Buné said before turning his attention back to Cadmus. *Michael will clear the way for you. You'll be able to end this before it's too late.*

"But how?" Cadmus asked, and the specter threw up his hands and smiled.

I don't have the answer. I just believe in you. Now, Buné said, his form flickering slightly so his arms were at his sides. *Do your job as a reaper.*

"Buné, no, I can't."

You took Azrael's soul, Cadmus. I can sense it. To fight Niccolo and Adonai, you'll need to take mine, too. Claim your inheritance and become the True Reaper, Cadmus. Take your place as a new god. Buné offered him one last sad smile. *And besides, you know I don't want to end up like Lucy.*

"You know about that..." From the disappointed look on the ghost's face, Cadmus realized that Buné had known all along. With his next thought, Cadmus brought his scythe behind him and prepared to reap the soul of his teacher, the fallen angel who had treated him like family.

Thank you, Cadmus. Thank you for giving this old angel some hope.

Knowing he had no time, Cadmus swept his ethereal weapon through Buné's shade, claiming his power and all the souls tied to his spirit. It was not nearly as monumental as Azrael's inheritance, but Cadmus could tell that it was a substantial source of power. For a long moment he was distracted by thousands of new memories, but he eventually turned his attention to the archangel standing by.

"So you'll clear the way for me?" Cadmus asked, forcing Michael to realize his role in this last effort.

Turning to look at the path to the capitol, Michael found that what remained of the Heavenly Host was between them and their goal.

"I'm hoping that means I just have to talk to them," he said under his breath.

"And if it means more than that?" Cadmus asked skeptically, but once Michael turned to him, his resolve was evident.

"Then it means more than that," Michael stated before letting out his wings and jumping high into the air, leaving Cadmus to stare up at him. Looking at the angels spread out before them, Michael tried to find the right words, to counteract the speech he had given them at the beginning of this battle. After a moment, he realized there were no right words.

There was no best way to convince soldiers to turn against their god.

"Men and women, angels and demons, I am Michael, the archangel!" he shouted, his words echoing across the expanse of Heaven. "This war is *over*. The Apocalypse has ended and there is *no* victor! What lies before us are two possible futures! *One*, we allow Adonai to end this world and move on to a new dimension by himself. The *other* is that Cadmus, the Grim Reaper and *God of Death*, stops Adonai and we take back our future!

"I will not blame you if you decide to stay loyal to your god, but I *urge you* to join us. I urge you to consider a future where humanity, angels and demons are all free to exist in peace. And although I do not wish to spill more blood, I will cut anyone down who stands in the path of this new god," Michael declared, letting his sword burn bright and letting his righteous inferno rage through the heavens. "Make your choice, my friends, but know this."

"If you stand against us, I will have no mercy."

———

"Go on, have your moment. I'll wait," Adonai mocked them as he folded his hands over the end of his staff and watched both devils.

Ignoring the deity entirely, Niccolo pushed himself to his feet and watched as Lucifer turned around. He waited for some sign that this was not the real Lucifer, that it was just a shallow clone created by

Adonai, but Niccolo could see the pain and guilt in the fallen angel's eyes.

"How? How are you here, Scratch?" he asked, gulping down air as a maelstrom of emotions threw his mind into chaos. Looking down, the radiant angel shook his head before setting his hands on his hips.

"Oh, this'll be good," Adonai muttered, causing Lucifer to whip around and point at him with Lux.

"We'll tear you apart in a moment, you *tyrant*." He breathed hard for a moment, but then turned back to Niccolo with regret. "Niccolo, I'm sorry, but this is how it had to be."

"What did you do?" Niccolo asked, giving into his anger. That Lucifer somehow found some way to resurrect himself through him only forced the point home; Niccolo was just another soul for Lucifer to manipulate. "You used me *again*. You couldn't stop once you were dead, could you?"

"No, Niccolo, but I won't apologize. It was necessary. I gave you my memories so you could see *why*." Lucifer walked forward, letting his weapons flicker out of existence to remove their inherent hostility. "That god does not deserve his throne, and I would do anything to remove him from the world."

"So that you could be king, is that it?" Niccolo asked, and he could see the pain work through Lucifer's face.

"*No*. No, Niccolo, that's not what I want at all. I didn't even know that this *could* happen," Lucifer said as he gestured toward himself. "Adonai's *destruction* is all I wanted and I... I had to create the kind of person who could accomplish that. That was you, Niccolo. I could see it the first time I met you, over the hundreds of years I've known you. You were supposed to be the one who finally tore out this bastard's heart."

"And yet you're here all the same, Scratch." Niccolo glared at his mentor, and it was met with a loud snort from Adonai.

"Yeah, Lucy, go ahead and explain that one. Tell Niccolo how you were living off him for this whole year." With a raised eyebrow,

Adonai looked at them both before sighing. "Unless, of course, you don't understand it yourself."

"No," Lucifer admitted as he faced Niccolo. "I know how it happened. I just didn't know it would. It was never my intention, Nico."

"Get on with it," Niccolo responded, crossing his arms. "At least tell me the truth."

"You're right, I owe you that," Lucifer said with a sigh, avoiding eye contact by staring at the ground. "When my powers manifested in you, it wasn't a mistake. Once Plague died, there was a void within your soul. Once I saw that, I filled in the gap and... that's how you were able to use Lux and Morningstar, that's how you inherited my wings. At that point, our souls became wrapped up in each other and... you gave me part of your life, Niccolo."

"You're skipping ahead," Adonai interrupted, smiling over the edge of his fingers and chuckling softly. "That wasn't your first crime, Lucy. You didn't just show up after Azazel killed his pretty, little horse. You were already siphoning off power."

"I didn't know that!" Lucifer snapped, his weapons forming along with his words. "I *thought* I was guiding him, helping him through it all!"

"Pshaw." Adonai waved off Lucifer's intentions before making eye contact with Niccolo. "Ever since that day in the Overlook, Lucy here has been wrapped around your soul, absorbing scraps of your life and the souls you consumed in your journey. You should thank him, though."

"I should thank him?"

"Yeah, if he hadn't crawled into your body, Azazel would have killed you. Why do you think you survived getting stabbed in the heart? Did you think you were just *special*? I mean, you obviously *are* —Lucy and I can agree on that one—but the heart and the mind are the focal points for the soul," Adonai said before setting his staff to the side and gesturing toward Lucifer with an open hand. "You lived because my son took the hit, which delayed his recovery significantly."

"He *what*?" Niccolo shouted without thinking, causing Lucifer to turn back. He could see the worry, the compassion and the affection this fallen angel had for him, and Niccolo's fury evaporated before Lucifer even answered.

"I couldn't let you die, Nico. Not there, not to Zel. And when you lost Plague, I may have been selfish and took his spot but... I gave you what I could in return." Tears formed against Lucifer's willpower as he explained. "I gave you the tools you needed to lead an army."

"He's such a softie," Adonai said as he picked his nose, flicking a gob of mucus to the side. "Always cared for you monkeys and couldn't stick with any of his plans as a result. He honestly might have won the rebellion if he didn't have that damned sense of responsibility."

"That *responsibility* is exactly what you lack, *father*." Lucifer snarled out the title without reverence. "And even though I didn't have the power to stop you, I knew I had the *responsibility* to forge someone who could. Cadmus and Niccolo are greater than you and I could ever be, even if they're *monkeys*."

"Hey, I'm not knocking it," Adonai said, putting out his hand. "That's why I wanted to take Nico with me. Ever since Zel told me about your plan, I just *knew* you were onto something. That's why I got Sabrael to give him the arm. That's why I set up everything with Beleth and Azazel back on Earth. It wasn't a bad idea, you just didn't have *perspective*."

"Perspective? *You* speak about perspective," Lucifer said, covering his face with his left hand and laughing in dismay. When he lowered his hand, Lucifer brought his shield forward, let out his brilliant wings, and nodded toward his adopted son. "I think it's about time Niccolo and I give you a lesson on *perspective*."

"Hah, you really think you're going to teach *me*? You were watching as Niccolo tried to use your weapons against me. What makes you think that when you're separated that I won't just *crush* you?" Adonai asked, but his smile disappeared once he saw the satisfaction on Lucifer's face.

"Because Niccolo never knew how to truly use my weapons, or even his own power. You were right, Adonai. I *was* a parasite. Every being Niccolo killed with my weapons, every soul he consumed, went directly to me. By tying my soul to Niccolo's, I achieved something no other angel could." Lucifer narrowed his gaze and gave him a wild grin. "I removed my own limitations."

"You *cheeky* little devil," Adonai said, returning his son's grin and tapping his staff against the ground. "You've just made this so much more exciting. *However,* that leaves poor Niccolo worse off than before."

"Not in the slightest," Lucifer said, shrugging as if nothing was wrong. "Niccolo's strength has always come from *himself*, no matter what anybody thinks. His defiant spirit protected him when Sabrael turned him into a leper, forced him through the ranks of Hell, allowed him to conquer Earth, and has brought him to God's doorstep. Now that I'm not *holding him back*, we'll get to see his incredible potential."

"Interesting theory, Lucy, but how is he going to match either of us like that? He's a human with no weapons. He doesn't even have your sword." Adonai dismissively pointed at Niccolo and made him fume with anger.

However, that anger abandoned him once Lucifer turned to Niccolo with a sly smile.

"Then you didn't see how he tore off his arm and formed another in its place. Niccolo is no longer limited by our rules—*your* rules, Adonai. His concept of self is so strong—his spirit is so *powerful*—that his body is a construct of his own willpower."

"What the hell does that mean?" Niccolo asked.

"It means that if you want to fly, *fly*. If you want to create a sword, you just have to will it into existence. It means, Nico," Lucifer said, glowing with pride for his second son, "that if you want to join me in tearing down a god, you just have to believe you *can*."

"That is ridiculous, Lucy, and I'm an expert in ridiculous. I have billions of years of losing my mind under my belt. Just why do you think any of th—" Adonai started, but he lost his ability to speak when viridian energy surrounded the lowly human. Niccolo looked at his own hands, seeing his skin shimmer as untold power surged beneath the surface, and with a light hop, he tried to fly.

Even Lucifer was surprised when Niccolo hung in the air, gravity holding no power over him. A brilliant green aura surrounded him, and after a moment, Niccolo let energy condense in his hand. It was as if his arm had never been torn off, and his bastard sword bubbled into existence. Looking from the blade to his other hand, Niccolo finally realized that Lucifer was telling the truth, that his only limitation was his desire and sense of self.

When Niccolo turned his attention back at the awestruck deity, he couldn't stop himself from smiling.

"Scratch... how do you know all this?" Niccolo asked, turning to face the fallen angel, who had joined him in the air and now set a hand on his shoulder.

"I *don't,* Niccolo. I just had faith. I've *always* had faith in you. I used you—I admit it—and I'm only here now because I took advantage of you, but *all* of my plans, my ambitions... it was all because I believed in you. And even though... even though we may not win, even if we die..." Lucifer paused, ignoring Adonai, whose fury was palpable.

"I want you to know *that* will never change. Until I draw my last breath, until I truly die, you have someone who believes in you. I know now, Niccolo, that raising you—that teaching you—was my true purpose. I waited for you for two million years, Niccolo, and seeing you now is my proudest moment."

"Scratch," Niccolo started, but they were interrupted by a loud crash. Turning to face their creator, they found a spoiled brat in the middle of a tantrum, slamming his staff against the ground and sending splinters of marble everywhere. When he stopped striking the ground, they could see Adonai's face red with anger.

437

"*Enough* of this! Enough chatter, enough babbling! Lucy, you should be dead, and Niccolo is nothing more than a goddamn monkey! Even if I have to *drag* you to the new universe, Nico, you're coming with me! Even if it's just to spit in your face for eternity!"

"You're right, Adonai. Enough of this." Niccolo let his aura shine even brighter as he made eye contact with the petulant deity. And as he looked down on Adonai, Niccolo finally realized that this body was merely a vessel, that the scars from his leprosy were just ornamentation.

Continuing to look down at Adonai in smug satisfaction, the leprosy on his face flaked off, ruined skin floating away before disappearing in the wind. After a moment, Niccolo looked down at Adonai with both eyes, his pupils shining with viridian light.

"Like I care for your parlor tricks!" Adonai shouted, and it was less than a second before the tyrant god was in front of them and swinging his massive staff down at them. If he had been anything lesser, if he had lost his confidence, Niccolo would have been liquefied by the force of the strike.

Instead, he threw his arm forward and slammed his fist into the staff, causing the weapon to fly backward and take Adonai with it, who recovered in mid-air twenty feet away.

"How's that for a trick?" Niccolo asked, but Adonai was not amused.

Flexing his muscles so hard that the veins of his arm popped out, Adonai swept the staff horizontally in an effort to catch Niccolo in his midsection. Taking his chances, Niccolo prepared for the power behind the strike and tried to meet it, letting the staff hit him along the ribs. Although he could feel his bones crack and creak, he was able to remain in the air and wrapped his arm along the circumference of the staff, his sword flickering out of existence now that he didn't need it.

"Won't deny you have power, but what good is that?" Adonai tried to move the staff out of Niccolo's grip and failed, but he stopped moving once Niccolo shook his head.

"A distraction, you idiot," Niccolo taunted, and Adonai looked to his side just in time to see Lucifer dive through the air and drag Lux along his massive right arm. Against Adonai's every expectation, a deep red gash opened up as the radiant edge ran along his arm, sending out a spurt of divine blood as Adonai lost his grip on the staff.

"How did you..." Adonai immediately grabbed onto his upper arm with his left hand, but Lucifer only laughed as he flew around Adonai and cut deep into his back.

"I *told* you, Father! I removed my limitations," Lucifer said before circling around to the front, holding Lux vertical as he gathered energy. Once he was satisfied, he sent down an arc of energy that slammed into Adonai's chest and caused him to drop down five feet.

"This is impossible!" Adonai shouted, but then he saw Niccolo rushing past Lucifer with a giant staff held in both hands.

"Keep telling yourself while we beat you to death!" Niccolo shouted in glee as he brought down the massive weapon, crashing it into Adonai's skull and causing him to plummet to the ground. When he landed, Adonai's body let out a massive shockwave. A dust cloud formed at the impact, shrouding him, and so Lucifer and Niccolo waited in the air.

"You will not beat me to death." Adonai growled at them, and a thunderclap filled the air, dispersing the dust cloud and showing a very angry god looking up at them. After Adonai brought his hands back down, Lucifer and Niccolo could see that the wounds they had given him had already healed. "You will not lay a hand on me again."

"That's a bold fucking claim." Niccolo scoffed, but when he turned to Lucifer, he could see alarm spread through his face.

"Shit," Lucifer exclaimed before turning to Niccolo and flying toward him, slamming his hand into Niccolo's chest and sending him sprawling through the air. He had been caught completely flat-footed, and when Niccolo recovered, he immediately looked at Lucifer in frustration. However, he saw why Lucifer had pushed him less than a second later.

A giant slab had rocketed past Niccolo's last airborne position, still rising into the air impossibly fast.

Watching as the rock carried Lucifer higher into the sky, Niccolo almost could not comprehend the shadow that rushed past him. If he had blinked, Niccolo would have missed it entirely, but then he saw that it had been Adonai on his way to intercept the giant slab. Four hundred feet in the air, Adonai got in front of the rock's flight path and then threw his divine fist into and *through* the stone, shattering it and sending a broken devil back along its trajectory.

Before Niccolo could fly forward to save Lucifer, he was grabbed out of the air and jerked around so he could see the giant face of Adonai glaring down at him.

"I will make you suffer, Niccolo."

Adonai flew through the air, taking his opponent with him, and Niccolo only had the strength to hit Adonai's nose a few times with his fist. Although there was a satisfying crack, Niccolo watched Adonai's face immediately rearrange itself back to normal, and it was the last thing he saw before he was engulfed by burning, bright light.

"How does it *feel*, Niccolo? How does the heat of a *star* treat you?" Adonai taunted, and it momentarily distracted Niccolo from the intense pain.

In that instant, he realized that Adonai had plunged him into the middle of one of the miniature suns that decorated the heavens, but he stopped being able to think shortly after that. He felt his skin crackling and burning away, felt the flames consuming him, and he panicked. This felt like dying, worse than when he had fallen to the Pestilence Quarter, bathed in hellfire.

It felt like the end.

"I will not allow this!"

Lucifer's harmonious voices broke through Niccolo's world of pain, and seconds later Niccolo had been pulled out of the burning star and he was able to think again. Someone's shoulder was buried in his armpit, holding him up in the air, and once he was able to see, Niccolo realized it was Lucifer. Niccolo could not fully comprehend it in his current state—his eyes had burned away during Adonai's attack and had only partially healed—but he didn't have the time to fully recover. As soon as Niccolo lifted his head to look at his second father with new eyes, Lucifer was suddenly ripped away from him and thrown to the ground.

Recovering himself midair and steadying himself with his hands even though he did not need to, Niccolo looked down to find that Adonai was beating Lucifer over and over again with his giant fists. Only between Adonai's strikes was Niccolo able to see Lucifer, and the bruised and battered angel looked like he was barely alive. His fury building in him all over again, Niccolo was covered in energy as he dove down to attack Adonai.

"No, Nico! Be patient!"

Adonai quickly whipped around and backhanded Niccolo once he was in range, sending him tumbling along the ground and breaking bones from the sudden change in inertia. However, because of his new power, Niccolo was able to spring off a broken wrist and halt himself instantly once he was in the air, and his limbs healed as soon as he took another breath. However, what he saw stole the breath from those vestigial lungs.

Standing up and chuckling, Adonai held Lucifer's arms up in each hand, his broken body hanging limp by his wrists. Shocking Niccolo further was the second set of arms that appeared at the top of Adonai's shoulders, each malicious hand pinching the crest of Lucifer's wings.

"See, Niccolo? This is why you need to be patient," he said before pulling at Lucifer's radiant wings, causing the fallen angel to scream in agony.

Instantaneously, Niccolo recalled the gruesome sight of Tamiel's mutilation, his golden wings popping before the skin tore away. It was like he was seeing it all over again, but then Adonai outdid himself. Once Lucifer's wings were torn away, Adonai used his new arms to grab hold of Lucifer's torso, and Niccolo realized what that cruel god intended. However, as fast as Niccolo flew, he did not have enough time.

In a sickening display, Adonai tore Lucifer's arms off, one of them falling away at the shoulder, the other separating at the elbow.

"You *monster*!" Niccolo screamed as he closed the distance and capitalized on Adonai's malicious joy. Throwing his fist into Adonai's face, he sent the titan through the air and quickly followed, using his powerful legs in conjunction with his hands to pry Adonai's fingers off Lucifer's body. Once he had freed the fallen angel, Niccolo grabbed Lucifer out of the air and set him down.

This was a mistake, as Adonai quickly recovered and then swung his shin directly into Niccolo's chest, launching him into the air. Niccolo flipped over, determined to find Adonai's next avenue of approach, but his eternal enemy was on him in an instant. Slamming his knee into Niccolo's gut, Adonai forced the air from him before grabbing the back of his head and throwing him back to the ground.

"I told you, Nico. He would never lay a hand on me again."

Adonai breathed heavily as he stalked toward Niccolo's crash site. Once he was able to sit up, Niccolo realized that Lucifer was sprawled out on the ground nearby, and rational thought abandoned him. Crawling toward Lucifer—not realizing that fingers and ribs and toes had been broken in his landing—he unintentionally ignored the deity looking at him with skepticism. "Oh, c'mon, that's just pathetic."

"Scratch..."

Niccolo focused on the fallen angel who was lying still on the ground. Although Niccolo had lost him once before, the pain of it had been so much, and he could not bear feeling that emotion again. Now that he had Lucifer back, the very concept of him dying again was too much for Niccolo to handle. Azazel had stolen Niccolo's happiness and his sense of belonging, and now Adonai was poised to do it all over again. Slipping into his old life for a moment, Niccolo prayed—even if his god was the one responsible—and he just wished that Lucifer was still alive. Niccolo could handle so much pain if it meant that Scratch was still breathing.

Once he was within a foot of Lucifer, however, a giant fist crashed into the angel's chest and broke most of his ribs. Niccolo watched as it rose into the air, dripping blood, and he looked down at the ground with tears in his eyes. His world was sorrow for a moment, but that sorrow eventually gave way to anger. With such fury dominating his mind, Niccolo turned around to see Adonai looming over him, the smirk on his face showing just how little he respected this moment.

"That was an angel without limits, Nico. That was a fallen angel who had lived for billions of years who had *somehow* found a way around my rules, and he lies broken. He was the *firstborn*, one of the strongest creatures in existence, and I don't even have a scar or a wound to show for it." Adonai leaned down, his face dominating Niccolo's entire perspective. "What makes you think a human without limits will fare better?"

"What makes you think he won't?" an unexpected voice answered, and Adonai's face was ripped from Niccolo's vision as a radiant fist crushed Adonai's face and sent the monster flying. Looking at the owner of the newly-formed arm, Niccolo was amazed to see Lucifer standing above him, triumphant even as he was covered in blood. It was enough to give Niccolo hope.

Until Lucifer collapsed, unable to stop his fall with his remaining strength.

"Scratch!" Within just a moment, Niccolo crawled over to Lucifer's maimed body and gather the angel's head into his lap, holding his hand to Lucifer's face. Although he didn't want to look, Niccolo found that Lucifer's right arm was still completely gone, his ribcage was still irrevocably damaged, and the wreckage of his wings pulsed lifeblood onto the ground. Confused by the entire affair, Niccolo hyperventilated until Lucifer brought a shaking hand up to his face.

"It's fine, Nico. It will all be fine." Despite Lucifer's consolations, Niccolo shook his head and tried to force away the tears.

"He's going to win, Scratch. You're dying and then it will just be me. I can't fight him alone," Niccolo argued, but Lucifer gave him a weak smile.

"The opposite, actually. You were always supposed to fight him alone." He swallowed down blood, but a small amount trickled out from the corner of his lips. "I was never supposed to be here."

"What are you talking about—"

"It was just supposed to be you, Nico. That's why you lost everything, lost me, lost Plague, Camilla, everyone. As much as I hate the thing, the Leviathan was right. By removing your humanity, you have become so much more. Our champion, the strongest soul on this planet. I... I..." Lucifer hesitated, coughing up blood. Flecks of it landed on Niccolo's face, and Lucifer did his best to wipe them away with his new hand. "I held you back, Niccolo."

"Scratch, no, you never held me back," Niccolo said, earning a smile from his adoptive father.

"Not in life, maybe, but Adonai was right. I was a parasite. I stole from you all the energy and potential you should have gained since coming to Earth," Lucifer admitted, but then he stared through Niccolo. "And I still have it."

"You still have it?" Niccolo asked, but then it dawned on him what Lucifer was actually saying. Shaking his head, Niccolo gritted his teeth and looked back at Adonai, who was picking himself up from where he had landed. "No, Scratch, I won't."

"You *have* to, Nico. Neither of us can beat him like this, but if I give my power to you—the power that should have been yours the entire *time*—you... you will be strong enough..." Lucifer gasped in pain as his ribcage popped out and his lungs inflated to fill the space, healing in spite of his wishes.

"No, I'm not going to lose you again!"

"You didn't lose me last time," Lucifer argued, causing Niccolo to look back at him with tears in his eyes. "This whole fight proves that

I was there the entire time, and it proves that I was wrong. I'm your last tie to your humanity, the only thing keeping you from becoming a god."

"No—"

"*Yes*, Nico. This was never my fight. I had my war and lost, and part of me was stubborn enough to think I could try again." Lucifer shook his head at his own foolishness. "Even if I *can* heal from these wounds, I shouldn't. My time is over."

"Scratch, there has to be another way!"

"I have faith in you, Nico," he said, certain as he curled his fingers around the back of Niccolo's neck. "I could not have asked for a better son, and I'm glad that we can finally have a proper goodbye."

"I..." Niccolo tried to find some way to convince Lucifer, but he finally realized the truth. Looking down, Niccolo made teary eye contact. "I love you, Scratch."

"And I love you, Niccolo," Lucifer said with a smile, breaking Niccolo's heart as he guided his son's hand into his chest. Feeling the power dwelling in the devil's heart, Niccolo looked away as he crushed it between his fingers. Lucifer gasped in that last moment, but he was still alive as he pulled himself up to look at Niccolo one last time. "Go save the world I could not."

"*I will end you both!*"

Adonai's shout echoed throughout the chamber, but Niccolo could not have cared any less. He just stared into Lucifer's golden eyes as the life departed, his father dying in front of him for the second time. Once Niccolo saw his eyes glass over, he used his fingers to close Lucifer's eyelids before setting his head down on the ground and laying the angel's remaining hand on top of the gaping hole Niccolo had created.

When Adonai's arm came down like a hammer, twenty tons of force coming down to crush his enemy, Niccolo caught Adonai's wrist and held him there. Completely surprised by the sudden stop, Adonai only watched as golden energy flowed from Lucifer's body and joined Niccolo's green aura, licking around him like a bonfire.

It seemed like his body shook with anger, but Adonai quickly realized that Niccolo's skin—his entire body—was just barely containing the power of this new being. Although Adonai tried to retrieve his hand, Niccolo squeezed tighter and crushed his wrist, forcing an agonized yelp from the insolent god.

"You are still outmatched. You are *nothing*. You're just a *human*," Adonai said, considering what tactic he would use next, but he could *feel* the absolute confidence flowing from this human soul. Twisting his arm, Niccolo snapped Adonai's wrist even further and brought him to the ground, forcing a god to look up at him as Lucifer's power continued to leak into the air around them.

"If I'm just a human, then why are you afraid?" Niccolo asked, at which point Adonai could take no more.

Throwing his other fist forward and propelling Niccolo through the air, Adonai forced him to release his grip. After willing his body to heal—the bones rearranging themselves before Niccolo could stop his momentum and interrupt—Adonai laughed to the heavens.

"Afraid? *Afraid?*" Stomping with his foot, Adonai bellowed further as he gave into laughter. "Why would I be afraid of a flying monkey?"

"I'm not a flying monkey, tyrant!" Niccolo declared, his grief falling away as hatred took its place. "I am something *new!* Something *unknown!* Cowards *always* fear the unknown!"

"I am no coward, Niccolo. I am *God*," Adonai stated, his voice firm as he let divine energy course through his body, forcing his physical vessel to expand and become stronger and more powerful than ever before.

By the time he was finished with his transformation, Adonai was a hundred feet tall and looking down at his opponent. "*Tell me, Niccolo, what are you?*"

"What am I?" Niccolo was unafraid even as Adonai towered over him.

"*Yes, Niccolo. What are you? A human? A devil? You've used so many names and titles now.*" Adonai crouched down, supporting himself with massive arms as he obscured Niccolo in shadow. Only the green and gold aura surrounding his body allowed Niccolo to avoid getting absorbed in the complete darkness.

"They're just words," Niccolo said as he flew up to attack Adonai's face, uppercutting the deity and forcing him back to his feet.

Although it was satisfying, it left Niccolo completely open to Adonai's counterattack. The giant creature threw out his hand to capture Niccolo, which he avoided, but he didn't expect the foot that fell down on him and crushed him against the ground. Unable to move, Adonai stomped him two more times, obliterating bones to dust and forcing blood out of Niccolo's mouth. Although the bones quickly healed and the blood soon replaced itself, the pain was overwhelming.

"*Just words,*" Adonai said with a laugh, breathing back in drool that had escaped his mouth. "*That's all you have, Niccolo. Just words. You've lost everything, you stupid human. You've lost Lucifer **twice**, you lost Camilla **twice**, you lost Paimon, you lost **Cadmus!** You even lost **Plague!** Tell me, Niccolo, how does it feel to lose a creature tied to your very soul?*"

"You will not say his name... I will... I will... " Niccolo muttered as he picked himself up to his knees, as Adonai lifted his foot to crush him one last time.

"*You will **what**, Nico? You've lost everything, including this fight and this war. No matter what titles you use, no matter what words you say. You're not a human anymore. You're not a devil, and all the titles and words won't help you now. Hell, ever since Plague died, you can't even call yourself a Horseman of the Apocalypse. I mean, really, Nico...*" Adonai lowered his foot slowly to crush Niccolo.

"*What's a Horseman without a horse?*"

"Just a man..." Niccolo said as he raised his hand to meet Adonai's foot, "with *nothing* left to lose."

"*Words again. A shame,*" Adonai said, his voice full of condescension before pushing down with all his might.

Once his foot met the ground, Adonai felt a small degree of satisfaction, but then regret filtered in. After all this, he really *was* going to be alone in his new universe. There would be no rival, no companion for him in the Void and the vacuum of space. Sighing, Adonai was struggling to think up another option when he felt something tickle the bottom of his foot. Looking down, the deity was confused until he felt a massive surge of power beneath him.

With a powerful explosion of green energy, Niccolo burst from the ground and pushed against Adonai's foot, throwing his opponent off balance before settling himself fifty feet in the air. Once Adonai was able to regain his footing, he looked at the furious, miniscule human and gritted his teeth so hard that one of them cracked.

"Why do you persist in this stupidity!" The force of Adonai's breath battered the flying soul, but Niccolo met his fury and sent out a terrifying shockwave before responding.

"Because I lost *everything*, Adonai!" he shouted, pointing at the giant with a hand brimming with celestial energy. "You stole it *all*, and I will not let you get away with it! Your life ends here, *today*, and *nothing* will stop me from tearing out your heart!"

"What makes you think you can, you dirty fucking ape!" Adonai replied, stomping on the ground and causing an earthquake in his throne room. *"I created you—I created **all** of you—and this universe would not exist without me!"*

"Then your purpose is over," Niccolo growled, gathering energy in his relatively tiny frame.

*"I crushed you once, Niccolo. I am so much larger than you, stronger than you, and just because you have a fancy aura does **not** mean you can meet me as an equal!"* Adonai screamed, but then Niccolo shocked him by laughing.

"Equals? *Equals?* We are not *equals*, Adonai! I will destroy you if it's the last thing I do!" Niccolo shouted, yelling as energy poured into him and caused his body to erupt with shining emerald light.

Before Adonai's eyes, this lowly human's form expanded and

grew—much like Adonai's own body—and it was not long before Niccolo stood there, just as tall as Adonai.

"*How could you possibly...*" Adonai muttered, but Niccolo rushed forward and slammed his fist into Adonai's jaw, snapping the bone on impact and causing him to fall onto his back. Feeling pain in his stomach, Adonai looked down to see that he had fallen onto his throne and that the upper half was just peeking out of the torn skin of his gut.

"Possible means nothing to me anymore, you fool," Niccolo said as he walked over, sending tremors through the ground with every step. When he leaned over to pull Adonai up—the wound caused by his throne gushing out blood before it started to heal—the tyrant god could only look up at this spirit of vengeance. "I will kill you, Adonai. I would like to say it's for everyone I lost, but it's not."

"*It's not?*" Adonai asked, too shocked to be angry.

"No, you bastard, this is for *me*. In these moments, I'm going to be selfish. You have caused me pain. You have caused me misery. Scratch may have manipulated me, but you—*you* pulled my strings like a puppet for centuries," Niccolo said before shaking Adonai by the neck. "*You* don't get to make the rules anymore. *You* don't get to end the world. *You* get to die and it's going to me who kills you."

"*You fool...*" Adonai said, laughing softly at first before bursting into hysterics. Grabbing hold of Niccolo's wrist, Adonai pulled himself up so he could stand eye-to-eye with this human upstart. "*If you kill me, you **end** the world.*"

"What are you talking about..."

"*I'm the only thing keeping the Void at bay. Without me, the walls come down, the monsters come in and the world ends. In short: you kill me, Nico, you end the world **anyway**.*" Adonai laughed and set his hand on Niccolo's shoulder, supporting his weight on the gigantic human.

"So be it," Niccolo muttered, and Adonai opened his eyes just in time to see Niccolo throwing his hand forward, intending to plunge it into his ribcage.

Unable to think of a better option, Adonai released the energy inflating his body and shrunk down, past his usual size and becoming only six feet tall. He was about to fly away and avoid Niccolo's fury, but then a boot struck his face and staggered him. Spitting out blood coming from his newly-broken nose, Adonai looked up to see that Niccolo had reduced himself to the same size.

"There is no running, Adonai." Niccolo rushed forward, twisting his body so he could throw his shin into Adonai's gut. Taking the hit, Adonai caught Niccolo's leg and spun around with the intention of throwing him into an upturned boulder, but Niccolo leaned into the clinch and battered Adonai's face with rapid jabs until he let go. Floating there, Niccolo fumed as Adonai tried to stay standing. "I told you that I would kill you."

"Why? I already told you! If I die, so does this universe! It makes no sense! All of humanity will die if you kill me, so why the *fuck* are you still *trying*?" Adonai demanded answers, but he was met with a snarl from his opponent.

"I don't care about them, anymore. I'm not human. I'm not a devil. I'm not even a Horseman," Niccolo said in a low voice as he approached Adonai, avoiding the god's reckless counters. "I'm a *monster*, Adonai, and I will not be satisfied until my prey is dead."

"Niccolo, don't!" another voice interrupted them, causing Niccolo to turn in alarm. Standing there panting was someone who should have been a stranger. He had white hair, bright blue eyes, his skin seemed weathered, even his voice sounded like it didn't belong to him, but Niccolo knew exactly who had come to join them.

"Cadmus..." he said, and it was enough of a distraction that he was left open to an attack. Immediately his limbs were seized, and Niccolo turned to see Adonai smiling down at him—his bloodlust taking complete control—and he had grown back his second pair of arms. Each hand was clamped down on his wrists and ankles, and Niccolo already felt the strain on his body as Adonai started to pull.

"Any last words, Niccolo?" Adonai asked, but that only caused Niccolo to explode with anger.

Gnashing his teeth, Niccolo pulled his limbs back and Adonai was not strong enough to stop him. After Adonai lost his grip, Niccolo brought in his arms and legs until he was curled in on himself, and then he threw out his limbs in a catastrophic display of power, buffeting his onlookers with an emerald tornado of cosmic energy.

"I will destroy you, Adonai. I will fulfill my promise."

Niccolo stomped toward Adonai, who was ten yards away and using all of his strength to stay standing against the onslaught of energy. The wind tore at him like knives, and Adonai had to lift all of his arms just to guard his face.

"Niccolo, if he dies, the world ends!" Cadmus shouted as he ran from the entrance, but Niccolo only looked back at him in resignation. That was absolutely the wrong reaction, and so he continued on in denial. "I came back to stop this! I came back to stop you from doing this! *Please!*"

"You can't stop this. This is how it always had to be," Niccolo said before turning back to Adonai and sending out a blast of green plasma that knocked him off his feet. "You shouldn't have come back, Cadmus. You should have stayed dead."

"You don't mean that!" Cadmus shouted over the roar of the cataclysm surrounding them. "You're Niccolo da Firenze! You're a Horseman of the Apocalypse! You're *my friend*, Nico! You don't want to do this! There's another way! Just stop!"

"I'm sorry, Cadmus," Niccolo whispered as he came to a stop above Adonai, the coward still on his back and scrambling to get away. In a swift movement, Niccolo jumped forward until he was on top of his opponent, knocking away his limbs and grabbing Adonai's throat with his left hand. "But I *do* want to do this. Even if there is another way, this is *my* way."

"Niccolo, please, think about this!" Cadmus shouted, arcs of electricity running along the throne room once he slammed the end of his scythe against the ground. As he desperately tried to sway his friend, Cadmus did not notice the outpouring of blue energy swirling around him and crashing against Niccolo's aura. "If you don't stop now, you're worse than Adonai ever was! If you don't stop, you don't leave me any choice!"

"Choice..." Niccolo muttered, watching the fear dance in Adonai's eyes. "They never gave us a choice. It's what we wanted all along. The right to choose, the right to own our future."

"I'm sorry, Cadmus, but I'm going to be selfish. This is my choice."

Then Niccolo threw down his right arm, brimming with destructive power and intending the destruction of Adonai's heart. In that last moment, Niccolo looked at Adonai and saw delicious, satisfying terror, and smiled. If this was the end of the world, at least it ended his way; at least he was able to have his vengeance. With that smile on his face, Niccolo didn't even notice the reaper stretch out his hands and release a tidal wave of celestial energy.

"*Stop!*"

CADMUS.

"Go away," he whispered, but he could feel Mercy inching closer. Cadmus was still kneeling on the ground, supporting himself with shaking arms, and he certainly did not want company. After what Cadmus did—after what Niccolo forced him to do—the last thing he wanted was to talk about it.

"Cadmus." The rasp came audibly this time, so Cadmus whipped his head around and tears streaked down his face.

"What the *hell* do you want?" he shouted, unable to hear the souls that had echoed his voice only moments before. "Just what do you want, Mercy? Do you want me to feel better? Do you want me to see what I've done and not think of myself as a monster?"

"You are not a monster," Mercy argued, but that only caused Cadmus to jump to his feet and jab an index finger into his face.

"Yes, I am! I *am* a monster! I'm not human anymore, that's for fucking sure, and I... I just betrayed my best friend. I'm awful... I..."

"...saved the world," Mercy finished the statement for him. Feeling the admiration and love flowing from his horse, Cadmus was taken from his anger. "You did not have a choice, Master. This much is evident. What you have done here is the best possible thing."

"The best possible thing, Mercy?" Cadmus asked in dismay, turning to point at the still gods wrapped up in each other just a few feet away. As he looked down at them, they both appeared as statues, not even breathing. "How is *this* the best possible thing?"

"You did not kill them, although it was within your power," Mercy argued, stepping forward until he was beside his Horseman. "Even though Niccolo betrayed you and left you for dead, you still gave him your own form of mercy. He was too far gone, willing to destroy the world, but you left him alive."

"What kind of life is *this*?" Cadmus asked, his voice weak as he looked down on his best friend. "He will be frozen in time, stuck like this for eternity. He'll never breathe, never laugh, never speak, never walk, never do *anything* again. I turned my best friend into a glorified rock."

"Which is more than he deserved. You could have killed him, perhaps... you *should* have killed him."

"I couldn't, Mercy, and you know that."

"I am well aware, and I do not fault you for this. It proves that you are still human when it counts, and that you are a much better god than what came before," Mercy rattled before turning back to look at the creatures beneath them. Niccolo's fingers were poised just above Adonai's chest; Adonai's face was etched with terror. "However, you have given yourself a weakness."

"Weakness? What are you talking about?"

"Although this was the humane course," Mercy said, turning around so he did not have to face the frozen gods, "your existence will forever be chained to this place."

"Chained to this place?" Cadmus asked as he walked up to Mercy's side. "How am I chained here?"

"Your manipulation of time is not absolute, Master, even if it is beyond comprehension. This you know well. You have stopped time for not one, but *two* deities, and it requires concentration."

"Yeah, but—"

"*Constant* concentration," Mercy interrupted, looking at Cadmus with shining blue eyes. "If you had harvested Niccolo's power and locked Adonai away, this would not be as difficult, but your compassion has given you a monumental task. You will not be able to sleep, to rest, to ever feel comfort again."

"Mercy..."

"For the rest of eternity, you will guard these two destructive creatures. It will take everything you have—it will take constant vigilance—but this is the course you have chosen. I do not envy you, Master, but I admire you. More importantly," Mercy said as he set his skull against the reaper's forehead. "I have faith that you will succeed."

"I..." Cadmus stammered, but then the weight of it hit him all at once. He had used most of his massive reservoir of power in order to stop Niccolo and Adonai, and the hazy remnants of his display still floated around their arena. Even then, Cadmus felt untold power surging underneath his skin, but it did not take long for him to realize that Mercy was correct. For Niccolo and Adonai to stay prisoner, Cadmus would never be able to stop focusing on keeping their prison intact.

It was more than just daunting.

"You're right," Cadmus said as he leaned into his horse's touch, feeling affection and trust flowing between them, and it was almost enough for him to avoid despair. However, Cadmus knew it was only a momentary retreat, and so he stepped back and let himself drift back to reality. Staring straight into Mercy's eyes, he sighed heavily. "*How* are you right?"

"I am part of your soul, Cadmus. Everything I know comes from—"

"No. That's only partly true," Cadmus said, staring analytically at his old friend. "You know more—*always* know more—than you should. Who were you?"

"Master—"

"*Who were you*, Mercy? I'm not asking out of anger. You're still my friend, but I need to know." Cadmus stared down his horse and waited for his answer. After a moment, the stallion looked away and pawed at the ground.

"I was... I was an angel named Raziel. I was Adonai's keeper of secrets," Mercy said before lifting his head and staring at Cadmus with bright, blue eyes, which seemed to be a permanent change. "All of the horses were angels who died in the First Rebellion. Barbas... he linked what remained of our souls to these beasts, removing our memories in the process."

"And you got them back the more powerful I got..." Cadmus said, causing the horse to break eye contact.

"You were always intelligent, Cadmus. There is no need to show off." Mercy turned back to the frozen gods forever locked in combat. "You have already displayed power beyond imagination."

"And so you knew everything? Everything that Adonai ever told you?" Cadmus asked, drawing the bright gaze of his stallion.

"Everything and more, Master. Secrets filtered to the Void from every soul, in life and in death, and it was my duty to relay that information to Adonai. That was how he gained his rumored omniscience. Every soul you harvested allowed me to reclaim my memories and my powers."

"So you've been keeping secrets from me this entire time." Cadmus was frustrated as he looked down at his feet, but then he felt Mercy's nose tap his forehead. Looking up, Cadmus was surprised when he felt Mercy's dignified sense of purpose flow through their connection.

"*Never*. When I learned those secrets, you were notified as soon as it was appropriate. I did not want you dismayed by information that could only hurt you. I did not want to distract you as you took your place as the guardian of humanity. My secrets—all of the secrets I will learn—they are all yours."

"And why? Why would you give me those secrets?" Cadmus asked, causing his friend to tilt his head.

"I was the keeper of secrets to God. I have never had an issue giving you those secrets because, deep within my soul, I always knew my true master," he said, the statement shocking enough for Cadmus to drop his arms. "This was ordained, Cadmus. Time itself yearned for you."

"Mercy..."

"It is appropriate, Master. That is why I tell you this now, as you have become the god you were meant to be," Mercy said before turning to look at the entrance, wordlessly beckoning Cadmus to take his place on the saddle. "I do not know what the future holds, reaper, but your reign begins on the other side of those doors."

"What the future holds..." Cadmus repeated, turning his gaze on Niccolo and Adonai. Before that moment, Cadmus had no idea what he was going to do to stop either of them, but his soul had instinctively known his only option.

As much as he hated leaving Niccolo here suspended for all eternity, Cadmus realized that Mercy was correct; this was the best possible outcome. Because, before his descent into madness and rage, Niccolo had wanted to give humanity a better future. That had been their dream, their reason for rising up against a cruel tyrant; this was their *purpose*.

And even though that stubborn man no longer existed, Cadmus promised he would make that dream a reality.

"So," Cadmus said as he threw his leg over the saddle and took his place on Mercy's back. "When did you know you used to be Raziel?"

"Only after you inherited Azrael's burden," Mercy admitted as he carried Cadmus to the entrance. "Once I saw the memories of all those angels, I was able to see my life from a different perspective."

"And you chose to hold that back," Cadmus muttered, feeling the shame flow from his horse.

"It was not necessary to tell you. Would you forgive me?" Mercy asked, and Cadmus was surprised to feel worry prevalent in his horse's tone. Setting his hand against Mercy's long neck, Cadmus rubbed weathered fingers along his mane.

"Of course, I do. I trust you, even when you lie to me," Cadmus said with a smile, unaware that they were only thirty feet from the doors now.

"I will not lie again, Master," Mercy promised, drawing out a chuckle from his rider.

"It's fine, Raziel, you're allowed to lie. If you want, we can try to figure out some way to return you to your angelic bo—"

"No, Master," Mercy interrupted, coming to a stop just a few yards from the doorway. "I much prefer being the horse of the Pale Rider. It is an honor."

"An honor..." Cadmus looked ahead and sighed. "I don't really see it that way."

"Gods tend to have differing perspectives," Mercy said as he brought Cadmus across the threshold, confusing his rider just as a whole new world opened up before them.

"Cadmus, look out!"

Michael had shouted from the side, and Cadmus looked from the archangel to all the others gathered there, demon and angel alike. So confused by the sight, Cadmus almost didn't hear the roar coming from above or feel the heat surrounding him. Only after a few dangerous seconds did Cadmus finally look up to find a giant green dragon roaring at him. When it lunged forward and opened its cavernous maw, everyone gathered there thought Cadmus would be Asmodeus' next victim.

That was until Cadmus raised his hand and curled his fingers, sending out a wave of blue energy that slammed into the giant dragon and the rest of his audience. Focusing on the old angel buried deep in the creature's scales, Cadmus knew he had enough strength to do this one last thing.

When Cadmus lifted his hand higher and caused the great dragon to float in the air, there was no soul in the audience who did not look on in wonder. Clenching his fingers tighter and letting his considerable power flow around him, Cadmus murmured in a language he did not know, syllables that had been long forgotten. Although Asmodeus screamed in protest, Cadmus continued the chant and squeezed his fingers around whatever nebulous thing was in his grasp, and for a long moment it seemed like time had stood still.

What some of his audience did not understand was that Cadmus had truly stopped it.

Slamming his scythe against the ground, Cadmus exerted his will on the airborne dragon and clenched his fist entirely, creating a localized distortion of space and time. His audience gaped up at the sight as the enormous creature twisted and contorted, at times shrinking and expanding before Cadmus exerted even more of his will. Then—while the creature screamed—the dragon withered away, becoming smaller and smaller until it was the size of a human.

"Asmodeus!" Cadmus shouted as he struck the ground again, this time with the blade of his scythe. A crack formed along the ground until it was underneath the relatively small dragon, and then blue flames burst out of the crevice and surrounded the floating creature. Even Cadmus was surprised to see the scales fall away, the arms and legs snapping back and forth and reforming into human limbs, and then the wings withdrew into the angel's back.

To Cadmus' wonder and the surprise of everyone in the audience, an unconscious—but breathing—Asmodeus drifted to the ground next to the crevice. After a few moments, the demon king stirred, and it was only seconds more until Paimon fell to his side and gathered his head in her lap. Touching his face and feeling his warmth, Paimon laughed in relief before looking up at Cadmus with happy tears. Her smile made him feel lighter, but one look at his face was enough for that smile to fall away.

"Cadmus... is Niccolo..." she tried, but she could not give life to the question.

"Adonai and Niccolo have been trapped." Cadmus started by speaking to Paimon, but he quickly realized that thousands of immortal creatures were looking at him for answers. "They will be locked in that throne room for all eternity."

"For those of you who don't know," Cadmus began, taking a deep breath so he would not lose his nerve. "My name is Cadmus. I was the Horseman of Death."

"Death..." a weak voice came from the crowd.

"Death..." another murmur joined it.

"There is no end of the world!" Cadmus declared with a sweep of his scythe. "We have *stopped* the Apocalypse! From this moment on, there is no god to tell you what to do, what to think. From this point, you have the *choice*. The choice to do whatever you want, live however you want."

"Are you the new god?" a stranger asked, and Cadmus turned to see it was a cowering angel. Knowing that fear too well and that he did not want to be responsible for it, Cadmus shook his head.

"I am *not* divine!" Cadmus stated, turning from the angel to incorporate the rest of his audience. "I'm just a man. Just like so many of you! From now on, there *is* no god! God led us to this moment—to this awful war—because he was a cruel tyrant.

"In this world, we will live and work together," he said before looking down, remembering the friend he had left behind. "We will live on. We will remember our fallen brothers and sisters, and we will remember what they died for."

"They died to give us this choice! They died to give us this freedom!" Cadmus boomed out, his voice echoing through the expanse of Heaven. "We will not desecrate their memory! We will create a new age, a new age of freedom, a new age of knowledge, a new age of choice, an age without God! This..."

He faltered as his grief bubbled to the surface. Once he looked down and found the faces of friends and enemies, alike, Cadmus regained his confidence and lifted his scythe to the sky.

"This is the beginning of the Age of Humanity!" he declared, almost surprised by the cheers that rose to meet him.

Looking down from his weapon, he found that almost everyone gathered there was cheering, yelling, and smiling. When he turned to Paimon, she was nodding at him with tears in her eyes, but then she turned her attention on Asmodeus once he sputtered awake. Facing Michael, Cadmus saw the archangel looking at him with respect and holding his burning blade to the sky.

Cadmus smiled at the silent exchange, but then he heard a rumble from his side and turned to see Astaroth send a blast of energy into the sky. He was confused at first, but then Astaroth looked at him out of the corner of his eye and nodded at the gathered crowd. Then—the sight somehow shocking him after all that he had seen—Cadmus saw why Astaroth was so pleased. Cadmus could only watch as thousands of angels, demons and humans all lifted their weapons to the sky, their chanting echoing through the heavens.

In that moment Cadmus wished to be somewhere else, to be someone else, but he could not take away their victory or their champion. Instead, he accepted his responsibility and sat up straighter in the saddle, lifting his scythe and letting it shine with blue light. This was not what he wanted, but he could give them their moment. Closing his eyes, Cadmus let their emotion and joy flow over him, and he unintentionally repeated their chant.

"Long Live Death."

EPILOGUE: AN AGE OF ENLIGHTENMENT

"You know, Nico, it really is incredible," Cadmus muttered, turning to face the frozen man straddled over his eternal enemy. Rubbing his face with a wrinkled hand and feeling the stubble irritating his skin, Cadmus leaned on his scythe and gave into fatigue.

It had been so many years, so many nights without sleep, and it all weighed on the reaper. Still, it was worth it. These two monsters grappling in front of him looked eternally youthful, eternally furious, but Cadmus had stopped them. Whether or not he was older, more weathered and more tired than he had ever been, Cadmus knew that it had been the right choice. Niccolo was not dead, the universe had been saved, and humanity had flourished.

His own, personal pain was nothing in comparison.

"Just incredible," he grumbled, lifting his scythe and then folding his legs underneath him so he could sit. "Just a couple centuries and it's like they're a whole different species. When we were alive, humans were content to just survive, but they're so *advanced* now.

"Well, relatively," Cadmus said as he looked down at Adonai. That monster deserved to die, but he would stay here for eternity

461

because of his actions. "Without Adonai keeping them down—destroying their spirit and their drive—they're really starting to gain momentum.

"God, you would love it, Nico. So much artwork, so many ideas..." he said, looking off into the distance before leaning toward his best friend. "They're *finally* realizing the nature of the universe and there was this man, Leonardo. Oh, Nico, he's absolutely insane, but damnit if he isn't brilliant. Part of me thinks an angel or demon is helping him out, but I think I'll let it slide. I know I told them no interfering, but it's so interesting to see.

"Oh, don't you judge me," Cadmus added quickly before wagging his finger at Niccolo's frozen face. "I've been alive a long time, and I deserve some distractions. A little rule-*bending* from time to time isn't terrible. Hell, if you were in my place, you'd do a hell of a lot more than that!

"If you were in my place..." Cadmus said as he looked down at his cloak, which had gathered around his legs. "Maybe you should be in my place. There are times when I think I'm failing, you know. When I overthink it and I just—I just feel like a failure. I feel like I'm not living up to everyone's desires.

"You wouldn't worry about that, would you, Nico?" Cadmus let loose a light chuckle. "You wouldn't give a damn. Even if you *were* failing, you'd just convince yourself you weren't and that everybody can just eat crow. You were always so confident, even if you didn't deserve to be that way. Almost thought Marchosias would rip you apart the first time we met him.

"Marchosias," Cadmus mumbled, remembering the werewolf and his friend. "Always regretted that. Worked through it in my brain a thousand times and there were so many things I could have done that would have saved him. So many things I could have done to save Yeshua.

"I had enough time, Nico, even if everyone tells me I didn't," Cadmus admitted, a tear stubbornly refusing to fall from his right eye. "Because I didn't stay and help them, Yeshua and Diogenes didn't make it. Seems wrong to make it through the apocalypse without Jesus Christ, doesn't it?

"But that's what he wanted. Wanted to save one soul," the reaper said before sniffing and reclaiming his tear. "Protected William until he could stand on his feet and Seere did the rest. Only reason *he* didn't die was because Asmodeus scared the angels away. Just... sometimes you have to think."

"Paimon's doing alright, by the way. Thought you would want to know," Cadmus said, nodding to the entrance of the throne room. "We don't talk much anymore, but her side project is thriving. It'll be good for them, I think. Can't leave humanity *completely* unsupervised. William's keeping her company, actually. They're... well, I'm sure you don't want to know about that."

"Cadmus, you're needed," Mercy's voice interrupted, and Cadmus disregarded it with an absent-minded wave.

"I'm always needed, old friend. Can't I ever get a moment's peace?"

"No. That is not your role," Mercy stated simply before bowing out of the conversation and leaving Cadmus with his thoughts. Surrendering to his horse, Cadmus uncrossed his legs and pushed himself to his feet with the aid of his scythe.

"Guess it's time to go, then. Maybe next time I come up here, I can tell you about how the monarchies are starting to fall. Exciting times, Niccolo. I'm not sure what they're going to do next." Cadmus laughed and shook his head at the world's antics. Sighing in content, Cadmus looked down and saw unfathomable anger still etched into his friend's face.

"I'm sorry, Nico. I'm always going to be sorry. This wasn't fair and it's definitely not what I wanted. You just... you just didn't give me a choice. I'd give anything to have you back, sharing this life with me. I hope you know that."

"Master—"

"One second!" Cadmus shouted, pointing behind him with a thin finger. "I just need to... I need this.

"It was all worth it, Niccolo. All of it. All the pain, all the grief, all the guilt, even the manipulation. It was all worth it to see what humanity is capable of when a cruel god isn't holding them down. They have such *potential*. Just like... just like you and me. We became gods, and we did it for them. Even if you lost sight of that, this is why we were fighting. This was why we suffered for so long.

"We were the Horsemen of the Apocalypse, Niccolo, and we did end that world. What they didn't tell us—what we didn't know until the end—was that we were going to create a new one," Cadmus said as he stepped forward and placed his hand on Niccolo's face. "We did this, Nico, even if you don't get to see it. We saved them all.

"I'll come back in a few years, and... well, I'll give you another update," Cadmus said as he retrieved his hand and then approached his horse, using his scythe as a walking stick. Once he was at Mercy's side, he looked back at his prisoners and sighed. "I won't leave you alone, Nico. Not for long. I'll always be here for you. I owe you more than that, but it's all I can give you.

"Goodbye, old friend," Cadmus said as he pulled himself up on Mercy's saddle, fatigue setting in and causing him to breathe heavily once he was seated. Pretending to be stronger, Cadmus sat up and urged Mercy forward, away from the gods he had frozen in time. He didn't know if Niccolo heard a single thing he had said, but he had to hope. If he didn't hold onto that, he sincerely doubted he would last through the ages.

So Cadmus hoped, feeling his spirit pulled in a hundred directions as people cried out in pain, their last moments carved into his mind even if he was not the one to reap them. This was what kept him going; kept him strong in the face of eternity. If Niccolo was alive, if he could listen, then Cadmus could tell him stories. And as long as he believed Niccolo could hear him, Cadmus was not alone.

If he had turned around in that moment, in that moment of weakness, Cadmus would have seen a glimmer in Niccolo's eye. He might have imagined it, might have convinced himself that he had imagined it, but he would have seen it.

However, Cadmus did not turn. He did not see a glimmer in Niccolo's eye, imagined or otherwise. He just looked ahead—beyond the doors of Adonai's throne room and the expanse of Heaven—and reveled in the possibilities. He felt the warmth of the sun and the excitement that comes from leading a world out of darkness. If Cadmus held onto all those feelings, onto his hope and his memories, he would be able to carry this burden.

As blue energy surged around him, Cadmus prepared himself to travel through the Void and felt the first cracks in reality. Dimensional travel had become easy—Cadmus had *needed* it to become easy—but that never took away the fear that came with it. Since it was so easy, Cadmus had no real justification to stay away, but it was always so painful. Even if Niccolo gave him hope, Cadmus' heart broke with every visit. And just like every other visit, Cadmus made the same promise before disappearing into the Void.

"Goodbye, Niccolo. I'll be back soon."

DRAMATIS PERSONAE

DRAMATIS PERSONAE FOR IN DEFIANCE OF HEAVEN

Adonai: The creator of Earth and Heaven, and that only served to inflate his ego.

Ajax: The Horseman of War, and in life he was known as Ajax the Greater from the Trojan War. He spends most of his time in the War Quarter fighting, drinking or both.

Amdusias: A King of Hell and the stoic twin brother of Asmodeus. He is known for weather manipulation, and he rules over a kingdom suffering through an eternal winter.

Amon: One of the Demonic Seers, along with his brother Räum, Amon relayed the prophecy for the Apocalypse. He has a raven's head along with other avian aspects.

Andras: A former human who abandoned his shape to look more like an owl. He is known as an information broker throughout Dis, the capital of Hell.

Antonio Gherardini: A successful merchant in medieval Firenze and the father of Camilla Gherardini, Niccolo's first love.

Asmodeus: A King of Hell and the light-hearted twin brother of Amdusias. He has access to pyrokinesis and has taken on draconic aspects since his fall to Hell, suiting himself to his volcanic kingdom.

Astaroth: Lucifer's more martial twin, Adonai created him to be a general in the war against the Nephilim. Even though he is not one of the Kings, he works diligently to keep Hell from falling apart.

Azazel: One of Lucifer's best friends, he is a Fallen Angel who appears as a satyr with a reptilian tail, and he generally keeps Lucifer company in the palace.

Azrael: The Angelic Reaper, who harvested all the souls of the angels who died during Lucifer's rebellion.

Bael: A King of Hell who appears as an anthropomorphized toad with venomous horns. He generally does not commit to either side of a conflict and focuses on self-preservation. Most of his realm is silt and swampland, a breeding ground for all the insects he loves to eat.

Balam: A King of Hell who appears as a gigantic humanoid hybrid between a bear and goat. He is known for his strength and lack of intelligence, and his kingdom resembles a redwood forest with sparse wildlife. Balam has a habit of hunting anything that moves.

Baphomet: An entity from another dimension, he currently resides in Purgatory and acts as a gatekeeper for a secret entrance to Heaven.

Barbas: The leader of the Pestilence Quarter in Dis, the capital of Hell. He acts as a mentor for Niccolo, helping him find his place in Hell after his death.

Beleth: A King of Hell, known for his intelligence and sadism. He always wears obsidian plate mail, and he has mastery over many schools of magic. He had a giant fortress built in the center of his dark kingdom, surrounded by a deep network of mines where his subjects endlessly toil.

Belial: A King of Hell, called the Eveningstar to serve as a foil to Lucifer. He appears as a reanimated corpse, and he consistently blames Lucifer for their fall to Hell. His kingdom is a cold, barren wasteland, and his ostentatious palace is the only permanent structure.

Buer: The Head Librarian in the Famine Quarter and the preeminent scholar in all of Hell. He appears as an aged centaur, though that is purely an affectation.

Buné: The leader of the Death Quarter in Dis, the capital of Hell. He acts as a mentor for Cadmus, and he is one of the only angels who could ever reap souls.

Cadmus: The Horseman of Death and Niccolo's best friend in Hell. He was an early Christian who was executed via gladiator combat.

Camilla Gherardini: The daughter of a merchant in medieval Firenze, and Niccolo's first love.

Carlo Vespucci: A wealthy merchant in medieval Firenze, and Niccolo's father.

Cimeries: One of two Hell Knights, former humans who protect Lucifer from lesser threats. She claimed Cimeries after her first life as Hippolyta, the legendary Amazon.

Crocell: The Slayer of Dis, a Fallen Angel tasked with exterminating feral demons so that human reapers are not in danger. He wields a trident and is attuned to electricity and water.

Diogenes: The Horseman of Famine. In life, he was a Greek philosopher who rejected the norms of society. He is often accompanied by Manes, a stray dog, and Despair, his horse.

Eligos: The leader of the War Quarter of Dis, the capital of Hell. A giant warrior with a shifting weapon, he generally spends his time presiding over the fighting pits.

Furcas: One of two Hell Knights, former humans who protect Lucifer from lesser threats. One of the older humans to fall to Hell, he still wears the trophies of monsters he has killed.

Fury: The horse who serves as the mount for the Horseman of War.

Gabriel: One of the archangels, and he is generally seen as a messenger throughout Heaven.

Giovanni Simonetti: A minor noble in conflict with Niccolo during his time as a leper.

The Leviathan: A terrifying entity from another dimension who acts as a deterrent for violence between the Kings of Hell.

Lilith: The first angel to ally themselves with Lucifer, eventually becoming the High Queen of Hell. She dies in the process of giving birth to Mammon.

Lorenzo Innocenti: An enigmatic merchant who operates out of medieval Firenze and Napoli. While he seems to assist Niccolo, no one else finds him trustworthy.

Lü Bu: The first Horseman of Pestilence, and a legendary warrior from the Three Kingdoms period of Chinese history.

Lucifer: An archangel who rebelled against Adonai so he might enlighten humanity.

Currently rules as the High King in Dis, the capital of Hell, but he is also known as the Firstborn and the Morningstar.

Mammon: Known as the Hellborn, Mammon is the only child born to Lucifer and Lilith, who he killed during childbirth.

Marchosias: A former human who usually appears as a werewolf wreathed in shadows. For more than a thousand years, he worked for Astaroth along with Phenex, his longtime friend.

Marco: A man who enjoys life too much, he is often seen offering unsolicited advice to Niccolo, his best friend in Firenze.

Mercy: The sentient horse who serves as the mount for Cadmus, the Horseman of Death.

Michael: One of the archangels and the General for the Heavenly Host. His morality is constantly tested while in service to Adonai's tyranny.

Mitzrael: A sadistic Seraphim who took great pleasure in fighting against Lucifer and his allies, even after they had surrendered. He was sent to Earth along with Nithael to stop the Horsemen.

Moloch: A refugee from another dimension, like the Leviathan, who made his home in Hell long before Lucifer and his armies fell.

Niccolo Vespucci: The current Horseman of Pestilence and a former merchant prince from medieval Firenze.

Nithael: An officer from Heaven sent to Earth along with Mitzrael to stop the Horsemen.

Paimon: A King of Hell who appears as a seductive blonde woman. Before the Fall, she was known as "the Butcher" for how savagely she fought against the Nephilim. She has made her kingdom along a tropical beachfront where she can remember the warmth of Heaven.

Phenex: A former human who acts humble despite an immense capacity for pyrokinesis. For more than a thousand years, he worked for Astaroth along with Marchosias, his longtime friend.

Plague: The sentient horse who serves as the mount for Niccolo, the Horseman of Pestilence.

Purson: A King of Hell who appears as a hybrid between snake and human. He rules over a desert kingdom, so he often seeks reasons to visit anywhere else.

Räum: One of the Demonic Seers, along with his brother Amon, Räum relayed the prophecy for the Apocalypse. He had a crow's head, and his prophecies were considered more accurate.

Ronové: The leader of the Famine Quarter of Dis, the capital of Hell. Appearing as a squat demon with a long staff, Ronové is considered a master of rhetoric.

Sabrael: One of the archangels, and he is usually preoccupied with his experiments. Adonai gleefully encourages him to commit atrocities against humans, demons and even other angels.

Sathariel: A pacifist angel, she was romantically linked to Lucifer before the rebellion, eventually becoming a Watcher along with Tamiel for the sin of staying neutral.

Seere: The first human to fall to Hell, he has spent thousands of years fighting and honing his skills. While he initially refused to become the Horseman of War, it was always his to claim.

Sitri: A former human who took full advantage of their second life and became a shapeshifting socialite. All gossip eventually goes through Sitri, usually for a price.

Solomon: Said to be the first human reaper, which could be expected of King Solomon.

Tamiel: Considered Adonai's favorite before the rebellion, he and Sathariel were considered Watchers and were banished to prehistoric Earth.

Uriel: The most violent of the archangels, Uriel is more than happy to punish anyone who has displeased Adonai in any way.

Valefor: An aggressive Fallen Angel who was considered powerful even before he turned feral.

Viné: A King of Hell who comes across as an implacable shrew, but she can form blades from her bones that will rip most people to shreds. Her kingdom is a lush rainforest, and seldom few souls who venture into those depths ever return. Whether or not Viné is involved is a mystery.

William Combe: The estranged son of a petty lord in medieval England who is recruited to guide the Horsemen to Stonehenge.

Ymir: The leader of the Nephilim, whose story indirectly influenced the Jotun in Nordic mythology.

Zagan: A King of Hell who appears as a giant with bull horns, and he consistently maintains a buzz off a bottle of wine that perpetually refills itself. His kingdom is mountainous and he holds court in a hollow within the central range, but grapes grow freely within the valleys.